DAUGHTER OF DAYBREAK

JUNIPER ARDEN

Flamespringer Press

DAUGHTER OF DAYBREAK. Text copyright © 2024 by Juniper Arden.
Map copyright © 2022 by David Steindl.
Cover art and design by bukovero.com.

ISBN 979-8-9872417-4-5 (hc) — ISBN 979-8-9872417-3-8 (pb) — ISBN 979-8-9872417-5-2 (ebook)

Library of Congress Control Number: 2024917138

First Edition: October 2024
Printed in the United States of America
10 9 8 7 6 5 4 3 2 1

For the latest news about the author and upcoming releases, visit www.juniperarden.com.

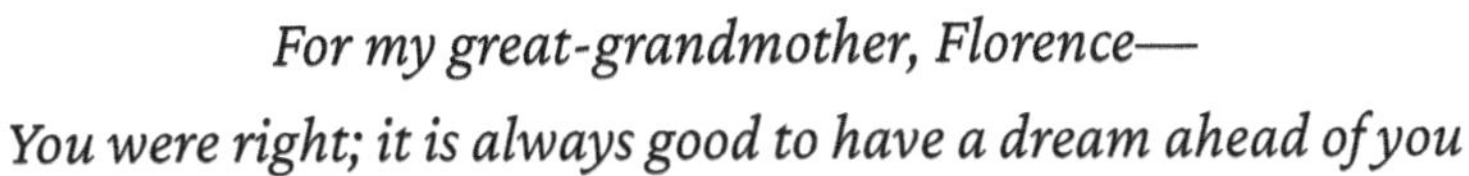

For my great-grandmother, Florence—
You were right; it is always good to have a dream ahead of you

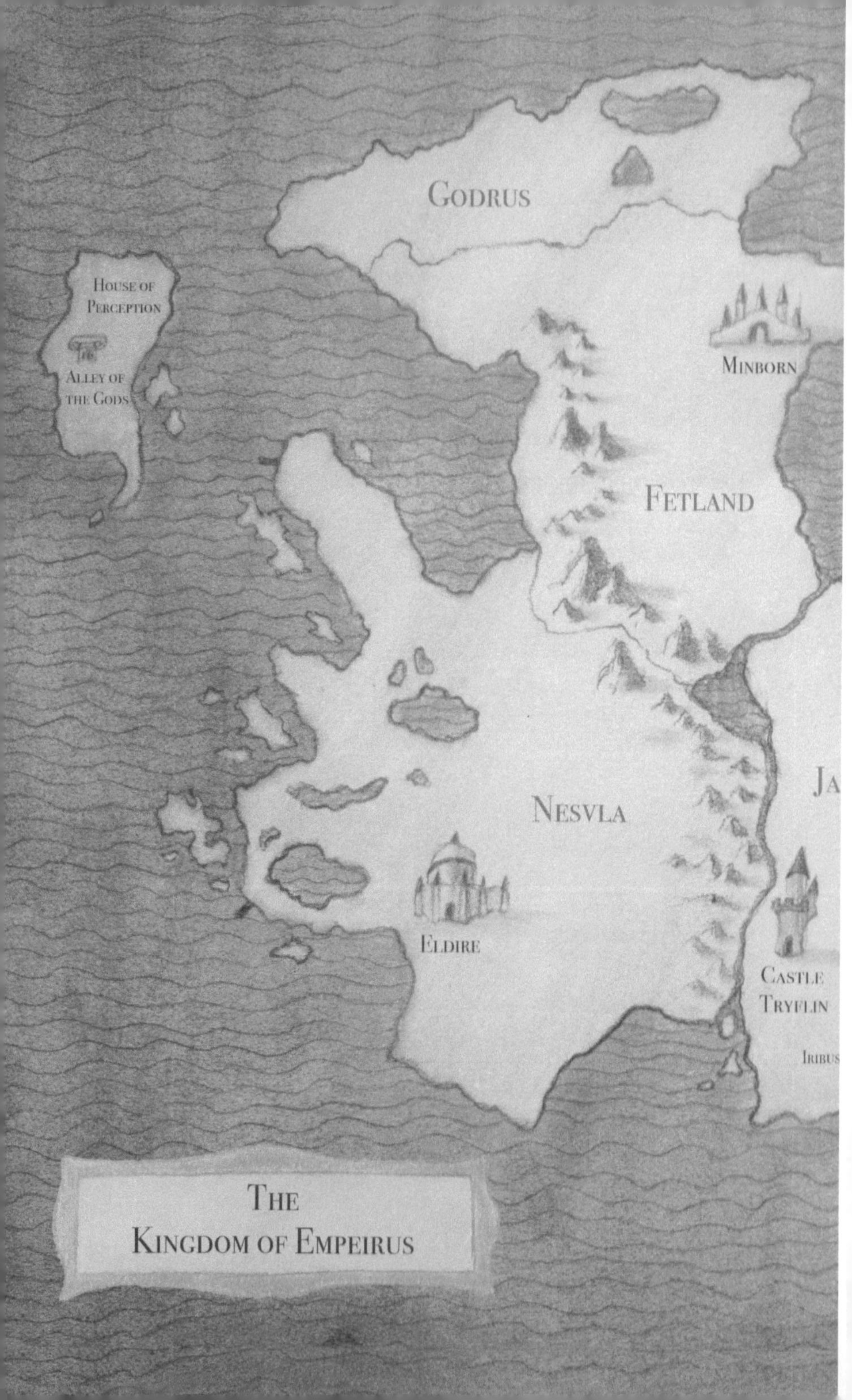

GODRUS
HOUSE OF PERCEPTION
The ALLEY OF THE GODS
MINBORN
FETLAND
NESVLA
ELDIRE
JA
CASTLE TRYFLIN
IRIBUS
THE KINGDOM OF EMPEIRUS

SAVEK COAST
EMPEIRUS
VIR
LARKINGSPORT
Sapphire
GOORDEN'S BEACH
CIRCUS
CALLEEIT

Pronunciation Guide

People

Aimelie: aim-ell-ee
Annora: a-nor-a
Anzac: ann-zak
Belline: bell-een
Calix: kay-lix
Calleeit: ca-lee-it
Dimity: dim-it-ee
Elouthera: el-oo-ther-a
Gissaira: ji-zair-a
Ione: ee-own-ee
Jedda: jed-a
Modgen: maw-jen
Renai: ren-ay

Places

Empeirus: em-pier-us
Godrus: god-rus
Javir: ja-veer
Nesvla: nes-vla
Savek: sa-vek
Tryflin: trif-lin

DAUGHTER
OF
DAYBREAK

PROLOGUE

The flames dance in a million different directions, the reflection of their persimmon embers bouncing off her baby-blue eyes. Her fingers graze the smooth pendant of Linden's necklace for the hundredth time today, the golden metal warm from the heat of the fire and her trembling touch. Sitting on a heap of rags, Princess Aimelie Larking watches the former Royal Jeweler put away the last of his remaining belongings, his graying brow furrowed seriously as he turns to face her yet again.

"Your Highness," Urayus Helva begins. "I know it is not my place to say, but delaying the inevitable will not eliminate it."

The youngest princess is as silent as she had been

yesterday when her slippered feet carried her away from the harbor to the temporary safety of her friend's forge. Her golden curls are tangled from running, and her head aches from the misery of losing both of her sisters and the love of her life. *Should I have known? Should I have been able to predict something this improbable after knowing Annalise and Adrianna for most of their lives? And Linden ...*

Aimelie dips her forehead down to the dirt floor of the blacksmith's forge. Her heart has not yet been able to comprehend the events of yesterday afternoon. It seems like a lifetime ago that Melie's royal mentor had deemed it necessary for her to find Annalise while he stayed behind at Larking Castle. *I can only imagine the hell my love will face with Dria now.* For as much torture as Linden experienced working as a servant for Queen Adrianna before, there will surely be more of it working for the Dark Goddess, Jedda. What that will mean for Linden's safety and well-being ... Aimelie tries not to let herself think about that much.

Urayus closes the last of his satchels, his horse's neigh audible from outside the wooden door. Sighing, the burly blacksmith seats himself on the chair beside Aimelie's place on the floor.

"I don't know what to think of it either," he admits. "But there are many times in life when we don't know what to think, just yet."

The crackle of the fire is his only response. Aimelie's doe eyes drift from the flames to meet his gaze.

The blacksmith leans forward to rest his elbows on his knees. "The day the Crimson Queen stripped me of my title as Royal Jeweler, I exploded." Urayus swallows. "I knew I was skilled. I knew I was admired. My work was of the finest in the kingdom. I knew why she did it, but I couldn't fathom *how* she could.

"One night, I drank myself into oblivion and woke up face down in a pile of what I wanted to believe was mud." He shakes his head, fighting a faint smile. "It was enough to make me realize that I had let her win. That same day, I went into town and found myself a new home, one where I could start anew. Not a year later, I fashioned myself this business and a new life of my own." Urayus gestures to the forge around them.

"And now you're leaving," Aimelie points out.

Her friend chuckles. "This is exactly my point, Princess. What the gods grant us is only part of what determines our fate. The rest is what we make of it. We must adapt." Urayus stands with a groan. "It is my time to leave this city, Your Highness. Whatever these gods have in store, I want to be with my family in Godrus to face it."

The princess works a thread loose from the orange fabric of her skirts. "I don't know if I have it in me to face those gods again," she whispers. Her mind churns at the reflection of a marble Throne Room, of Adrianna and Annalise trading fire and ice like it is something humans are supposed to do.

The light of the glowing fire shifts against Urayus's face. "You do," he states simply, tossing a bag over his muscled shoulder. "You have your mother's heart."

She doesn't know how, but hearing the declaration warms Melie's broken heart, if even just a little. Maybe it is the fraction of her soul that still clings to the hope of a brighter future, but something urges her to stand from her throne of rags. "I suppose this is goodbye, then." Aimelie smooths out the pleats of her dress.

"I suppose so," Urayus replies. His tired eyes fall on the leather satchel pressing against Melie's waist, the one that holds the crown he forged for the true heir of Empeirus, Princess Annalise Larking. He reaches into his bag to pull out a gray cloak, handing it to Aimelie with a sort of gentleness few are likely to see from him. "It's starting to get cold out this time of year."

Aimelie nods, trying not to let her emotions get the best of her. *I might never see him again*, she realizes. *Just like I might never see Linden again, either.* "Thank you for all your help. And thank you for your advice. I shall never forget it."

Urayus offers a weathered grin. "Take care of yourself, Princess. If you need me, I'll be in Godrus." He opens the wooden door of his forge for the last time. "The gods be with you—and on your side."

Aimelie watches the door close, listening to the sounds of a horse ready to pull its cart. Before her, only the empty forge stands witness to her rumination, the weight of the blacksmith's words sinking in at last. "We must adapt," Aimelie repeats to herself out loud, her eyes darting between her new gray cloak and the orange silk of her gown.

She sets down the cloak and the satchel before beginning to undo the laces of her bodice, then her skirt, until all that remains is her simple white underdress. *Better for blending in,* the princess notes. The satchel finds its way to her hip once again, and Melie fastens the enormous cloak over her shoulders. Gathering up her previous dress, she takes a shallow breath, willing her arms to thrust them into the open hearth.

Aimelie watches as the orange fabric is devoured by the matching flames until they are nothing but ash, her hand clutching the golden necklace beneath her cloak. When the fire has been satiated, Aimelie lets herself out of Urayus Helva's former home and back into the world that had similarly scorched her fragile heart.

The town is bustling with horses and people, most of whom seem to be headed away from the capital. *Fleeing,* Aimelie corrects. *And I'm going to be one of them.* The only difference between the princess and the townsfolk is that, instead of running away from gods and goddesses, Melie is running in pursuit of one.

So many people, she thinks. *How many will stay to endure what Adrianna and Desmond have to offer? And, while the individual territories of the kingdom maintain some of their own rights, the Empeirian throne still rules above them all. Wherever they go, they will still be subject to Adrianna's— or Jedda's—schemes, as long as they are still within the king- dom.* Aimelie swallows. *But even outside of it, in Calleeit …* She reflects on the supernatural powers both of her sisters put to use at the castle yesterday. *A god's reach may extend beyond any border.*

All around the castle, the cobblestone streets are barren and deserted, with only a few guards standing watch in their traditional spots. Aimelie averts her eyes to keep from being identified, pulling Urayus's cloak down over her forehead as she approaches the docks once again. There isn't a soul to be seen where Linden had said his goodbyes yesterday afternoon, and, by the luck of some gods, the wooden dinghy still waits for her exactly where it had before.

Carefully lowering herself into the boat, Melie unties its ropes and begins to paddle. The Falvedrie Sea is calm today, its usual swirling gray waters lapping at the hull of her vessel with a languid sort of energy. Had Aimelie been accustomed to rowing boats regularly, such a voyage may have been easier for her, but the adrenaline in her veins keeps her arms pumping.

The marshes are to her right now, and from looking at the map a hundred times since she sent Captain Ivo and Master Tasman there years ago, she knows exactly where to turn. After ramming the hull of the dinghy into the muddy banks, Aimelie makes landfall in her ivory slippers, watching them turn brown from the earth. She waits for a moment to ensure she has not been followed and continues to push her way through the dense vegetation and mud.

Just ahead, beyond the tree line, the watchtower climbs into the sky, its base surrounded by a light fog. Aimelie's heartbeat quickens, her body suddenly aware of the weight of the satchel on her shoulder. *She could be in there*, the youngest princess hopes and frets at the same time. She turns her freckled face to the skies, watching a black crow fly overhead before moving another footstep closer to the tower.

The feeling of a blade pressed against her neck would have her spewing a vicious scream if it wasn't muffled by someone's rough hand.

"Who are you, and what the hell are you doing here?" the familiar voice asks from behind her ear.

Aimelie's chest rises and falls faster than ever before. For a moment, she believes she might pass out, until an elderly man hobbles his way into her field of view.

"For the gods' sakes, Ivo, let her go! It's the princess," Master Tasman whispers to the former Captain of the Royal Guard.

Ivo immediately drops his hand and blade, apologizing profusely in hushed tones.

Aimelie nearly collapses, taking some time to collect herself. "You are forgiven, Ivo," the princess finally musters. *Why aren't they taking refuge inside of the watchtower?*

"You shouldn't be here, Your Highness," Tasman warns her. "You should be leaving Empeirus, too. We were just on our way out."

"Your way out?" Aimelie glances around in search of her sister, but no one else is in sight.

Ivo sheathes his dagger. "Unless you have someplace to be, I suggest you come with us."

"I shall, but ..." she swallows. "I've come for Annalise."

The former master taps his cane. "Then, I'm afraid you're too late. They left at sunrise this morning."

The youngest princess furrows a brow. "*They?*"

Tasman adjusts the strap of the small bag on his shoulder. "She and the former Master of the High Council, Oliver McHenry," he clarifies, taking another step. "The rest of the gods willing, they should be on their way to the Savek Coast by now."

Master McHenry? The Savek Coast? Why would she have fled Empeirus with a man who was once part of Adrianna's inner circle? Aimelie hikes up her skirts to catch up with her two colleagues. "So, we're meeting them there, then?"

"Gods, no." Ivo spits.

Aimelie's head spins. "Then where are we going?"

Tasman pauses his hobbling to remove a letter from his robes, his wrinkled eyes gleaming with delight as he hands her the parchment. "To meet an old friend."

Part I

Ripple

ANNALISE

Annalise Larking blinks her brown eyes at the bright afternoon sun, squinting as they adjust in the salty air. Her shaky hands grip the wooden railing of the ship's stairs in a deadlock—not only to keep from falling as the vessel sways, but to force herself above decks for the first time in a week.

It has been ten days since Annalise's and Oliver McHenry's hurried departure from Empeirus, and the lost princess has spent the majority of their journey to the Savek Coast hiding belowdecks with her face buried in a book. *Anything to keep my mind off the endless waves,* she thinks anxiously. Time has not healed her traumatic history with the Falvedrie Sea, and she isn't confident enough to face it unless she has to. Anna shirks a memory from her childhood, one of a rocky cliff face and greedy waves and lungs filled with seawater. *How strong would a wave have to be to throw me overboard and pummel me with its waters once again?*

The princess toes her way up the wooden steps cautiously, willing her muscles to move her away from the comforts of the cabin. Trembling, she pads across the wooden planks and immediately takes a seat on an empty cargo box. She breathes in and out, fixing her gaze on the solid boards beneath her feet, if only to remind herself that not all ground is made of water. The sound of footsteps has the princess lifting her stare to find a man stalking toward her, a generous smile blooming beneath his pine-green eyes.

"It's nice to get some fresh air, once in a while," Oliver jokes, gathering up some rope before her.

Annalise can't help but snort. While her fears had been enough to keep her in darkness for days, Oliver has been working alongside the crew every moment he can. He rises at dawn, works all day, and is back in his cot come nighttime. Though their makeshift beds are beside one another, the two of them haven't spoken much—a consequence of Oliver's busy schedule and protecting Annalise's anonymity.

"I figured I should get some sunlight," Anna quips. "I'm starting to look like a porcelain doll next to you."

The former Master of the High Council chuckles, the

faintest freckles making a shy appearance beneath his newly acquired tan. "I don't think it's that extreme."

Annalise pushes back a lock of her brown hair, even wavier now from the briny sea winds. She watches as her newest ally finds a seat on the other half of her wooden cargo box, setting the rope in a neat stack beside him.

"You know I'm not particularly fond of the ocean," she points out, daring a glance at the ceaseless white caps.

Oliver nods. "I know. I'm sorry."

He should be sorry, it was his bloody idea. The Goddess of Wisdom and Justice sifts through her thoughts, back to their last few days in Empeirus. Back to the Throne Room, to Adrianna's ice beam, to the way her sister in blood and bond had looked before they both collapsed in a heap atop the smooth, white marble. Their fight had left Dimity's body ravaged, and even now, she can sense that her body is still recovering.

"Trust me when I say that this place is not safe for you anymore," Anna remembers Master Tasman, her former tutor, warning her the day before she and Oliver left the watchtower. *And he was right,* Annalise thinks as she bobs for the millionth time to the rock of the Falvedrie Sea, peering at every stranger's face that she had memorized from day one. *If anyone on this ship learned of my true identity—royal or godly—what would they do?*

Getting on the ship was easy. Like Oliver had mentioned at the watchtower, he knows a great number of sailors. It was even easier to board considering that after the battle at Larking Castle, people didn't seem to be asking many questions. Especially not when most of the Empeirians around the capital were also lining up at the docks to get the hell away from either of the incarnated goddesses. All Oliver had to do was slip them a handful of coins, and they didn't even think twice about his bounty.

"They're not the most honorable folk, but they'll get us to the Savek Coast faster than any other crew leaving from the Royal Harbor," he had assured her.

Annalise wants to believe him, but her mind is not the kind made for trusting. *The Savek Coast,* the goddess frets. *A totally different territory, with a practically total stranger.* She turns to Oliver. *He can't be too bad, though. He did carry me out of the castle after watching me spray fire from my palms, when everyone else was horrified to so much as glance in my direction.*

"You did say this was only supposed to be a ten-day trip, right?" Anna jumps as a larger wave splashes against the hull of the ship, droplets leaping onto the hem of her skirts. "How much longer do you think we have?"

Oliver rolls his neck. "It shouldn't be too much longer. See the difference in the water?" He gestures to the Falvedrie Sea. "Near Empeirus, the waves are a grayish-blue. But in the north, the color changes to a deep cobalt."

The princess manages to tear her brown eyes from the

deck of the ship to find that the waves have indeed transitioned into a beautiful dark blue.

They sit in silence, as this is usually how their conversations go. A few sentences here and there, but nothing substantial. Annalise desperately wants to press him further about his background, about the Savek Coast, about why he is a mortal who seems to be unfazed by helping a deity train to take down her fiery counterpart. But those are not things best discussed in public—especially not on a boat in the middle of the ocean with too many suspicious ears close by.

Annalise looks back to find Oliver spinning the silver ring on his pinky finger while he stares out into the sea. It is something he does a lot; sometimes, it seems, without even realizing it. "That's a nice ring," Anna comments, admiring the feather embossed in the center of the band.

Oliver opens his mouth to reply, but the ship captain booms across the deck.

"Land, ho!" he shouts in a Fetlandish tongue, the rest of the passengers joining in on a round of victorious bellows as the first sight of solid ground creeps into view.

Annalise could cry tears of joy. "Thank the gods!" She laughs inwardly at the irony of such a phrase. "I'll pack our things," she tells Oliver, before descending into the safety of the dark cabin.

She isn't the only one to have this idea. The dozens of other passengers have also gone belowdecks to gather their belongings, packing the innards of the ship like a school of fish. Hands rifle through their bags to ensure nothing will be left behind, their voices enough to drown out the noise of the waves.

The lost princess shoulders her way past her temporary roommates until she reaches her and Oliver's cots. They didn't bring much, only enough of the necessities to get them through their voyage. Annalise collects her book from her makeshift bed and stuffs it in her rucksack, doing the same with Oliver's clothes. Cleaning up the last of his shirts, she looks up at the giggle of a toddler, whose mother sweeps her up into her arms with excitement.

Anna's heart withers as she thinks back to a time when she had her own mother to hold her. It withers even more when her thoughts drift to Narelle, the courtesan who had all but taken over that role after she had run away from the castle the day her royal parents were pronounced dead. *Narelle, I promise I will find you!*

Captain Ivo told her that Adrianna would need to keep Narelle alive to use as leverage, but Anna can't imagine, tries *not* to imagine, the things that her sister has already done. *All of this, because of me.* The guilt is more nauseating than her seasickness. Still, Annalise reminds herself that she is doing everything she can to save Narelle and the world, as futile as her efforts feel at the moment.

The other passengers slowly filter out of the cabin,

Annalise at their heels with both bags in her hands, brimming with angst to leave this wooden hell at long last. Ascending the stairs for the last time, she joins the end of the line to wait for her turn to exit the ship. Oliver meets her there, looking more nervous than usual.

"Is something the matter?" the goddess questions.

"No," he answers quickly. "It's just that ... I haven't exactly visited home in a while."

Annalise pauses. "How long is 'a while?'" She twiddles her fingers.

Oliver runs a hand through his dark brown hair. "About four years."

An exasperated sound escapes Anna. "*Four* years?" She pins her eyes in the direction of a rocky beach looming ever closer, its large harbor ready for their ship to dock. "You didn't think to mention that before?"

He shrugs, shaking his head. "We shouldn't have any issues. After my parents died, I left for Empeirus, and my sister moved in with her husband's family once she got married. The house has only been vacant for about six months."

Her mind scrambling for purchase, the princess picks up her rucksack as the line ahead of them begins to move. She watches the deckhands leap onto the docks, tying down ropes to secure the ship on both ends. *Sweet, precious land!* Anna can feel her heart beating in her chest when the woman in front of her steps off the ship. It is everything she can do to contain her elation as she makes her way to the ramp and—

A sword blocks her line of exit. She turns back to Oliver, who drops his bag.

"Not so fast, McHenry." The grimy ship captain smiles. "I think this ship could use some work, don't you? Might be something I'll look into when I collect your ransom."

Annalise scoffs. "His ransom? You mean, if you don't get your hands melted off by Queen Adrianna before you can collect it."

Captain Garin spits. "Who said anything about Queen Adrianna?"

Around them, the deckhands watch in silent intrigue.

"You might be wanted by the Empeirian Crown," Garin continues, "but there are many who would pay a fair price to have one of Adrianna's highest pawns in their arsenal." His gray eyes trail the length of Annalise's body. "And maybe a mistress, too."

Good gods. They are pirates. My newest ally has placed us in the hands of bloody pirates! The goddess's hand twitches, and she can feel heat beginning to pulse through her veins.

Oliver moves in front of her. "Fine. You can take us."

Annalise chokes. "What—"

"Under one condition," he continues. Oliver kicks his

bag to the side, squaring his shoulders. "You defeat me in a duel."

The princess gawks, her brown eyes wide.

And the ship captain begins to laugh, his deckhands joining in, their humorous sounds swelling like the waves they have just sailed over. "You want to challenge a pirate to a *duel?*" Garin doubles over in laughter. "I never thought you were the brightest, McHenry, but I didn't expect you to be that stupid."

"Then perhaps you will go easy on me," Oliver retorts. "If you win, you can take us to the highest bidder and take your cut. But if you lose ..." His pine-green eyes glance around for a moment. "We both walk free, and we take your ship."

Oh, good heavens! Annalise doesn't know whether to laugh with the rest of the crew or cry for her safety. *What is he doing? Does he know how ridiculous this sounds?*

Captain Garin regroups, extending a hand. "Very well, Oliver McHenry. Let us shake on it and be done. Odren, give him your sword, will you? He'll only need it for a moment."

Oliver retrieves the deckhand's sword, obviously much less cared for than Garin's, and turns to Annalise. "However bad it looks, please don't use your powers," he warns her.

She can only nod before the fight begins.

OLIVER

His first parry is one of the worst Oliver has executed, perhaps in his entire life. The clang of metal vibrates up his arms, which buckle from the intense ferocity of Captain Garin's blow. *Have I gotten that bad?* Oliver thinks with surprise. After all, years of laborious training with his uncle had made wielding the sword like second nature to him.

"You're just like your father," Isaac would admonish him. *"A natural with the blade, but too much of a diplomat to drop the pen for it."*

Were Oliver anything like his uncle, he would have undoubtedly made another high-ranking commander in the Royal Guard. But, were Oliver anything like his uncle, he might also be dead from it.

"Come now, McHenry. You don't want to embarrass

yourself in front of your lady, would you?" Captain Garin quips, his faded eyes giving away his next move.

Oliver returns the attack, warming up to the familiar back and forth of dueling. The crew watches them, none daring to interrupt as they continue to trade swings. Even Annalise witnesses patiently as she clutches the straps of her rucksack. As Oliver's boots slide over the wooden deck, he wonders how much longer he should keep up the ruse. His arms are getting tired from being out of practice, and—

A sharp pain across the left side of his chest catches him off guard, and he quickly blocks the subsequent attack before it gets even worse. *Good gods,* Oliver curses. *Uncle Isaac would throttle me for that.* He takes a step back as the deckhands begin to cheer on their captain, their hollers soon forgotten when Oliver dares a swift glance at the flicker of embers blooming under one of Annalise's palms. The sight is enough for him to realize that he needs to end this now, for as dangerous as dueling with a pirate is, exposing the princess's true identity is far worse.

Captain Garin takes a moment to gloat to his crew, waving his hands in the air to get another rise out of them for additional encouragement. *Not yet. That would be too cheap of a shot.* Oliver pretends to be calculating his next move, the one he has had planned since they first began their skirmish.

"Is that blood on your shirt, I see?" Captain Garin

mocks him. "I warned you before, Oliver. Courtiers have no place picking fights with pirates. They belong with the rest of the fools who think they can do something useful without getting their hands dirty."

In the blink of an eye, Oliver uses the force of his entire body to parry Garin's next attack, striking again above the pirate's sword with a swing so hard, it drives the blade down to the wooden boards of the deck. Oliver slams a boot over the metal while bringing his own weapon directly before the captain's neck.

Captain Garin swallows. The crowd goes silent. Annalise gives what sounds like a sob of relief.

"Perhaps I was wrong about you," the pirate admits in a voice much quieter than before. He eyes the point of Oliver's blade warily, raising his hands in a pose of submission. "I yield."

"No," Oliver clarifies. "You lost." He lets his pine-green eyes unnerve the captain for a moment longer. "We had a deal," Oliver reminds him.

Captain Garin closes his bloodshot eyes. "Indeed." Without a word, he unhooks the small golden pin from his tattered shirt and extends it to his opponent.

Oliver takes the pin, running a finger over the ornate ship's wheel. He tosses Garin's sword back to him, beholding the captain retreat to the docks. The rest of the crew exchanges anxious glances as Oliver restores his own blade to its rightful owner.

"For those of you who still pledge allegiance to your previous captain, you may leave," Oliver announces. "All others who wish to remain employed on this ship will be subject to my agenda, but may also leave as you please. You will be compensated for your work."

The sailors whisper, some nodding and some shaking their heads. After a few more moments, the first of the deckhands leave. A few more join in, following Garin onto the shore. Oliver reaches into his pocket, counting out a decent sum. To the remaining crew members, he passes out the coin. "I'll be back in a few days to check on things. I trust that you'll keep her clean and tidy."

"What will you call her?" a sailor asks from the fidgeting crew.

Oliver throws his bag over his shoulder. "Pardon?"

"What will you call the ship? Will you keep her old name or give her a new one?"

Oliver signals for Annalise to make her way onto the dock. *I hadn't thought about that.* Following the lost princess off the ramp, he responds to his new employee, "How about *Anna's Revenge?*" He watches as Annalise tenses ahead of him, her fists clenching at her sides while they walk toward the shore. He can tell she is bursting with questions, but she waits until they are out of earshot to ask her first one.

"Who the hell are you?" Annalise snaps, her brown eyes narrowing in suspicion.

Oliver raises his eyebrows. "I—"

"A man of court doesn't just challenge a pirate to a duel and then live to take his ship. Besides, your fighting technique is far too disciplined to be learned from back-alley quarrels."

Oliver hides a smile. "Thank you." He realizes all at once how little they truly know about each other. "My uncle taught me. He was a commander in the Royal Guard." Seashells crunch beneath his boots when they finally set foot on dry land.

"I can see that. I used to watch the Guard train when I was younger." Annalise glances back at the ship—*Our ship*, Oliver thinks with some discomfort—and tightens the straps on her rucksack. "What if they take it back?" she dares to ask.

The former master lets out a shallow sigh, then shrugs. "Then I'll be glad I wouldn't have trusted them on future voyages." *And a little disappointed to lose such a nicely sized ship.*

They approach the livery stable now, the pungent scent of hay and horses filling their nostrils. Oliver grabs a few coins from his pocket.

"Got here just in time!" The stable hand exclaims. "Only one left for hire."

The horse is of average build, but should be well-equipped for reaching Oliver's family home. Oliver pays the man, then mounts the chestnut-haired horse, extending a hand to help Annalise up. Hesitantly, she wraps her arms around his torso while Oliver steers the horse toward the main road.

The stable hand laughs boisterously. "Don't act like you've never touched him before!"

Even Oliver blushes at the crude implication until Annalise turns back to the merchant.

"He's my brother," she quips back at him.

The man's eyes grow wider than a full moon.

Oliver can't help but crack a laugh at the terrible joke, giving the reigns a snap to send them on their merry way. "You have a strange sense of humor for being a member of the Royal Family," he tells her quietly.

"Six years in the slums will do that to you," Annalise chuckles. "By the way, you're bleeding."

Oliver darts his evergreen eyes down to the slash on his left pectoral muscle, the fabric of his shirt torn above it. It is small but fairly deep, and hurts more than it should. "I'll take care of it."

The two outlaws ride in silence except for the constant clicking of their horse's hooves. They begin to crest the hill when the familiar sight of Oliver's hometown creeps into view, his heartbeat quickening. It has been four years since Oliver made the journey back to his birthplace, and if it were up to him, his last visit would have been just that—his last. But with his sister living with her husband this past year, his family's empty house shouldn't pose much of an issue. *Only the memories will remain to haunt me.*

Oliver follows the worn cobblestone street through town, rounding the path of markets by a route he knows like the back of his hand. *Cordel*, he smiles. *So similar to Larkingsport, yet so different.* The coastal town on the shoreline of the Savek Coast also sprawls along the Falvedrie Sea, but is far cooler and usually quite windy. Gone are the gaudy nobles' outfits, which have instead been replaced with simple garments better suited for work. Cordel's patrons are mostly sailors, which is part of why Oliver's father wanted to reside here after retirement instead of remaining in Empeirus.

"Have we decided on a backstory?" Annalise whispers from behind his shoulder.

"You didn't want to go with the sibling one?"

She snorts. "Too much to learn. Having to come up with a shared family history would be too complex."

Very true. Oliver ponders for a moment, the signs of town finally disappearing from view. "I might have something; I just need to think about it a little more." He spots another livery stable, preparing to dismantle their horse. "We can walk the rest of the way."

About a mile from town, a quaint house sits high above a rocky coastline. Its long sidewalk meanders through fresh green grass until it meets the dirt road running parallel to it. There are other small houses on the road, but none closer than the length of two houses apart. Privacy is important to the Savekian people. *Yet another difference between here and Empeirus.*

"So, this is it?" Annalise asks enthusiastically.

Oliver offers a half smile, his pulse hastening with every step. "It is." Stepping foot on the front porch, he kneels to find the spare key hidden beneath a garden pot. *Thank the gods that it's still there.* Taking a breath of fresh air, Oliver fits the key into the lock and is just about to give the door handle a twist, when he swears that he hears voices on the other side.

"Is everything okay?" the princess questions.

Oliver pauses. "Yes ... No. Do you hear—"

The front door opens under a forceful hand, its owner meeting Oliver's stare with her own pine-green eyes. *Damn it.* Any man with a conscience knows that look means to run, but if Oliver had one, he wouldn't be at his family home with an outlawed royal goddess.

"Well, well," his sister drawls, her auburn hair glowing in the afternoon sun. "How long has it been, Oliver?"

"Harper," he says by way of greeting. "It's been four years."

"*Four* years!" Harper repeats. "And to what do we owe the pleasure?"

Oliver swallows. *Why is she here right now? Is she just visiting?*

A young voice calls out excitedly from inside the door. "Uncle Oliver!" The red-haired girl darts through the doorway, jumping into Oliver's arms.

"Wren!" Oliver exclaims, straining to withhold tears. "I missed you so much. Gods, look how much you've grown."

"Funny, how they do that over time," Harper snarks.

Oliver tries to ignore the sting. "I thought you and Evan were living in Cape Dright?" He watches as his sister's face transforms into a different kind of anger.

"Daddy is on a trip to Wembleton!" Wren tells Oliver. "Will you come inside to play?"

His heart breaks in two. *So, that's why she's here.* Oliver wonders what Evan did, his jaw clenching at every possible scenario. He never liked his brother-in-law much.

"I'm sorry, Harper."

"Wren, go inside and get the baskets ready for picking, will you?" Harper closes the door once her daughter runs back into the house. "If he knows what's good for him, he'll be on that trip for the rest of his life." Her green eyes dart from Oliver, to Annalise, then back to Oliver again.

She wants an explanation, he realizes. "You remember

my friend Marcus from the Royal Guard? This is his sister
…" *Gods, what was her name?*

"Piper." Annalise reaches to shake Harper's hand.

Sure, Piper. "Last month, Marcus was fatally wounded
during a conflict on the Javirian border, gods rest his soul.
With everything that happened at Larking Castle a couple
of weeks ago, I offered for his sister to flee the capital with
me." Oliver drops his voice slightly lower. "He asked me to
take care of her, since he was the last of their family."

Harper assesses her brother's travel companion with
little interest. "There's an inn down the street."

"Harper, wait!" Oliver catches the closing door under his
palm, pushing into the entryway. "Please, you don't understand. We don't have the coin to stay at an inn. Everything
happened so fast! We needed to get away in a hurry and."

"I don't need your sob story, Oliver. Believe me, I've
heard enough of them. And it isn't her that bothers me,
it's *you*. You know what you did."

"I didn't do anything! It's what I *didn't* do that you
blame me for."

"Exactly! Your insolence cost them their—"

"Mommy," Wren interrupts, dropping her baskets to
peer up at Harper with teary eyes. "I miss Daddy."

Oliver watches Harper pick up her daughter, rocking
her side to side for one second, then two. Stubbornly, she
meets her brother's gaze. "If you plan on staying here,

you'll need to work for it. I can hardly find enough time to take care of Wren."

Oliver closes his green eyes. "Harper, I will gladly help with everything I can. Piper will, too."

His sister nods. She places Wren back down and motions to Annalise to step inside. "Please excuse the mess. I'll have Wren clean up tonight after dinner." She brushes back a lock of auburn hair. "Everything is where it always has been," Harper tells Oliver, "except that I'm in Mom and Dad's old room. Wren has mine, but yours is untouched."

Annalise and Oliver pad down the hallway, pausing before an oak door.

Oliver turns the knob to reveal his old bedroom, a mirror image of what it had looked like four years ago. The curtains are still drawn, letting pale fingers of sunlight trace their way across the rug and the hardwood floor. He finds Annalise with her brown eyes locked on the singular bed.

"I can stay in the living room," Oliver quickly declares. He sets down his rucksack, taking a deep breath as his gaze travels outside his window and across the waves of the cobalt sea. His fingers slide over the grain of the windowsill, his mind replaying the day over and over again. *It couldn't have been my fault. I can't control everything.*

A soft pressure on his arm startles him, and Annalise quickly withdraws her hand. "Everything all right?"

Oliver nods. "Of course." He looks down at her other hand to find it presenting a small metal tin.

"For your cut," the princess instructs him quietly, before continuing to unpack the belongings in her bag.

MODGEN

"C'mon, is that all you've got?" A shirtless Modgen Sprightly spits blood on the fighting pit floor. "I've known Fetlandish women with more balls than you!"

The responding grunt of his opponent has Modgen readying for an attack, the lanky form of his body dripping with sweat as he drops to the dirt and rolls aside. From the ground, he kicks the huge Javirian man behind the knee, leaping at the opportunity to wrap his arms around his neck before being elbowed in the ribs. *Gods, Anna. This had better be worth it!*

He wastes no time. In a matter of seconds, the former Royal Treasurer drives his palm into the bottom of the man's nose and follows it with a quick punch to the throat. The crowd is hysterical when they watch the

Javirian collapse on the ground, clutching his neck. When the victory is called, Modgen gladly accepts the hefty sum, its weight pressing heavily into his marred hand.

Usually, any kind of physical conflict would be enough to send him sprinting for the hills—especially after his encounter with Captain Desmond Jrehart in the Royal Gardens—but when Modgen spent every last bit of coin that Annalise had given him for his journey, he needed to turn to some ... less-than-royal career paths.

"Go find Elouthera," she said. *"It won't be easy,"* she said.

And Annalise was right. Trying to find a goddess under the cover of an entirely different name and human body somewhere in the territory of Javir was like trying to find a day when Queen Adrianna wasn't willing to light the world on fire. *Then again, finding Dimity was easy enough.*

It isn't that Modgen wants to avoid thinking about his childhood best friend turning out to be the Goddess of Wisdom and Justice, only that if he tries wrapping his mind around the concept, it sends his head spinning with unwanted questions: *Has Annalise secretly been keeping this from me since we were young? Does she have magical powers that allow her to cheat during* halsen? *If a human kissed her, would they be electrocuted?*

The outlaw reels in his thoughts to focus on the task at hand, tugging on a stained tunic as he pushes through the fighting pit's exit. Modgen's only saving grace lies in the cryptic pieces of information Annalise was able to grant him before he departed from Empeirus: *"She's in Javir. Somewhere near the coast. I saw the Oronian Clock-tower, and heard the sound of water nearby..."* Which means that the Goddess of Dreams and Mystery could be in any number of coastal Javirian towns surrounding the famous landmark.

And so far, I haven't found a trace of her in any.

Modgen runs a hand through his reddish curls while his eyes adjust to the glow of the sun. A thick smoke greets his nose just outside the fighting pit building, twining its way through the air from a nearby vendor. Whether it's the legal kind or not, Modgen has no idea. His tired feet carry him across the main cobblestone road and down various winding paths, avoiding beady stares like he does Anzac's temples, until he reaches his destination near the harbor.

Taking a breath of humid sea air, Modgen trades a few of his hard-earned coins for a small loaf of bread and some salted fish. The Javirian salesman gives his familiar curt nod before his customer begins walking back through town. He makes this trek almost daily now. Sometimes because he feels like it, but mostly because it's the only thing he can afford on a fighting man's wages.

Chewing on his only meal of the day, Modgen broods over Annalise's situation. He recalls their final moments at the watchtower, the way she had looked just before stepping aboard a galley with Oliver McHenry. Stoic, but uncertain. As much Modgen wants to believe that his dearest friend can save the world, he can't help the occasional doubt from clawing its way in. There is always the risk of Annalise being found out while she is in the Savek Coast, but what if she fails at training her powers? *Or worse—what if she has her own agenda and should not be trusted?* Modgen nearly chokes on his last bite of bread.

Still, the most harrowing thought is the one he tries to run from most; the one that could result in Annalise losing her battle against Adrianna: *What if I can't find Elouthera?* He rounds a corner, tripping over a cobblestone and bumping into a girl wearing purple robes.

"Careful, there," she chides. "Be glad I'm not one of Edris's boys."

Modgen brushes his shoulder, wondering who the hell Edris is. "My apologies."

Another Nev. The nomads have always had a presence in Javir, but Modgen swears they have been growing in number by the day. Their notorious wagons draped in amethyst cloths have begun to plague the inner workings of Oron, especially near Modgen's lodgings—if they could be called such.

On the main road running through town, the ramshackle structure someone has enough nerve to call a hostelry stands tucked between two buildings of similar condition. Oron itself isn't a very wealthy town—which is surprising to Modgen, considering that it is home to many famous Javirian landmarks—but the district he has chosen to take residence in is particularly unfortunate. *Alas, there is not much that can be afforded when you earn your keep in the ring.*

Despite how dire his situation may seem, Modgen tries to find the best in it, as he usually does with most things. Trying out the local cuisine and sightseeing have both been enjoyable parts of his divine endeavor, and the former Royal Treasurer likes to take advantage of these as much as possible—so long as money permits.

One block from his temporary home lies a specific attraction that he often finds himself drawn to. '*Ig Dalosh O Ferrio,*' or 'The Road of Glory' in the Empeirian tongue, is a strip of town that is home to four major landmarks, the Oronian Clocktower included. In a few steps, his worn boots carry him there once more, mulling over the same vague phrase that Annalise had shared with him weeks before: *"I saw the Oronian Clocktower ..."*

It is ornate and beautiful, in a gothic sort of way. Each golden hand of the clock ticks with precise rhythm, the glass behind them a ghost compared to the dark gray of the rest of the building. Even the outside brick seems to emanate an eerie sort of mood, some of its sooty hue marred by what looks to be an occasional blood stain. And every sharp turret, every curve and grinning gargoyle seems to look down from the rooftop and mock him and his futile mission.

Modgen can't help feeling a little down on his luck. He knows Annalise was likely telling him the truth, but who is to say that she wasn't wrong in her judgment? Surely, visions can be hard to read. *Perhaps she misinterpreted? Or perhaps the vision could have changed by now?* He rubs the crooks between his cobalt-blue eyes and his nose, trying desperately to breathe away his growing frustrations.

Two guards stand watch outside the elaborate oval doorway of the Oronian Clocktower, which obviously isn't open to the public. But no matter how many times the red-haired man passes the landmark, nothing looks out of the ordinary. In fact, Modgen has scoured the entire town looking for signs of Elouthera, but the only things he finds are dead ends. A female with unspeakable powers? Just another Nev. A dangerous woman with a bounty on her head? Turned out to be a Calleetian pirate. How is Modgen supposed to find a goddess without her mortal name? *I don't even know what she looks like, for the gods' sakes!*

Turning back to the cobblestone street, his attention catches on a clamor of horse hooves, his eyes lingering on the rider in front. If his gaudy attire or chiseled jaw doesn't give away his authority, the way he carries himself certainly does. The man dismantles his horse, his black boots thudding against the ground with unrivaled vigor.

"How is she holding up?" he questions one of the guards.

"Which one? Your sister or the witch?"

A snarl from the leader. "Who the hell do you think I mean?" The man moves the single stride it takes to close the gap between them, twisting the fabric of the guard's shirt into a fist. "I have everything riding on this, Fenz. Don't muck it up." He shoves the man backward, watching him stumble in shock. "Now, how is she?"

Modgen pretends to be interested in the mud caked between the cobblestones.

The guard swallows. "Very good, sir. We've kept her under wraps, as you've requested."

"Good. Our travel plans are almost in place. If she gives you any trouble, let me know." The muscular man turns to remount his horse.

"Edris!" the guard calls out. "What will become of your sister?"

Edris offers a sinister grin. "Leave her to me," he orders, snapping the reigns before he and his gang disappear through one of the back alleys of Oron.

Edris, Modgen reflects. *The same name that Nev mentioned earlier today.* Crimes in Javir are more common than snowflakes in Godrus, but this man and his posse seem to be up to something far larger than petty theft. *A witch in the clocktower ...* Modgen casually surveys the windows of the building, with guards on each side of the doorway. *Whoever is in there must be important,* he notes with growing curiosity.

Modgen watches the minute hand of the clock reach the hour, a matching chime echoing through the alleys to inform those too far away to see. *I don't know. It seems like too much of a risk.* Sighing, he continues down the road toward his decrepit home when on the third ring, he stops dead in his tracks.

The scream is faint and muffled, but loud enough to hear until it is drowned out by the next note. It doesn't sound like it is from ground level, but rather from the top of the clocktower itself. At first, Modgen thinks he is imagining things, but a swift glance at the guards' suspicious faces tells him everything he needs to know: *There is a so-called witch in the Oronian Clocktower who is guarded under the command of a powerful gang. How much more conspicuous does it get?*

Modgen may not have had much luck before, but the odds of finding another situation with this many parallels are slim to none. He feels in his pocket for his measly earnings from today's fight, already half gone from his daily meal. *I suppose I really don't have much to lose.* His boots are worn, his shirt is dirty, and his eyes are tired. *I need to take this chance. And then, gods willing, I will be able to leave this place.*

As he reaches the front door of his battered lodgings, Modgen looks back toward The Road of Glory. The highest turrets of the Oronian Clocktower can be seen from here, cresting just above the rooftops of other dark, gloomy, Javirian buildings. *If I'm really doing this, I'm going to need to find a way in.*

A sensual call from the balcony next door breaks his concentration, his cobalt gaze switching from the courtesan above to the drunken man walking zig-zags on the street below her. Modgen thinks back to a similar environment in the slums of Empeirus, back to an old bakery, a man with pine-green eyes, and crimson servant's attire. By the time the man stumbles into the bottom of the brothel, Modgen already has an idea weaving its way together.

While the sun sets behind the skyline, he breathes in the balmy Javirian air, weighing his bag of coins in his hand and wondering how hard it would be to find smoke bombs in this part of the kingdom.

ADRIANNA

"**A**gain!" Desmond Jrehart chants for the fortieth time this session. His piercing silver eyes drill holes through Queen Adrianna Larking's head while she concentrates on maintaining her wilting form.

She thrusts her palm forward with the last of her remaining strength, watching the shard of ice sail through the air with the feeble force of a child. It dips just before Desmond's palm, crashing to its doom like Adrianna's confidence.

Her lover drops his hand, surveying the shattered ice before him. "Perhaps that's enough for today," Desmond admonishes.

"Don't patronize me," Dria spits. "I'll be done when I want to be."

"Then you can practice aiming at the castle walls, because I'm exhausted." The Captain of the Royal Guard turns toward the exit of the White Garden. Their relationship has been like this for some time now, dampened by the intensity of their incessant training.

Adrianna's body writhes with agony, her brows beaded with sweat. "You don't think I can do it, do you?"

Desmond stops in his tracks. "What did you just say?"

The queen hides her trembling arms. "I said," a pause for breath, "you don't think I can defeat her."

The captain scoffs, backtracking a step toward his paramour. "Never once have I doubted your capabilities, Jedda." He sighs quietly, dropping his voice to a level reserved only for her. "I know losing to Annalise that day in the castle was a blow to your self-esteem. But you must realize that the only person doubting yourself, is you."

Adrianna blinks her icy-blue eyes, watching as the God of Darkness and Decay stalks out of the garden successfully this time. *Maybe he's right*, she acknowledges, feeling both dread and relief. She stands alone before the White Garden Pond, watching her reflection ripple in the waves while she rolls out her aching wrists.

The day that Annalise defeated both Adrianna and Desmond two weeks ago wasn't only devastating to the Dark Goddess's ego, but a rude awakening that even with Desmond, her power wasn't enough. *Annalise may have been outnumbered, but we were outsmarted.* She clenches her fists at the thought of Dimity smashing a glass case above Anzac's head, at the way it crushed him against the marble floors of the Throne Room. *And if she finds Elouthera, things could quickly turn from bad to worse.*

Adrianna's only hope lies in the memory of Annalise at the end of their battle, at how her body also looked like it was deteriorating from the inside out. *I can't be the only one having such a long recovery period from the use of my powers.* Which is why Jedda has turned to practicing her divine magic with Anzac, pushing herself past the pain and the fatigue to train at least once daily.

A drop of cold rain lands on the queen's fair nose, startling her from her dour thoughts. It is still too warm for snow, but the chill autumn air promises to grant some soon. Adrianna pulls herself from introspection in time to spot her lady-in-waiting padding across the lawn.

"Your Godliness." Renai curtsies in her gray silk gown.

Jedda rolls her eyes. "Please, Renai. I thought we went over this already. 'Your Majesty' will do just as well." The Crimson Queen links her arm through Renai's, guiding them back toward the castle. "Walk with me."

"If it pleases you, Your Majesty." A playful smile, one that quickly fades once she recognizes the frail condition of her queen. "I'm afraid I don't have the most uplifting news. There is still no word of your sister."

Adrianna smiles weakly. "I wasn't expecting Annalise to reappear out of thin air."

"I wasn't talking about Annalise," Renai clarifies. "I was talking about Princess Aimelie."

The queen walks quietly, trying to ignore the heavy weight in the pit of her stomach. Her younger sister had bolted the day she and Desmond had exposed their godly forms, and things have not been the same since. The castle has indeed been lonely without her presence, but it pains her more to know that her only remaining family has chosen to side against her. Adrianna digs her nails into the palm of her free hand. *I always knew she would choose Annalise. Everyone always does.*

Renai senses her queen's disappointment and takes Adrianna's hands. "We will keep looking, Your Majesty. She can't have gotten far."

The Queen of Empeirus nods, taking a breath of cold air before entering the castle's Great Hall.

"But, I also have some good news," Renai continues. "Desmond's contact in the Iribus Circus has successfully captured the goddess Elouthera. Plans for her arrival by ship are being made as we speak."

Adrianna's blue eyes narrow. "Elouthera," she repeats, the name burning on her tongue. She had forgotten about Desmond's contact in Javir. *I can't believe it actually worked.* Her mind flashes back to a conversation with a courtesan, to one phrase she divulged in particular: *She fled to Javir!* The queen snorts. "Perhaps there was some merit to what Narelle had mentioned." She turns back to Renai. "Where there is one, there is bound to be the other. Maybe Annalise will crawl out of the Javirian woodwork too, if the gods are good." Dria smiles ironically.

"My hopes are high." Renai shoots her a foxlike grin. "And so are the Nevs'."

The queen's smile disappears. *The Nevs.* As little as Adrianna trusts her outlawed sister, she trusts the Nevs even less—especially her latest contact in the fortunetelling cult, Cyndeya Kutchrik. Dria never expected a nomadic oracle to be anything short of mysterious, but to wear a lock of hair around her neck ... *My hair,* Adrianna thinks with a shutter. It bothers her more than she wants to admit. "I am sure Cyndeya has placed her very best in Javir. Edris Sharpkey has been made aware of our alliance, so there shouldn't be any cause for issue between them."

The pages open the doors to the Throne Room, and all eyes fall on the queen. *Well, the few eyes that have stayed to partake in court under the Dark Goddess.* While the number of courtiers has dwindled after the incident at Larking Castle, not much else about them has. *They are still the same tittering fools, all fighting over a scrap of my attention.* "Tell me, Renai," Dria asks in hushed tones, "why are they still here? They know what I am. Why haven't they fled with the rest of their ilk?"

Renai shrugs her thin shoulders. "Power. Fame. Greed."

"And why are *you* still here?"

The queen's lady-in-waiting smirks. "Who said my reasons had to be any different?"

Adrianna snorts, departing from her childhood friend to take her seat on the throne while the rest of her court follows suit.

Lady Elmington is the first to speak. "Your Godliness, it is our duty to aid you in protecting your queenhood, but how is this possible if Princess Annalise—or, *Dimity*, rather—is nowhere to be found? How can we make the most beneficial decisions without knowing her whereabouts?"

Queen Adrianna ignores the woman's use of her "godly" title and nods. For a moment, she actually feels something like gratitude. *How odd would it be to feel this every day, to have people that care about your well-being?* Dria's mind wanders back to the way everyone seemed to care about her older sister, and even Aimelie. *What made them more likable than me?*

Adrianna frames her response with a smile, however serpentine it may look. "I appreciate your concern over my safety, my lady. After all, knowing that my traitorous sister is loose somewhere in the kingdom is distressing news for everyone, considering that she murdered our royal parents." A cold gaze out the far window, the one that Annalise climbed out of only weeks ago. "I fear this world has changed her, made her into something else entirely, far from the Dimity I've known my whole immortal life."

She stands from her throne, sighing while she brushes out the folds of her crimson dress with weak arms. "Many of you know me as Jedda, the Dark Goddess. But such a title is not meant to be feared. Just as there is light, there is darkness, and we need each to survive. It is only when one causes an imbalance that we need to worry." Adrianna steps aimlessly about the dais.

"Dimity's attempt to take control of the Empeirian throne has caused chaos, rattling the grounds of the entire kingdom," the queen continues. "It is true that we need to guard against Annalise, but to learn where she has been hiding, we may have to do just the opposite."

"Your Majesty," Cyndeya Kutchrik chimes in beneath purple robes. "If your sister desires the throne, it is likely that she will expose herself in due time."

"Waiting for her to turn up at my door would almost guarantee her enough time to obtain an army and alliances, neither of which I am inclined to deal with," Dria rebukes.

The occultist tilts her round face, narrowing her

citrine eyes. "Then you will need something quite enticing to draw her out."

The Queen of Empeirus chuckles, seating herself back on her crimson throne. "That, I do, Cyndeya." Adrianna smiles. "That, I do." Her icy-blue eyes fall to her spymaster with glee. "Calix," she calls. "How fares our precious courtesan?"

ANNALISE

Another wave skims its way across the rocky shore of Cordel Beach, Annalise's body tensing again from its proximity. The princess feels like they have been walking for close to a mile, but it is better this way, to be sure they are hidden from prying eyes. *I don't know how Savekian folk are, but in Empeirus, word spreads like wildfire.*

"How about here?" Oliver points to what looks to be a small cave visible only from its entrance.

Anna steps over a large rock, sucking in a breath as a tendril of seawater finds its way around her boot. "Perfect." She tries to ignore the sound of the Falvedrie Sea behind them as she follows her friend inside.

It has been almost two weeks since Annalise's showdown with her sister at Larking Castle, and the princess's godly powers have remained dormant ever since. Now, with the opportunity to train them, she is almost afraid of facing them again. *Afraid of how my body will react again. Afraid of not being good enough to win against Adrianna and Desmond. Afraid of reminding myself that I am actually a goddess incarnate, and not just a normal human being.*

The inside of the cave is cool with moisture, its jagged ceiling dripping occasionally with chilly droplets of water. But despite a gruff welcome, its sandy floor is smooth and nearly even, making it ideal for training purposes.

"We just have to make sure to leave before the tide comes back in. Unless you want to swim out of here?" Oliver gives her a knowing smile.

The princess shivers. "No, thank you." Annalise turns to survey the cave, locking her brown eyes on a stalactite hanging from the ceiling. She turns her gaze back to find Oliver observing her with his hands in his pockets. "Well, don't watch me!"

The former Master of the High Council laughs, throwing his hands up in submission. "Fine. I'll just watch the waves instead of a goddess wielding magical powers in human form."

Annalise sighs in frustration, pressing her thumb and forefinger to the bridge of her elegant nose. "I haven't used them since I faced my sister."

Oliver kicks a pebble across the beige sand. "And you're nervous?"

The goddess shrugs. "Last time didn't exactly offer the smoothest period of recovery." Annalise flexes her hands to focus on the magic flowing through her veins, remembering how much her muscles ached in the days after her battle at the castle. "But I have to get better if I want to win. I *need* to win." Losing wouldn't just mean the potential loss of taking back the Empeirian throne, but the ultimate failure of saving Earth from being destroyed. *That is, if Elouthera and I can't sway Jedda and Anzac to our side.*

Focusing her energy on the stalactite, Annalise finds the fire within her body and releases what she thinks will be an epic arrow of flame—only to watch it sputter into a few embers. She drops her hands. *How could I have gotten so much worse?* Regrouping herself, the goddess tries again, pushing her body to produce what turns out to be even fewer flames than before.

"Perhaps you aren't fully recovered yet?" Oliver suggests.

The goddess rubs her wrists in irritation. Her stomach tightens even more at the fact that she already feels exhausted from what should have been a small output of energy. Disappointedly, Annalise takes a seat on a nearby rock in the sand. "Maybe you're right. Maybe I'm not fully healed yet."

Oliver watches the ceiling drip in silence, his ever-green eyes falling on the spot where her embers dissipated into the sand. "Does your magic hurt your body every time you use it?"

Anna runs a finger in the sand. "Not necessarily." She thinks back to her room in the watchtower, to when she levitated a cup of tea in front of her desk. "It only seems to affect me when I need to summon a lot of it."

He rubs the back of his neck. "And you were feeling otherwise well before you tried using your powers today?"

"I thought I was. My body wasn't sore anymore." Annalise stands from her rock, dusting the sand off her dress.

Oliver slips his hands back into his pockets. "Is there any chance that strengthening your body would make it easier to summon larger amounts of magic?"

The princess huffs a laugh, watching the waves creep slowly inland. "You mean, by getting physically stronger?"

A nod.

Annalise thinks for a minute, at how the idea might have some merit. *If levitating a teacup doesn't seem to faze my body, but working up enough magic to blow Adrianna to bits does ...* "I suppose that could be a sound assumption, especially since I was feeling fine before I started today. Summoning the elements is harder than working with ones that already exist in some form or other, so this would have been a more moderate task."

"Then, maybe you should start there."

Annalise watches a white gull cry over the cobalt waters, its body swooping down to grab tonight's dinner from the sea. "All right, I'll do it. Under one condition."

Oliver raises a brow.

"You train me to fight without magic, the way you did on the ship."

Her comrade pauses, reading the sincerity in Anna's expression. "I'm by no means up to Desmond's standards," Oliver admits, "but I can at least show you the basics."

"Really?" Annalise grins with excitement, eager to shift her attention away from her divinity and toward something she can progress at, toward something human.

"Of course." Oliver begins the trek outside the cave with Anna following closely behind. When his feet hit the stretch of smooth sand, he shoots a smile at the goddess. "We can start with an easy run back to the house."

"A run—" Annalise starts to protest, but Oliver's boots are already flicking up sand yards in front of her. *Damn him!* Groaning, she launches her body forward to catch up to him, blocking out the nearby waves as she inches her way to his side.

Annalise brushes out her dark brown waves, staring back at her reflection in the mirror of Oliver's old bedroom. Her dark eyes are tired from today's training, but strangely enough, her soul feels … lighter. It's almost like taking a break from thinking about her dire responsibilities has helped give Anna some much-needed peace of mind.

The eldest Larking princess adjusts a dress sleeve, frowning at the state of her attire. In their haste to leave Empeirus, Annalise and Oliver thought it best to travel light, and she only brought two dresses. *One for travel and one for more formal occasions, such as dinner, I suppose.* But even the nicer of the two gowns has begun to show its age, a few blue threads working loose from its square neckline.

Sighing, the goddess unlocks the bedroom door, nearly tripping over a child sprinting down the hallway. "I'm sorry," Annalise breathes, mostly to herself, now that Wren has already made her way to the dinner table.

"Please excuse her." Harper throws a towel over her shoulder, pushing a platter of cod and potatoes to the center of the table. "She hasn't gotten out of her wild phase yet."

Anna smiles. "I wish I had half her energy. Can I help you with anything?"

A sharp glance around the room. "Well, you could go tell your boyfriend that dinner is ready, since he's still not out."

"Oh." The princess blushes, picking at the loose threads of her dress. "It's not like that. We aren't …"

Harper waits with an entirely different set of pine-green eyes.

"It's complicated," Annalise musters.

"What is?" Oliver's voice startles her from behind.

Harper grins wider than Anna has seen her grin yet, turning to grab a pitcher of water from the kitchen. "Life," she responds, calling Wren to the table.

Annalise pulls up a chair next to Oliver, trying to suppress any residual awkwardness from her and Harper's conversation. "Everything looks wonderful. Thank you."

A swat of her hand. "You're too polite," Harper smirks. "Where did you say you were from again, Piper?"

"Empeirus," Annalise answers, remembering Oliver's ruse from yesterday.

"Right. That's how you and my brother met. Through his friend Marcus, who he showed more care for than his actual family for the past four years."

"Harper, enough." Oliver levels his gaze at his sister, tightening his jaw. "If you want to have this conversation, we can have it outside, away from Wren."

"Why not in front of her, so she can understand what really happened that day?" Harper's auburn hair glows in the light of the fireplace.

Oliver sets down his fork. "I will not discuss the

details of our parents' deaths before my niece." He stands from the table. "If you'll excuse me, I think it's best if I have my dinner outside, where I won't be an imposition to anyone."

Annalise regards him with wide eyes as he takes his plate toward the back porch, pausing at the door.

"You're welcome for the fish, by the way," Oliver grumbles, slipping into the brisk night air.

Wren quietly resumes her meal, but Annalise turns her attention to Harper, whose face seems to be smattered with something like guilt. The princess knows better than to ask, so she does her best to finish her food in silence and excuse herself from the table, taking a few extra minutes to clean her dishes and put them on a shelf with the others. Quietly, after she watches Harper take Wren down the hall for a bath, Anna opens the door to the back porch.

It is a chilly night, the breeze coming off the Falvedrie Sea getting colder by the day, but the sky is clear enough to see a thousand twinkling stars. Annalise's brown gaze takes in the constellations with appreciation, her arms wrapped around her abdomen in a futile attempt to keep warm. "Is this what you stayed out here for?"

Oliver gives what might be considered a half smile from his spot on a bench. "Not exactly." His stare drifts back to the sea, to what will likely be the horizon at daybreak.

Tapping her fingers against her leg, the princess nervously decides to take a seat beside him. She opens her mouth, but nothing comes out.

By the grace of the gods, Oliver opens his, too. "You asked about my ring while we were on the ship." He slides the silver band from his pinky finger, the embossed feather hardly visible in the starlight.

"I remember. I said it was a nice ring."

A genuine half smile. "It was my father's. He gave it to me when I was sixteen, after I joined the Royal Guard. It was a family heirloom. That's why it has the feather, from our family crest."

Annalise nods silently, waiting for him to continue.

"I'm sorry you had to hear us argue at dinner." Oliver's tone is soft, his face to the ocean. He slips the ring back onto his hand, toying with it uneasily. "Harper blames me for our parents' deaths. And maybe there's a part of me that blames me for it, too."

Anna's heart sinks to her stomach, the loss of her own parents coming to mind.

"My parents were like most Savekians. They lived for the sea, were bred for full sails and a deck beneath their feet. But even the most skillful sailors are no match for Mother Nature, especially during a surprise storm." Oliver places his hands on the edge of the bench beneath them.

"One day, about four years ago, Harper and I got into a fight. It was a petty argument like we usually had, but this one happened to be on my birthday. At seventeen, I was more self-absorbed than I should have been, and I set sail without telling anyone. I spent hours on the sea by myself, waiting until the last of my anger had fizzled out, and I returned home. Only, by the time I made it back, my parents had already left." He sighs, stealing a breath to finish his story.

"Harper told me that when they saw one of our sailboats gone, our parents decided to go out looking for me. What they didn't know was that there was a massive, unexpected storm moving ..." Oliver presses a hand to his mouth, taking a moment to restore his composure. "They were found in the rubble where their boat wrecked, about half a mile from here."

A stray tear splashes onto the blue fabric of Annalise's dress, her hand quickly wiping the others away from her porcelain cheeks. "I'm sorry," is all she can offer. She wonders at how he can still look at the Falvedrie Sea, at how he can continue to set foot on ships and sail over its waters knowing that it had taken his parents' lives. "It wasn't your fault," Anna tells him, and from the way his expression changes, she can tell it is something he needs to hear.

Oliver takes a deep breath, closing his evergreen eyes in the darkness of the night.

A memory tugs on Annalise's mind—more specifically, a particular face. It is blurred from time, but

Annalise remembers the way his green eyes looked almost as patient as Oliver's own. She faces him with curiosity. "Was your father Edmund McHenry?"

Oliver quickly meets Annalise's gaze. "He was."

A bright smile. "I would often sit in on council meetings when I turned thirteen. Your father was the shipmaster during my father's reign. If I remember correctly, they seemed to be rather good friends."

The former master huffs a laugh, returning her smile in the late autumn air. He leans back on his hands to get a better view of the beautiful night sky. "I wonder what they would think of us, being friends."

The princess follows Oliver's gaze to the stars, mirroring his position. "Me too." Annalise smiles faintly at the heavens. "Me too."

VEGA

Vega Kutchrik observes with narrow eyes as Eden Sharpkey is thrown to the ground for the third time this week.

"Careful with the bindings," Edris Sharpkey orders the guard. "Her wrists might be raw from the other ones."

A simmering rage takes hold in Vega's stomach. Even though she doesn't know the aerialist well, her lime-green eyes can clearly see what is going on—and the Goddess of Dreams and Mystery doesn't like it one bit. "Can't you find any willing participants? Or does everyone find you that repulsive?"

Eden's twin brother saunters past the doorway of their cell in his usual finery. "Anzac did say you had a dark side, Elouthera." He stops a healthy distance from Vega, whose arms are strapped into her own binding-like contraption. "Maybe before I return you to him, you'll let me explore it?"

Vega's hands tighten into fists, her up-tilted eyes meeting his own. "When I break out of this, you'll be the first to go."

A low whistle. "I don't think you'll be that lucky." Edris turns on a booted heel to face Eden's guard. "Boat leaves on the hour. I want the goddess in the carriage mere minutes before it does. The less time we keep her outside this clocktower, the better. Leave Eden here." The leader of the Iribus Circus faces Vega once more. "I'll be waiting for you when you get to the ship." He smiles, a disgusting, twisted thing.

Elouthera's stare could shatter glass as Edris departs from the jail cell with his guard in tow. It has been a little over two weeks since she and Eden had been caught on the streets of Javir looking for a ship that would take them to Empeirus. *Well, now I have one waiting for me, only it's under control of a criminal working for my godly counterpart.* Vega curls her bound hands into fists. *Anzac,* she curses silently. *Of course, Jedda's protector has found yet another way to keep me from being united with Dimity.*

Vega remembers the day she was captured by Edris's men and the unfortunate events that led up to it. From Christa, her false friend and shadow pawn watching Vega fall into the Javirian Sea, to meeting Eden Sharpkey once she reached the deceptive safety of the Javirian shore.

Vega senses a stare and shifts her attention toward the mismatched gaze of her new acquaintance.

"Nothing," Eden tells her quietly in her Javirian accent. "He told me nothing about Anzac or his plans."

Their attempt to gain information from Edris Sharpkey has been unsuccessful, leaving them only with the dissatisfying knowledge that he is taking Vega to Empeirus, and that Eden will be chained here for what will likely be the rest of her days.

Elouthera sighs. "When Anzac finds me, he will kill me."

The circus performer glances at her bound hands. "It is a better fate than others," Eden replies.

Gods, the Sharpkeys. The moment Eden spilled that her mother was Laraya Sharpkey, Vega knew she was damned. Said to be the most gifted seer in history, Laraya was the infamous leader of the Iribus Circus, an elite group of performers that has been bred for generations of entertainment, and perhaps more than that. Rumor has it that after Laraya managed to eliminate a surprise ploy, planned before Queen Annora's coronation, the circus continued to be used as the Empeirian throne's secret guard. Conspirators swear that the group performs stunts by day and executes Queen Adrianna's dirty work by night.

Whether or not the claim is true, Vega hasn't an inkling, but she wants nothing to do with it. Getting involved with this lot can only draw her further from her original plans of finding Dimity. *But considering that Edris is in the business of holding hostages and working for Anzac, it might be safe to assume that there is some substance to the hearsay.*

Anzac. Vega releases a frustrated sigh, a few strands of her jet-black hair leaping forward. *Could it be?* A memory tugs at her mind, one from what felt like Dimity herself. *"I will be Earth's champion no matter what."* A blonde woman in a crimson dress, a ruby-adorned crown glittering atop her head. A battle of fire and ice. A man beside her, weaving shadows out of darkness. *Could it be that Jedda is the queen?* The man from Dimity's shared vision was obviously Anzac, but Vega isn't familiar enough with Empeirian politics to guess who he might be in this mortal lifetime. *His silver eyes looked like they could cut steel.*

She doesn't know what exactly went down the day Edris locked her up in this clocktower, but Vega knows two things for certain: Jedda and Anzac are in Empeirus, and Dimity is still alive. *I can feel that she is far away, but the bond is still there.* The goddess often wonders who her allied deity is in this lifetime, but amidst her ongoing confinement, she mostly wonders how they will get to each other. *I need my hands to manipulate objects, and I need time to concentrate on altering minds. How am I supposed to break free if they keep me locked in this contraption and under the watch of multiple guards?*

A groan from Eden catches her attention, and Vega finds her wincing from pain. The goddess dips her forehead, feeling guilty for not being able to save everyone in the world from such tragedies. "I'm sorry," is all she can muster.

"No," Eden manages. "My head ..." She closes her mismatched eyes. "I see the color red."

Normally, Vega wouldn't have given this woman the time of day, but considering that Eden's last vision had some merit, she tries to be more open-minded. *Her last vision foretold Edris and his men coming to usurp us, albeit in a very non-direct way. Besides, playing into this game makes captivity just slightly less boring.* "Can you see anything else?"

Another wince, then a deep breath. Eden relaxes her eyebrows. "It takes the shape of a knight." Her blue and gold eyes meet Vega's own. "Vega, we are going to be saved!"

The goddess stares. *Perhaps two weeks is the tipping point for madness.* She manages a small laugh. "Eden, the last time you saw a gray cloud and we were taken hostage in a clocktower. Seeing a knight could mean anything. Your brother could come back later disguised as a knight."

Eden shakes her head but says nothing. Vega doesn't want to crush her dreams, but wishful thinking won't get them out of this nightmare; using their brains will. *Think, Vega. Think!* She closes her lime-green eyes before she hears another moan, this one deeper than before. Vega looks up at her cellmate.

"That wasn't me," Eden declares.

The two of them glance around the room, but no one is to be seen.

"It must have come from outside," Vega gathers. She closes her eyes once again.

Another groan, then a short yell and a bang, followed by coughing. This time, the sound comes from the stairwell on the other side of their cell's door. The sound of running, then walking. A moment of quiet.

Vega opens her eyes. "I—"

The wooden door bursts into a million pieces, the splinters raining around them in a cloud of smoke. Elouthera's heart thunders in her chest, her cat-like eyes wide awake and taking in every inch of the scene that she can. Watching a shape take form through the haze, Vega prepares for Anzac himself to make an early appearance, her breathing almost loud enough to drown out the shadow's coughing on the other side of the room.

He's taller than I expected, is the first ridiculous thing that pops into her head when he breaks through the smoke. The second is, *I don't remember him having red hair in that vision.*

"Good gods!" The lanky man coughs, waving a hand through the air. "I've got to get out of this territory."

The women look at each other in appalled silence.

"My apologies," the intruder begins. He turns his cobalt eyes to the sky. "I know this is going to sound absolutely insane, but I'm looking for—"

Vega's lime-green gaze meets his own.

"Elouthera," he finishes, looking entranced by her for some reason or another. *Maybe it's this bizarre contraption.*

Eden's mismatched eyes fill with excitement. "The red knight!" she mouths from her post across the room.

"Who's asking?" Vega snaps.

The man checks behind him before briskly moving forward to undo Eden's bindings. "Annalise—or Dimity —sent me on her behalf."

Dimity! Lazarus, almighty! "Annalise," Vega begins, the man setting to work on her own system of confinement. "Wasn't that the name of the lost princess?"

Their savior chuckles. "I suppose word doesn't travel well to clocktower jail cells." He lends Elouthera a hand to help her stand up. "Dimity *is* the lost princess."

"And who are you?" Eden questions while Vega stares blankly at such a bold statement.

"Me?" The redhead grins. "Modgen Sprightly, childhood best friend of Dimity and Javirian fighting pit extraordinaire, at your service."

It is Vega's turn to say, "Good gods!"

Modgen winks. "Do you think you can show me that you have powers? You know, so I don't rescue the wrong goddess or anything."

The sound of a bellow comes from outside.

"I don't think we have time for that," Vega replies, grabbing Eden's arm. "Get us out of here." *I don't care who you bloody are, at least being outside this clocktower will give us a fighting chance.*

The women follow their new accomplice down the winding clocktower stairs, stepping over the occasional unconscious guard until they reach the main level. For the second time today, Vega's heart beats faster than a Calleetian ballad, her mind scrambling for purchase over all the new information she has just learned and the thrill of breaking free from this gods-forsaken prison.

Modgen rounds the corner, only to come face-to-face with a boisterous guard. "What the hell do you think you're doing?" He greets the guard with a punch to the throat, but no sooner does he try to do it again than the guard slips out a dirk.

In a moment, Elouthera sees what she needs to do, and does it. The goddess lunges forward, clamping her hand over the hilt and using her other hand to catch the puddle of silver she transforms it into. With the man distracted by fear, she manipulates the puddle into a band of metal and slams it over the guard's eyes, making sure the circle meets at the other side to keep him from being able to pull it off.

"Go!" Elouthera yells at Modgen, pushing him out the clocktower entrance.

"I only brought one horse!" he yells at them. "I didn't anticipate there being two of you!"

"We'll take this one!" Vega unties a black horse from a post, reassuring herself that she is freeing it from whatever cruelty the Javirian guards had put it through. She throws her tiny foot over the saddle, helping Eden up as soon as she is situated.

Modgen trots his brown steed beside Vega and Eden's, escalating it to a canter as they navigate the cobblestone roads of the town. *Oron*, Vega soon realizes after reading a few shop signs. She whips her gaze behind her and Eden to ensure they aren't being followed, but the only people watching seem to be some civilians and a small group of Nevs.

What am I doing? Vega finds herself thinking while her stolen horse follows Modgen's. As grateful as she is for the redheaded man freeing her, she can't help wondering if she has traded one form of danger for another, however unlikely that notion may be. The goddess examines Modgen's swaying figure, sending up a prayer to Lazarus that he is, indeed, taking her to Dimity.

At the edge of town, the three reach a fork in the road. To Vega's surprise, Modgen turns left instead of right. "You missed the sign for Empeirus," she points out, assuming that is where Dimity still is.

"That's because we're not going to Empeirus," Modgen Sprightly concedes. "We're going to Nesvla."

AIMELIE

"Princess, I said to wait for us!" Ivo yells thirty feet behind her, but if Aimelie has to hold her bladder any longer, she fears it is likely to burst. *And given recent events, I have no more doubts that anything is possible.*

The princess scurries along, leaving Tasman and Ivo with her singular bag as her slippered feet climb the granite steps of Eldric Castle. *It's even more beautiful than in the paintings,* Melie thinks with some delight. Finely dressed courtiers dot the corridor, the chill air of late autumn drifting through the castle doors each time they open and shut. The golden domed ceilings are wide and cavernous, but oddly comforting compared to the drafty heights of Larking Castle. It is the first bastion of normalcy that she has felt in almost a week, since the happenings at her own castle home.

"Your Highness." A page clad in orange meets Aimelie in the grand hallway with a bow so low, she swears his nose may hit the ground. "My queen is awaiting your arrival in her Throne Room. If you would please follow me, Princess?" The page waits for her nod of approval before leading her down the orange carpet to a set of thick doors, the mahogany decorated with scenes in gold leaf. He gives a few taps on the right door in a discreet pattern.

Aimelie waits a bit impatiently while the pages on the other side undoubtedly announce her arrival. Master Tasman and Captain Ivo hadn't shared much about the Eldrics, only that they were close friends with her late parents. *In truth, I'm more concerned about where the nearest chamber pot is.*

The behemoth doors groan, opening up to a lovely Throne Room in shades of persimmon. At the head of the dais, a shimmering throne sits occupied by a handsome woman, perhaps no older than thirty-eight years, with skin pale as moonlight and eyes like the sea. Her cloth-of-gold gown must have cost a fortune, and for a moment, Aimelie blushes through her freckles at the tattered gray cloak that Urayus had gifted her.

The princess curtsies gracefully, as she has been taught to her entire life. "Your Grace." She smiles politely.

"Your Highness." Queen Minerva rises from her

throne, making her way toward Melie. Her posture is pin-straight, the spitting portrait of a ruler with her thick black hair decorated in golden pins.

Does her head even move an inch while she walks? Her crown looks as if it is floating.

The Queen of Nesvla takes Aimelie's porcelain hands in her own. "Lazarus almighty." Her blue eyes well with tears. "I never thought I'd see the day!" Queen Minerva embraces the princess, taking a moment to study her face. "You must be dreadfully tired from all of your travel, but I can't wait any longer." She gestures to the young man to the right of the throne, his features so similar to the queen's. "Princess Annalise, allow me to introduce you to—"

"Your Grace, this is not Princess Annalise," Tasman interrupts through heavy breaths.

Aimelie turns to find Tasman at her left and presses a hand to her lips.

"Ivo told you to wait for us," he whispers disappointedly.

Queen Minerva releases a huff of air, blinking her blue eyes with something like embarrassment or annoyance. She clears her throat. "My apologies, my lady. Perhaps we should start with introductions, shall we?"

Aimelie swallows her questions. "Your Grace, I am Princess Aimelie Larking, youngest daughter of the late King Tiberius and Queen Annora Larking." She watches as the Nesvlan queen nods in recognition, her mind seeming to piece things together a bit more. "And this is the former Master of the High Council, Tasman Rigfeld, and the former Captain of the Royal Guard, Ivo Drandian."

Queen Minerva smiles. "Now things make more sense. Master Tasman, Captain Ivo; it is good to see old friends again." She turns her regal gaze toward the young man beside her throne once more. "My son, Darren Eldric, the Crown Prince of Nesvla," she finishes at last.

The Crown Prince of Nesvla, Aimelie mulls. The princess reads Prince Darren cautiously as they exchange a bow and a curtsy, her large doe eyes soaking in every bit of his demeanor. While his blue eyes and pitch-black hair are a mirror image of his mother's, the prince is taller and seems to walk with even more self-assurance, if such a thing could be possible.

"My lady." Darren Eldric smirks at Aimelie.

"My lord," Aimelie responds courteously, with hardly more than a glance in his direction.

"Well, then." Queen Minerva claps her hands together excitedly. "Perhaps we can catch up a bit more after you've had time to recover from your journey? My servants will show you to your living quarters, and we can reconvene at dinner."

"Very well, Your Grace" Tasman bows, Ivo and Aimelie following suit. On their way out of the Throne Room, the old man places a frail hand on the princess's cloaked shoulder, the other on his cane. "She was not expecting you to be here in Annalise's stead."

Aimelie presses her blonde brows together. "Yes, why *was* she expecting me to be my sister? You said she was with Master McHenry in the Savek Coast." The princess couldn't help but notice how much less excited the queen was upon discovering her true identity.

Tasman sighs. "Better to speak of this once she arrives," he dodges her question.

"And when will she be arriving?"

"When she finishes her training," Ivo grunts. "The gods know when that will be."

Of course, her training. I guess goddesses need to train. Is there anything else I don't know about?

The servants lead them up a series of golden carpeted staircases, every wall filled with gleaming artwork and intricate sconces that seem to brighten the atmosphere. They reach the top, Aimelie and the others following their guides down a corridor with several mahogany doors.

"Your Highness." The female servant gestures with a hand, opening the heavy door to what is presumably her chambers. *Or, Annalise's,* the princess notes with awkwardness.

Aimelie follows the servant inside, leaving Tasman and Ivo for the first time in nearly a week.

"If you need anything, Your Highness, please don't hesitate to ask. I shall be stationed just at the end of the hall." The girl curtsies, turning to the door before Aimelie makes to remove her fraying cloak, the gray fabric swinging open to reveal her underdress.

"Wait." Melie stops her, a blush staining her fair cheeks. "Would you happen to know where to find me a new dress?"

The Great Hall bursts with fervor, each of its occupants scrambling to take a seat before the arrival of the Nesvlan queen. As the chirps of nobles and royalty swell with each guest's arrival, a fireplace roars along the wall, its flames staving off the brisk autumn air to make for a more intimate atmosphere. Aimelie can feel the heat turning her freckled cheeks red when she takes the seat which would have been reserved for her sister, Annalise—the seat directly to the right of Prince Darren.

She tries to ignore his existence, only to meet three daunting pairs of eyes seated across from her.

"You're human, right?" the young girl with black hair asks, her blue eyes wide with interest.

Aimelie glances left, then right. "I believe so."

"But your sisters, they aren't!" The girl and her two friends giggle with excitement. "Were you shocked when you found out? Do you feel left out because *you* don't have any magical powers? Tell us, what is it like being related to actual *goddesses*?"

Melie blushes. "It's a bit like being a zoo animal, I suppose."

"That's enough questioning, Briar," Prince Darren cuts in, turning to face Aimelie. "I apologize for my sister's unyielding curiosity. It gets the best of her, at times." He takes a sip of wine. "As one of the youngest princesses in the kingdom, I'm afraid she hasn't had much experience in diplomatic affairs."

Aimelie swats her hand. "She is welcome to ask all the questions she wants. I just can't guarantee I'll have all the answers."

The dinner guests rise when Queen Minerva enters the room, reseating themselves once she takes her chair at the head of the table.

"So, it's true, then? All the rumors we heard about a battle at Larking Castle?" Darren observes Aimelie with his nosy blue gaze.

"Honestly, Darren," Minerva asks from the head of the table. "Can't you think of something more polite to talk about?"

"You mean, like the weather?"

Ivo clears his throat a few seats down. "Whatever you heard, Your Highness, I'm sure it's at least partially true. Princess Annalise is Dimity; Queen Adrianna is Jedda; and Desmond, that arrogant Captain of the Royal Guard, is

Anzac. I didn't believe any of it until the princess showed me her magic firsthand."

"Speaking of Princess Annalise," the queen cuts in, "we really should begin making arrangements."

Tasman starts. "Yes, about that—"

"The sooner we get things moving, the better." Queen Minerva swats away one of her eager servants and his platter of appetizers.

Tasman taps his cane thoughtfully on the ground. "I have not yet discussed the matter with Annalise."

The queen's blue eyes stare blankly at him. Darren gawks, peering around the table to gauge other witnesses' opinions.

What hasn't he discussed with Annalise? After a few uncomfortable seconds, Aimelie thinks it best to break the silence. "I'm certain my sister will be here as soon as she can, but until then, perhaps we should start considering the possibility of alliances. Adrianna isn't well-loved, so Annalise should already have the upper hand there. But not every territory may be comfortable getting involved in a war of unknown proportions."

"War? Who said anything about war?" Queen Minerva presses her perplexed brows together.

The table looks to Princess Aimelie, who offers an anxious breath of laughter. "Your Grace, this is no childish quarrel! This is a dispute between two goddesses over the throne of the Empeirian Kingdom. Wars have broken out over situations far more trivial."

"The princess is right," Tasman agrees. "The more prepared we are for Princess Annalise's arrival, the better her situation will be against Queen Adrianna."

Prince Darren leans back in his seat to assess the man. "And how exactly would you advise us to prepare?"

"I feel that Princess Aimelie would be better suited to address your question, Your Highness."

Melie simpers while appreciating Tasman's compliment. "Well, as I mentioned before, alliances are going to be critical. Javir would be out of the question, but—"

"Negotiating alliances will give the impression that a war is imminent," Queen Minerva cuts the princess off, taking another sip from her golden chalice. "Besides, I never affirmed that the Nesvlan throne would wish to partake in such a matter."

You're kidding! You want so badly to help Annalise, but you don't want to get your hands dirty when she needs you to. Princess Aimelie feigns a smile and nods. "Your Grace."

"That's enough political talk for our first dinner," the Queen of Nesvla beams politely as she fans herself. "Briar, how was your dance lesson, today?"

While the Nesvlan family shares tidbits of their royal lives, Aimelie finds her eyes settling on the flames of the Great Hall fireplace. *They won't be of any help, despite their eagerness for Annalise's arrival,* the youngest princess thinks disappointedly. *Annalise will be on her own again, only hiding in a different castle with fancier decorations.*

Looking around the table, Melie realizes that this is almost exactly like her experience at home in Empeirus. Royals and nobles laughing, all neglecting to confront the demons that no one wants to face, the same demons that are eating their people alive. *These are the kinds of beings that served in Adrianna's court; they just fly a different banner.*

To her right, Master Tasman watches her with keen eyes, likely recognizing the same terrible truth. But something in his gaze makes her feel just a little more hopeful, especially when she catches the hint of a smile tugging at his lips.

When the Nesvlan queen calls for dancing to commence, Aimelie excuses herself under the ruse of an upset stomach. Maybe it was the honest chat with Urayus Helva last week, or the way that Tasman had recommended her own opinion at dinner instead of his, but for the first time in her life, Aimelie doesn't feel like she needs to wait for someone to help her solve a problem.

Closing the ornate door to her chambers, the princess levels her blue eyes on the stationery at her desk. *Annalise can try working out a deal with the Nesvlans, but if she needs allies, I'm going to have to take matters into my own hands.*

ANNALISE

Annalise stretches slowly, every muscle in her body aching with a soreness different from the kind her magic induces. The princess groans, pulling the sheets back over her shoulders until her brown eyes catch a glimpse of sunlight slipping out from behind the curtains.

Gods! Anna stumbles painfully out of bed, scrambling to change into her tunic and pants. She has just enough time to take care of some necessities before sprinting to the kitchen, wincing as she swipes an apple from the fruit basket. Stealing a bite of her meager breakfast, the goddess takes the steps down the back porch in twos. *Hopefully, I'm not too late*, she worries. But the sight of the golden sun hovering above the horizon does little to soothe her anxiety, its fingers of light sparkling over the Falvedrie Sea in silent jest.

"I'm sorry I'm late," Annalise apologizes with a mouth stuffed with apple. "I didn't mean to sleep in, I was just so tired."

Oliver McHenry grins his usual winsome smile, one that Annalise has grown more familiar with while residing at his family home. "I'm sure you needed the rest. Besides, I might be pushing you too hard."

The princess swallows her apple. "I *need* to be pushed. How else will I be able to keep up with—" She stops herself from speaking Adrianna's name aloud. The Savekian people might be known for leading private lives, but you never know when one might decide it is more interesting to eavesdrop.

Oliver hands her a dull sword. "But you also need to rest to grow." He uses the flat side of his blade to tap her right calve. "Ready your stance."

Annalise adjusts her footing, remembering the lessons he had taught her over the past few weeks. While setting aside her magic training is a hard thing for her to do, Anna understands the necessity of getting physically stronger to wield it. *And besides, learning a different kind of self-defense isn't a bad thing, either.*

Her friend mirrors her position across the cool sand. "I'm ready when you are."

Breathing out, Annalise makes the first move. Oliver

parries it easily. She continues dealing the different attacks he has shown her, responding to his own with compounding frustration. *Oliver has years of experience on me. I'm never going to be good competition for him.* Still, Anna forces herself to keep moving, to keep strengthening the muscles that will help her use her magic. A bead of sweat trickles down the side of her forehead, and the princess pauses to catch her breath.

Oliver rolls his neck. "I think you need more time to recover. You're getting fatigued more quickly than usual."

Anna shoots him a dark glare. "I think you're wrong."

"And I think you think I'm wrong because you know I'm right," he playfully retorts with a grin.

Annalise returns his smile, readying her stance once again. Only this time, she lets him deal the first blow. In the fraction of a second the goddess has to think, she remembers the way Oliver moved that day he was dueling with Captain Garin. She replays the way he caught him by surprise, the way he must have analyzed the pirate's fighting habits and defeated him by breaking the pattern. Annalise waits for Oliver to advance again, but this time, decides to try something different.

Instead of practicing the same sequence of moves that they have been, Anna uses Oliver's energy against him, similar to the way she had against Jedda at the castle. Displacing the force of his attack in a way they hadn't gone over yet, Annalise catches him by surprise when she continues to build her movements into a storm of advances.

Oliver has only a moment to block her before he regains his footing on the sand. Joining in on her ferocity, he reciprocates her swings and slashes until their movements meld into a fluid dance reserved only for the Falvedrie Sea. On a whim, Oliver throws in a few new attacks of his own, his pine-green eyes gleaming with entertainment as he watches Annalise somehow manage to evade them.

Burning with exhaustion, the princess lifts her weapon above her head for an overhead strike, ready to achieve a victory at long last, until Oliver thrusts his sword toward her stomach, the weight of Annalise's upraised blade just enough to help her trip backward over a misfortunately placed rock.

Groaning on her back, the princess brings her brown eyes to the sword pointed at her abdomen, letting the back of her head hit the sand. "I yield."

A low whistle from the bottom of the porch steps. "You weren't kidding when you said it was complicated." Harper approaches, carrying Wren on one of her curvy hips.

Annalise blushes as Oliver hauls her off the Savekian sand.

"Harper," he greets her. "Can I help you with something?"

Harper waits until Wren's feet hit the sand, watching her retrieve a stray piece of driftwood and begin using it like a sword. "Actually, I came down here for Piper. I have to make a trip to town, and thought it might be nice to have a day out, instead of ..." She gestures with her hands and lets her green eyes assess them curiously. "... whatever this is."

Anna considers her invitation. *I suppose I need a little more rest, anyway.* "I'd be happy to join you."

"Great," Harper smiles. "Oliver, I'm leaving Wren with you. It's a ladies' day."

"Oh ..."

"Uncle Oliver!" Wren jumps into his arms. "Will you teach me how to fight?"

Oliver sets his niece back down on the beach. "Of course I can." He grabs two pieces of driftwood from the sand. "First things first ..."

His voice trails off the farther Annalise walks back to the house, but when she turns to find him adjusting Wren's little hands around the driftwood, her heart is warmed, nonetheless.

Annalise fidgets with the empty basket in her hand while she and Harper walk the dirt path into Cordel. Though her time spent at Oliver's home had made her much more comfortable around him—and even Wren, for that matter—the princess still hasn't made much headway when it comes to Harper. It isn't that Oliver's sister is *rude* by any means. It is only that, about ninety percent of the time, she can make the goddess feel the slightest bit intimidated. Anna picks at the straw coming loose on her basket's handle, remembering the way Harper shamelessly reamed out Oliver at dinner a few nights ago. *I don't even know what I could talk about with her.*

"So," Harper breaks the silence. "Were you close with your brother?"

Oh, right! I can talk to her about my imaginary brother while I pretend to be someone I'm not for the third time in my life. Annalise pushes back a lock of brown hair. "Not terribly, but enough that I mourn his absence with every passing day."

Harper nods, shifting a basket on her hip. "You must think I'm a horrible sister after dinner on Tuesday."

The princess betrays a hint of a smile, thinking about Adrianna and their most recent quarrel. "Believe me, you could be a lot worse."

A soft hum of laughter. Harper is quiet for a moment as they encroach on the outskirts of town. "I know it wasn't really his fault." She lets her eyes sink toward the dirt. "Maybe I just want him to apologize, anyway."

Annalise reads Harper's evergreen gaze, her heart fracturing from the empathy of losing her own parents.

Only, in my case, my sibling was *responsible for their deaths.* "Does he know that's what you want?" The goddess grasps her basket a bit more loosely.

Harper's auburn hair shines in the late fall sunlight, a few strands floating on the salty air. "Probably not."

The town of Cordel is bustling today, even more than it was upon Annalise's first encounter with it the day she arrived in the Savek Coast. Merchant stands are brimming with food and fabrics, customers crowding every cranny of space before the storefronts. An uplifting tune coming from a trio of lutists swells above the business, and something about the whole scene brings a smile to Anna's elegant lips.

"Where to first?" she asks Harper over the noise.

"You get the fruit, and I'll get the cheese," Harper yells back. She digs into a coin purse, offering Annalise her currency, but the princess refuses to take it.

"I'll get the fruit, and you get the cheese," Annalise confirms with a smile.

The women part ways, each retrieving their assigned groceries before they reconvene at the edge of the market, heading for the center of town for a more serene atmosphere. In the center of the square, a beautiful white fountain sprays water from under a statue of Ione, the Goddess of Purity.

"Oliver and I used to play in this fountain when we

were kids," Harper informs her. "We got scolded at, of course, but it was fun nonetheless."

Annalise chuckles, switching her full basket to her other hand. "I never had Oliver pegged as the rule-breaking type."

Harper snorts. "You mean, instead of being the overly polite, chivalrous, man-of-court type?" She grins, shaking her head. "In all honesty, I envy him. I'd kill for half his patience." Her green eyes trace the sky. "He truly is a gentleman, and he'd do anything for you. Hell, maybe he should have been born a prince."

Annalise bites her lip, watching the water tumble to the bottom of the fountain. "Maybe," she responds coyly.

A skitter of movement across the tiled ground catches their attention. A few yards away, a small group of Nevs stand in a corner whispering, the blonde woman in the center observing Annalise with a mysterious gaze. *Does she know?* the goddess thinks, wondering if this woman can see right through her disguise. The thought is enough to make breathing difficult.

"What the hell are you looking at, Nev?" Harper spits from across the town square. "Why don't you find someone else's mind to pry open before I do the same to yours?"

The three oracles turn around to face the opposite direction, moving collectively toward the other end of the square.

Annalise exhales a discreet sigh of relief.

"Anyway, I brought you along today because I wanted to make sure you had something nice to wear for next week." Harper nudges her chin in the direction of a quaint storefront.

The princess squeezes her eyebrows together. "What's happening next week?"

Harper stops. "You're kidding, right? Don't you celebrate the Last Harvest in Empeirus?"

Ah. Have I been so deep into my training that I'm now forgetting major holidays? "We do," Annalise rubs the back of her neck. "I just didn't realize it was coming up so fast."

Harper leads her into a boutique stuffed from floor to ceiling with dresses and jewelry, many of which are decorated using seashells from the Falvedrie Sea. The merchant gives them a kind greeting, and Annalise follows Oliver's sister between racks of fine garments.

"Cordel holds a celebration that is probably minuscule compared to the ones in Empeirus, but they're still a great deal of fun." Harper sets down her basket of cheese to survey a gray dress with silver trim, holding it up to Anna's figure. "Do you like to dance?"

Annalise laughs, mostly because she doesn't, but also because somehow, she is having fun with this stranger. "I will if I have to."

"Oh, you'll have to," Harper smirks, returning the gray

dress to the rack. "But don't worry, my brother is a good dancer."

The goddess chokes on a laugh as Harper pulls another gown, this one a soft rose. "A good dancer?" Annalise repeats.

"Oh, yes. Growing up with a parent on the High Council, we each had the gift of a privileged education. Oliver knows all the traditional court dances, as well as Savekian ones. So, when it comes to festivals around here, ladies flock to him." Harper rolls her green eyes. "Which is why I'm going to make sure you're better dressed than any of them."

Annalise's eyes grow wide. "I'm sorry?"

Harper shakes her head at the rose gown, setting it aside in exchange for another. "I know you don't seem like you enjoy being the center of attention, but trust me, it's for the best. As soon as they see Oliver at the festival, all the single women will make a beeline for him. He's an attractive suitor in this town, you know."

"I see." Annalise blinks. "Harper, I'm not sure you understand. Oliver and I aren't courting. We're just friends."

The feisty woman turns to face Annalise, landing a hand on her full hip. A glimmer of humor sparkles in Harper's eyes when they meet her own. "I don't believe you."

The princess gawks. *I'm not sure I can close my jaw.* "How ..."

"Let me rephrase that. I might believe that *you* feel that way, but Oliver certainly doesn't."

"And how would you know that?"

"Easy. Of all the women who have shown interest in my little brother, he's never brought one home."

Annalise is silent, her stomach tying itself in knots. She shakes her head, recalling her fake identity. "I had nowhere to go after Marcus passed—"

"I'm sure that's true, but Oliver wouldn't have volunteered to have you live with him if he wasn't at all interested in you." Harper moves to a different rack of dresses. "He could have just as easily helped you find a place to stay in Cordel. Or, you could have taken the initiative, too." A pointed glance.

This ruse is getting more difficult to pull off by the second. I wish I could just tell her the truth. Maybe then it would make more sense to her. But even though Annalise knows the real reason behind Oliver taking her to his family home, she can't help recognizing the logic in Harper's words. *Could his sister be right? Is there a deeper motive behind why Oliver is helping me this much? There is no denying that he is risking a lot.*

"Ah," Harper holds up a gorgeous navy gown with a moderately low neckline. Along the square collar is a combination of beads, cowry shells, and small white pearls. "What do you think about this one?" she asks confidently.

Slowly, Annalise turns to look at herself in the floor mirror, watching the silk fabric catch the afternoon light. "It's beautiful," she affirms while holding it flush against her body, thinking for half a moment how she almost looks like a princess again.

NARELLE

"My old mum was born in Drum, and no wiser was I!

I worked for fun but had no one, and now I'm going to die!"

Narelle Lambric listens to the prisoner descend into madness, pressing her dirt-stained forehead against the iron bars of her cell. Whether singing in the dungeon helps boost morale has yet to be determined. But little can help the aches, pains, and unspeakable torture the former courtesan has endured during her month-and-a-half long stay in the depths of Larking Castle.

"A stone unturned left me spurned, and—"

"Will you *shut up*?" Narelle's neighbor spits from where he lays on the dirt floor. Few would be able to recognize him with his shoulder-length hair and beard, but Narelle remembers those copper eyes as clear as day. *"It's no trouble, really, Narelle. I just thought I'd drop in to see if she came by,"* he had informed her at the Sapphire so long ago.

Robbin Flangham told Narelle everything when she was thrown into the cell adjacent to his own. Everything from his spying for the queen to his life before that, when he was a petty jewel thief caught red-handed in Adrianna's chambers. Narelle still isn't sure if she would call him a friend, but in the darkness of the dungeon, his company has been appreciated. *And perhaps the only thing keeping me from turning into a singing madwoman.*

A beetle skitters across the toe of Narelle's filthy slipper, stained from blood and the gods know what else. While her interrogation time has nearly vanished, she doesn't like to get her hopes up too high that they are permanently over. In truth, she doesn't like to get her hopes up about much anymore.

"Favorite color?" Robbin asks from his side of the bars.

"Yellow. Favorite season?"

"Winter. Why yellow?"

"Because it's happy and comforting. Why winter?"

"Because it's cold, and I usually run hot."

Narelle sits herself on her bed of hay, using a rock to carve another line on the stone wall behind it. This is how every morning has gone since she arrived. She and Robbin ask each other questions in a futile attempt to hold on to their sanity, and Narelle does her best to keep track of how long she has been down here, though it may be in her best interest to ignore that number.

"Give it up, Narelle." The fruit merchant makes his next move on their dirt-and-stone chessboard.

The former courtesan narrows her hazel eyes, once sultry and full of life. "I don't think I'm doing that badly."

Robbin pins his bloodshot gaze on her own. "I wasn't talking about the game."

His pointed glance at the carved tally of days makes Narelle's stomach twist. "It was my choice."

"And a bad one, at that." Robbin waits for her to make her move.

Long ago, her heart would have fractured with each passing day that she waited for Annalise Larking to rescue her from the grasp of Queen Adrianna. But that was before her heart was obliterated, before her hope in humanity was shattered by Calix and the queen. *I'm surprised the spymaster hasn't tried to cut out my heart yet, to make sure I'm still alive.*

Narelle presses a hand to her bruised rib, undoubtedly broken, and winces as she pushes her makeshift rook forward.

Robbin notices her discomfort while he assesses their dirt board. "Was it worth it?" he asks with tired eyes.

"Was it worth it," Narelle repeats, a smile of sadness tugging at her split lips. *You mean the spying, the correspon-*

dence …? Her mind flashes back to fresh parchment and a peculiar stamp and Calix in her bed, back to a window seat and a girl with dark hair in the pouring rain. She flicks her eyes up at Robbin. "I hope so," she whispers desperately. "I really hope so."

The puddle of cloth lands on Narelle's abdomen with just enough force that it wakes her from a dead sleep. *What time is it?* No sunlight makes it into the dungeon, but based on their last mealtime, she thinks everyone should still be sleeping. When her hazel eyes finally blink themselves awake, she can make out an unfamiliar figure standing at the door of her open cell.

"Get up!" the female voice orders, but Narelle has never seen this woman before. No, not with her unsettling citrine eyes and long, flowing robes.

This woman is a Nev. "Who are you?"

"Now is not the time for questions if you want to escape. Put the robes on and get up."

All around them, fellow prisoners begin to open their eyes from their own dreams. *If they figure out what is going on, they will make enough noise to draw the attention of the next guards.* Quickly, Narelle slips the robes over her frail body, pulling the hood over her head. She turns to her left, watching Robbin shifting on his pile of hay. "What about him?"

"He is of no use to me. Now, hurry. The next round of guards begins in a few minutes."

But Narelle pauses mid-step, replaying the words in her head. "How am I of use to you?"

A sigh. "You are a former employee of the Sapphire, are you not?"

"I am."

"Then, you know Princess Annalise Larking. Now, walk with me or I will lock this cell with you in it."

Princess Annalise Larking. Narelle's heart skips a beat. *Piper! By the gods, I never thought she could do it, but she* did *get someone to rescue me!* A pang of guilt shadows whatever happiness Narelle had been enjoying when she glances back to find Robbin, now awake in his cell. "He knows her, too."

The Nev stops in her tracks, eyeing the merchant with something like distaste. "I only brought one robe, so he'll have to use mine," she complains, unlocking Robbin's cell and tossing him the clump of fabric.

"My old mum was born in Drum, and no wiser was I!" their neighbor sings.

Robbin pushes Narelle at the sound of the madman's alarm, tailing the Nev as she climbs the flights of stairs it takes to reach the dungeon's entrance. By the top, they are all winded, but the Nev coaxes them to follow after witnessing the last set of guards disappear around a corner. Silently, with only the sound of their ragged breathing piercing the night, the party reaches a door to outside, conveniently leading to a large caravan with two horses at the ready.

"Follow my lead," the Nev whispers, approaching the stable hand.

Narelle couldn't care less about what she has to do; her mind is too engrossed by the sensation of the cool, fresh air against her skin and the whinny and neigh of horses. A tear spills onto one of her tan cheeks. *What things you miss after so long in the darkness.*

"A bit late at night for departure, don't you think?" a burly man questions, watching the oracle run a hand down one of the black horses' manes.

"My girls and I have decided to get an early start on our trip. Staying cooped up in a castle is simply not our way."

"*Hmph.* And where are you headed?"

An eerie smile creeps into the Nev's face, her black dress shimmering in the faint light of the half-moon. "Lord Elmans," she says, moving close enough to run a long nail down his cheek. "Don't you know who we Nevs are? There is no map we follow but our own. But, not to worry, my dear. We'll be back in a few days' time." Grinning at his discomfort, she gestures to Narelle and Robbin to get inside the caravan, following in their wake.

Besides a typical carriage-style seating arrangement, purple and black fabric lines the interior of the caravan, accented by what looks to be trinkets and shards of bone hanging from its walls. On the singular shelves behind each seat, an array of crystals and oddities are on display, one of which looks to be a human skull.

Narelle might be ill if her stomach wasn't so empty.

With the door in her hand, the Nev calls to their drivers. "To wherever the wind takes us!" the witch orders, before taking a seat across from her prisoners and tapping the top of the caravan's roof. Her citrine eyes fall on Narelle while she crosses her full legs.

"Who are you?" the former courtesan can't help asking, her blood thrumming with disbelief from speaking to another human besides Robbin for the first time in over a month. "Why did Annalise send you to retrieve me? You don't look like the kind of company she keeps."

A stale chuckle. "That's because Princess Annalise doesn't know who I am."

Narelle feels Robbin shift slightly, her own chest tightening with suspicion. *Where is she taking us?*

"You can call me Cyndeya Kutchrik, High Priestess of the Nevs." The oracle observes her with glowing eyes. "You've been in the dungeon for a good while, Narelle Lambric. Tell me, what is the last thing you remember about the lost princess?"

Narelle closes her eyes, pressing a tan hand to her ribs over a rough stretch of road. "She was hiding at the watchtower across from Larking Castle." Her hazel gaze opens. "Why?"

Cyndeya offers a caliginous grin. "Oh, my dear," she begins mysteriously. "You're in for quite a tale."

VEGA

Vega rolls herself off the blanket, rising beside the steady campfire. She can't sleep very well in the wilderness—can't sleep very well *period*—but it would serve her travel companions better if she walked off some of her energy rather than wake them up with her restless movements. *After all, Modgen only brought one blanket, so there isn't much room to sleep, anyway.*

With light steps, the goddess incarnate tip-toes away from Eden and Modgen, trying her best to avoid stepping on any dried leaves. Into the forest she goes, the silhouettes of trees blending into blackness the deeper her green gaze travels. With the campfire a healthy distance away, Vega finds herself appreciating the night sky like she used to so long ago in Wembleton. *Gods, how different of a time that was. Back before I was on this journey, before I was taken hostage by Edris, before I had known about Christa.*

Elouthera takes a breath, trying to feel out the bond between herself and Dimity—or Annalise, as Modgen had mentioned at the clocktower. *The lost princess of Empeirus. What a powerful position to be born into.* Silently, she follows the bond across a long span of distance, and she knows that her divine ally is still far away.

The sound of footsteps has her turning to see who she's woken up, but the black shadow moving toward her doesn't look a bit like Modgen or Eden. "Hey—"

The shadow jumps forward to catch Vega's sleeve, the half-moon in the sky offering enough light to make out the purple color of the woman's robes. *A Nev!* Vega can feel a rope scratching at her hand, her wrist stretching out of place while she tries to free herself of the bond. She risks a glance back at the campsite, listening to the bellows of her friends as two additional Nevs ambush them in their sleep, binding their hands behind their backs. Vega grits her teeth. "Let ... go!"

The Nev smiles, holding her end of the rope taut. In the moonlight, her eyes seem to glow with ecstasy while she easily maintains her footing.

The goddess can feel her wrist threatening to dislocate, the pain in her joint getting worse by the second. *It's only a matter of time before I give in, and if that happens, there's no way I'll be able to get away.* Placing her free hand on the binding, Vega uses her manipulation to separate the threads around her wrist with near-perfect execution.

The release of the rope snaps the Nev backward with wicked force, the woman stumbling until she falls on her back and doesn't move.

Vega's breathing is audible, the chill air clouding around her mouth. *Why isn't she getting back up?* Cautiously, she moves toward the oracle to get a closer look. *Oh gods!* Vega covers her mouth. A trickle of blood dribbles its way along the jagged rock beneath the Nev's head, her face completely emotionless. *Oh gods,* she thinks again. In the distance, the goddess can see the other Nevs prepare to make camp where Vega's had once been. She scampers a bit closer to make out their muffled conversation.

"How much longer do you think she'll be?" the taller Nev asks her accomplice. "She just relieved herself an hour ago."

"I have a better question," Modgen Sprightly asks, tied up like Eden to a nearby tree. "What the hell do you want with *us* if you're after that goddess?"

The shorter Nev rolls her eyes. "You're her allies. If you've been traveling together, you'll likely know where she's run off to."

"And if we don't?"

The oracle approaches Modgen slowly, her purple robes skimming the late-autumn leaves. "I'm sure we'll find some use for you," she ventures, untying the coin purse from his hip. "Especially if you're keeping the company of Miss Sharpkey, over here."

Damn. So, they must be working with Edris. Elouthera presses her back behind a tree. *Which means ...* The Goddess of Dreams and Mystery bites her lip. *The Nevs must be trying to recapture me and Eden.*

Modgen watches with discomfort, and possibly something like anguish, as the shorter Nev unties his bag. "Come on," he pleads. "I didn't think Nevs were the thieving type."

The taller oracle extends her palm to receive the pouch from her accomplice. "Then you thought wrong." One by one, she counts the small sum of coins that Modgen had been transporting until her eyes grow wide at something on the bottom of the bag. Intrigued, the Nev gingerly withdraws a silver necklace, the cobalt sapphire on its chain glinting from the fire's glow.

Gods, that has to be worth something substantial! Elouthera notes.

Defeated, Modgen closes his blue eyes in silence.

"What do we have here?" The taller Nev holds the necklace up to get a better view.

"Ooh, give it here! I want to read it!"

A swat at the shorter woman's greedy hands. "I found it; I get to read it." The taller Nev shuts her eyes, holding the silver and sapphire in a tan hand. A gasp as her dark eyes fly open. "Awe, this was Mommy's, wasn't it? And what an interesting woman she was."

The campfire light melds with Modgen's reddish curls until they look to be flames themselves. "This must be fun for you."

The Nev chuckles darkly until her mouth drops agape. "What is it, Lillian? Tell me; tell me!"

Lillian smiles, a sickening, devious grin staining her face. She drops the necklace back into the coin purse, the ground crunching beneath her feet as she approaches Modgen's tree. "Maybe we aren't so unlucky to miss out on Elouthera, considering that we've managed to capture two fine prizes, already. What say you to that, *son of secrets?*"

What the hell is that supposed to mean? Elouthera wonders.

For a moment, all that can be heard is the crackle of the fire and the faraway howl of a coyote, until Modgen's blank stare erupts into a cacophony of laughter.

"Tell me," his cobalt eyes twinkle with humor. "What do you Nevs smoke to come up with such bizarre fortunes?"

Lillian exchanges a glance with her comrade, pressing a hand to her heart. "He doesn't know." She feigns sympathy. "Don't worry, sweetheart. We'll make good use of your remains."

Okay, this might be where I need to make my move.

Focusing on the details of the deceased Nev's face and hair, Vega manipulates her own to match them to the best of her ability. *Lazarus, forgive me.* She robs the female of her purple robes, slipping them over her dirty prison attire. Anxiously, Vega steals another look at the campfire, her hazel eyes and blonde hair nothing like her true features. *There are two Nevs and only one of me. I will need to take out at least one of them to increase my odds.*

The goddess rounds the tree, making loud steps through the thicket as the women peer over the roaring fire.

"Finally." The shorter oracle gestures graciously. "What took you so long?"

Vega stops a healthy distance away. "I think you should see this," she beckons, before turning to lead the shorter Nev into the woods.

"You should see Lillian right now." The Nev smiles, unaware of whom she is speaking with. "She's in her element, interrogating hostages. Said we found some pretty valuable people, though, even if we didn't catch the goddess." The oracle meets Vega behind a tree. "So, what is it you wanted to show me?"

"Right there," Vega points in front of them. "Do you see them? I think they're footprints."

As soon as the Nev moves in front of her, the goddess smashes the side of her head into the tree trunk, the female unconscious after the third blow. She unties the belt around the oracle's waist and uses it as a gag, quickly binding her hands with the remains of first Nev's rope before traipsing back to the campfire. Vega can hear the blood in her ears when Lillian's eyes fall on her own.

"Did you find something?"

"False alarm."

"And where is Glenda?"

"Said it was her turn to relieve herself," Vega lies.

"Hmph," Lillian musters, turning back to her hostages. "Now, where were we?" She looks to Eden, whose mismatched eyes are flooded with fear. "We'll make sure you get back in Edris's safe hands. But, as for you …" The Nev uses a long, pointed nail to lift Modgen's pale chin. "I have plans for you far beyond your wildest imagination."

Modgen forces a grin. "I'm flattered, really. But you're not my type."

The fortune teller snorts. "Very funny." A large bowl sits empty on the ground below him, the only thing between Vega's ally and her enemy. "Your mother's necklace may be worth a small fortune, but your blood is priceless." Lillian unsheathes a small dagger.

Oh, no. This can't be good.

Modgen's eyes begin to fill with the same crippling anxiety that Eden's seem to exude.

"I've heard the rumors, but never thought I'd have the opportunity to see if they were true. Well, here's to making history." Lillian lifts the dagger to Modgen's neck while her other hand struggles to keep his chin high.

Quick as an asp, Vega launches herself forward, locking her arms around the Nev's throat while the woman stumbles backward from the weight. Lillian's height keeps Vega's feet off the ground, a tactic that serves the goddess well until the oracle collapses backward on the ground, crushing Vega's head against the dirt. Somewhere on the outskirts of reality, Vega can sense her manipulations wearing off while she and the Nev muster enough balance to stand.

Lillian coughs, her dark eyes brimming with fury as she whispers through heavy breaths, "*You.*"

The oracle charges at her, and Vega leaps to the side at the last minute, sprinting toward Modgen to grab the dagger off the ground.

Lillian rises from the leaves, her dark eyes still bloodshot from choking. "You wouldn't dare."

Elouthera extends the blade between them, its tip facing downward. "You have a choice: Leave us at once, or suffer my wrath."

"I knew you'd come back," the Nev smirks deviously. "There's just something about Kutchrik women that drives them to the occult."

Vega stops. *Kutchrik women?*

"Oh, don't act so surprised. You look just like her, only smaller and without those citrine eyes."

Vega's stomach roils, her breaths turning shallow. "You know my mother?"

Lillian laughs. "Who wouldn't? She's only our High Priestess."

Somewhere behind her, a male voice reaches Vega's ears. "Don't listen to her. She's just trying to buy herself time."

Their High Priestess. The dagger feels heavier than it had before, the power of her arm withering by the second. *Their High Priestess.* "And what was she planning to do with me?" the goddess dares to ask.

The Nev reaches into her purple robes. "You know, I'm not sure, since I don't think she knows Elouthera is her daughter." Lillian advances in a flash, wielding another dagger ready to spill blood.

With the Nev approaching fast, Vega has hardly a second to think before she throws out her free hand and—

Lillian slows her pace, her dark eyes twitching while her knees buckle to the ground. Elouthera grasps at the threads of her mind, focusing on keeping the Nev from attacking as she closes the two steps it takes to pull the dagger from her hand. With her enemy still grounded, Vega slips one of the daggers into her robes and carefully moves Lillian's wrists behind her back. She manipulates the remaining blade into cuffs, tightly binding the Nev's hands.

When Vega lets go of her mind, Lillian releases a scream of fury in her mad attempt to free her hands from the closed metal. "You wretched—"

"Save it." Elouthera stops her, using the dagger she kept to cut Modgen free. "Don't make me gag you."

Modgen rolls out his wrists, reaching down to retrieve his stolen coin purse from the ground. "I owe you my life," he acknowledges earnestly.

Vega smiles beneath weary eyes. "Don't mention it." *I'm just glad none of us had our throats cut open.*

When she finishes cutting Eden's ropes, the three outlaws quickly pack up their belongings from the campsite, ignoring the droning screams of Lillian, which are sure to wake the dead. *And the unconscious Nev I left tied up in the woods.* The goddess tries not to think about the other oracle, whose unconsciousness seems to be permanent.

"What you really owe me is an explanation," Vega tells Modgen while she wraps Eden in the robes she stole. "Who are you, and what in the world makes your blood so special?"

Dimity's friend mounts his chestnut horse, but for once, he seems to be at a loss for words. "I don't know," he admits quietly. "I really don't know."

ANNALISE

"O*f.*" Annalise releases the last ounce of air she has left in her lungs as Harper laces the back of her navy silk gown.

"And you're all set," Harper confirms. Her pine-green eyes survey the goddess once more before pushing her back onto the vanity seat. "Just as soon as I add a little more of this around your eyes," she mostly tells herself, retrieving the small tin of kohl.

"I'm sure this will do," Annalise tries convincing Harper to be satisfied with her appearance. "Any more of that and I might start scaring off Oliver instead of his admirers."

A feigned look of pain. "Do you think I would make you look *bad?*"

The princess can't decide whether to grin or grimace.

"Well, to be fair, I haven't exactly known you long enough to make that judgment."

A courteous knock on the door tears the women from their conversation.

"I told you already, I'm just doing the finishing touches!" Harper yells through the thick wood.

"Do you think it's possible to hurry up? Wren says she's starving," Oliver responds from the other side.

His sister rolls her eyes. "I fed that girl two hours ago and she's already hungry again." Harper swipes a dash more kohl along the top rims of Annalise's eyes. "She's probably just being dramatic, as usual." Oliver's sister sets down her brush to get a final view of Annalise's face. A strange smile passes over her lips, and for a moment, she almost looks like a proud mother.

Anna shifts nervously. "Do I look presentable?"

Harper nods. "Oh, yes. They are going to hate you."

"*What?* Who?" Annalise's heart skips a beat when she spins around to face the mirror, only to realize exactly what Harper is talking about. Staring at her reflection, she stands to smooth out the silk fabric of her gown, the curls of her dark hair spilling over a full bust. The shape of her perfect lips is now emphasized by a deep red stain; Annalise knows that the other women at this party will most definitely not want to be her friend.

"I added a few extra decorations to the back of your hair," Harper mentions to her, holding out some coin-sized sand dollars. "I think they complement the shells along the neckline of your dress nicely."

Annalise blinks, her dark eyes appearing even darker from the makeup. "Harper, you did an amazing job. How can I repay you?"

Harper adds one of the sand dollar pins to her auburn updo, smiling with a glow the princess rarely gets to see. "Just make them jealous," she grins deviously.

Another knock at the door, this one impatient and eager.

"Okay, okay!" Harper turns the handle, scooping up Wren into her arms. "Come on, little bird. Let's go get you something to eat."

Annalise takes one last look at herself in the mirror, thinking back to the last time she was so dressed up for an occasion. *It was probably six years ago, when I was still living at the castle and my parents were still alive.* One might think that she would be used to taking pride in her appearance, but hiding in the slums for so long made it wiser to choose discretion over beauty.

The princess takes a breath, exiting the doorway to find Oliver reading a book at the dining table.

He drops it when his green eyes find hers. "Good gods." Oliver smiles broadly from his seat. "You look ..."

"Don't say it," Anna whispers harshly.

"Like a princess," he finishes smugly.

A soft groan. Annalise glances out the front window,

watching Harper and Wren begin the trek to Cordel's Last Harvest festivities. "You can thank Harper. None of this was my idea, but she did a good job, nonetheless."

"Well, it's not like she had to work very hard."

The princess widens her brown eyes.

Oliver rubs the back of his neck, seeming to rethink his last statement. "She's always been rather good at getting cleaned up." He shrugs, rising from the table to give Annalise a better view of his perfectly tailored outfit, the cut of his doublet accentuating his physique more than she would like.

Annalise leads their way out the front door, Oliver falling behind to lock up. She swallows. "You look nice, too, if I may say so."

He chuckles, offering his arm to escort her. "You may."

Flustered, Annalise takes his arm. The two of them walk alone to the festival, the late autumn sun just beginning to sink below the horizon. "This wasn't part of the plan," Anna whispers to him anxiously.

Oliver meets her gaze sidelong. "We've been training almost every day since we've arrived," he whispers back. "I think it's okay to take the day off."

Maybe he's right, Annalise supposes. *Besides, I'm already feeling stronger. One day out of our entire training regimen is not going to cost me the war.*

Up ahead, the lights of lanterns and bonfires can be seen in town, the scent of apples and cinnamon blanketing the atmosphere on the sea winds. There must be hundreds of enthusiastic visitors, each one dressed in their finest attire to celebrate the end of autumn before the year descends into the freezing clutches of winter. And above the raucous of so many guests are the sounds of lively string instruments, their strumming far more energetic than anything Anna has ever heard in Empeirus.

One by one, their heads turn as Oliver and Annalise make their way into the thicket of town, curious eyes catching a glimpse of some of the most finely dressed patrons at the festival.

"Everything all right?" he asks her quietly, waving casually to a stranger wearing a tidy blue outfit.

"Of course," Annalise declares. "Why wouldn't it be?"

He gives her hand a tap with his free index finger. "You keep drumming your thumb against my arm. Are you nervous?"

Yes. "Not at all. What do I have to be nervous about?"

Oliver smirks. "I don't know. Maybe you can't dance."

A roll of her brown eyes. "For the gods' sakes, Oliver. Considering my background, I should be able to dance better than you."

His green eyes sparkle. "*Should,*" he repeats, leading her toward the center of the flighty music. "How about you prove it?"

Annalise stops, watching him release her arm to move a few steps in front of her—only to be stormed by a lovely blonde lady. The goddess has only two seconds to observe before a young man approaches her as well, taking her hand in his without a single word.

"My lady, let me show you how it's really done." The confident man pulls Annalise into the trill of the next song, and what commences, she can only describe as absolute madness.

The crowd swarms to the orchestra, the sound of vigorous strumming an apparent sign to commence jumping in place. Annalise grips the stranger's hands as loosely as she can while her dark eyes search for Oliver, but he is lost in the masses. Before she can turn to look again, the man places a hand on her waist, guiding her to jump in a circle with him like the rest of the dancers.

"Are you ready, my lady?" the man asks her over the loud music.

"Ready for what?" Annalise yells. She can hardly get her bearings before he leads her to the right, nearly tripping over her feet when he turns them in the opposite direction.

Gods, this is worse than a nightmare!

Like a prayer immediately answered, a brusque hand pulls the stranger backward, freeing Annalise from his grip at last.

"What the hell is this about, McHenry?" the man spits.

Smoothly, Oliver closes the gap between himself and

Annalise, placing one hand on her waist and the other in her own. "You were practically killing her, Felix. Besides, I can't let you have all the fun."

Annalise releases a breath of gratitude. "Gods bless you, Oliver." She smiles widely in the light of the hanging lanterns. The music continues to blare into the evening sky, dozens of couples dancing their way into the chaos.

"May I?" Oliver asks politely.

"As long as you don't dance anything like Felix does."

His answering smile is full of amusement and something else when he pulls the goddess flush against him, to a distance made for sharing secrets. "I'll try to give you some direction as we go."

Annalise watches his green eyes count the steps of the nearby dancers, trying not to think about his hand pressed against the small of her back.

"And … *jump!*" Oliver hops them into the line of dancers, keeping the princess taut against his chest as they transition into sweeping circles, each couple moving in unison to create a spinning ring of dancers. The former master meets her dark gaze once more. "When I tell you, you'll spin to the center of the circle."

"Okay." Annalise laughs nervously over the vivacious energy of the music.

As the other dancers ready their positions, Oliver releases her waist. "Now!"

Annalise does her best to twirl in synchronicity with

the other ladies, each of their free hands reaching toward the center of the circle at the height of their spin. A giddy laugh escapes her mouth when she spins back into Oliver's arms. "Dances aren't half this energetic in Empeirus," she divulges between jumps.

"I know." Oliver grins. "But they should be." He leads her back into the sweeping circles they had made before, and Annalise finds herself catching on to the pattern.

"I take it you're going to spin me again?"

"You would be correct." Oliver removes his hand from Anna's waist to send her twirling back toward the middle of the ring of dancers, waiting for her hand to take its place back on his shoulder. "The last part of this dance is the same, but after you spin back in, I'll dip you. Is that all right?"

Annalise presses her brows together above a cheerful grin. "Why wouldn't it be?"

Oliver gives a huff of laughter before the two of them move through the familiar sequence of events, their bodies moving in unison to the intense, strumming beat.

Annalise spins toward the center of the dancers, her navy silk gown glittering in the dusk light. Twirling back in, she nearly falls backward into Oliver's arms when he leans her to the ground in a dip much deeper than she had anticipated. She doesn't know why, but something about his expression makes her smile even deeper. When the music stops, Oliver helps her stand, the dancers taking turns to exchange bows and curtsies. Annalise reclaims his arm as they walk toward the line of vendor stands.

"Did I do better than Felix?" Oliver asks playfully.

Annalise snorts, stopping to purchase a bag of chocolate-covered caramels from a merchant. "I don't think he sets the bar very high, Oliver." She allows herself a modest grin. "But your sister was right. You are a good dancer."

A sidelong glance. "Harper told you that? That's the nicest thing she's had to say about me in years."

Anna pops a caramel into her mouth, her dark eyes glowing as she savors the soft, melt-in-your-mouth candy. "Lazarus, almighty!" the princess swears with a mouthful of chocolate. "Have you ever had one of these?"

"I think I've eaten more of those than I should have during the first twelve years of my life," Oliver japes while he eyes the offered bag. "But, I will have one because they're my favorite."

Annalise chuckles, letting him take a caramel. "So, who was that pretty lady who was talking to you while I was off dancing with Felix?"

His pine-green eyes meet her own. "Who? The woman with blonde hair?"

Annalise nods, chewing on another piece of candy.

"I have no idea. But something about her just doesn't sit well with me."

I guess Harper was right. He is an attractive suitor in this town. Anna tilts her bag of chocolates in his direction again. "I thought maybe she was an old love interest, or something like that."

Oliver huffs a laugh, stealing a second caramel. "No." He takes in the glow of the hanging lanterns while they walk down the line of merchant stands. "There was one, but it wasn't anything too serious."

Anna lifts a brow. "Oh?"

Oliver shrugs. "We were young. That was before I joined the Royal Guard, so I had just turned sixteen."

For some reason, a pang of jealousy thrums through Annalise's veins. She tries to smother it with the taste of more chocolates. "What happened, if you don't mind me asking?"

Her friend is quiet for a moment, but he forces a polite smile. "She cheated on me."

Annalise's heart fractures. *Oh, gods. I am such an idiot.* "I am so sorry."

"Don't be." Oliver waves a hand. "There's a reason why we weren't supposed to end up together." He pilfers another caramel from the bag. "What about you? Did you leave any heartbroken suitors back at home?"

"You mean, in the slums?" Annalise shares a laugh with him. "You know as well as I that a fake identity isn't exactly conducive to courting."

A hum of contemplation. "What if they already know your true identity?"

Annalise gives him a smug smirk. "Wouldn't you like to know?"

Oliver chokes on a laugh.

"*Wren!*"

The two of them look up to find a concerned Harper racing toward them in her rose-gold gown. She grabs Oliver by the arms. "It's Wren. I can't find her anywhere. I've been looking for the past twenty minutes, at least, and—"

"Breathe, Harper," Oliver instructs his sister, his own evergreen eyes roving over the surrounding festival. "Have you checked the house?"

"No. I was going to go there next." Harper palms the side of her face, worry staining every inch of it.

Oliver helps turn her around. "I can do one more look around here. Piper, would you be kind enough to walk back to the house with my sister?"

"Of course." Annalise places a gentle hand on Harper's back.

"What kind of mother am I if can't even keep track of my own child?" Harper verges on the edge of tears. "One minute, she was right beside me, and the next ..." She shakes her head. "The gods would never forgive me if I couldn't find her. *I* would never forgive me."

The princess rubs her back. "She could very well have run back to the house. Just try to take some deep breaths."

Harper attempts to recompose herself on their walk back from Cordel. "This just isn't like Wren, though." She wipes a tear from her eye. "That's what has me worried."

ANNALISE

Annalise Larking follows Harper into her family home, her heart pounding against her chest as she begins to share in Harper's worries over Wren's whereabouts. "If you look downstairs, I'll look up here," Anna tells her as calmly as she can.

Harper follows her suggestion, calling out her daughter's name while she descends the staircase to the lower level. "Wren, this isn't funny!"

Annalise pads down the hallway, searching each of the three bedrooms and even the bathroom to no avail. "Come on, Wren!" She grimaces at the stupidity of her following bribe: "I have chocolates!" The princess hears the basement door open and close, the sound giving her the idea that Harper has gone out to the beach. Setting down her bag of candy, Anna makes to head downstairs as well, until a scream stops her dead in her tracks. *Harper!*

Faster than she thought possible, Annalise bolts to the backdoor, flinging it open with unparalleled speed. She wills her slippered feet to carry her down the steps as quickly as they can, her dark eyes searching frantically within her field of view. "Harper?" Annalise yells out, but only the empty beach is witness to her trepidation—until she walks to the right of the stairs.

"*Please!*" Harper is on her knees, crying to three women. "I'll do *anything*! Is it coin that you want? I'll give you everything I have, just please don't hurt her!"

Annalise beholds one of the women's faces. In a matter of seconds, her mind finally pieces things together. *The pretty blonde woman who was pestering Oliver at the festival earlier. She was one of the Nevs in the town square that day Harper and I went to the shops.*

"There you are." The Nev smiles sadistically above the dagger she has pressed into Wren's little throat, a whimper escaping the young girl's mouth. "We've been waiting for you."

Anna's body moves before she can think, splaying her hands toward the blonde woman and her two accomplices.

"Uh-uh-uh," the oracle taunts her condescendingly, pushing the blade deeper into Wren's pale skin. "Try to make a move, and so will I."

"Oh, gods!" Harper drops her hands on the sand and sobs.

A wicked smirk. "We'll let her go." The blonde woman turns to Annalise. "All you have to do is come with us. A simple trade."

Annalise locks her jaw, slowly lowering her trembling hands to her sides.

"Wise choice." The Nev nods at her partners, both wearing the cult's customary purple robes, a pair of iron cuffs in one of the women's hands.

Annalise can hear her heartbeat in her ears when the irons lock around her wrists, but she doesn't take her eyes off Wren until the oracle lets her fly back into Harper's arms.

"Now, was that so hard?"

The princess watches Harper cradle her daughter, soaking Wren's shoulder in tears. She turns back to the blonde woman. "Did Adrianna send you?"

The Nev gives a derisive laugh. "Who else can fulfill such a high bounty? But don't worry, we'll see you home soon enough, Your Highness."

Dria. A feeling of rage has Annalise curling her fists, wondering how hard it would be to take down three women at the same time. *My powers aren't honed yet, but once I'm far enough away from Harper and Wren—*

"Your Highness?" Harper looks up from Wren's auburn hair, then makes a beeline back to the house.

"I am so sorry," Anna whispers beneath teary eyes, but Harper is already gone. The ropes tug forward on her irons. Tripping over her navy dress, the goddess drills holes into the back of the blonde Nev's head. "Who else knows where I am?"

"Just yours truly, that I know of." The oracle raises her arms into the air, stretching as she leads the group across the sand in her dark maroon gown. She cackles, savoring the victory of capturing the kingdom's most wanted. "I can't wait to see how the queen intends to end you. Honestly, I can't believe we found you." An obnoxious snort. "Lillian's team has nothing on—"

The whirr of an arrow stops when it splits cleanly through the side of her head, the blonde woman's mouth stuck on a word she will never be able to speak again.

Good gods! Annalise and her other captors jump back while the Nev's body collapses to the sand, Anna's heart leaping to her throat. The oracles' pause gives her just enough time to decide one thing: she will fight for her life, or die trying.

With her hands still bound, the princess throws an elbow to her right, cracking the Nev in the face before she drives the base of her palm into the other woman's nose. In a flash, the first Nev makes to reach for her arm, until another arrow spears its way through her heart, the oracle falling in a heap beside the blonde woman. In the fraction of a second Annalise has before the final Nev pulls her rope, she swears she sees a blur of navy run across the cliff face.

With her hand latched around Anna's rope, the remaining oracle reaches into her purple robe, the gleam of a blade shining in the last light of the sun. "Funny thing about your bounty," her sinister voice lilts. "The queen never specified whether she requires you dead or alive."

Annalise dodges the first advance, desperately trying to recall all her training with Oliver. *Only, with Oliver, I wasn't fighting with my hands bound, and without a sword!* The oracle's movements are too fast to keep up with using her untrained magic, but somewhere in the back of her racing mind, Annalise remembers the way she changed the dynamic of her fighting when she started using Oliver's momentum against him.

Anna evades the next thrust, this time using her elbow to knock the oracle's arm away from her body. The dagger falls from the Nev's hand, her body swinging from the movement. Annalise launches herself forward, lacing the chains between her irons around the oracle's neck and managing to maneuver behind her back. Her opponent throws an elbow into her side, sending Annalise stumbling onto her back to drag them both to the sand.

When the wind rushes back into her lungs, the princess tightens the chains around the Nev's neck, using almost all her strength to roll their bodies over. The action would have been successful if the Nev hadn't used the momentum to continue their movement, each of the women taking turns on the sand until Annalise ends up on top. Kneeling on the oracle's back, Anna drives her knee into the back of the Nev's head, her wrists aching from the irons pressing into her skin while she pulls the chain tighter. *Oh, gods,* she cries silently. *Please forgive me.*

The Nev chokes into the sand, the goddess doing everything she can to hold her down.

Suddenly, Annalise screams, her brown eyes darting to her leg to find a small knife jutting out the side of her left thigh. The searing pain is enough to loosen her grip around the Nev's neck, her enemy collecting the blade from Anna's leg before the princess lurches to her right to avoid the oracle's next attempt. Annalise lands on the sand just in time to find the Nev raising the dagger over her body. The princess's only option is to throw out her hands, turning her face away as she tries summoning her magic as quickly as possible.

Anna hears the sound of metal piercing bone, followed by a breathless groan.

She opens her eyes to witness a sword protruding from the Nev's chest, red blood sputtering from her lips onto the hem of her navy dress. Slowly, the oracle slides off the blade to rest on the beach like her sisters, a horrified Annalise watching blood drip from the honed steel.

Oliver meets her gaze with serious eyes. "Are you ..."

Annalise jolts her body to the side, emptying the contents of her stomach onto the sand. She spits, heaving until she collapses onto her back again, silently observing Oliver search the woman with the arrow in her chest. He returns with a key, unlocking her irons and examining her leg. The princess rolls out her marred wrists as he gently presses a hand near the wound to get a closer look.

"*Gods, damn it!*" she curses into the evening air, her nails filling with grains of sand.

Oliver frowns. "We need to take care of that." He looks around at the three corpses. "But first, we need to take care of this."

Grasping his arm, the princess hauls herself off the ground, balancing most of her weight on her good leg. While Oliver drags the bodies into a pile closer to the cliff face, Annalise tries to focus through the pain, using her magic to move any bloodied sand toward the ocean. When she reaches the corpses, the goddess says a quick prayer before lighting them ablaze, ensuring all three are engulfed in flames.

The orange fire glints off Oliver's solemn gaze, his lips set in grave dismay. "What will the gods think of me, now?" he asks quietly, as they turn back for the house.

Annalise holds a hand over her thigh to stop the blood from spilling. "Well," she winces, "I can tell you that this one is very grateful for you saving her life."

He presses his lips together. "At the cost of taking three."

The princess is silent for a moment, attempting to hold back painful groans with every other footstep. "They threatened to kill Wren if I didn't go with them." Another wince. "And then, they actually *tried* to kill me. What you did was just ..."

Oliver adjusts the sword at his hip. "It doesn't make what I did any less wrong. It's a burden I will carry for the rest of my life."

"I know you will. If you didn't, you'd be on Adrianna's side." Annalise meets his sidelong glance, hoping that if only for a second, she can put his mind at ease. In the light of the dying sun, Anna catches a glimpse of her blood trailing a few feet behind them, a thin stream now trickling over the edge of her slipper. She groans, both from pain and inconvenience, pushing the crimson sand into the Falvedrie Sea, its mouth incessantly hungry at the shoreline.

"Here," Oliver tells her as he moves to her good side, placing a hand around her back and under her knees.

"Oh, you don't have to—"

The former master lifts her from the beach, carrying her with relative ease. "I can focus on the walking if you can focus on the blood."

"I suppose I can't argue with that."

They say very little on their jaunt back to the house, Annalise's hands already aching from the use of her magic. It is a welcome distraction from her leg, but the goddess knows she will feel it tenfold tomorrow. Just before they reach the porch steps, an unpleasant thought crosses Annalise's mind: *What are the chances that Harper will let us back in?* Underneath the selfishness of the idea is the fact that Anna was the one responsible for all of this, including little Wren's near-death experience. *If it weren't for me, Oliver and his family would never have been troubled by tonight's horrific events.* Her heart sinks when she realizes the indisputable notion that she cannot stay here any longer.

They ascend the wooden stairs in silence, Oliver carefully lowering Annalise to the ground. When he reaches the back door, the princess holds her breath for an invitation that may never come, but Harper opens it on the third knock. Her green eyes peruse their expressions, one of pain and the other of solemness, before giving them a curt nod to enter.

Harper locks the door behind them. "I had to make sure you were alone." She watches suspiciously as Annalise clutches her thigh. "I didn't think you'd be back."

The princess leans her weight on her right foot. "We've only come to collect our things." A determined glance at Oliver. "We're leaving tomorrow morning." She watches his eyes widen as Harper grabs three glasses and a bottle of liquor from the cabinet.

"Where's Wren?" Oliver inquires.

"In bed." Slowly, Harper seats herself on one of the sofas, pouring the brandy with tired eyes. "Where will you go?"

Annalise peers down at the floorboards to find a small puddle of blood collecting beneath her shoe. "Eldric Castle." She presses her hand harder against her thigh while Oliver disappears down the hallway. "We can stay the night at an inn before we depart."

Harper laughs faintly into her glass. "I'm sure that won't be necessary, if the rumors are true."

The princess pushes her brows together.

"It is 'Your Highness,' is it not? The lost princess, Annalise Larking." Harper takes a swig of the amber liquid. "They say you are the goddess Dimity incarnate."

Annalise closes her brown eyes, opening them to find Oliver returning with a box of medical supplies. "That would be correct," she confirms.

"Well, then, I'd say that if I keep Wren within my line of sight, we should be well-equipped to take on any intruders for one more night."

The princess bows her head, nodding solemnly. "Thank you."

"Don't thank me yet." Harper smiles softly in the candlelight. "I have to mend your leg."

Anna shoots Oliver a confused look as he drapes a sheet over the sofa across from Harper's. "My sister used to be a nurse before she had Wren," he explains, helping the goddess sit.

"What a lucky coincidence." Annalise smiles back at Harper, retrieving her glass of brandy and watching her rifle through the medical box.

Oliver steals his own glass from the table, sinking exhaustedly into the cushions on the opposite sofa. "The gods willing, our ship will still be in the same place we left it."

Anna smirks tiredly. "And its crew." Her stomach twists when Harper lifts her skirt to expose the gaping cut, frowning at its depth.

"Ha!" Harper huffs. "That'll leave a mark. Not very princess-like," she quips over a damp cloth. "But I wouldn't say you're the average princess, anyway."

Annalise turns to her left to find Oliver nursing his drink, a modest smile half-hidden by the lip of his glass.

"Why Eldric Castle?" Harper pries.

"I don't know." The princess takes another sip of her liquor. "It's where we were told to reconvene once my training was completed." A heavy sigh. "Though it's looking like I'm going to have to postpone my progress until we arrive."

"Here, Oliver." Harper chucks a bloodied shoe at his feet. "Maybe you can try to wash the stains out while I do this next part." She threads a fine needle, adding an additional rag beneath the princess's leg. Her hand at the ready, Harper eyes the remaining brandy in Annalise's glass, a frown tugging at the corners of her mouth. "On second thought, you may want to finish that, first."

Part II

Wave

ADRIANNA

Adrianna slams against her feathered bed, the sound of her moans reverberating against her chamber walls. The Captain of the Royal Guard finishes, his breath tickling her neck before he rolls onto his back. Dria watches his chest rise and fall with satisfied eyes.

For weeks, she and Desmond had been drowning in anxiety over Annalise's whereabouts, a thought that has made them wrought with exhaustion. But Dria's plan should lay their worries to rest, so long as the Goddess of Wisdom and Justice is not as wise as people say she is.

"Do you think she will fall for it?" Adrianna asks her captain, slipping on a loose nightdress.

Desmond stretches deeply on the bed, his muscles

shifting in the dim candlelight. "There's only one way to find out."

The Dark Goddess fills her chalice with a bright red wine, waving a lazy finger to swirl it with her magic. She hasn't mentioned her plan publicly for risk of having the ploy exposed. *The last thing I want is for Annalise to discover my idea before I get the chance to execute it.*

Slowly, Desmond stands to dress before his queen, Adrianna's hands interlacing behind his neck. She presses a few kisses to his tan shoulders, then to the scar on the side of his forehead, meeting his quicksilver gaze. A look of something like sadness falls across Dria's face. "They like Annalise," she notes in a small voice.

"The people, you mean?" Desmond runs a thumb across her cheekbone. He waits for an answer that doesn't come.

Adrianna drops her stare to the bedpost behind him, her fair skin flushed from physical exertion. "They don't like me."

The captain lifts her chin. "Why do you care what they think?" He lowers his voice to a near-whisper. "We're immortals; it doesn't really matter what—"

"It matters for *my reign*, Desmond," Adrianna seethes. "They don't have to love me, but I need them to at least like me. If they don't, they will choose my sister over me every single time." She grits her teeth. "It matters."

Desmond sighs, nodding slightly. "You make a valid

point, Dria. But getting the kingdom on your side doesn't just happen overnight. It takes time to expose Annalise's faults, to begin having them question their old ways of thinking." He bends to scoop up his queen, carrying her to the bed. "What *does* happen overnight is sleep, which you need desperately."

A groan as her captain lays her back onto the sheets. "I swear, if I had the option, I would stay up for the entire remainder of my life," Adrianna spits. "Damn this mortal body."

Desmond pulls the golden fabric over her shoulders, pushing back her blonde hair with a gentle caress.

"I would get so much more done," Dria sighs heavily, a yawn creeping into the last few syllables as she closes her eyes for the most peaceful sleep she has gotten in weeks.

Queen Adrianna emerges into the Throne Room with Desmond at her side, the chattering of her courtiers coming to a halt while she claims her throne. She had her handmaid lace her up in one of her finer gowns today, her body rejuvenated from both hope and a day of recovery. Flicking her blonde braid behind a shoulder, the queen surveys her court. *No Cyndeya, today?* she notices with some dissatisfaction.

"Lords and ladies!" Dria announces. "I have considered heavily your concern over my wellbeing—and the wellbeing of the kingdom—in regard to my sister Annalise's potential plotting." The queen forces a smile. "I am … honored by your worries. To help prevent Princess Annalise from attacking out of thin air, I have devised a plan to lure her directly to Larking Castle."

A chorus of grumbles and murmurs.

Adrianna raises her hand. "I know what you are thinking. But the advantage of such a situation is that we have time on our side. We will not bait her to the castle until we have sufficient methods of detaining her."

"Your Majesty," Lord Earlmence, her royal ambassador chimes in. "What do you plan on doing with her once she arrives?"

The shipmaster interrupts. "Your Godliness, might I suggest pacifying the threat entirely? Who knows when she should strike again."

"She cannot *kill* her," Lord Earlmence appalls. "Were you not paying attention when Her Majesty explained how there must be a balance between light and darkness?"

Blushing, Adrianna reflects on what she had told them during her last time holding court. *Maybe killing her would lead to some sort of godly consequence that I know nothing of.* "I will need to take unique measures to ensure that she is no longer a threat, but I will spare her life." She ignores the baffled look from Desmond. "By providing her with accommodations in the most secure part of the dungeon, her followers should, in effect, lose hope."

The shipmaster shifts in his seat, looking down his nose at the marble floor.

"Very well, Your Majesty." Lord Earlmence hides a smile. "And what is your plan for doing so?"

Queen Adrianna lands her icy-blue eyes on her spymaster. "Calix, my dear. Bring me the courtesan."

Calix disappears after a curt bow, journeying into the heart of the dungeon to retrieve Adrianna's most prized possession.

How many other people know so much about the last six years of Annalise's life? I think I've learned more about my sister from Narelle than I had when Annalise lived with me in this castle. Dria waits quietly, resting her head on a hand before realizing that such an action may not portray a queen who is interested in others' problems. She straightens her posture, eyeing her court once more. "Are there any other issues that you wish to discuss today?"

Renai stands in her usual confident manner. "Your Majesty, there are many townsfolk who wish to attend court but are too fearful to bask in your presence. I wonder if it might be a fair idea to take a walk through the town one day, perhaps handing out gifts to show them your true nature."

Adrianna chokes on a laugh.

Her lady-in-waiting lifts her brows as if trying to explain that she is serious.

"Oh, yes. Of course! That sounds like a great idea," Dria lies, wondering what the cheapest gift is that she can hand out.

In the middle of her thoughts, Calix comes bursting through the Throne Room doors, his gray eyes overflowing with alarm. "She's gone," her spymaster divulges, the chest of his rail-thin body heaving with distress. "Narelle Lambric and Robbin Flangham are gone!"

The court is silent as death, every attendee turning to face the queen on her dais.

"Gone?" Adrianna grips the arms of her throne to tether her to reality. A nervous smile. "That's impossible. You had her locked away in one of the most secure cells. It should have been guarded twenty-four hours per day. Was it not?"

Calix stalks to the front of the dais, his knees cracking against the marble. "I have failed you, Your Majesty." Her spymaster's body shakes while he lowers his black ringlets. "I do not deserve the privilege of living. Take it, my queen. *Take my head!*"

But Adrianna's blue eyes surf her crowd of courtiers once more, her gaze lingering on one empty seat in particular. "Where is Cyndeya?" she asks calmly.

The court whispers, tittering with suspense until a worn-looking man stands from the back of the room.

"Your Majesty." Lord Elmans's trembling is visible even from a distance. "I didn't put two and two together until just now. I beg you to forgive me—"

"Where *is* she?" Adrianna has lost her patience.

The stable hand swallows. "A few nights ago, I was asked to ready horses for one of the Nevs' small caravans. I didn't think anything of it; she told me she was going out for a short trip."

The queen stifles a scream. "And was she alone?"

"Well, no. She was with two of her ... Nevs." Lord Elmans covers his mouth in realization of both his complete insolence and the looming wrath of a godly queen.

Normally, Adrianna would have had him beheaded on sight, without thinking twice about it. But something like self-control encourages her to ponder the situation more. *If I kill him, my court will be even smaller, and I'm already low on allies. Besides, I do believe he had no idea of Cyndeya's actual motives. Just look at him. He's the kind of man who is afraid of his own shadow.*

"Your Majesty." Desmond puts a hand on his golden sword. "Shall I—"

"That won't be necessary, Captain." Adrianna folds her hands together on her lap, the perfect picture of a ruler. "I trust that each of you has learned the price of carelessness." She points a glance at Calix and her stable hand, tempering a flare of anger. "From this second forward, there will be no more trusting oracles, as they have so clearly chosen to side with my sister." She turns to Desmond and her guards. "Collect the remaining Nevs from the area and bring them here when you are done." *I have special plans for those ones.*

Dria stands from her throne, her belly filling with fire. "Effective immediately, I hereby outlaw the Nevs from the kingdom. Any who chose to remain practicing oracles running the risk of punishment."

Her guards shift slightly, the sound of their golden metal clinking from the movement.

"What kind of punishment, Your Majesty?" Lord Earlmence questions hesitantly.

For a fleeting moment, Adrianna finds herself on the brink of choosing between mercy and aggression, but the fire in her blood melts away any remnants of charity. *Perhaps this is my true nature, Renai.* An emotion like fear has the royal ambassador standing an inch taller when Adrianna answers him with an unflinching gaze.

"Death."

AIMELIE

Golden light shines through the stained glass of the corridor, the walls dwarfing Aimelie Larking at nearly thirty feet tall. She walks politely beside Master Tasman and Prince Darren, the soft morning sun illuminating her blonde curls like they, themselves, are part of the decorative window designs.

"Your sister," Prince Darren starts. "Would you say she is more forward or reserved?"

Aimelie smiles slightly. As much as she dislikes Darren Eldric, it is kind of him to inquire about Annalise, however annoyed he may be over her current absence. "It has been years since I've had the pleasure of speaking with her, but I would say that Annalise is the kind of person who is reserved until she has something important to discuss. Then, she can be quite passionate."

A crude smirk. "Let us hope her to be the latter."

Princess Aimelie shoots him a look of confusion. She still hasn't been told why Tasman and Ivo have asked for her sister to meet them at Eldric Castle, but the expression on Darren's face begins to stir an idea.

"How does your own sister fare?" the princess asks the Crown Prince of Nesvla.

Darren shrugs. "Briar is ill almost monthly. I'm sure she'll be better soon enough."

So kind and considerate, Melie observes dreadfully. She turns to Tasman. "We've been walking for a while, Master. Perhaps we should return to the tearoom for some of that delightful Nesvlan tea?"

Master Tasman chuckles, his wrinkled blue eyes glittering with humor. "Is this how princesses call a man old?" He taps his black cane on the ground. "Very well, Your Highness. We can return—if only for that delightful Nesvlan tea."

Aimelie rolls her blue doe eyes with a playful smile, blushing at his wit until a page approaches them from the opposite end of the hallway.

"Your Highness." He bows before Princess Aimelie, offering two pieces of parchment sealed with the stamp of Empeirus.

Melie contains a squeal, her heart beating with unrivaled giddiness as she retrieves her letters.

"You're a popular princess," Prince Darren notes with egotistical blue eyes. "Who might those be from?"

Like I would tell you. "My love," Aimelie brushes her thumb over the correspondence. "Master Tasman, I may have to postpone my meeting you for tea. I will be back soon, I promise!" She bids a temporary goodbye to her former tutor and the prince, trying not to jaunt too quickly back to her Nesvlan chambers.

As casually as she can, Aimelie slips behind her mahogany door, taking a seat at her stationery desk. While it is true that the first letter has come from Linden, the second is from a ... less acceptable source. She pushes the alternate piece of parchment aside to read what news her paramour has sent.

My dearest A.,

Things are quiet here these days. The queen's allies seem to be few and far between, especially with a shrinking court—at least, so I hear from the other servants.

My love for you, however, remains unchanged, and perhaps has grown from your absence. At night, I dream of your golden curls and your gentle touch, only to wake cold and alone. I pray to the gods that I will be back by your side sooner than I can imagine.

I love you always,

L.

The princess wipes a tear from her baby-blue eyes, trying to ignore the guilt of not being able to hold Linden in her arms. *At least I have given him the ravens as a means to communicate with me.* Still, her mind can't ignore the fact that parchment is a cheap substitute for love. Aimelie slides the opened letter to the other side of her desk, intending to respond after she reads the second one.

The letter has been closed with Empeirian wax and the kingdom's stamp, as Melie had requested for anonymity. With a poised swipe, she breaks the crimson seal, opening the paper to reveal a scrolling hand in clear, black ink. Line by line, Aimelie reads the letter with eyes wide as saucers. *She has offered to meet.* A shallow breath of disbelief. *Queen Haraja wants to meet.* She hasn't exactly decided that contacting the Queen of Calleeit was indeed a good idea, but the affirmation that Haraja is inclined to speak with her gives her hope that it was.

After a long and bloody feud ended almost four years ago, Calleeit has been operating as its own territory, separate from the Kingdom of Empeirus. And because the War on the Horns started due to Adrianna's missteps, communication between Empeirus and Calleeit has been almost nonexistent since then. *Perhaps since they achieved the freedom that they wanted, they don't see a need to hold off on correspondence anymore.* But the idea that Aimelie has broken the years-long silence between the island territory and the Empeirian kingdom with a single letter gives her hope. *Maybe they are less set in their ways than they are rumored to be.*

A light knock at the door draws the princess's attention from her desk. She stands, closing the letters and slipping them into the leather satchel with Annalise's crown. "Come in," she permits.

Her servant enters on quiet feet, curtsying with a feline grace. But it isn't her formalities that Aimelie is distracted by. In the servant's arms is a stack of fabric swatches and a bouquet of various flowers. The girl steps a foot forward, nudging a pink rose away with her chin. "Your Highness, in light of Princess Annalise's current absence, Queen Minerva thought it best if you began making some preliminary decisions in her stead."

An uncomfortable smile. "I'm sorry ..." Aimelie shakes her head in shock, finally beginning to understand Annalise's situation. "I'm not sure I understand. The queen wants me to make decisions for my sister?"

The girl nods. "Yes, Your Highness. Regarding the royal wedding."

Aimelie blinks her large blue eyes. "Will you excuse me for one moment?"

The princess takes the stairs down to the tearoom in twos, dodging golden platters of teacups with boiling annoyance. Prince Darren spots her passing his table, but Aimelie isn't in the mood to talk. *Not to him, anyway.*

"What's the matter, my lady? Wasn't your love letter satisfying enough?"

The princess ignores Darren as she crosses the room

to the corner table, where Master Tasman quietly sips his tea. Aimelie pulls up a chair before he can stand at her arrival.

"She doesn't know," Melie whispers angrily, more of a statement than a question.

The old master frowns, carefully placing his teacup back on its saucer. "You've heard."

"You know, of all the characteristics of an elderly master, I never thought one could be so secretive." Aimelie watches Tasman sigh heavily, paying attention to his every expression. "So, when are you going to tell Annalise that she is to marry Prince Darren Eldric? The moment she arrives? Or perhaps the day of the wedding would be just as acceptable."

"I didn't have the time, Your Highness," Tasman stresses through his white beard. "Before Princess Annalise and Master McHenry left, I mentioned that Ivo and I were going to look for potential alliances. Your sister's betrothal was viewed as null after her presumed death, but upon hearing of her return—" He coughs into the sleeve of his tunic. "What was I supposed to do? Write to her? Something like this is best discussed in person, not in ink. Besides, there would be too many risks involved with communicating over such a long distance."

Aimelie hides a blush, her stomach tightening from the idea of her own dangerous correspondence. She dares a glance in Darren's direction, dropping her voice to a whisper. "I don't know him very well, Tasman. But he doesn't seem to be the kind of person that Annalise would—"

"That is not a decision for us to make, Princess." Tasman's faded blue eyes turn serious. "I know you would do better than to encroach on such matters." He waits for Aimelie to give him a short nod. "The only thing we can do is wait for Annalise's arrival, which hopefully won't be too much longer."

The youngest Larking princess sits back in her chair, waiving away a servant's offer for tea. "Do you think she will be happy?" she poses her most pressing question to the old man.

Tasman finishes his last drop of tea, sliding the empty cup to the edge of the table. "I dare say she will be elated at the news of a powerful alliance."

Aimelie turns her miserable eyes to the window, watching the Nesvlan Sea churn like her thoughts. She knows her sister, knows that Annalise has always strived to be dutiful no matter how undesirable a situation may be—an attribute that will only be escalated if the state of the world is at stake. Her gaze settles on Tasman's empty teacup. "How romantic," is the only comment Aimelie can offer him.

VEGA

Vega beholds Modgen on his chestnut horse, stubbornly continuing down the path to Nesvla. "I'm serious, Modgen. She doesn't look well."

Modgen slows his steed to assess Eden, who lifts her pallid face with eyes less alert than usual. He releases a sigh. "It's hard to tell, considering she isn't typically bursting with energy."

"I'm fine," Eden lies, shivering behind Vega's back.

The redhaired man maneuvers his horse to face the direction they came from. "There was a stable that we passed not too far from here. I'm sure there will be a place nearby to hunker down for the night."

Hopefully. If not for Eden's sake, then for the sake of my legs.

They ride to the stable in silence, the sun casting

shadows on the surrounding autumn leaves as Vega's black horse trails Modgen's. Upon greeting the stable hand, she and Eden dismount, the latter gripping her stolen purple robes to fight off a chill.

The stable hand pauses. "Haven't you heard about the queen's decree?" he asks suspiciously. "Queen Adrianna outlawed the Nevs not a week ago. I wouldn't let any of the guards see you."

Elouthera squints in the sunlight. "*Outlawed*, you say?"

The man nods sternly.

Lazarus, almighty. I suppose that's good news for us. The goddess offers a curt smile to the guard before Eden disappointedly removes her robes, exchanging them for an extra shirt that Modgen had packed.

Modgen cracks his neck. "If you ask me, I think the whole kingdom is better off without those madwomen running around. They have all those magical powers, and for what? To tell you you're going to die in three weeks?"

Passively, Eden kicks a rock. "It's been passed down through generations that the Nevs originated as a way to bring clarity to human existence."

Modgen shoots her a bewildered glance. "Originated from where?"

"From the gods," Vega answers.

A nod from Eden. "When the gods were dissatisfied with how slowly humans were maturing, they blessed a select few with the power to see glimpses of the future; to help others realize the consequences of their actions so they could be given another chance to redeem themselves."

Elouthera assesses her with great curiosity, shocked at how much her acquaintance is speaking. "You know quite a bit about this story," she points out with wrinkled brows.

The aerialist shrugs. "My mother was blessed with the second sight, and so was I. Though, I haven't exactly mastered it as well as she had."

Ah, yes. Laraya Sharpkey, the woman who spurred the Empeirian throne's interest in using the Iribus Circus as their personal line of defense—and a probable spy ring.

"Pardon my pessimism," Modgen shakes his reddish locks, "but I think the gods were right. I don't think we were mature enough to handle even *that* gift."

Vega snorts. "What makes you say that? Because a Nev almost cut out your throat?" She tucks a piece of jet-black hair behind her ear. "Maybe you're right. Maybe we are better off without them."

Eden sniffles. "But isn't your mother one of them? I thought I heard she was their High Pr—"

"Yes, she is one of them, and they are worth far more to her than I will ever be." Elouthera blushes at her sharpness, but somehow, saying the phrase out loud makes it just a fraction more bearable. She finds her lime-green eyes lingering on a sign not far ahead. "There," she points. "That looks like an inn."

Modgen Sprightly leads the way into the Javirian inn, perhaps one of the nicest ones Vega has seen in the territory so far. A serving wench sits seductively on the bar, stealing the cigar out of a patron's mouth, but overall, the atmosphere looks far less dangerous than the inns near Oron. Modgen reaches into his coin, frowning at the shallow depth. Vega would gladly offer her own currency if it hadn't been left in Wembleton.

"One room, please." Modgen hesitantly hands over a small sum, noting the innkeeper's raised brow and pointed glance at the two women beside him. He flashes him an awkward grin. "I'm trying something new."

He accepts the key, turning around just in time to catch Vega's glittering stare.

"I'm beginning to question the kind of company Dimity keeps," the goddess admits bluntly.

Modgen shrugs. "If I'm being honest, I'd say I'm the worst of the bunch."

The group ascends the rickety staircase, Modgen opening the door with a swift flick of a wrist. While the room isn't the most luxurious that Vega has stayed in, it doesn't look unclean. *It could be worse, I suppose.* Her position on the matter changes when Vega observes the bed, which is hardly large enough to fit two people who are closer than friends.

"You two can have the bed; I'll make camp on the floor," Modgen offers, setting down his rucksack.

Vega rubs the back of her neck. *I don't want to sleep next to either of them, but I definitely don't want to get sick.* "I might just stay on the floor, too. I don't think now would be the best time to fall ill, right before I finally get to meet Dimity."

"Uh-huh," Modgen smirks.

The goddess flushes. "Don't flatter yourself."

"It was the smoke bombs, wasn't it?"

Vega scoffs, rolling her cat-like eyes. "You're insufferable, you know that?" She retrieves a canteen for Eden, giving her the last of their water, and changes the subject. "We need to get more food. How much coin do we have left?"

Modgen gives his coin purse a light shake. "Enough." He turns his tall form to the door, making to leave without so much as a goodbye.

"Aren't you going to wait for me?" Vega watches in disbelief.

"I figured you would rather stay with Eden."

Vega darts a glance back at the aerialist, who has tucked herself into bed.

Eden waves her hand. "Go ahead," she tells them in her Javirian accent. "I'll be fine."

The master manipulator finds herself back in the late afternoon sunlight, a chill breeze making her skin prickle.

The town isn't nearly as dismal as Oron was—a fact evidenced by the condition of the inn—but the gray stonework of the buildings is as good an indicator as any that they still haven't escaped Javir.

Far in the distance, a Goliath statue catches Vega's eye, its stone face marred by time and weather. Despite its imperfections, the foundation stands proudly enough that she and Modgen can make it out even from their location at the bottom of the hill. Vega waits for her travel companion to finish bartering for their meat and cheese before posing her question: "Would you like to go for a walk?"

Modgen swings a bag over his lean-muscled shoulder. "I thought we were already on one."

She doesn't know why, but something about the statement makes her stomach sink. "I wanted to apologize for what I said earlier." A blush rises to Vega's pale cheeks. "You're not insufferable."

"Oh, I know I'm insufferable," Modgen replies with a grin. "I just thought you needed some space. I know I'm not the easiest person to get along with." He murmurs under his breath, "Just ask the Captain of the Royal Guard."

That's right, Vega remembers. *Modgen was childhood friends with Dimity—or Annalise, the lost princess.* "You and Princess Annalise were close, I take it?"

A softer smile, one that is less arrogant and more kind.

"Very. My mother was Queen Annora's lady-in-waiting, so we spent a lot of time together growing up."

Vega nods, appreciating that his response isn't dripping with sarcasm. *Maybe he isn't as obnoxious as he's led me to believe.* She rubs her arms to fight off the cold from a rogue wind. "When you say 'very,' does that mean ...?"

"No, no." Modgen shakes his head. "Not like that."

The goddess nods again, trying to think of something else to pry about in a vain attempt to learn more about Dimity's life. *I've spent all this time wondering who this life has made her, and now I don't even know what to ask.*

"Where are we walking to?" The redhead interrupts her thoughts.

"To the statue on top of the hill."

Modgen adjusts the bag on his shoulder. "My turn to ask a question." He smiles with delight.

Oh, great. This will be fun. Vega prepares for the worst; for him to ask about her poor relationship with her mother or her nonexistent friends or if she has any suitors waiting for her back at her family estate.

"Who did you inherit your eye color from? I've never seen anything like them before."

Elouthera pauses, regarding him with a baffled gaze. "That's what you want to ask me?"

He raises a reddish brow. "I can ask you something more difficult if you want?"

Despite herself, Vega laughs. "My father. Bright green

is prevalent in the Kutchrik line." A sidelong glance. "Where do you get your red hair?"

Modgen's smile slowly withers, his cobalt eyes falling to the cobblestones.

Oh, gods. "You don't have to answer, I just thought—"

"No, it's okay," Modgen reassures her. He walks with her a few more paces before deigning an answer. "I always thought it came from my father. Or maybe, that's just how I've always imagined him." A shrug of his shoulders. "He left when I was a baby. Anyway, my mother had brown hair, like both of her parents, so ..." He turns his palms up to suggest he has no better idea.

Vega regrets asking the question now even more than she had after his first reaction to it. "I'm so sorry," is all the goddess can muster.

But Modgen bats a hand. "We all have our demons," he says, restoring himself to his typical upbeat demeanor. "We're almost to the top."

"Yes, we are," Vega agrees as the bottom of the enormous statue comes into view. On the front of the foundation is an inscription, the Javirian words chiseled into the gray stone.

Modgen runs his hand over its rough texture. "I don't speak Javirian, but if I had to guess, I would say it's—"

"Medrios," Elouthera says quietly, in awe of his towering height. Almost thirty feet in the air, the God of Streams and Sea watches over the coastal Javirian village, the tines of his trident piercing the sky in silent warning. *So serious, so stoic.*

"They could have given him more clothes." Modgen observes the measly amount of fabric barely covering the god's lower half. "Please tell me this isn't how he dresses in the immortal world."

Vega shoots him an amused look. "Only on holidays."

Modgen's laugh echoes off the gray stone, so at odds with the statue's dour expression. "What is he really like?" he questions her, the freckles on his cheeks dancing with childlike curiosity.

The goddess smiles, assessing Medrios's stone face. "Pretty much like this. Very stern. And very powerful."

"Mmm." Modgen is quiet for a moment. "And what about Dimity?"

Vega's lime-green eyes grow brighter. "Hopeful. Wise. Ready to give herself to defend a just cause."

Modgen gives a half smile that has Vega feeling just the slightest bit more comfortable with him. "Then she hasn't changed much."

Just down the hill, a group of three horsemen can be seen trotting into town, the sound of hooves reaching Vega's small ears. *That can't be good.* "We should move," she encourages, starting her way back down the cobblestone path.

"Who do you think they are? Edris's men?"

Vega shrugs. "Whoever they are, they don't look friendly. And they're headed toward the inn."

"Gods, damn it." Modgen shakes his head. "What a waste of coin."

Vega whirls in his direction. "Poor Eden is sick, and all you can think about is money?"

"My apologies." He frowns, toying with the leather buckle on his rucksack. "It's a habit left over from being Royal Treasurer."

DESMOND

The Captain of the Royal Guard stands proudly beside his queen on the dais, his heart beating in anticipation. *They should be bringing her in any minute.* Desmond tries hiding a satisfied grin, the corners of his lips subtly destroying his efforts. He eyes the end of the Throne Room with a quicksilver gaze, waiting for Edris's men to drag the goddess to them at long last.

Elouthera, Desmond thinks pleasantly to himself. *How long have I waited for this moment?* Were the Goddess of Dreams and Mystery anything like Dimity, perhaps she would have learned the importance of surrounding herself with a wall of allies. *But Elouthera has always been accustomed to working better on her own, which made her that much easier to find.*

The God of Darkness and Decay allows himself to reflect on his immortal memories, to a time spent tangled with silver hair and full lips and skin pale as the moon. For a moment, he almost feels sorry that it didn't work out between them. *Maybe I should have told her about me and Jedda. Maybe she didn't deserve that kind of fate.*

But Desmond brushes off any lingering guilt, listening to the groan of the enormous mahogany doors as they open to a band of four men, each desperately gripping the rope in their hands while they tug along a small figure behind them. The captain smiles deeply.

"Welcome, Elouthera," Adrianna sneers from her crimson throne. "I do hope you'll find your living quarters accommodating. Though I dare say the dungeon gets quite drafty this time of year." She waves a hand at the men. "Let us take a closer look at her mortal form."

Edris Sharpkey's men move away from the center, being careful not to let go of Elouthera's bindings. Between them stands a tiny woman with jet-black hair, her face blocked from the lowering of her head.

"I'm flattered at your discretion, but you don't need to keep bowing your head." Adrianna beams confidently. "Show us your face."

The woman doesn't budge.

The Dark Goddess frowns from her throne. "I hope you can tell that I'm not in the habit of repeating myself."

The queen traces a circle in the air, a silent command for Edris's gang to follow the instruction themselves. In a matter of seconds, the woman is forced to the marble floor, her small chin tilted upward by way of the hand tugging on her short black hair.

Desmond's heart stops.

Adrianna opens her mouth. "Well," she begins happily. "I suppose this is the face of the goddess they call *Vega*."

"It's not her. It's *not her*." the captain whispers to himself, first in shock, then in anger.

The queen turns her blonde curls his way. "What did you say?"

Pinching the bridge of his tan nose, Desmond steps down from the dais to get a better look at the woman's face, scowling when her eyes are a muddy shade of hazel. "This isn't Vega," the captain bitterly informs Adrianna.

His lover is quiet, observing the party above a blush red enough to match her dress.

"You're right. I'm not Vega. I'm Elouthera." The woman has the nerve to lie to their faces.

"Drop the game, wench," Desmond orders. "You really thought you could fool me? I've seen Elouthera *with my own eyes*," he seethes.

The woman shrugs. "Edris told me you wouldn't be able to tell the difference."

Desmond grits his teeth, storing away that bit of dark anger as a gift for the leader of the Iribus Circus. He rests a hand on his sword. "And you were foolish enough to believe him."

A snort. "I believed the amount of coin he was offering me."

"Did he mention you can't take it with you?" Before she can answer, Anzac draws his blade, skewering it from under her chin to the crown of her black hair.

"Desmond!" Adrianna cries from the throne, watching as the small woman drops to the floor like the hope of Edris's remaining men.

Anzac eyes them warily. "Who else knew about Edris's scheme?"

The men raise their hands in surrender, shaking their heads while the leader pipes up. "We promise, Captain, none of us knew anything about it!"

Desmond sheathes his sword. "Good. I expect Edris to claim the same thing when I meet him in Javir."

"I beg your pardon." Adrianna straightens her spine with concern in her icy eyes.

The captain stops at the foot of the dais. "This can't go on any longer, my queen," he tells her quietly. "I failed with Christa, and now with Edris ..." He shakes his char-coal-black hair. "We need to find Elouthera before she finds Dimity."

"I agree," says Adrianna, with a look of disappointment. "But Edris obviously doesn't have her in his possession anymore. Why go to him first?"

Desmond signals for his guards to herd Edris's men together; the sound of irons locking is music to his ears. "Because I need to remind him who's working for who in our little agreement. And once he realizes that truth, he is going to need to make amends for his mistake."

The gold-adorned castle guards lead Edris's men away, their captors broken and silent.

Adrianna stands from her throne, meeting her paramour on the white marble. Together, their footsteps flow to a side door, leaving the small woman's body for the servants to retrieve. "How will we make him pay for what he's done?"

The sound of Desmond's own golden armor echoes about the corridor adjacent to the Great Hall. "Edris Sharpkey leads an infamous gang in southern Javir."

"I know that," Adrianna cuts in. "He is the leader of the Iribus Circus, as well."

A nod. "My idea is that he can redeem himself by swaying the Javirian army to join his militia, rallying to the cause of the Empeirian throne."

Dria shoots him a patronizing glance. "You really think that will work?"

Desmond sighs, running a hand through his charcoal

hair. "If it doesn't, at least we can say that we tried. And if it does, then we will have an entire army—plus our own, here in Empeirus—looking for both Elouthera and Dimity."

The queen is introspective, pulling at the skin around her nails as she walks beside him.

"You're nervous," Anzac notes, stopping to hold her hands with his own.

Adrianna rolls her icy-blue eyes. "I'm not worried about *you*," she whispers through perfect lips. "I'm just a little concerned about … "

Desmond follows her gaze back to the Throne Room, remembering the last two times that Princess Annalise waltzed into their home and lived to tell the tale. Gently, he cups the side of her ivory face, ensuring that no one else is around. "I will make sure that this castle is guarded with my finest men, day and night. Nobody will get through without you knowing about it." A loving smile. "And if they somehow manage to, you are an incredibly powerful goddess with the ability to melt their faces off."

The queen laughs, the afternoon sun illuminating the graceful curve of her cheekbones. Desmond's silver eyes fall to her lips, but the sound of footfalls has him resuming a more appropriate position. They continue toward the Great Hall, waiting for a servant to pass before continuing with their conversation.

"It's been decades since the Iribus Circus has been

called into use, you know," Adrianna breaks the silence. "The last time they were recruited to help the throne was during the lifetime of Laraya Sharpkey. That was during my parents' reign."

The captain nods, reflecting on the familiar story. *Laraya Sharpkey, Protector of the Throne.* While the public knows the Iribus Circus for their superhuman strength and agility, members of the Royal Family recognize them as the throne's secret line of defense—as was the case with Edris's mother, Laraya. Blessed with the second sight, Laraya Sharpkey dreamed of a surprise attack on young Queen Annora. Combined with a healthy knowledge of self-defense, the aerialist took down eight armed men the night before Annora's coronation. Ever since, the Iribus Circus has been privately heralded as the Empeirian throne's most capable guard, though they continue to train under the guise of common circus performers.

"Let us hope that Edris takes after his mother." Desmond rounds the doorway to the Great Hall, taking a seat near Adrianna at the head of the table.

"How long will you be gone?" the queen asks him, a servant pouring them each a glass of ruby-red wine.

Desmond takes a sip of his own, savoring its full body. "A few weeks, I'd presume." He eyes her longingly. "I don't think I could stand being apart from you any longer than that."

His affection earns him a closed smile, one full of seduction and dark secrets. Adrianna takes a drink from her chalice before standing and luring him out of his seat. "Very well." Dria playfully tugs him back toward the entrance of the Great Hall. "Then I want to make every second count before you have to leave."

NARELLE

"Where will you go?" Narelle asks Robbin, who adjusts his cap over a freshly-shaven face. Despite his long months in the dungeon, he has cleaned up well, with the only physical evidence of his imprisonment being his emaciated form.

Robbin Flangham shoots the courtesan a weak grin. "To wherever the wind takes me, I guess. I hear Fetland isn't so bad if you want to lead a quieter life." He glances at Cyndeya, who has given them a bastion of privacy while changing horses at a stable. "You're sure you don't want to tag along?"

A snort. "I think I've had enough of your cheap jokes during our confinement." Narelle's hazel eyes twinkle with humor. "But I will miss you."

Robbin offers her a warm smile, and it is only then that the former courtesan wonders if she will ever see him again. His grin freezes over when he watches Cyndeya slip extra coins to the stable hand in town. "I don't trust her, Narelle. If you decide to stay with her, you'd better sleep with one eye open. That's if she even sleeps, at all."

Narelle nods, her chestnut hair finally brushed back into a smooth, low bun. "If I've learned anything by now, it's that there are very few people in this world that we can trust."

"There's a principle I couldn't agree with more." Robbin slips his hands into his pockets. "If you live to see Piper—I mean, Princess Annalise—again …" His copper eyes betray a hint of sadness at her name. "Give her my best, will you?"

"You mean, after you spied on her for Queen Adrianna?"

Robbin turns his guilty gaze to the ground, kicking a pebble in introspection. "I'll be the first to admit that I'm not a perfect person, Narelle. But I do sincerely wish her well."

Maybe it was the weeks spent talking with him through iron bars, or the honest expression of his tired face, but somehow, Narelle believes him. The whinnies of two new horses tear her eyes away, and she can see that Cyndeya and her drivers are almost ready to continue their voyage through Empeirus.

"Well." Narelle takes in the last of her conversation with the former fruit merchant, and bids him farewell. "The gods be with you."

"And with you," Robbin returns the blessing.

For a split second, Narelle feels like she could cry until Robbin pulls her into a close embrace. She tries to hide her shock when Robbin pulls away, only to have him steal one of the sweetest kisses she has ever experienced in all her profession. When his lips leave hers, Narelle watches him stalk away with his hands back in his pockets. "What was that for?" she asks under a crimson blush.

"For putting up with my cheap jokes," Robbin calls back to her, spinning back around to continue on his way.

Even after years of hiding emotions, Narelle can't keep a bright smile from blooming across her lovely face.

The only thing that breaks it is the sound of Cyndeya's voice.

"Are you hungry?" the High Priestess of the Nevs calls to her from outside of her caravan.

Narelle follows Cyndeya and her two Nevs into a small tavern, its tables cleaner than any ale house she has ever seen. *Or maybe it just seems that way, after eating off a dirt floor for the past month and a half.* The group makes it a few steps into the empty room before Narelle notices the barkeep's wide eyes.

"Good day," Cyndeya greets him with little interest. "Whatever you have is fine." She seats herself without waiting for an acknowledgment, encouraging the others to do the same.

Narelle observes the man hurriedly fill their drinks before bringing them to the table, his hands trembling slightly as he sets down four mugs of ale. She thinks he is going to make for the kitchen, but is caught off guard when he remains at their table, pulling at the button on his faded doublet.

"You ..." The barkeep swallows anxiously, his eyes darting back and forth between his guests. "You haven't heard?"

Cyndeya sets down her mug of ale. "Heard what?"

The man peeks at the closed door, then the windows. "It's the queen. She's outlawed the presence of the Nevs."

Narelle chokes. "When was this?"

"Almost a week ago." The barkeep drops his voice to a whisper. "Said the punishment would be death, if you're caught."

"Death, you say?" one of the other Nevs chimes in. "High Priestess, did you know of this?"

Cyndeya taps her long nails along the wood of the table. "Did I know there would be consequences? Of course. Did I know it would mean death? Unfortunately, not."

Narelle narrows her hazel eyes. "You told me Adrianna was the Dark Goddess. You weren't expecting her to reciprocate your wrongdoings with confetti and cakes, were you?"

"How *dare* you speak to the High Priestess like that," the smaller Nev criticizes Narelle. "You should be cowering in fear."

The former courtesan presses a hand to her slowly mending ribs. "There is little I fear these days, my lady." But when Narelle shifts her focus on Cyndeya, her tune suddenly changes. *There is little I fear, except for maybe that.*

With her citrine eyes closed, the High Priestess slowly moves the fingers of her free hand in the air while her others clutch a small glass vial around her neck. Looking more closely, Narelle can make out a few locks of golden hair within the bottle, her sanity waning at the sight of a crackling blue energy seeping into Cyndeya's fingertips. It takes almost every ounce of self-determination Narelle has to glance at the barkeep, who seems to have regained his composure.

Cyndeya's orange eyes pop open, her hands relaxing once she tucks the vial back into her purple robes. "Now, where were we?"

The barkeep scratches his head. "Ah, I believe I was about to go prepare your food!" He returns to the kitchen with a casual step.

Narelle's gaze roves to the High Priestess. "What the hell was that?"

Cyndeya lifts her hands in feigned surrender. "Just saving us a bit of trouble and him a bit of nerves."

"You're a witch," Narelle spits, reconsidering Robbin's offer to flee with him. *I wonder how long it would take to catch up to him.*

The Nevs laugh haughtily, the taller one flipping her black hair over her shoulder. "You didn't know that's what Nevs are?"

Narelle shakes her head. "I didn't think they were the kind that disregarded free will. That's some sort of black magic." She watches Cyndeya with disdain.

"Speaking of free will," the High Priestess begins. "Our options just got a whole lot more limited if we want to avoid the queen's punishment. I was prepared to be on the run, but to disappear altogether ..." For the first time since Narelle has known her, Cyndeya relents dissatisfaction. "We will need a new plan."

"Your food," the barkeep declares, serving them a hearty beef stew with a hunk of bread before happily returning to the bar.

"A plan?" Narelle blows on a spoonful of stew, conjuring up her own ways to survive without these witches. "And what might that be?"

"What do you care, *whore?*" The taller Nev's comment has Narelle dropping her spoon with a clatter, spinning her head in her direction.

"That's enough, Melda," Cyndeya scolds her before

turning to Narelle. "Please forgive her insolence. She doesn't get enough attention being my driver, it seems."

Narelle ignores the Nev's excuses. She returns to her bowl, dunking a piece of bread in the broth.

"But she gives me an idea."

All three women meet the High Priestess's glittering eyes.

Cyndeya's smile is serpentine. "Our interests are still the same. But to find the lost princess, the Nevs will need to continue our efforts to … collect information, if you will. If we cannot waltz around as the oracles Lazarus knows we are, then we will just have to find another sort of guise." Dark intrigue creeps into Cyndeya's full face while she holds a stare with Narelle. "My proposal is this: You teach my girls how to pose as courtesans, where they will be stationed throughout the kingdom to continue their duties. And in return, I will give you firsthand information on Annalise's whereabouts, and any other knowledge you may seek."

It is the drivers' turns to drop their spoons. "And what if we don't want to chain ourselves to a bedpost?" the shorter oracle questions.

"Then you will be stripped of your responsibilities and banned from the Nevs." Cyndeya offers them a frown. "But those who wish to endure will be rewarded handsomely, should Princess Annalise restore our legality once she takes her rightful place on the throne. My ladies, we

Nevs may be proud, but we are not infallible. In times such as these, we must show our strength by adapting, lest the queen destroy us entirely." She takes a swig of ale. "We cannot let that happen."

The women are silent; Narelle pushes around a potato in her stew. *Robbin might be right not to trust her, but with such a wide network of spies, how could I turn down my best shot at finding Annalise?* "Very well," Narelle extends her bruised hand to the High Priestess.

Cyndeya shakes it with an esoteric grin. "Excellent." She casts her gaze on her two drivers. "Melda, Iris. Prepare a meeting at the Southern Hall of Javir. Many will be in hiding already, but burning robes isn't enough to take the Nev out of a woman."

"Yes, High Priestess," Melda and Iris respond in unison, standing to exit the tavern.

Narelle watches Cyndeya finish the last of her bread. "Do you think it will work?" she asks quietly.

Cyndeya shrugs. "Many will likely bolt, but the strong few will stay." She leans back in her rickety chair. "Where do you think she is, the lost princess?"

Narelle can't imagine that Annalise is anywhere in Empeirus, by now. *Especially with the recent feud between herself and Adrianna.* The former courtesan offers the oracle a fragile smile. "To wherever the wind has taken her, I suppose."

ANNALISE

Annalise pads across the wooden deck with slightly more confidence than she had on her trip to the Savek Coast, her leather boots clunking softly against the rocking ship. *Anna's Revenge*, the lost princess thinks amusedly. *What a terrible joke.* She forces a stare out into the waves, the cobalt color of the sea now faded from traveling so far south. Her mind flutters back to a time when she tried practicing her control over the element of water, then back to her failed attempts to spray fire in a secluded cave. The goddess swallows. *I'm not ready.*

It has been a little over two weeks since she and Oliver had departed the McHenrys' family home in the Savek Coast, and Annalise has not exactly been thrilled about it.

Of course, she will miss the beautiful rocky shoreline and the delightful chocolate-covered caramels and spinning to drums under one hundred hanging lanterns. But most pressing is the fact that the Goddess of Wisdom and Justice has not yet completed the training of her powers, which could mean the difference between life and death should she come face-to-face with Adrianna or Desmond once again.

At the front of the hull stands Master Oliver McHenry, his attractive form outlined by the sun's brutal rays. Annalise tries to divert her eyes to more important matters, like the massive strip of land looming just beyond.

"Look at you, so close to the sea." Oliver beams when Annalise rolls her eyes. "You wouldn't have been caught dead standing here on our way to the Savek Coast."

Anna grips the ship's railing tightly, attempting to look more at ease than she feels. "The north has changed me."

Her friend laughs, flashing a winsome smile as he walks with the princess toward the wheel. "Then I hope the west doesn't change you back. Hann, Ric!" Oliver calls to some of his deckhands. "Ready her for arrival. We'll be on Nesvlan soil sooner than you think."

Thank Lazarus for the crew that remained during our time at Oliver's home. Although a few stragglers abandoned hope for their ship's new management, most of the original deckhands who agreed to stay after Oliver and Captain Garin's duel were found waiting for their next round of coin.

Oliver takes the wheel in his hands, surveying the approaching land with his evergreen eyes. "Almost there," he states quietly, the matching wheel pinned to his shirt sturdy in the sea breeze.

Annalise smiles at the pin Garin had surrendered to Oliver after losing their duel. "Should I call you Captain McHenry now?"

An admonishing glance. "Oliver is fine."

The princess cracks a laugh. "I'm asking so I know how to properly introduce you to others. I wasn't sure if you preferred your political title or the one you acquired from a duel," Annalise quips sarcastically, watching him fight the humor tugging at his lips.

"Lady Piper," Ric addresses Annalise. "We can help carry up your things if you need."

The princess offers a kind smile. "Thank you, Ric, but I'm afraid I only have one bag." Anna pats him on the shoulder before venturing belowdecks to retrieve her meager inventory, reemerging in the fresh air only when *Anna's Revenge* makes landfall. She regards the ship's crew tying up the large vessel, laying down the wooden walkway that will lead her to the destination Master

Tasman had whispered to her what feels like so long ago: *You must meet us in Eldric Castle once you've completed your training.*

Oliver passes out compensation to each member of his crew, thanking them for their hard work during such a long journey. While he descends into the cabin to grab his own belongings, Annalise finds her gaze settling on the distant golden domes of Eldric Castle, the rest of the walls obstructed by trees full of orange and crimson leaves. A salty breeze gusts off the Nesvlan Sea, fluttering a few strands of Anna's earthy locks.

"Do you think they'll be expecting you?" Oliver asks when he returns to her side, taking her own bag to slip over his shoulder.

Annalise swallows her growing trepidation. "I really hope so."

Carefully, the princess and the former master make their way down to the dock, meeting a pair of heavily armored guards at the edge of solid ground.

"State your business," the shorter one grunts suspiciously.

Oliver and Anna exchange glances. The goddess straightens her spine.

"We were instructed by a friend of the Nesvlan crown to reconvene here—by Master Tasman, namely."

The taller guard snorts. "Yeah? And who might you be?"

"Princess Annalise, rightful heir to the Empeirian throne."

The guards scramble, each of them bowing as they murmur endless apologies. While the taller guard calls for a carriage, the other takes their bags, helping Annalise up the step when their transportation arrives. Oliver follows her in, taking a seat on the opposite side before the guard closes the door, tapping twice on the side of the carriage.

Annalise eyes the long sword at Oliver's hip, her anxiety rekindling while a stranger drives them into uncharted territory. "Will you keep that on you?" she asks quietly.

"I will. Do you have yours?"

Anna pats the dagger through her cloak, its sheath held up by the leather belt tight around her waist. "I do." It belonged to the Nev that nearly killed her that night on the beach, the one who gave her a lovely scar on her left thigh. The goddess would have let it be, but after seeing how slowly it takes for her to summon powers at the nonce, Annalise thought it best to have an alternative form of self-defense. *And to be fair, I dare say I earned it.*

The sound of wheels rumbling over cobblestones fills Annalise's ears while she slides back in her seat, propping up her boots beside Oliver. She lies here with her eyes closed, gently drifting side-to-side with the movement of the carriage.

"Not interested in sightseeing, I gather?" Oliver asks from his bench.

Anna opens a brown eye. "Not interested in being here, honestly."

A hum of contemplation.

The princess allows herself a peek out the window, her spirits slightly lifted at the sight of stable land. "I'm not ready, Oliver," Annalise admits to him in a whisper. She meets his pine-green gaze with a fearful expression she seldom lets others see.

Oliver presses his lips together, nodding in acknowledgment. "I wouldn't worry, Annalise. There are few things in this world that we are truly ready for."

Before she can respond, the carriage comes to a halt. This time, a different guard opens the door to help Annalise out, one dressed in finer armor than the first two. After taking a few steps back into the chill Nesvlan air, the princess can see why.

The golden domes of Eldric Castle tower before them, the structure's steps lined by the same orange and crimson trees that Annalise had seen earlier from the ship. All along the castle's white granite stairs are men and women dressed in luxurious finery, dotting the way up to its remarkably elaborate doors. Annalise watches each of the noblewomen flaunt their lace-trimmed parasols, their enormous gowns trailing behind them while they cling to the arms of their escorts.

Tasman is here? Anna's confused expression must be evident, because Oliver seems to read her thoughts.

"A bit more lavish than the fashion back in Empeirus," he states within Anna's earshot. Oliver offers his arm, which the princess accepts as she continues to take in the view of the castle.

The guards follow with their bags in hand, tailing their voyage up the castle steps in silence. Upon reaching the main entrance, they relay information to two other guards and a page, who welcome Annalise and Oliver into a beautiful orange corridor with unbridled enthusiasm.

"Queen Minerva will be overjoyed to finally make your acquaintance, Your Highness," the page beams widely. "Of course, we can always delay your meeting if you wish to make adjustments to your presentation?"

The princess exchanges an uncomfortable glance with Oliver.

"To hell with their presentation," an elderly voice interrupts from the left, a black cane willing his frail body to move with a speed Annalise hasn't seen since her childhood.

"Master Tasman!" Anna releases Oliver's arm to embrace her former tutor before allowing him to shake her companion's hand.

Tasman takes Annalise's shoulder, ignoring the presence of the royal page. "Your Highness, there is something we need to discuss. I didn't want to put it off until now, but—"

Walking around the corner just ahead, the princess can make out Captain Ivo and a young woman with a head full of honey-blonde curls, her large blue eyes evident even from a distance. For half a moment, Annalise laughs at herself for almost thinking her to be her youngest sister.

My gods! It can't be!

But a double-take confirms her suspicions. Anna's mouth drops agape, meeting Tasman's gaze to ensure that she isn't going insane.

Princess Aimelie Larking stops dead in her tracks, a sob spilling from her lips as she runs full speed into her eldest sister's arms.

Trembling, Annalise clutches her tightly, the floral scent of Aimelie's perfume filling her nose while she fails to fight back tears.

"They told me you were gone, but I never believed them," Melie cries into her shoulder, her own body shaking with emotions. "I *knew* it was you that day in the Throne Room."

Annalise sobs, her mind still having trouble processing the fact that she is holding her little sister for the first time in six long years. "I didn't want to let myself believe it, but I saw you, too." Anna releases Aimelie to get a closer look at her beautiful face. Her features have matured significantly since she was eleven, but the youngest princess still maintains her familiar youthful appearance of doe eyes and freckles.

"We have so much to catch up on," Aimelie beams before she pulls away, eyeing Oliver with a sort of hesitant approach. "Master McHenry," she greets him suspiciously.

Ivo places a hand on Melie's shoulder. "Not to worry, Your Highness. Master McHenry has proven himself to be a trustworthy ally, despite his former source of employment."

Annalise bows her head in greeting at her Captain of the Royal Guard, who reciprocates the gesture. "Your Highness," Captain Ivo smiles honestly.

"I'm terribly sorry to spoil the moment," the royal page interrupts, "but I've just received word that the queen is awaiting your arrival in her Throne Room." He pins his cheerful eyes on Annalise.

The eldest princess balks. "Right." Anna frowns at her black cloak and tattered blue dress. *It will have to do.* Hesitantly, she follows the page to the immense doors with an unusually high-strung Tasman.

"Your Highness," Master Tasman begins, "I wanted desperately to discuss this matter in private, before your introduction to the queen."

"It's really no problem, Tasman. I've dried most of my

tears." Annalise uses her fingers to smooth out a few of her earthy locks.

The old master coughs. "I'm not speaking of Princess Aimelie."

Anna narrows her brown eyes slightly. "There is another matter?"

The royal page knocks a few times on the right door.

"Annalise," Tasman taps his cane against the floor. "Do you remember when I told you that we were looking for alliances?"

When the princess opens her mouth, so, too, does the page open the door. Annalise Larking turns to face the Nesvlan Throne Room, its walls glittering with gold as rich as the orange velvet runner leading to the dais. Her heart stops when her dark gaze makes it to the throne.

"Could it be?" Queen Minerva rises in a gown of the finest silk. She brings her hands to her heart, padding softly down the dais until she meets Annalise on the orange fabric, shooting a glance at the old master. "Can you confirm, Master Tasman?"

"It is she, Your Grace."

Why does she need Tasman to confirm this? "Queen Minerva." Annalise reluctantly returns her smile, curtsying in her travel clothes.

"Princess Annalise," Minerva reciprocates the gesture before looking down her nose at the cluster of servants on the side of the Throne Room. "For the gods' sakes, will someone be kind enough to take Her Highness' cloak?"

The Nesvlan queen's formalities are almost enough to distract Annalise from the tall figure near the throne, his black hair and sea-blue eyes a perfect reflection of Minerva's.

Wait, my cloak? Oh gods, no— "Your Grace," Annalise tries to stop her. "That really won't be necessary."

The queen bats a jeweled hand. "Nonsense. Bernard will take it."

Annalise can feel Oliver's eyes waiting for her to expose the rest of her travel outfit. She shoots him a side-long glance, offering the slightest hint of a shrug. Unclasping her black cloak, Anna hands it over to the servant, letting the world bask in the fashion choices of the kingdom's most wanted. The princess savors every moment of Queen Minerva's appalled expression until the man beside the throne opens his mouth.

"Well, I'm sure she cleans up nicely," he smirks.

Annalise fights the embers crackling through her blood. "I'm sure you do, too." She smiles sweetly.

"Princess Annalise," Queen Minerva attempts to diffuse the situation. "It is my absolute honor to finally introduce you to my son, Darren Eldric, the Crown Prince of Nesvla—and your betrothed."

The embers sputter out like a candle in a cold wind.

My what? Hopelessly, Annalise turns to Master Tasman, her mind too full of shock to voice a word.

"It has come to my attention that such an arrangement was not conveyed to you," the queen explains. "Please accept my sincerest apologies. The contract King Ryatt and I drew up with your late parents was thought to be null and void until your emergence a couple of months ago." Queen Minerva offers a kind smile. "We are very grateful to have you here, Princess Annalise."

Prince Darren Eldric saunters casually down the dais with more pep in his step than a man on his wedding night. He takes one of Annalise's near-trembling hands, bringing it to his lips as he bows before her. "My lady." His blue eyes gleam with ornery delight.

"My lord," is all Annalise can muster before he releases her hand with princely precision.

Queen Minerva shifts her attention to Oliver, who seems almost as perplexed as Annalise. "And who do we have here?"

"Master Oliver McHenry, Your Grace." He bows almost deep enough to hide his confusion.

"'Master,' as in 'Master of the High Council?'" Prince Darren tilts his head. "I recall you being stripped of your title once Queen Adrianna put a bounty on your head. But you still go by 'Master?'"

"That's because he's Master of *my* High Council, now," Annalise decides at this moment.

A slow, analyzing glare from Prince Darren. "I see."

Suddenly, even the ties on Anna's loose travel dress feel suffocating. "Your Grace. Your Highness. I do hope you won't mind if I excuse myself to clean up a bit."

"Not at all." Queen Minerva offers another overly-accommodating grin. "Bernard, will you please show Princess Annalise and Master McHenry to their respective chambers?"

Annalise can hardly manage a curtsy before they leave, Princess Aimelie wordlessly taking her arm. They ascend a few flights of stairs, reaching Anna's new chambers to the right of Melie's. Annalise half-listens to her youngest sister spew something about how fine Nesvlan tea is while Bernard stalks away with Oliver. Anna's eyes meet his for a split second before he disappears behind a corner.

"Anyway, I'm rambling." Aimelie beams beneath her freckles. "How about I let you rest for a little, and you can let me know when you're ready to meet in the tearoom?"

Annalise nods, summoning a grin before her sister embraces her once more. When Aimelie leaves her, Anna enters her chambers, slowly closing the mahogany door while her brown eyes glaze over the gaudiness of the chosen decor. With only the sound of her heavy boots, Annalise passes under a golden chandelier, catching her reflection in the crystal before removing her leather belt and tossing it onto the bed.

The goddess runs a hand over the cloth-of-gold fabric, feeling every crevice and ripple against her palm, her blood somehow thrumming with power, ready for use. She tries to tame it, tries to wash it away with a deep breath and a quick prayer until her hand wanders across the blankets and runs into a feather pillow. In a spurt of unwarranted anger, Annalise shoves her face into it, smothering her screams with the Nesvlan silk until it is all she can do but collapse.

DESMOND

Captain Desmond Jrehart dismounts his horse with all the fury of a madman, slamming his boots into the gray cobblestones of the Javirian street. While days of travel have honed his rage into a sharpness he somehow relishes, his veins are ready to burst at the first sign of his newest traitor. Prowling to his destination with unrivaled stealth, the God of Darkness and Decay eavesdrops on the conversation of some tittering courtesans, their black robes glistening behind a veil of sweet smoke.

"I heard he took out every one of the guards," the first woman notes. "Didn't even need help; he just went in on his own and came out with her like a knight from a fairytale."

"A knight!" the second woman swoons. "We need more of those around here. What did he look like?"

"Well, I wasn't out that day, but Bree heard it from a Nev that he was this tall, lanky gent with hair red like wildfire."

A moan. "Sounds handsome."

Desmond snorts. *Sounds like—* He stops in his tracks, whirling toward the courtesans. "This red-haired man, what did he do?" the captain asks viciously.

The women exchange glances. "You haven't heard?" The first one blows a ring of smoke toward the stars. "He broke into the Oronian Clocktower—the one Edris had been using as a cell for that witch—and he took out all of Sharpkey's men."

It can't be ... "Which way did they go?" Anzac curls his muscled fists.

"Like I said before, I wasn't there."

The two courtesans reenter what Desmond presumes to be The Onyx before a younger voice pipes up from his left.

"I was," another courtesan claims from her seat on a tree stump. "They stole a couple of horses, then headed that way." The blonde woman points west toward the road to Nesvla.

Nesvla? Why go there? But Desmond doesn't have time to indulge in mental gymnastics right now. Digging into his coin purse, he tosses the courtesan a golden sun before heading to his true target. The captain slinks into the shadows, following the map of the city he had memorized earlier, passing dark alleys and archways. He shoulders a bend, then—

"*Gods!*" Anzac grunts, trying to muffle a scream when a man on the run slashes at his pocket, disappearing around a moonlit corner. "What the hell is wrong with you people?" He clutches the wound, not terribly deep, but just as painful. *He was probably a pickpocket, looking for some more coin.* The realization is enough to make the god's dark mood even darker, a sentiment he tucks away just for Edris Sharpkey.

The entrance to the Iribus Circus is a wall of crimson and white stripes, the heavy fabric swaying in the wind. But Desmond isn't going in that way, isn't going to knock on the front door like a typical guest would.

Desmond isn't a typical guest.

The god rounds the back of the enormous tent to the building connected to it, the blood rushing in his ears as he uses a fraction of his magic to form a shadow pawn—a small girl of only about six or seven years, who he has tap on the wrought iron door a few times. Desmond waits, his scar glistening in the moonlight while he listens through the little girl's ears under the cover of a dark alley.

"What the hell do you want?" The well-muscled man slides a hand over his drunken face. "I don't have any coin for you."

Anzac makes the child smile, her sweet face glowing in the torchlight. "I know you don't. But *I* have something for *you*."

Edris Sharpkey snorts, stumbling forward just enough for Desmond to glimpse the half-empty bottle in his hand from a few feet away. "And what might that be?" he slurs.

Discreetly, the captain moves from his spot in the alley, slipping into the shadows to pose as a civilian while he continues his puppetry.

"I have a message for you," the girl chirps, her kind eyes slowly losing color. "A wise man once said that no man should be feared so much as the gods who created him. Do you know why that is?"

A huff of intoxicated laughter. "I—" Edris squints more closely, watching the features of the street urchin's face beginning to melt down her round cheeks, her eyes turning to liquid ebony.

"It's because no man is half as powerful as his creators, no matter how strong he thinks himself to be." Anzac lets the girl burst into shadows, each bolt of blackness firing through the air with a hair-raising scream.

Edris jumps back with a bellow, clutching the doorframe with white fingers. "Please, I beg you!"

"Who do you beg?" The faceless voice around his body whispers while Desmond moves toward the door.

"I beg ..." Edris falls to his knees, the sweat beading above his dirty-blonde brow. "I beg ..."

A roll of thunder finds its way to the Javirian night sky, the corresponding lightning flashing around Anzac's strapping figure. "You beg *me*," he finishes for him, hauling him upright by his nightshirt and smashing his bottle against the wall.

"*Please*," Edris sobs through drunken tears. "I had no choice! I couldn't go back on my promise. I couldn't let my men show up empty-handed!"

"You should have called off our arrangement. You should have owned up to your mistake like a true man would," Anzac spits at his face. "But you *never* should have played a god." Desmond summons a blade made of shadow, angling it just beneath the gang leader's neck.

"*Gods, no!*" Edris screams in the balmy air. "I'll do whatever you want! Connections, coin, you name it! Just let me live!"

With a devilish smile, Anzac lets the blade vanish into dust, dropping Edris to the ground when he releases his shirt collar. Slowly, Desmond advances a step, pulling him back by his hair to get a better look at his mortified face. "I'm glad we're on the same page, Edris Sharpkey. I need a Javirian army, and you are going to raise it for me."

NARELLE

Narelle points her hazel eyes out of the carriage window, their behemoth caravan now stripped of its purple cloths in exchange for a fragment of anonymity. Her side aches from the bounce of wheels over cobblestones, but the pain isn't nearly as sharp as it had been in the weeks prior. *And even then, it isn't anything compared to the other blows I've suffered.* "What exactly did you do at Larking Castle?" Narelle asks Cyndeya quietly.

The High Priestess sighs, smoothing out the wrinkles of her new black gown. "Not all pasts were made for sharing, my lady." She eyes the former courtesan carefully, watching Narelle shrink from her gaze. "But finding you was an added benefit of the position."

Narelle opens her perfect mouth, the carriage coming

to a halt before she can voice her thoughts. *Her freeing me is the reason Queen Adrianna has banished the Nevs,* she frets. *I know Cyndeya wants me to help her find Annalise, but that's a high price to pay if it means outlawing the very women who work for you.* Narelle rises from her seat, exiting the carriage to be greeted by the chill air of autumnal Javir and a trove of tall hemlocks. In the distance, a raven caws its way across the gray skies, one of its inky feathers dropping to her feet on a heavy wind.

Cyndeya Kutchrik follows her, the hair-filled vial she typically wears around her neck now hidden between her full bust. "It's just ahead, through the brush," the oracle divulges, pausing for a moment to wait for her carriage drivers to catch up.

With a gentle hand, Narelle pushes the stray branches aside, exposing a painted black door set within a tree trunk. *What is this, some kind of fairytale forest?* She turns the knob with a cautious hand, preparing herself for whatever may lie on the other side. *What if this is some kind of trap?* But the High Priestess stands at her side, and Calix has taken most of the fear from her. *After all, what is there to fear after looking death in the eye?*

The painted door opens to a dark staircase, its steps spiraling downward within the hollowed tree trunk.

"Melda, the light," Cyndeya instructs her Nev. The High Priestess passes the lantern to Narelle, letting her lead the way down the tightly placed stairs until they reach the bottom, where the sound of voices spews from a short doorway beaming with light.

Narelle dips her head to clear the entrance, avoiding wild roots clawing their way through the shallow dirt tunnel until at last, the world opens up to an impressive underground cave. *Gods*, Narelle swears internally. *This is surreal!*

The Southern Hall of Javir is no less than twice Narelle's height and illuminated by twenty or so lanterns hanging from various roots, throwing light at every inch of the earthen hall. Along the left wall are dozens of purple cushions, almost all of them taken by sullen Nevs in their outlawed robes. Narelle watches their eyes light up when they spot their High Priestess making her way to the opposite wall, to a large makeshift throne decorated in swatches of jewel-toned fabric and metallic pendants.

"High Priestess!" one Nev calls out from her seat on the floor. "You must help us!"

Cyndeya pushes her way past the other women, dragging Narelle with her until she claims her place on the throne. She orders Narelle to stand by her side while Melda and Iris find an empty cushion to seat themselves on.

"What have we done to deserve this fate?" another oracle cries over the chaos of the hall.

Narelle waits for a response that never comes from Cyndeya's sealed lips. *She isn't going to tell them*, she thinks with no small amount of shock. *She isn't going to admit that her choice to free me is what cost all these women their livelihoods.* Narelle swallows her bitter disappointment when the High Priestess raises a hand, the eyes of every Nev darting between their leader and the former courtesan.

"Ladies," Cyndeya begins in a sad tone. "Thank you for meeting me here." A dramatic sigh. "Indeed, the decree made by Queen Adrianna is a dismal one, and despite her own godly background, I do hope that her partial mortality will enable her to experience the justice of her ill intent. As we know, karma comes for us all."

"Karma comes for us all!" the Nevs repeat with passionate reverence.

The High Priestess toys with the chain around her neck. "There are things in this world that a Nev can fall victim to. Death. Illness." A pointed look at Narelle. "Torture." Solemnly, Cyndeya pulls the necklace over her head, running pale fingers over the glass vial while she stares at the lock of blonde hair. "But they don't have to fall victim to the law." The oracle rises from her chair, adjusting the skirts over her curvy hips. "We Nevs have dwelled on this planet for as long as history has been recorded. Our line will not end here," Cyndeya declares fiercely.

"But how can it not?" a Nev asks from the ground. "We're no use spying for the throne anymore."

So, that's what Cyndeya was doing at the castle.

"And now, with the decree ..." the woman shakes her head. "There are guards everywhere. It's only a matter of time before they catch us telling fortunes, even if we burn our robes."

"I wasn't talking about telling fortunes." The High Priestess turns her citrine gaze to Narelle, whose skin rises in goosebumps despite her heavy cloak. "If we mean to survive, we are going to need a visible change of occupation. We must go someplace where no one will suspect us to flee, where no one will bat an eye at anything we do or say." An intentional pause. "Somewhere like a brothel."

Whispers fill the cave, the seated Nevs listening to Cyndeya with suspicious eyes.

A brunette chimes in. "You want us to become courtesans?" The question comes out more like a statement.

Narelle darts her hazel eyes around the hall, silently waiting for Cyndeya's next sentence.

The High Priestess shakes her head. "I don't want this for any of you. But we cannot be snuffed out like a candle beneath the queen's fingers."

Oh Robbin, maybe I should have just run away with you and left this nonsense behind. Narelle pinches the bridge of her nose. *The only thing keeping me here is that I would miss out on my best chance at finding Annalise.*

"Somewhere in this kingdom, the goddess Dimity is in hiding under the name Princess Annalise, rallying troops of her own to take down Jedda—Queen Adrianna, if you will." Cyndeya walks before her oracles. "Whether Dimity would abolish the decree that made practicing our talents illicit, I haven't the slightest idea. But, if we agree to help the Goddess of Wisdom and Justice regain the Empeirian throne—say, by collecting vital information for her across the kingdom—she will at least be indebted to us, and the chance of her restoring the Nevs' legality should be greatly enhanced."

"And if it isn't?" a tall Nev from the front row asks, her dark eyes flickering with distaste. "My girls and I didn't exactly have the best luck with Elouthera."

The High Priestess stops her pacing. "I beg your pardon, Lillian." Cyndeya locks her citrine stare on the peeved oracle.

Lillian exchanges worn glances with the shorter girl next to her, the fabric of their purple robes frayed and tattered. "We found her in the woods along a path headed toward Nesvla, right after that red-haired man freed her and Edris's sister from the Oronian Clocktower. My group followed them for a while until we caught them unawares in the middle of the night." Lillian's expression turns sour.

The shorter Nev stands from her cushion, pushing back the sleeves of her robe. "That goddess took out one of our girls and still managed to tie us both up before escaping with her friends." She rubs the imaginary rope around her wrists. "I don't want to risk that kind of treatment again, especially not after selling my body for the gods know how long."

A flicker of introspection in Cyndeya's round face. "Nesvla, you say ..." The High Priestess trails off before coercing her thoughts back to reality. "I'm convinced that Elouthera wouldn't have attacked you if you were trying to help her rather than capture her, and I would apply the same logic to Dimity. But, regardless, I must remind you all that this is not an order."

Cyndeya floats before her chair, eyeing each of them with total sincerity. "Anyone who wishes to adapt to this new way of life will continue to be led by myself, with the help of Princess Annalise's former caregiver, Narelle Lambric. Those of you who choose not to pursue this path will be banned from the Nevs and must give up their robes to be burned."

Gasps spill from gossiping lips at the latter option.

The High Priestess sits herself on her throne, sighing from the movement. "The choice is entirely yours."

Lillian is the first to stand. Sullenly, she strips herself of her robes, tossing them to the center of the cave before exiting without a word. Her friend is the next, adding her own robe to the pile, followed by several others. One by one, the Nevs filter out of the cave, their hall which was once filled from wall to wall now breathable from so much empty space.

Gods, this is less than half of the original count, Narelle notes with wide eyes.

Quietly, Cyndeya surveys her thirty-or-so girls, each waiting patiently for instruction. "What I see are the strongest of the strong," she tells them with a back rigid and tall. "You are the reason why we Nevs will never fall. My lady," the High Priestess casts her gaze on Narelle, "the floor is all yours."

ANNALISE

Sylvie finishes lacing up the back of Annalise's corset, examining the gold fabric with satisfaction. "This should serve well to impress the prince," the handmaid smirks.

Above the princess's dark waves sit a multitude of shimmering golden pins, glowing in the Nesvlan sun. "I had no idea the Eldrics had such fine taste."

"Oh, yes." Sylvie fluffs out the bottom of Annalise's skirts. "But you don't need to worry. You could show up in your underdress and your beauty would still be apparent."

The princess smiles weakly at the compliment, recalling Darren Eldric's snide remark about her travel clothes yesterday. *Beauty isn't all I will need to get along with the Crown Prince of Nesvla.* "What can you tell me about Prince Darren?" she pries with interest.

Sylvie laughs. "Nothing that you haven't already heard, I'm sure."

What the hell is that supposed to mean? Anna presses a hand to her corseted stomach. "I'm afraid I haven't heard much. Living in exile for six years makes it rather difficult to stay in the political loop."

The handmaid balks. "I am so sorry, Your Highness; I didn't mean—"

"There is nothing to apologize for, Sylvie." Annalise watches her resume placing a citrine and gold necklace around her neck. "I suppose I'm not like many other royals—I can stand speaking plainly, once in a while."

A kind smile. "Very well, Your Highness." Sylvie walks a circle around the princess for a final look at her work. She nods, her dark eyes meeting Annalise's own. "Prince Darren is a fine man," she begins quietly, "but like all princes, he appreciates being appreciated." A shy shrug. "Perhaps, if you were trying to win his affections, you could start by paying him some compliments."

Win his affections? Shouldn't he be winning mine, after his insult yesterday afternoon? "Thank you, Sylvie." Annalise waits for her handmaid to open the door before heading downstairs to the tearoom, where she finds herself drawn to a marvelous view of the Nesvlan Sea. *He "appreciates being appreciated,"* the princess rehashes. *Doesn't everyone?*

Annalise was hoping Sylvie would spill something more substantial about the prince, but even her hand-maid seems to be as spurious as the Nesvlan family she has been promised to marry into. Pausing for a moment to gather her wits, Anna can take all of two breaths before she catches a tall shadow in the corner of her eye.

"My lady," Darren Eldric greets her. "I had a feeling I'd find you here." The prince bows while Annalise offers him a curtsy, his sea-blue eyes beholding Sylvie's efforts with acute interest. "I hear the winds aren't as harrowing as they were yesterday, if you would care to join me for a walk about the gardens?"

Annalise cracks her knuckles behind her back, ignoring the impoliteness of the prince's gaze. At any other time, she would have searched for an excuse not to accept his invitation, but they are the only two in the tearoom this early in the day. "I would be delighted," she lies.

"Splendid." Darren grins handsomely, offering her his arm. They walk in tense silence for a moment, the prince leading their way toward a set of arched doors. "About yesterday," Darren starts. "I'm afraid I said something I shouldn't have, and I wanted to apologize for it."

Anna raises a brow. *An apology? I wasn't expecting him*

to be capable of such a thing. "I appreciate that, my lord. And I, too, would like to apologize for my insolence."

The Crown Prince of Nesvla bats his free hand. "It wasn't unwarranted." He glances sidelong at the princess. "Though, I dare say I was right—you do clean up nicely."

Annalise's eyes narrow suspiciously above a slight smile. "As do you."

Past the arched doorway, the world opens up to a magnificently manicured lawn accented by high and low shrubs. Orange and crimson trees stand watch along the perimeter of the castle gardens with climbing white vines twining their way around the bark, the sight like something from a storybook. Annalise and Darren take the white granite path between the first set of shrubs, the former breathing in the salty sea breeze off the coast ahead.

"So," Prince Darren begins again. "Six years in the slums, I've heard. That must have been tough."

The princess huffs a laugh. "It was. So is this." Annalise gestures to her golden gown and finds Darren eyeing her in confusion, the breeze running through his night-black hair. Anna swallows, hoping he doesn't recognize the truth hiding in her words. "I don't remember the last time I was dressed from head to toe in finery."

"Mmm." Darren nods as though he understands. "Then you're forgetting the first rule of being a royal," he quips with her. "It doesn't matter what you think or know, as long as you make it look easy."

Before she can respond, two figures emerge from the opposite side of the garden, one in particular whose presence unwillingly catches Anna's eye with his form-fitting doublet and styled brown hair. Darren and Annalise pause their walk to face Captain Ivo and Master McHenry, who exchange pleasantries with more politeness than she is used to seeing from them.

"A beautiful day now that the wind has died down, isn't it?" Prince Darren makes small conversation with Anna's allies.

The princess would continue with the formalities if she had the patience. "Captain Ivo, have you had any word from Lord Sprightly?" She hasn't forgotten about Modgen's brave mission to find Elouthera in Javir.

Ivo clenches his jaw. "I'm afraid not, Your Highness. We pray for his safe return—and Elouthera's."

She tries not to get discouraged, if only to maintain her composure. *Gods, protect him. I don't like him doing this alone.*

"Ah, I forgot about your higher purpose." Prince Darren grins widely. "So many responsibilities for one person."

Anna's eyes light up at her opportunity. "Indeed, there are many." The goddess meets Oliver's eyes at last.

"Master McHenry, I was wondering when we might resume my training?"

Prince Darren stiffens. "Training?"

"I was teaching Princess Annalise basic sword fighting, Your Highness," Oliver explains. "We hypothesize that the stronger she is physically, the easier it will be to wield her godly powers."

"Sword fighting," Darren chuckles. "For a princess?" He runs a hand through his black hair at the awkward realization that he is the only one laughing. "I don't know why we don't teach more of them! In fact, we have one of the finest instructors right here, in Eldric. I can call on him after our walk."

Annalise's smile vanishes. "Actually, I—"

"Sir Albert Renwick, I believe his name is. You'll like him. I've heard great things about his teaching style."

The princess frowns, searching Oliver's green eyes for any kind of help to get her out of this mess.

"I'm sure Prince Darren's connection will be far better suited for the task than myself." Oliver forces a smile. "If you would excuse me, Your Highnesses, Captain Ivo. I have a letter in need of writing." Her Master of the High Council bows elegantly while Annalise tries to ignore the feeling of an invisible punch to her stomach.

When Captain Ivo relinquishes from the party, Annalise is left alone again with her future husband, the hand around his arm burning with desire to let go.

"And again," Sir Renwick repeats, watching Annalise swing her blade with fizzling energy, her arms nearly trembling from training for half an hour. "And once more …"

The goddess strikes the straw man again, this time making a small indentation in the burlap cloth. It has only been two days since Prince Darren's decision to hire Annalise's personal trainer, but she already feels annoyed with the ceaseless repetition of his teaching. *At least with Oliver, I was able to practice more than one movement at a time. Besides, the point of this isn't really to master the art of the blade, but rather to help me become stronger for the sake of my powers.*

Her instructor turns to face her reddened cheeks. "Are you getting tired, Your Highness?"

Yes, tired of you. Annalise lowers her sword, wiping the sweat from her brow. "Perhaps we should resume on the morrow," she says through heavy breaths.

Sir Renwick smiles kindly. "Of course, Your Highness. I will be present at the same time as today, as long as it suits you."

Anna nods. "It suits me fine." She curtsies, an awkward movement in the tunic and pants she had Sylvie order her. While her new instructor exits the dirt training ring, the princess blots her forehead with the sleeve of her white undershirt, taking note of her solitude. She picks up her canteen, draining half the water before deciding where to hide next.

The choice is easy: head somewhere less traveled, or risk being stuffed back into a gown that she can't breathe in half the time. Annalise chooses the first option, sneaking through the tall hedges to take the path to the beach, savoring the sound of nothing but the Nesvlan Sea with only a few seagulls to keep her company. She jaunts away from the beach entrance, seating herself on a stretch of flat sand dotted with white shells.

It isn't that Annalise wants to avoid everyone—she would love to spend more time catching up with Aimelie and the others—it is only that she hasn't had much time to process the way her life was turned upside down in the blink of an eye. *I didn't know,* Anna mulls. *My parents never mentioned anything to me about my betrothal when I was young.* But if the princess is being honest with herself, that isn't the only thing bothering her.

I still haven't heard from Modgen, she frets, *or ... Narelle.* Annalise's stomach is swallowed in guilt at the thought of her friends, who are as close as family. *What if Modgen is lost, or has been captured by Adrianna's forces? What if Narelle is being tortured, while I sit here, doing nothing to help? Or worse ...* The princess presses a porcelain hand to her lips. *What if they're dead?*

If Annalise could do anything to help either of their

cases, she would. But right now, there isn't much she can do, considering that she hardly knows the Eldrics and isn't about to ask Prince Darren for any favors. *I hardly trust him as it is.* She picks up a shell, using it to trace a shoddy design in the sand before chucking it into the sea. *There is one thing I can do to help, even if may take a while to reap its rewards.*

She hoists herself from the ground, dusting off her backside while she stamps her leather boots into softer sand. The Nesvlan Sea laps against the shore with its grayish waters, calmer today than it has been with the high winds of those prior. Closing her brown eyes, Annalise focuses on the power surging through her veins, extending her palms above the feeble waves lapping at her boots. Slowly, the goddess spreads her fingers, drawing tiny tendrils of seawater from the top of the surface.

Trying to ignore her anxiety, Annalise forges the water into a wall before her, separating herself from the rest of the Nesvlan Sea. The barricade wavers, but the princess can't help smiling at the increased ease of using her magic, her body already feeling so much stronger than the time she had used them against Adrianna that day in the castle.

The sound of fast footsteps snaps her concentration, the watery structure collapsing with it. Whipping her dark locks to the left, Annalise catches a glimpse of Oliver

McHenry taking a morning jog, the rhythm of his footfalls growing fainter the farther away he runs. Her friend shrinks away in the distance, and Annalise's muscles suddenly feel tired from all her training today.

Without a second glance at the Nesvlan Sea, the princess drops her hands, carrying her heavy limbs back to the castle and putting up little argument when Sylvie tries to stuff her into another frivolous gown.

VEGA

"What do you mean, they're gone?" Modgen Sprightly spits at the stable hand with eyes as stormy as a raging sea. "We *gave you our coin.*" He stares at the empty stable where their horses had been left while they spent the night near the Nesvlan border.

The stable hand throws up his hands. "They were Empeirian guards, threatening me for my last two horses. What was I supposed to tell them? 'No?'"

"*Precisely!*" The redhead slaps the man's forehead, retrieving their coin. Bitterly, he shoves their currency back into his own coin purse, while Eden counts the blackbirds in the sky. "What the hell are we supposed to do now? Walk to Dimity?"

Now there's something I don't want to try. "There must

be a better way." Vega sighs deeply, letting her lime-green eyes peruse the busy Javirian street, listening to the sounds of civilians headed out to pray at their local temples. Just across the intersection sits a large carriage, its door opening under the hand of a tan woman with chestnut hair. *What if* ... Elouthera pulls Modgen's sleeve. "Maybe we can hitch a ride?"

Modgen glances at the woman warily. "And risk exposing our identities? I don't know."

"What other choice do we have?" Vega's hands land on her small hips. "The stable hand said the next livery stable isn't for another five miles. Who's to say that we'll make it there before the sun sets if we don't travel by horse?"

He runs a hand through his reddish curls. "All right," he relents. "Who wants to be the one to go ask her?"

Eden and Vega share unenthused glances, leaving Modgen to stalk across the bustling street, his rage almost as bright as his hair.

What am I doing? Vega chastises herself. *He traveled all this way to rescue me; the least I can do is try to repay him for his efforts.* She moves to go with him until a muscled hand grabs hold of her shoulder.

"I'm seeing something," Eden whispers to her nervously. The aerialist points her mismatched eyes in the direction of the carriage. "It's someone with a dark presence about them."

The goddess tries not to roll her eyes. *She was right about us being captured by Edris's men, and again about Modgen coming to save us. Maybe there is some merit to her sub-par visions.* "Okay. What do they look like?"

A waving hand from Modgen encourages them to join his side of the road, cutting off Eden from further explanation. Vega holds onto Eden's arm as they manage their way through the crowds of people. "Do you see a color?" Vega pushes.

"No. No color at all. Just … shadows." Eden shivers as they clear the masses, meeting Modgen and the cloaked woman.

Shadows? Couldn't it be something more helpful, like a name, or an actual face? Vega nods, watching Modgen hand their new acquaintance a few coins. "Let me know if you pick up anything else. But for now, we'll keep our eyes open."

"Good news!" Modgen beams with a smile more radiant than the sun. "I explained our situation, and this kind lady has agreed that she and her lot will take us to the next livery stable. As it turns out, they are also headed for Nesvla."

Vega releases a breath of air she didn't know she was holding. "That's wonderful news!" The goddess extends a pale hand. "I'm Aleena," Vega lies, "and this is Eden. I believe you already met Modgen."

"I have." The tan woman smiles beautifully, shaking

Vega's hand. "I'm Narelle. The rest of the group should be back from the market any minute now."

She might just be seeing things, but Vega swears she catches Modgen freeze for one second, then two.

"I'm sorry—what did you say your name was again?" He presses a hand to his mouth.

"Narelle, my lord," the woman repeats.

A sturdy grip on Vega's elbow. "She's been looking for you," Eden whispers frantically.

Vega feigns a laugh to help downplay her friend's odd behavior. "It doesn't look like she has been, Eden," she responds in a low voice.

"Not her." The aerialist palms her face. "*Her.*" Eden points to a heavy-set woman of about fifty years, framed by two younger women with arms full of fresh fruit and cheese.

At first glance, Vega wouldn't have paid her much attention, if it weren't for Eden so insistently pointing her out. *But her cool demeanor, her secretive smile ...* Gone is her youthful appearance and supple skin, now replaced by deepened wrinkles and long black ringlets with a hint of silver emerging from their roots. Her citrine eyes are less vibrant than they had been during Vega's childhood, but no less sharp. *And her posture, the way she carries herself like she knows the thoughts of every person around her ...*

The goddess doesn't wait for her to get any closer before she grabs Modgen's wrist. "We need to go."

"Actually," Modgen slips out of her grip to eye Narelle more closely, "I think we might be in the right place."

No. No, no, no, no, no! Elouthera wipes her sweaty palms on her tunic. "I don't think you understand, Modgen. *I* need to get out of here."

Ignoring her, Modgen continues, "Narelle, you wouldn't happen to be from Empeirus, would you?"

Narelle balks, pressing a hand to her ribs. "I am. Why?" She narrows her hazel eyes.

Vega's throat starts to tighten while Modgen delays their leave. Her stomach turns sour enough that the goddess thinks she will be sick. "I'm leaving without you." On a heel, she whirls in the other direction.

"Wait, Vega!"

The goddess nearly trips at his accidental use of her name, exposing her ruse to the world around them, to the woman named Narelle, to—

The woman's citrine eyes glow with prideful joy, as if it was she who made the stars align for this event to fall in place. "Vega," Cyndeya Kutchrik whispers beneath sparkling tears, her lips quivering in futile attempts to keep them locked away.

"You know this woman?" Modgen questions from her left.

A surge of pain slashes through Vega's fragile heart. "Hello, Mother," is all her small voice can manage.

"Gods, is it true? Is my own daughter Elouthera, the Goddess of Dreams and Mysteries?"

Vega opens her lips just in time to have her words overtaken by a grunt. *Oh, not again!* She grabs Eden by the shoulders, who clutches her sandy hair with a death grip. "Just breathe through it, Eden," the goddess instructs her. "Let it come to you. Don't fight it."

"What's happening to her?" Narelle questions from the carriage.

Cyndeya squints at the young woman. "Eden," she whispers to herself.

"Just talk to me, Eden. Tell me what you see." Vega glances at Modgen for any kind of help, but his cobalt gaze seems to be pinned on something in the distance.

The aerialist flashes open her mismatched eyes. "A sword. A shadow." Eden takes a ragged breath. "A scar on his face."

"Well, shit." Modgen Sprightly moves toward Vega and Eden with a seriousness he rarely exudes. "We have to go."

"Oh, *now* we have to go?" Vega chides.

"Get in the carriage!" Modgen tells all the women, ignoring Vega's sarcastic remark to get a better look at something in the crowd.

Not something, Someone. Just across the street is a man on a black stallion, the scar down the side of his temple doing little to distract from his attractiveness. "Who is that?" Vega asks Modgen, until the world fades away, until a shared memory of a battle in Larking Castle has something inside her clicking into place at long last. *Is that ...?*

His silver eyes meet hers in a gaze dripping with contempt. Vega would run if she didn't know she was a powerful deity herself.

"You heard the boy, ready the horses!" Cyndeya commands the two women beside her, pushing Narelle and Eden into the carriage before she turns to grab Vega's hand. "I am so sorry, my dear, for my departure all those years ago—"

"*Get in the carriage!*" Modgen spits at the former Nev, leaving Vega with no choice but to face her mother in a confined space. He pushes the goddess in, shutting the door beside them before tapping the roof with anxious speed.

"Is everything all right?" Narelle worries from the seat across them.

"No," Modgen affirms, feeling out the dagger he has hidden inside his waistband.

Cyndeya regards her daughter intently. "I know what I did was wrong, Vega. I don't pretend that it wasn't. But if you can find any shred of forgiveness in your heart—" The High Priestess stops herself from losing her composure. "I would love another chance to be the mother you deserve."

Elouthera blinks her green eyes, trying to keep the world from spinning as the carriage whips forward.

"I don't think now is the best time, my lady." Modgen presses the back of his head against the seat, trying to avoid the window. "Gods, can't they go any faster?" He bangs on the roof of the carriage again, this time with even more purpose.

The group is quiet while the masses begin to disappear behind them, the carriage emerging into the emptiness of the dirt path to Nesvla. Vega would try taking a deeper breath to relax, if only Eden would stop fidgeting.

"What is that?" Eden asks fearfully.

Vega whips her jet-black hair in the direction of Modgen's window, witnessing something dark slipping its way over the glass. *A shadow*, the goddess realizes with no small amount of dread. It is her turn to smack the top of the carriage, urging their drivers to hurry the hell up.

Cyndeya relents a mysterious smile. "You act as though you are scared, daughter. If the rumors are true, you have nothing to fear. You are his equal."

"I desperately hope so," Modgen interjects.

Vega shoots her mother a look of disgust, the remnants of years of self-doubt and criticism. "You know nothing about me."

The shadow completely covers each of the windows, snuffing out the last of their light.

"He's here," Cyndeya whispers anxiously.

"Who?" Narelle whimpers.

The carriage comes to a halt.

Elouthera forces a long breath, gathering her wits enough to face her godly counterpart directly for the first time in all her mortal life. "Anzac."

In a flash of shrapnel and wood, the carriage doors are ripped off their hinges, leaving the five passengers exposed to the outside air. Modgen draws his dagger while Vega climbs over Eden to leap out the other side of the vehicle. The dirt road is empty, save for a few stray leaves that crunch beneath the manipulator's small boots.

Vega's eyes meet Modgen's. "Where are the drivers?" Before he can respond, a cloud of smoke rises ahead. Its ethereal movement sends shivers down the goddess's spine.

A choking sound from inside the clouds. The two drivers land in the dirt, their mouths dripping with blood.

Lazarus, help us!

With a dagger shaking in his pale hand, Modgen steps forward, making to move for the clouds.

"Don't you dare," Vega spits, yanking him back by the shirt collar. "He'll kill you in an instant. Besides," she sighs, "he's here for me." She pads toward the gray mist, waiting for the God of Darkness and Decay to expose himself.

It takes all of two seconds for his handsome form to

emerge, the shadows seeming to blacken with his appearance. Even from several yards away, she can see the light glint off his perfect teeth when he sends her a draconian grin.

"Hello, Elouthera," Anzac sings.

"Hello, Anzac," the goddess returns.

Anzac lets his silver eyes rove over her body. "You look ... well."

Vega smirks. "You still look like a prick."

A seductive laugh while he shifts his gaze to her fellow travelers. "And what have we here? A gift from Lazarus, I'd presume."

The goddess's face must reflect her confusion.

"I thought I'd be lucky to find you, let alone three of the kingdom's most wanted." Anzac removes a handkerchief to blot a few droplets of blood from his doublet. "Modgen Sprightly, Cyndeya Kutchrik, and Narelle Lambric. All I need now is to find Oliver McHenry and Princess Annalise, and my queen can rest easy." He shakes his head. "Lucky for me, I should be able to get their whereabouts from you once we're finished."

Vega dares a glance at the others, swallowing her shock as easily as burned toast. It isn't too appalling to know that Modgen or Narelle have some ties to her enemy—Vega hardly knows them—but her own mother? The goddess finds herself watching Cyndeya with an even deeper sense of betrayal than before. "You know Anzac?"

Cyndeya scoffs. "Of course I don't. Is it not beyond the scope of a dark god to conjure lies as easily as he does shadows?"

But Narelle pins her hazel eyes on Vega's up-tilted ones. "She's lying."

The High Priestess whirls on her colleague, her mask of self-assurance melting like the sweat on Modgen's brow. "That's a nice way to repay the person who saved you from a dungeon."

"I didn't know you were a black magic-wielding Nev. I thought Annalise had sent you!"

Annalise? Does she know— Elouthera has just enough time to exchange a glance with Modgen before Anzac makes his move. The shadow bolt sails past the goddess's head, disappearing down the dirt road while the goddess readies her advance. Quick as an asp, she scrounges some of the metal from the carriage wreckage to forge into arrow points, levitating them around herself in a rotating circle. She fires one immediately at Anzac's face, her jaw dropping when she observes his body transition from opaque to translucent, and back again. *What in the name of Lazarus?*

"It's a projection!" Eden calls from behind her.

She's right, Elouthera thinks miserably. *How are we supposed to fight a phantom?*

The false Anzac grins at the goddess, continuing to fling shadows from his fingertips.

Think, Vega! Outside of her thoughts, she hears Eden groaning while Cyndeya and Narelle move to take cover behind the skeleton of the carriage. Vega melds the arrows into a shield, blocking another one of Anzac's shots until a greedy hand pulls at her tunic.

"He's in the forest, to our right!" Eden tells her urgently.

A stray bolt slices across Vega's arm, the goddess wincing as she successfully staves off the other two. "How will you hold it off?" She darts her eyes in the direction of the forest. When they return to the shadow pawn, Vega freezes.

Standing at the edge of the destructed carriage is her mother, Cyndeya, with one hand outstretched as she whispers a slur of spells. She draws blue energy from the glass vial around her neck, and to the goddess's absolute shock, the shadow pawn struggles in its movements. *Is she—* Vega stops herself from the thought. *There is no way she can be manipulating its mind. I thought that was something only I could do, as a goddess.*

"Eden, stay here! I'll go with Vega." Modgen sprints into the forest with the goddess while Cyndeya continues to distract Anzac's projection, he and Vega taking up residence behind two tall pines. "Any chance Eden told you *where* in the forest he is?"

"No." But Vega doesn't need to look very hard. About twenty yards deeper, she can make out the silhouette of the black horse he was riding in town. "He's this way." She pulls Modgen's wrist to get a closer look, guiding him around fallen leaves to keep their feet from emitting any crunching sounds. Pressing a finger to her lips, Vega discreetly points to Anzac, who seems to be pushing rocks in the leaves. *Now, what do we do?*

Modgen's gesture seems to ask her the same thing.

At first, Vega fears she may have to take him on alone, at least holding him off while the others get away. But the Goddess of Dreams and Mystery might not have to get her hands too dirty, after all. *We can outrun him.* Silently, she extends her hand toward the horse, easily feeling out the threads of its mind until it begins to stir.

Anzac doesn't seem to budge; he only continues to concentrate on his stones.

Vega gives Modgen a look that says, *Get ready.* With poised hands, the goddess guides the horse toward them, letting it pause occasionally to make it seem as if it isn't being controlled. When the animal reaches them, Modgen hoists himself onto the horse, helping Vega take the seat behind him. They make it all of two steps before hearing Anzac mutter to himself.

"Where the hell ...?"

His attention is reason enough for Modgen to send the horse leaping into a gallop, the vicious sound of Anzac's screams echoing through the forest. Elouthera holds onto

Modgen while they resurface from the pine trees, the shadow pawn nowhere to be seen.

"*Get onto the horses!*" The goddess screams at the others, watching them scramble to unlatch the equines from their unusable vehicle.

Narelle claims one of them with Eden, while Cyndeya takes her own. Somewhere from the forest, a bolt of shadow flies past them, nearly missing one of the horses' hooves.

"*Go!*" Modgen yells, he and Vega's stolen stallion leading the way toward Nesvla with the God of Darkness and Decay nipping at their heels.

VEGA

"Here." Cyndeya opens the door to an old storefront using the amethyst-encrusted moon around her neck. "It used to be a place where we did readings, before the Nevs were banned. We should be safe here."

Vega rolls her cat-like eyes at her mother's confidence. "It's only a matter of time before Anzac finds us again. We won't be able to stay here long."

Modgen chortles, taking a seat on a dusty wooden chair. "I'm inclined to agree with you. The gods know how determined Desmond can be."

Vega pushes together her black brows. "Desmond?"

"His mortal name," Narelle explains. "Captain Desmond Jrehart of the Royal Guard."

Modgen sneers. "And let's not forget about Jedda—the illustrious Queen Adrianna."

Vega has had her suspicions about the Queen of Empeirus after the vision she was able to see through Dimity, but hearing the statement out loud makes it even more intimidating. *So, it is true.* "You mean to tell me that my archenemy has been ruling the kingdom for the past six years?" Vega palms her small forehead. "And you know Desmond *how* exactly?"

The four other travelers find their own seats at adjacent tables. Cyndeya looks away, but Modgen props his boots up on a chair. "I used to be the Royal Treasurer, and he wanted to push whatever mad plans Adrianna came up with. Naturally, we had our disagreements."

Vega shifts her gaze to Narelle.

"I never met him, but I know of him. He knows Adrianna wants me back, so that's reason enough for him to go after me." A somber gaze. "I was caught spying on them for Princess Annalise," she finishes quietly.

"Princess Annalise, who also happens to be the goddess Dimity," Cyndeya clarifies uselessly.

Elouthera shakes her head. "We know who she is. She's the reason we're headed for Nesvla."

Narelle's hazel eyes brighten. "You know Annalise?"

"Well, *I* know Annalise," Modgen chirps. "I grew up with her at the castle. My mission was to find Elouthera and meet her in Nesvla." He assesses Narelle with his cobalt eyes. "You're the courtesan who took her in, aren't you?"

"*Former* courtesan." She smiles faintly before squinting at Eden. "Well, then, who are you?"

Cyndeya cuts Eden off before she can speak. "Edris Sharpkey's sister, Eden." She adjusts her black dress. "Daughter of the infamous Laraya Sharpkey."

Vega narrows her green eyes. "And how do you know that?"

The High Priestess turns away from her daughter again, from annoyance or shame, Vega cannot tell. "The Nevs had a temporary alliance with Edris and his men. We were hoping to find Princess Annalise in Javir."

Eden flinches.

Vega grits her teeth. "You were working with Edris Sharpkey," the goddess restates viciously.

Cyndeya sighs. "I know what you're trying to do, Vega—"

"You knew that Edris had me locked up in the Oronian Clocktower, and you did nothing to stop him."

"I heard they captured a witch; I didn't know it was *you!*"

"Then there's one for the books. Something that my mother doesn't know, even with the all-knowing power of being High Priestess!" Vega clutches her bad arm, watching a thin trail of blood drip from where Anzac's shadow bolt had sliced it earlier. *I never wanted to see her again. Why is she here?*

Cyndeya sinks into silent dissatisfaction while Modgen digs into his rucksack, pulling out an old shirt and a canteen of water.

"And why were you trying to find Annalise, again?" Narelle asks the High Priestess, who visibly begins to sweat.

Vega's mother smirks. "I am under no obligation to share that information with you."

"Of course," Modgen japes. "I have heard that every good relationship is built on lies and secrets."

Cyndeya stands from her seat. "I'm going to get some air. If anyone else would like to join me, they can."

For once, Vega could not be more grateful for Modgen's presence. Cyndeya offers no response as the redhead blots her daughter's arm with a sort of tenderness the High Priestess hasn't shown Vega in years. "Thank you," the goddess tells him quietly, her pale cheeks turning the faintest shade of pink.

"For the bandage, or for telling off your mother?"

She pinches the bridge of her nose.

Modgen finishes tying the fabric around Vega's arm, the goddess lifting her gaze to find Eden shuffling toward the exit.

"I'll help keep an eye on her," the aerialist proclaims, closing the door behind her.

Good, Elouthera muses. *Somebody has to.* The Goddess of Dreams and Mystery releases a sigh, attempting to restore a thread of patience by closing her up-tilted eyes.

They flash open when a scream breaks out, the rest of the group hurdling to their feet to fling open the door.

Elouthera's heart skips a beat.

Standing in the middle of the dirt road is her mother, holding the blade of a dagger clean against Eden's neck.

"I'm done playing games, Vega," Cyndeya Kutchrik declares. "Let's forget about this godly nonsense. Come back with me to our estate in Nesvla. I'll make amends with your father; we can live like the family we should be!"

How pathetic does she think I am? All she has ever cared about is herself. Still, tears begin to threaten Vega's composure. She tries not to let them dampen her wits. "You don't want to be a family. You just want your fortune back now that the Nevs no longer suit you!"

Her mother snorts. "That sounds like something your father would say." Cyndeya shakes her jet-black ringlets. "I had high expectations that you would turn out to be wiser than him."

The goddess makes to move a step closer, but Modgen places a hand on her shoulder.

Cyndeya seethes. "I should have grabbed Lord Sprightly, instead. Maybe then, you would be more easily convinced. And if not, I could be on my merry way with the blood of a demigod."

Elouthera blinks, opening her mouth—

A ring of shadows whips around Cyndeya and Eden, rising into a whirling sphere.

Just across the road saunters Captain Desmond Jrehart, his body moving closer like the shadows in the alley behind him.

"*Eden!*" Vega screams into the wind, her jet-black hair fighting to obstruct her vision.

A strong hand reaches out from the abyss just long enough for Modgen to grab. With several tugs, he manages to pull a horrified Eden from the sphere. He corrals the others toward the alley opposite the one Anzac is in, urging them to run as quickly as they can.

Vega doesn't budge. Her lime-green gaze peers at the shadows transforming into a misty vortex, her mother clutching at her own throat beyond the veil. The dagger she had used to threaten Eden with drops to the ground, and even though Cyndeya's face is blurred from the spinning darkness, Vega swears she can see tears rolling down her cheeks. Vega's eyes fill with her own until an arm gently turns her around, pulling her away from the treachery of the scene.

The goddess struggles to keep up with the others, hindered by breath and guilt. *But how could I have stopped him?* Another, more unsettling question surfaces in her mind over resounding footfalls: *Should I have* tried *to stop him?* Her heart splinters as they round the corner of a building, stumbling into a nearby cemetery. Vega's feet nearly trip over a low gravestone. "Where are we going?" she asks through ragged breaths.

"As far away from Desmond as possible," Modgen replies.

Narelle stops to catch her breath. "We can't outrun him forever."

"She's right." Vega nods, searching for signs of Anzac in every direction. "I need to face him." She braces her hands on her knees. "Gods, is Dimity's life this hectic?"

Modgen laughs. "I'm pretty sure Adrianna spends every waking minute of the day hunting Annalise, especially after their tiff at Larking Castle."

Vega shakes her head. "I can't wait for you to fill me in."

A gasp from a closed-eyed Eden. "He's coming! I can see him near the shop we passed a few streets back."

Great. Think, Vega. You're a deity, too!

"Do you have a plan?" Narelle asks hopefully.

Elouthera bites her lip. "I might." With speedy execution, the goddess divulges her idea, ensuring that everyone is in their proper positions before Anzac can make his appearance. She hides behind a tall oak near the entrance of the graveyard, its elaborate wrought-iron gate the only thing separating it from the living world.

"He's here," Eden whispers to her before scampering back to a bush next to Modgen.

Vega waits patiently, letting their plan fall into place.

"What the hell is this?" Anzac asks with a smirk, stepping into the cemetery toward a frozen Narelle. "Where is she?"

The former courtesan stands alone, her black cloak flapping in the wind. "She kept running with the others."

A low laugh. "And you didn't think it was wise to do the same?"

"I'm sick of running," Narelle admits. "I'm sick of everything." She extends her wrists. "Take me back to Larking Castle. I'll tell you the rest of what I know."

Desmond tilts his handsome face, a devilish smile dancing about his lips. "Calix is good, but I don't think he works miracles."

A rock flies toward Anzac from his left, smacking him in the arm.

It is enough to tell Elouthera one thing: *It's not a projection.* Without warning, she latches onto the wrought-iron gate, melting it into a puddle of liquid metal that sails toward Anzac's feet. Before the god can cast any shadows, she flexes her fingers, lifting the liquid into an iron cell, its walls solid save for the few holes she left on top.

Desmond pounds violently against the side, spewing curse words from the confined space.

With continued concentration, Vega places a hand on the cell, manipulating two handles on the wall. Modgen and Narelle tug while Vega and Eden push the cell from the opposite side, slowly sliding the trap toward the back corner of the cemetery. *Should anyone find him here, they will need to melt him out. Either that, or recruit a small army to tip it over.*

"You wait until Adrianna finds out about this!" Desmond growls, his voice muffled from the iron walls.

Modgen shrugs. "You might be dead before she finds you."

His answering yell is enough for Vega to believe that Desmond doesn't want that fate. She places her hands on Eden and Narelle. "Come on," Vega insists. "Let's go before he figures out a way to get out of there."

The gang scurries out of the cemetery, retracing their steps until they reach the livery stable. Narelle hands the stable hands a few coins in exchange for their two horses —one of them still being Desmond's black stallion— before mounting them hastily. Vega would feel better if she didn't remember that they would be passing the place where her mother had suffocated. When she spots the first sight of the old fortune-telling house, she closes her lime-green eyes, going so far as to press her cheek to Modgen's back in an attempt to keep herself from looking.

Modgen pats one of her hands around his waist.

The halt of their horses has Vega opening her gaze again.

"What are you doing?" Eden asks as Narelle jumps down, presumably to examine the corpse.

A few seconds later, Narelle remounts their steed. She drops a glass vial necklace in Eden's hand—the one Vega had seen her mother use earlier. "Cyndeya rescued me from the dungeon, so I was working with her to help the Nevs disguise themselves as courtesans to collect intel for Annalise. Now that their High Priestess is gone, they have no leader." Her hazel eyes fall to Eden. "But you are the daughter of Laraya Sharpkey."

Eden's mismatched eyes widen at her implication. "No." An exaggerated shake of the head. "I'm a nobody, I—"

"That's not what I've seen so far," Narelle counters. "I promised Annalise that I would do whatever it takes to help her regain the throne. I failed the first time, but I'm not going to let that happen again." Her gaze falls on the necklace. "If you're willing, I will help you organize the Nevs so that when the time is right, Annalise will be prepared."

Vega and Modgen sit in silence, waiting for Eden to choose. *If she chooses to help Annalise by continuing Narelle's plans ...* Vega ponders on the thought. *A spy network that enormous could mean the difference between Dimity's ultimate failure or success in winning back the Empeirian throne.*

With a subtle sigh and an almost imperceivable straightening of her back, the aerialist gives Narelle a nod. "I accept your offer," Eden affirms in her Javirian accent, "so long as they accept me as their leader."

Narelle smiles broadly. "Very well, then. I am at your disposal, High Priestess."

ANNALISE

Annalise works a spot of royal-blue paint into her canvas, squinting to get a better view of her artwork as a whole. It isn't a perfect depiction of the beach by Oliver's house, but it could be worse. The eldest princess of Empeirus persists in adding white caps to the waves, enjoying the pleasant company of her youngest sister.

"It wasn't so long ago that this would have been a dream, painting with you." Aimelie smiles beautifully, dipping her brush in a pot of lemon yellow.

Anna beams. "You mean, you didn't paint with Dria?"

Melie laughs, tucking a honey-blonde curl behind her ear. "Things at the castle weren't as chipper after you disappeared. I did paint, but it was usually with—"

Aimelie blushes, stopping herself from finishing a sentence that Annalise is quite interested in hearing.

"With whom?" The goddess grins.

Aimelie sits back in her tufted chair, rubbing her arm for a moment. "Well, his name is Linden. He was the royal mentor that Adrianna assigned me ... and my eventual love interest."

Anna gasps, giving Melie a playful shove. "My little sister, courting her royal mentor!" She stifles a laugh. "Convention be damned."

Aimelie snorts, picking up her brush again. "You can say that again." She resumes, adding delicate rays around a bright sun before glancing sidelong at Annalise. "What about you? Did you meet anyone during our time apart?"

It is the goddess's turn to chortle. "The only men I generally spoke to were the ones I played *halsen* against for my income. Even if some caught my eye, I was too worried about exposing my identity."

"Hmm," Aimelie hums in thought. "What about Master McHenry?"

Annalise drops her brush, splattering blue paint onto the front of her dress. She curses, a servant presenting her with a damp cloth while she tries to recover with a bit of lighthearted laughter. "Whatever makes you think that?"

Aimelie presses her lips together under wide blue eyes. "I didn't." She tries hiding a smile. "I just figured I'd ask." Dotting the last of her wildflowers, Melie leans back for a final look at her canvas. "There. I think I'm finished."

"I think I am, too." Annalise rinses out her brush, failing to do the same with her embarrassment. She changes the subject. "You said you had something to show me?"

Her sister's doe eyes fill with excitement. "I do!" Melie grabs her arm. "Walk with me to my chambers."

The hike from the drawing room to Aimelie's chambers is a bit of a long one, but Annalise could not be happier. *To be reunited with Melie at last—and to have some fun without thinking about my duties—is truly a gift from the gods.* When they reach her mahogany door, the youngest princess opens it to a room very similar to Anna's own, decorated with lavish throw rugs and gold accents. Annalise follows her in, watching Melie scamper over to a leather satchel near her desk.

"I've been waiting so long to give this to you," Aimelie tells her with glassy eyes.

Annalise takes the satchel, eyeing it curiously. "It's ... a bag?"

Melie chuckles. "Open it up."

Carefully, Annalise opens the flap, reaching in a porcelain hand to grasp something solid and detailed. The princess pulls it out, fighting to withhold tears.

"I had the former royal jeweler make it using Father's original plans. Urayus Helva, if you remember."

"I remember." Anna wipes away stray tears, blinking to see the emerald and jet stones glimmer back at her. *How could she have organized this? To take our father's original papers to Urayus and have him forge this?* Many parts of Aimelie's plan could have gone awry. She meets her sister's doe eyes with an expression deep with gratitude. "Thank you."

Melie bats a hand, smiling gleefully. "Put it on!"

With trembling hands, Anna stares at her crown almost fearfully. "Why don't you do it?"

Her sister giggles, taking the silver in her hands and raising it above Annalise's head, letting it rest against her earthy brown waves. Melie grins wider than a proud mother as Annalise turns to face herself in the golden floor mirror.

Gods! Anna thinks, surprisingly. *It fits perfectly. And to know that my father designed it ...* The goddess shares her elation with her mortal sister, taking Melie's hand with a gorgeous smile.

"I thought you could wear it to the ball tomorrow."

Annalise's smile fades. *Right, the ball.* "You don't suppose I could get out of going, do you?"

Melie shoots her an admonishing look. "Annalise, it's being held in your honor."

A groan from the eldest princess, who gingerly removes her crown to place back in its satchel for safekeeping. "Very well." She faces the door before Melie places a hand on her arm.

"One more thing, while I have you here." Aimelie's demeanor turns serious, her voice dropping just above a whisper. "I wanted to talk to you about something I've been keeping under wraps for a while."

Annalise faces her sister fully.

"I've been around Dria long enough to know how important relations are—and which territories she will be able to rely on, should things escalate to ..." She darts her blue eyes back and forth. "A war." Melie shudders. "You can certainly pursue Nesvla as a potential alliance. But in the meantime, before you are wed to Prince Darren, I've decided to reach out to another territory. Somewhere ..." She bites a full lip. "Less predictable."

The goddess nods hesitantly. "Less predictable?" Anna thinks. "Like Wembleton?"

Aimelie squirms in her dress. "Even less than that." She reaches behind her to retrieve a worn piece of parchment with a broken seal, extending it to Annalise. "Calleeit."

Anna's dark eyes stare blankly at her sister, the letter in her hands suddenly weighing one hundred pounds. "Calleeit."

Melie nods while Anna skims through the letter. "Queen Haraja, herself, has requested a meeting to discuss details in the event that you need aid against Adrianna.”

Annalise presses a hand to her lips. *Calleeit*, she muses. *The one territory that would help take down Adrianna any day of the week, since the day she started the War on the Horns to try to keep it in the kingdom.* She shakes her head. “Where would we meet?”

“That’s what I wanted to discuss with you.” Aimelie takes the letter back. “*You* have plans here in Nesvla, but *I*—”

“There is no way I’m endorsing you to travel across the sea to negotiate in Calleeit,” Annalise interrupts. “Do you know how much they hate Adrianna? What are the chances they would take well to one of her sisters?”

“I know there has been bad blood between us for a long time,” Melie rebukes, “but things seem to have changed after they broke away from the kingdom. They got the freedom they wanted.”

The Goddess of Wisdom and Justice palms her elegant face. “What if,” Annalise closes her brown eyes for a moment to regroup. “What if you leave, and you never come back?”

The youngest princess nods slowly, as though she has been prepared for this question for some time, now. “I have had to live with that possibility for the past six years, when it pertained to you.” Aimelie takes Annalise’s hands, matching her gaze. "I am not the little girl I used to be, Annalise. And I will have Captain Ivo by my side, as well."

"Ivo? He knows of this plan?"

Melie nods. "I won't be alone."

Yes, though a single bodyguard may not be enough to protect you if this is indeed a trap. Clenching her jaw, Anna allows herself the tiniest nod of approval. "When would you leave?"

Melie slips the letter back in with her personal belongings. "A couple of weeks. I'd like to leave before winter."

Right, because the seas get rough during the winter, and, depending on the year, may even freeze over in some areas. "All right." Annalise sighs, straightening her posture. "You have my blessing." She smiles back at Aimelie, shifting her hourglass figure to the door.

"Annalise," Melie calls out to her before Anna's hand touches the doorknob. "Captain Ivo and Master Tasman are the only other ones who know."

The goddess meets her sister's baby-blue gaze, deigning her a nod of understanding before she twists the knob with a strong hand.

DESMOND

Anzac grunts loudly one more time as he pushes against the side of the iron cage, but even gods are subject to some laws of physics, and the metal doesn't budge. Heaving for air, he closes his silver eyes, wishing that Elouthera could have made the breathing holes on the top of his cage just the slightest bit larger.

Elouthera, Desmond seethes. His recent defeat wouldn't hurt so much if Annalise hadn't taken him down at the castle a few months ago. *First, Dimity; now Elouthera.* The God of Darkness and Decay swallows, ruminating on how he has been outsmarted for the second time by his and Jedda's opponents. *Am I that bad?*

A throb has him gripping the angry slash on his left thigh, just below where a functioning pocket used to be.

Damn thief! Anzac recalls the pickpocket who wounded him the night he scared the wits out of Edris Sharpkey. Pressing his charcoal-black curls into the cool iron, a light rain begins to trickle in through the holes above his head, dampening the arch of his brow. *I need to get out of here,* he worries.

Anzac hasn't had much time to recharge after his battle with Elouthera and taking down Cyndeya Kutchrik, but what energy the god has left will have to do. *If I had enough stamina left, I would use my pawns to free myself of this mad contraption.* Summoning his magic and a little hope, Anzac conjures a shadow in the shape of the same little girl he used with Edris, using her eyes to navigate the Javirian town with as much ease as he can manage. He walks her to the nearest house before the sprinkle of rain turns into a heavy downpour, the droplets streaming down the god's tan cheeks like the tears he will do anything to keep from falling.

He makes his shadow-child knock on the door, but there is no response. He tries again, this time with slightly more force. No answer. The god sighs from within his confinement, his frustration growing when he continues his attempts only to have rotten luck with the subsequent two houses. On the grass-covered bottom of his cell, puddles are forming on the ground. He decides to try one more house.

His pawn knocks on the door three times with authoritative speed, making for a fourth when it opens under the hand of a stocky man. "Please," Anzac makes her say. "You must help me. There is a man trapped in the cemetery just across the street."

A disbelieving grunt. "How many times will it take for you children to learn that ghosts aren't real?" The man slams the door, leaving Anzac's shadow in the rain.

This could take a while. The god scowls, wondering how long he can make it without food. He would pester Adrianna with a message through their bond, but he doesn't want to worry her. *Besides, how disappointed would Dria be if she learned that I had lost to Elouthera? And how long would it take for her to reach me? At least for now, I have water.* There is no better portrait of desperation than when the Captain of the Royal Guard opens his mouth to the sky, a hand pressed against the oozing flesh of his left leg.

ANNALISE

Anna's heart thumps in her chest while she listens to the royal page announce her name on the other side of the Great Hall doors, her newly acquired crown shimmering on her head like all the stars in the night sky.

"I now present to you Princess Annalise Larking, eldest daughter of the late King Tiberius and Queen Annora Larking, rightful heir to the Empeirian Throne."

The enormous, gold-gilded doors open with a groan, revealing the princess clad in an emerald-green gown. One by one, the nobles bow as Annalise passes them as gracefully as she can manage, her skirts skimming the orange velvet of the aisle runner until she reaches Prince Darren at the end of it.

"A powerful entrance for a powerful lady," Darren greets her, letting her slip a hand around his arm.

Anna musters a smile, trying not to feel the weight of a thousand lingering stares. "The last time I attended a ball was when I was fourteen."

A quick glance. "And the last time you rehearsed the Queen's Dance?"

Annalise's mind drifts back to an old watchtower and a bedroom filled with books and a shattered picture frame. "I'm sure it will come back to me." *Only this time, I'm hopeful nothing will explode.*

The music begins, cueing Darren and Annalise to initiate the Queen's Dance in front of an entire audience of greedy eyes. The princess would have practiced if she had known they would be performing the number tonight, but she does well enough. *It certainly isn't as fun as the dances in the Savek Coast, but at least I'm not smacking a straw man five hundred times in a row with Sir Albert Renwick.* When the last move is completed, the two exchange a bow and a curtsy, Annalise nearly cringing at the attention of the clapping onlookers.

At last, the hoard of guests dissipates, brooking the princess an opportunity to peruse the Great Hall. By the grace of the gods, Anna finds a table exploding with food, her stomach rumbling from hours of getting her hair and makeup done for this damned occasion. Her hand lands on a teacake covered in pastel purple icing, which she soon discovers to be lavender. *While the Nesvlans may not be the most welcoming people, their food certainly is.* Annalise indulges in second teacake, going so far as to lick the icing off her perfectly manicured fingertips.

"I hope this isn't an everyday occurrence," Darren notes with a plastered smile, waving to a wealthy couple across the room. "Or I may have to prohibit our chef from making so many sweets."

Annalise's eyes grow wide. "Or *what?*" she pushes.

A fake laugh while he continues to greet guests from a distance. "Or risk having you outgrow all the new dresses I've ordered for you."

Somewhere in the ether, Annalise can hear her deceased mother warning her to temper her anger. But she isn't particularly in the mood for tempering. Without a thought, Annalise eyes the wine in Darren's golden chalice, flicking a finger behind her back so it splashes up his nose the next time he goes to drink.

"*Gods!*" Prince Darren curses to himself, covering his dripping face while a servant rushes over to him with a napkin. "I didn't think I raised my hand that quickly."

The goddess hides a smug smirk when she comes face-to-face with Aimelie, Master Tasman, and Captain Ivo. Tasman, especially, beams at seeing Annalise in her crown, his wrinkled blue eyes tearing up at the sight. "Your parents would be so proud," he tells her with no small amount of happiness.

"I hope so," Anna admits, pilfering some brandy from a passing tray.

Before the goddess can draw another breath, Queen Minerva joins their posse, crossing their circle to press a light kiss to each one of Annalise's cheeks. "My darling, you two did *splendidly* dancing together! I knew this match was blessed by Lazarus from the start," the Nesvlan queen declares. She pins her cool blue eyes on Ivo. "Captain Ivo, you must come with me. There are a good many women here tonight; a few widows that I think would be absolutely perfect ..."

Darren drains the last of his wine, exchanging it for a full cup. "How many of these do you think I would have to drink to attain my mother's sense of accommodation?"

Too many to count.

"I think you've been quite accommodating during our time spent here," Aimelie chimes politely with Tasman nodding in agreement.

Prince Darren shakes his head. "That kind of attentiveness doesn't come naturally to the men in my family." A look at Annalise. "Soon, my lady, it will be *you* playing hostess and matchmaker on the same night!"

Anna joins in on the group's hearty laugh, her cheeks burning with ire before she turns in the opposite direction to swallow her brandy in a single gulp. The only witness is Master Oliver McHenry, who fails to hide his winsome smirk.

The princess excuses herself to greet her friend for the first time in days. "I'm sorry you had to see that." Annalise blushes.

"I wouldn't worry yourself too much. I'm not much of a gossip." Oliver offers her a warm smile, his pine-green eyes twinkling in the light of the ornate sconces. "You look beautiful, by the way."

Annalise could melt into the golden floorboards. *There's something Darren has never once told me.* "Thank you. You look very nice, yourself."

"Annalise!" Prince Darren waves a conceited hand. "You must come meet Lord and Lady Hamilton."

The princess grits her teeth. *If Adrianna doesn't kill me, my future husband surely will.* She gives Oliver an apologetic look, one that unintentionally lets her exhaustion shine through.

He reads it with ease. "I'll trade you, if you need." Her Master of the High Council extends his own glass of brandy.

Annalise chuckles, perhaps the only genuine laugh she has had all evening. "I probably shouldn't, though I appreciate the gesture." She curtsies, setting her empty glass on a serving tray before trudging back to her betrothed.

The clock strikes midnight, and every ounce of Annalise's impatience might as well be written on her face. *Gods, can't this be over already?* Her back aches, her feet are tired, and her crown is digging into her skull. In a desperate attempt to get back to her chambers, the goddess pulls Darren to the side. "My lord, I'm afraid I'm feeling rather tired. Would it be acceptable for me to retire for the evening?"

Prince Darren teeters on his feet with a smile much more enthusiastic than she had expected. "Of course, my lady. Allow me to escort you back." Setting down an empty chalice, he offers Annalise his arm, though it seems Darren is the one in need of her balance.

"What a wonderful evening," the princess lies, relieved that she is at last on her way to getting out of this corset.

Darren walks her up a flight of orange stairs. "Indeed, it was wonderful." He almost trips over the top step, catching his golden crown with his free hand. "You know, I never complimented you on your beauty," the prince slurs.

"Oh." Annalise frowns. "I'm not sure that's necessary. You probably won't remember it tomorrow, anyway." They start down a corridor that runs parallel to Anna's chambers on the other side of the floor, the hallway much darker than the torchlit stairwell. "I was thinking," the goddess begins, "I'm beginning to reconsider my lessons with Sir Renwick." She shrugs. "Maybe princesses just aren't meant to wield swords."

"Maybe I can show you what princesses *are* meant for." Without warning, Darren Eldric throws Annalise against the wall, locking his lips on her own.

Good gods!

The prince presses his body against hers, the taste of alcohol making its way into her mouth.

Annalise pushes him away enough for a breath of air, adrenaline flooding her limbs with every passing second. "What the *hell* do you think you're doing?"

Darren plants messy kisses down the side of Anna's neck that quickly descend toward the top of her bodice.

"Get *off* of me!" Annalise shouts, but her bellows are just as useless as her arms. Embers begin to crackle in her blood, but leaving that kind of mark on a prince would cost Annalise more than her betrothal. *Maybe if I can't push him away, I can bring him where I need him to be.* When Darren's hand moves a little too far south, the goddess makes just enough room between the two of them to drive her knee between his legs, watching him stumble backward in pain.

Darren meets her gaze with blue eyes cold as a Godrian winter. "You *bit*—"

"Is everything all right, Your Highness?" Oliver McHenry asks abruptly from the end of the hallway.

Annalise chokes back her tears. "No, actually; everything is *not* all right." She moves toward him without giving Darren a second glance. "Master McHenry, would you be so kind as to escort me back to my chambers?"

"It would be my honor, Your Highness." Oliver lends her his arm, failing to withhold a look of disdain from the prince.

Trembling, Annalise clutches his arm with both hands, trying not to think about the consequences of her actions. *Hopefully, he won't remember tomorrow.* She walks with Oliver in absolute silence until they round the corner.

"Are you all right?" he asks quietly.

The goddess huffs a laugh. "Perfectly. My future husband just tried to force himself on me after drinking three bottles of wine. I'm great." Annalise forces a smile, listening to the sound of her teeth chattering from fear.

Oliver only responds by placing his free hand gently over hers, the warmth of his skin melding with her own. Whether or not he means to fracture her heart, Annalise has no idea. It is only after she bids him goodnight and disappears behind her door that the princess sinks to the floor, running a thumb over the back of her hand with glassy eyes.

ADRIANNA

The pond is still and quiet, but Adrianna can see the trail of bubbles from a mile away. She kicks her bare feet, arms cutting through the water as she propels herself toward the source of the bubbles. Descending to the crack in the sandy bottom of the pond, Dria runs her hand across the spot where the bubbles seem to be originating. When the sand lifts and the water clears, she finds Desmond's face staring lifelessly back at her, his silver eyes pale and frozen.

"*Desmond!*" she screams underwater, her hands failing to pull him from the sand when something lurches her backward. Adrianna squirms in deft hands that restrain her, wasting another breath as she bellows his name again. Sometime during her ungraceful outburst, one of the hands had moved just above her heart, but the goddess cannot control her desperation.

"*Desmond!*" Adrianna screams through the water again, air bubbles spewing from her mouth. And when she tries to part her lips again, a slicing pain pierces her heart, the water around her body turning as red as her fury.

Adrianna wakes gasping, clutching the matted fabric of her nightdress. *Desmond!* she cries through the bond, praying to Lazarus for an answer.

No response.

Desmond! She rattles the tether connecting them with a sense of urgency she rarely lets anyone see.

No answer.

Tempering her desire to hyperventilate, Adrianna twists out of bed, calling on her handmaids to help her dress for the morning—which is already off to a horrendous start. *He always responds to me, no matter how busy he is.* The goddess slips her arms through crimson sleeves, grinding her jaw closed. Her Captain of the Royal Guard has been gone for one-and-a-half weeks now in an effort to find and beat into submission Edris Sharpkey after he sent them a false Elouthera. *One-and-a-half weeks, and he has communicated with me every day during that time.* Dria's heart begins to race. *What if something is wrong?*

"Would you like red or gold today, Your Majesty?" One of her maids holds up a selection of necklaces, which Adrianna could not care less about.

"The gold." She bats a hand, permitting the woman just enough time to clasp the back of the jewelry before storming into the hallway to find Renai.

She spots her lady-in-waiting flirting with a tall castle guard, one who will undoubtedly stumble his way into her chambers tonight.

"Your Majesty." Renai curtsies, her foxlike grin wide with self-assurance.

Adrianna doesn't have time for gossip. The queen grabs Renai's arm and drags her to a corner, meeting the woman's gaze with eyes cradled in dark circles. "I can't hear Desmond," Adrianna whispers.

Her lady-in-waiting snorts. "Me neither, Dria."

A frown of disgust. "That's not what I mean." Jedda darts her blue eyes left and right. "Anzac and I can communicate through our bond. Hear each other's thoughts and such. We've been doing so every day since he departed for Javir, only now ..." The goddess swallows. "I had a nightmare that he drowned at the bottom of a pond, and now I can't hear anything from him at all."

Renai looks more sympathetic as she takes Adrianna's hand. "Perhaps he's still asleep," she suggests. "If you still hear nothing from him by this afternoon, then we will start to worry. Does that sound reasonable?"

Hesitantly, the queen nods, turning to walk with her childhood friend to the Throne Room. *Because work never stops, even when your personal life is going to hell.* They take the turns of Larking Castle slowly, attempting to diffuse the tensity of this morning in a languish fashion. Dria would typically love a quiet time like this, if she wasn't fraught with riddling anxiety over the state of her paramour. Adrianna breaks away from Renai when they enter the Throne Room, taking her rightful place on the Empeirian throne with feigned poise.

It dissipates when one of her guards enters with a corpse, the Nev's blood smearing across the floor like the guts of a roach beneath Adrianna's high-heeled shoe.

"I thought I said I needed them alive," Adrianna sneers.

"This one was a fighter, Your Majesty. Couldn't even get her in irons." The guard bows gracefully.

Adrianna wrinkles her blonde brows, examining the woman's gray dress. "How do you know she was a Nev?"

"We found her doing a reading at the Dog's Head Tavern last night." He shakes his meaty head. "Some people just don't learn."

The queen props her head on her hand in silent contemplation. "Apparently not."

At the end of the Throne Room, a page announces the

presence of the royal courier, his absurd feathered cap almost large enough to hide the unsightliness of his ruddy nose. The old courier left shortly after Adrianna's battle with Annalise, and the queen has still not grown accustomed to his replacement. "Your Majesty." The man putzes down the aisle way. "A letter from Oron."

Oron? Where Edris Sharpkey lives, at the Iribus Circus? Dria snatches the letter, breaking the seal with primal aggression. *Maybe he sends word of Desmond ...* She unfolds the parchment, her icy-blue eyes glazing over a messy scroll before they rise again to meet her court. "Edris Sharpkey of the Iribus Circus has rallied the support of the Javirian throne on our behalf."

The queen's court rumbles with anxious fervor.

Adrianna continues. "In addition to Edris's men, the Empeirian throne now has the backing of the Javirian army." *Could he really have pulled this off?* "Captain Jrehart may have reminded Edris who is in charge after his previous ruse with Elouthera, but I'm not stupid enough to believe in the validity of this letter." The queen eyes the Royal Guard's next in line, now that her captain is away. "Send a few of our men to ensure that Edris is telling the truth. That we may, in fact, rely on the Javirian throne for aid."

"Yes, Your Majesty," Sir Braydenton replies dutifully.

Adrianna's eyes wander over her court, waiting for another issue to surface as she tries to cram down the fear rising in her throat. "If there is not anything else ..." The goddess dismisses her court, the hoard of fine silk and jewels disappearing through the enormous doors while Renai approaches her on the dais.

"Your Majesty," she begins slyly, "I have one more issue to raise." Haughtily, Renai slips a rolled piece of parchment from between her bust, unfurling it with care before presenting it to her queen. "One of the castle maids caught the letter while servicing his room. It was folded up in his desk, but thank the gods, she looked."

The letter hasn't yet been sealed, but Adrianna gets the feeling that it should have been. She opens it quickly, her icy-blue eyes growing with interest. "Who wrote this?" she dares to ask, her stare lingering on one sentence in particular:

My love for you continues to grow, even in your absence.

"A servant named Linden, Your Majesty. The mentor you entrusted to tutor Princess Aimelie on her royal duties." Renai opens her palm. "She also found this."

Dria examines the familiar silver and teal piece of jewelry. *Aimelie's ring?* Adrianna's mouth drops agape as she rereads the sentence three more times. *Aimelie ... is in love with Linden?* She blinks. "How long has this communication been going on? Have you confronted him yet?"

"No. I wanted to check with you first. We don't know how long they've been writing to each other, but I'm sure this isn't the first letter he's sent with details of the throne's agenda."

Dria traces back over the first two paragraphs, the ones spilling whatever information a servant is likely to hear in the castle about their monarch. *He's spying on me. For Aimelie.* While it doesn't seem like Linden has much to offer, the idea that her youngest sister has managed to gain some sort of foothold on Adrianna is unsettling. *And shocking*, the queen admits.

"Shall I have him brought here—"

"No," Dria cuts her off, something dampening her usual aggression. She finds her thumb brushing over the end of the letter, to the conclusion scrawled across the bottom of the paper:

My eternal love,

L.

Renai waits for her instruction, but Adrianna has had enough emotional exhaustion for one day. "Something must be done, but I need to think about it first."

A small chortle. "Think about it? What happened to the spontaneous, cut-out-your-throat girl that I grew up with?"

Adrianna's narrowed gaze is enough to remind Renai of her place, and she apologizes with a blush and a curtsy. When her friend leaves the Throne Room, Dria refolds the letter, watching the stained glass catch the early afternoon rays. The light warms her ivory face, so lost compared to what it used to be. She glances at the empty spot where Desmond usually stands, her heart burning with fear when she closes her blue eyes to desperately call on him once more.

She drops the letter on the marble floor when at last, there is a response.

Part III

Tsunami

ANNALISE

It was frivolous, the wedding gown they had selected for her to wear. Definitely not something that Annalise would have chosen for what should be the most important day of her life. The garish clumps of embroidered gold and white flowers adorn from the tops of her shoulders down to the train, with additional blooms added elsewhere in a rather randomized attempt to embody her godliness.

Annalise swallows deeply, observing herself in the mirror. *I am doing the right thing. I am doing the right thing for my kingdom, for my people, for my parents ...* A dangerous thought creeps into her mind, one that has her lips sinking into an even deeper frown: *But what about for myself?*

A memory surfaces, one from two nights ago, when

Prince Darren had her pinned in a darkened corridor, his body exploring hers in every spot she wishes she could have killed him over. Never in all her years in the slums would she have consented to go through with something as unfathomable as this, as marrying another man just because she was told to, much less marrying one whom she finds as repulsive as Darren Eldric. But it is Annalise's duty as the eldest daughter of King Tiberius and Queen Annora Larking, the very beings who she has shaped her character after. To disobey them, even in their death, would be a slight.

The lost princess shuts her dark eyes to take a breath, but it is no use. Annalise can feel the embers crackling in the pit of her stomach. She tries to stifle her anxiety, but remembers that for all her proposed grace, she is still part fire. Placing an ivory hand across her stomach, the seamstress bats her fingers away with an angry swat.

"Are you asking to be pricked, young lady?"

Anna cannot help but smirk at the brash woman. The old crone has no regard for formalities, but the goddess would not have it any other way. *After all, if nobody decides to treat me like a human, how will I ever know how it is like to live as one?* "I apologize, Libby," the princess speaks at last.

The seamstress rolls her wrinkled eyes. "An apology won't fix your squirming. You've been fidgeting ever since I began working on your bodice. I understand you are to be married soon, but I am old and half-blind, and if I stab you with a pin, I will be dead, too! Have you no sympathy for the elderly, girl?"

Annalise is awestruck, her mouth failing to form words. Staring at her reflection as half a dozen handmaids tend to her wedding dress, hair, and makeup has not given her the peace of mind she needs before marrying the Crown Prince of Nesvla. Her legs are shaking from standing for so long, her feet are sore from the heels they placed her in, and—

"Libby, it's well past your lunch break. I can take it from here." Sylvie watches Libby gather her sewing things before wordlessly leaving the room. Taking up a fresh needle and thread, Annalise's handmaid starts adding ivory beadwork to the top of the dress's bodice.

"I owe you," Anna whispers to Sylvie, but the woman simply laughs.

"You looked like you could use some help, Your Highness."

You have no idea. Upon no answer, her handmaid peeks from her work to examine Annalise's face, watching her appear lost in contemplation. The princess slowly looks at herself in the tall floor mirror before them. "Yes," Annalise replies quietly. "Yes, I could."

❧

It is nighttime before Annalise finds herself traipsing about the castle, searching for something to distract herself from the weight of the world pressing down upon her shoulders. She would pester Aimelie, but remembers that her youngest sister had excused herself from dinner with a grueling stomachache. *Hopefully, she will be feeling better in time for the wedding.*

The notion has Anna recalling Master Tasman's own indisposition, which she uses as an excuse to prolong her time away from the loneliness of her thoughts. She takes the steps in twos, letting her slippered feet carry her through torchlit hallways. Annalise makes to knock at Tasman's door but withholds her hand at the sound of a female voice on the other side.

"I don't see what the point of waiting is," Queen Minerva says in muffled tones. "The kingdom will find out eventually."

Master Tasman's soft voice responds with a sternness Annalise has rarely heard. "The point, Your Grace, is to give Queen Adrianna as little time to prepare for war as possible." A cough. "The moment she finds out Princess Annalise is marrying Prince Darren, the Queen of Empeirus will begin plaguing Nesvla with as many troops as she can."

"You cannot possibly be suggesting that we keep their marriage a secret for an indefinite amount of time."

"Not indefinitely, but for as long as is needed to make preparations for your own forces, Your Grace."

"My forces are well equipped for any quarrel, Master," Queen Minerva retorts. "Even if outnumbered, my Nesvlan army has more might than that of the rest of this kingdom combined." A tense pause. "I will have my pages spread the word first thing tomorrow. Goodnight, Master Tasman."

Annalise speedily raps on the door in an attempt to cover her eavesdropping. It opens to Queen Minerva's dissatisfied face. *Too late in the evening for ruses, I see.* "Queen Minerva," the princess curtsies.

"Princess Annalise," the Queen of Nesvla acknowledges with hardly so much as a glance.

The goddess waits for her to leave before entering Master Tasman's chambers, much less ornate than her own. She shuts the door. "What was that all about?" Annalise asks as casually as she can.

A heavy sigh, one which turns into a cough. "Nothing good," Tasman relents, though Anna heard every word. Her old master is cocooned in a small bed, his face even paler than usual.

"I came to check on you, to see how you are faring." She takes a seat in the chair beside his bed.

Tasman's lips form a smile. "I've been better, Your Highness."

Something in his words has Annalise's own smile

vanishing, her throat suddenly dry. She meets his wrinkled blue gaze with unbridled honesty. "I have, too."

A soft hum while the former master takes her hand. "You must promise me, Annalise," Master Tasman whispers to her. "Promise me that you will do the right thing for this kingdom—and for this world—no matter how unpopular the choice may be."

"Of course." Anna bows her dark waves, but Tasman shakes his head, pulling her closer.

"Queen Minerva is going to publicize your marriage to Prince Darren tomorrow." A rattling cough. "You know as well as I that Adrianna will begin preparations immediately—"

"I know," Annalise confirms. "I will be on my guard."

But Tasman does not seem satisfied. "No one else will be. None of the Eldrics, I mean."

Anna offers an anxious laugh. "Tasman, I don't know what you mean."

"I saw what happened the other night." Her former tutor saddens. "Not all of it, but enough."

Annalise closes her eyes, feeling a bright blush paint her cheeks.

Tasman grabs a piece of fabric, holding it against his mouth to cover his cough. When he pulls it away, red splotches stain the surface.

No. Gods, *no.* It takes everything for the goddess to swallow her tears.

Master Tasman's voice is hardly audible when he breathes his next sentence. "Darren Eldric is not the man your parents thought he would be."

Annalise guffaws, her brown eyes flying open. "Well, it's a little late for that now."

"It is never too late, Annalise." Tasman continues to hold her porcelain hand, meeting her gaze with wrinkled blue eyes. "I am in no position to give you orders, but I hope that you will trust your judgment. I believe you recognize the implications of this kind of marriage."

The princess is speechless. *Is he telling me not to go through with this?* Annalise shakes her head. "I have a duty, Tasman. And besides, I need this army—"

"As long as the Eldrics are still alive, they will not let you use their army. Queen Minerva said as much at dinner one night, before you arrived." A shallow sigh. "Aimelie and I didn't want to intervene with the possibility that you'd win them over, which is why she negotiated a potential alliance with Calleeit. In case this one failed."

Anna presses her free hand to her forehead, running it through her dark brown waves. *No army, no chance against Adrianna. But it isn't that simple. What about my reputation?* "What will they say about me? About a princess who calls off her betrothal for the sake of keeping her freedom?"

Tasman frowns in thought. "I don't know. But I do

have an idea of what they will say about you if you marry him."

The world spins, Annalise trying to wrap her head around the fact that one of her most trusted advisors is telling her not to marry the prince she has been promised to.

"It's time you started asking yourself what kind of characteristics your future king should possess," Tasman continues, watching her stare back in confusion. "Besides, how long will you be able to live with yourself knowing the truth of how you really feel?"

Anna shakes her head. "It doesn't matter how I feel; our parents struck a deal."

"I wasn't talking about Darren, Your Highness."

Her crimson blush grows brighter as the old man delights in a secret he chooses not to spill. *Could he know about my feelings for Oliver?* With great embarrassment, Anna diverts her eyes. "I don't know what you mean."

A light laugh. "A few months ago, gods and goddesses roaming our earth would have been labeled as absolute nonsense. The rules of this world have already been rewritten once; there is no reason why they cannot be rewritten again." Tasman's grin fades. "Your sister, Aimelie, she is wiser than she pretends to be." A look of seriousness. "She may be your biggest ally in this fight against Adrianna."

Annalise nods. "I do consider your own advice to be

paramount, Tasman." She lets her forehead fall toward the earth. "There are few times in this world when I do not feel like the lost princess."

Tasman cups her face with a weak hand. "Annalise," he offers her a gentle smile, "you are no princess. You are, in every sense of the word, the world."

DESMOND

He had done it, finally. Somehow, between aches and chills and an empty stomach, he had scrounged up enough of his energy to lead a group of farmers to him using a shadow of a man. The God of Darkness and Decay sits panting against an iron wall, one that begins to lift from the grass under the hands of three working men. A trickle of sweat slips down his temple, nearly missing his glassy eye.

Somewhere behind him, a beam of sunlight grows until it basks Anzac with all its golden glory; the light of freedom, the light of vengeance. But he can hardly think of that, not when his mind is swimming and his muscles are trembling and the gash on his thigh is oozing with the gods know what. The men seem to sense this and haul the captain to his unstable feet, two of them keeping him upright while the third sprints ahead. For what, Anzac has no idea. He hardly has any ideas, right now.

Dria, Desmond thinks longingly, remembering the last time he contacted her. He thinks it was yesterday, but can't be too certain. It doesn't matter, anyway, because the god hasn't the energy to send a message to her today. A sudden need to heave up whatever stomach contents he has left sends Desmond gagging onto the dirt road before him, the men at his side the only reason he still stands. Spitting, he can make out the blur of the third man waving them toward an old house, his vision swaying with every dragging step.

The porch, then a bed. The feel of cold, clean water on his face and neck. An elderly woman in a beige dress who cuts away the fabric of his pants to expose an angry, red wound. Anzac tries to focus harder on her face but sees only stars when she begins to drain the wound, his body shaking in agony.

"Dria?" Desmond asks a younger woman after catching his breath, one with fleeting features of blue eyes and honey-blonde hair.

The woman smiles, her voice lilting in his ears. "You should rest," he can make out behind the ringing in his head. "You should rest," she repeats, bringing a thick layer of ointment to his leg.

Desmond groans, shaking his head at the pain of her gentle touch. With double vision, he lays his head back down, cringing at the bowl of fluid beside him. "Where …" A shallow breath. "… is Dria?" the god whispers, the ceiling spinning as she covers his leg with what feels like a bandage.

The female hushes him, holding a cool rag to his forehead. "Go to sleep," she beckons in a tone as comforting as a mother's touch. "Go to sleep, and it will all be better."

AIMELIE

Captain Ivo stands before the behemoth vessel with his hands on his hips, letting his grayish eyes soak in their future method of transportation. "How much thought have you put into this, Princess?" He turns to face her seriously in the morning light.

Aimelie sighs. "Enough to make it real. Now, can you please spare me the lecture and go over our plans one more time?"

The former Captain of the Royal Guard presses his unpleased lips together, emphasizing the squareness of his jaw. "Two days after the royal wedding, we will depart for Calleeit, before the seas turn icy here in the north. What else is there to cover?"

She knows there isn't much to their plan, but it helps

Aimelie to hear it coming from Ivo's lips. *It makes it seem slightly less insane.* Master Tasman will be staying here in Nesvla, since rough seas don't make a good companion for the elderly, and Annalise will continue her duties as the future Princess of Nesvla. The only people set to travel with Aimelie are Captain Ivo and their limited crew, who have all agreed to keep their destination private—even from the Nesvlan throne. "Thank you, Captain."

Melie walks in tense silence back to Eldric Castle with Captain Ivo at her side. They make it all the way to the rose garden before sharing conversation again, the petals on the bushes decaying in the late autumn air. She tiptoes across the garden path, avoiding the rotting flowers for fear of dragging them along in her skirts. "How is Master Tasman feeling?" the youngest princess presses, hoping that his cough is finally clearing up.

A quiet grunt. "Says he's fine, but I think he still needs rest." Ivo shakes his head. "The man's as stubborn as your sister."

Aimelie can't help but snort, considering that Ivo is perhaps the most stubborn person she knows. The princess raises her baby-blue eyes to the golden domes of the castle, pondering on the state of Annalise's affairs. Just for fun, she decides to pester her friend for his unusually honest opinion. "What do you make of all this? The wedding, Prince Darren ... all of it."

His sidelong glance is about as reassuring as his

personality. "I think it would be more polite if I held my tongue, Your Highness."

Melie relents a faint smile, excusing herself when they reach the inside of the castle in hopes of finding the royal courier. He has scarcely been seen, lately, and while a small fear tries to take root in the back of her mind, the princess likes to believe that he has simply been sick. She rounds a corner to the main corridor, only to run straight into Queen Minerva.

"Good heavens!" cries the Nesvlan queen, keeping a teetering Aimelie upright.

Melie flushes the brightest shade of red. "Your Grace, I am terribly—"

"Oh, please don't worry yourself, dear! In fact, you're just the person I wanted to speak to." Minerva places a hand on her back, leading Aimelie down the hallway. "I've been looking for your sister this morning, but haven't found her anywhere in the castle or in the training ring with Sir Renwick. I was hoping you might have an idea of her whereabouts. My decorators have more questions for her regarding the wedding." A soft sigh. "If I didn't know any better, I'd say she is doing her best to avoid them."

Aimelie stops. "Nonsense, Your Grace." The princess shakes her blonde curls with a kind smile. "Annalise may be introverted, but she would never intentionally be rude.

Please, leave it to me. I will find her and let her know of your concerns."

A full grin. "The gods bless you, Princess Aimelie." Satisfied, Queen Minerva leaves the youngest princess with a pat on the hand and a new mission in mind.

Avoiding wedding planning, is she? Melie sucks in a breath of air. *The real question is does she know she is avoiding it, or is it merely by accident due to her busy training schedule?* Reeling in her thoughts, she nearly jumps at the sight of the royal courier, who in turn frowns at her excitement.

"I'm sorry, Your Highness, but I'm afraid I don't have anything for you today."

Aimelie's smile withers. "Thank you." She dismisses him. *Nothing today, nothing yesterday, nothing the day before that...* The princess tries not to remind herself that it has been over a week with no word from Linden, and thus welcomes the distraction of Queen Minerva's mission to find her sister. *Sometimes the birds take a while to arrive between destinations,* she tells herself. *I will not worry until two weeks have passed.*

The princess steps back into the chill Nesvlan morning, crossing her fingers that Annalise will be found somewhere on the castle grounds. *She would not have run away, right? Hopefully not without saying goodbye, first.* Aimelie scours the gardens, the training ring, even the small apple orchard not exactly on the Eldrics' property, but close by.

She pushes back a curl, frowning beneath her freckles. Down on her luck, Melie decides to pad back to Eldric Castle when a set of muddy footprints catches her eye, the trail disappearing past the gate to the beach.

Aimelie squints with curiosity as she opens the wrought iron gate, her doe eyes widening when she finds Annalise on the shoreline, constructing a watery cage around herself. One at a time, her eldest sister adds a thin stream of seawater to the collection of loops and holes, until she is enclosed by a liquid dome. Melie would be entranced enough to watch the magic for hours if a figure to her left didn't catch her eye.

The princess fails to hide a smirk. "Good morning, Master McHenry."

Her sister's Master of the High Council diverts his green gaze from Annalise, recovering himself with a polite smile. "Good morning, Your Highness."

Aimelie glances back at Annalise, taking a steadying breath. She still hasn't gotten used to her sisters' godly heritage, and watching Anna use her powers makes her more nervous than she wants to admit. *I should talk to her, but I don't want to interrupt.* "I haven't seen them since that day at the castle," she tries making small talk. "Her powers, I mean."

A light laugh. "They've gotten a bit more controlled, thankfully. This is the first time I've seen her use them since we arrived. I just so happened to catch her on my way back from a run."

Their conversation comes to a lull as they observe Annalise with quiet fascination, Melie's sister struggling to uphold the twenty different concentric rings she has above her head. Aimelie opens her mouth to continue speaking with Master McHenry, but stops when she finds his eyes locked onto her sister with a different sort of gaze. His lips say nothing, but his eyes speak volumes. "I had a feeling that's why she dropped the paintbrush."

"I'm sorry?"

Melie laughs, allowing herself a shake of the head. "I'm supposed to be heading to breakfast, soon," the princess tells him, ignoring Queen Minerva's mission. "Would you care to escort me?"

Master McHenry returns her smile. "Of course, Your Highness. I'm afraid I'm not in my finest attire, but I'd be happy to."

The youngest princess takes his arm, the two of them leaving Annalise on the beach with whatever little free time she has nowadays. Walking back to the castle for the second time today, Melie wonders what to talk about with Queen Adrianna's former master. *I never liked most of the men on Dria's High Council, but if Annalise finds that she can trust Master McHenry, then perhaps I can, too. Besides, Captain Ivo did say that he has proven himself.* Aimelie could approach any number of topics—*the wedding, the weather, the way Darren Eldric looks at him like he wants his head to explode*—but instead, the princess wants to learn more about Master McHenry. "So," Melie begins. "How long have you known my sister?"

The master thinks for a moment. "A few months, or so, Your Highness. Were you close with Princess Annalise growing up?"

"Oh yes, very." Aimelie gives him a bright smile. "You can lose the formalities, by the way. I'm just fine being called by my birth name like most other humans."

"Likewise." Oliver grins.

An awkward pause comes between them, a cool breeze raising goosebumps on Aimelie's porcelain skin. She presses him further. "She trained with you, my sister?"

"She did," Oliver responds happily. "Well, not so much her powers. I was teaching her how to sword fight, to help her get stronger so she could use her magic more effectively."

Melie raises her blonde brows, a smile blooming on her pretty lips. "It must have taken a great deal of trust to go with you to the Savek Coast," she ventures.

"To be fair, I don't think she had much of a choice." Oliver shrugs. "It was all part of Master Tasman's plan."

"My sister is a goddess," Aimelie says aloud. "If she felt like she wasn't in a good situation, she would have found a way to leave—which means she trusts you."

Oliver ponders the thought before nodding slightly.

"Which is more than I can say about her future prince," the princess adds bitterly.

The master glances at her sidelong. "I beg your pardon?"

Gods, I am so stupid. An embarrassed laugh. "My apologies." Aimelie blushes, shaking her head. "I've been quite stressed lately, which seems to be sapping my ability to make sound judgments."

Oliver's eyes sparkle with the slightest bit of humor. "We did nix the formalities."

Melie tries not to smile back, especially when Prince Darren Eldric rounds the corner like a soldier preparing for war. Quickly, she removes her hand from Oliver's arm, curtsying while he bows. "My lord," she greets him.

"My lady," Darren returns. A look of shameless derision. "Master McHenry."

"Your Highness." Oliver reflects the sentiment with a fire in his eyes that Aimelie has never seen him give before.

The prince's sea-blue gaze could cut steel. "I hope you don't mind me interrupting, but I've been instructed to hunt down my betrothed on my mother's account. She still needs to choose her gown for the wedding."

I wonder if it's common to have to "hunt down" your betrothed, or if all happy marriages begin with a bride on the run. "I apologize for your inconvenience, my lord,"

Aimelie starts. "I, too, have been tasked with this mission, but have had no luck with finding my sister."

Prince Darren's night-black hair billows in the crisp air, his eyes leveling on Oliver's own. "And what of you, Master? Have you seen my future bride this fine morning?"

Melie holds her breath to hear what words her sister's friend will choose, her stomach tightening with each passing second.

"I have not, Your Highness," Oliver lies perfectly.

A low snarl. "Very well," Darren spits at him, turning to bow to Aimelie. Just before his exit, he shoots Oliver one last look of vile. "I trust that if you do run into Princess Annalise, I will be the first to know."

"Undoubtedly." Oliver nods his head with more regality than the childish prince who storms back into the castle.

Aimelie blows out a sharp exhale of disgust, nudging Oliver to continue to walk them farther into the gardens, where she can delay bumping into the Nesvlan Royal Family again. Maybe it is the disappointment of watching Annalise go through with her parents' contract only because it is advantageous, or the insufferable behavior of Prince Darren, or the weight of not hearing back from Linden for so long, but Aimelie Larking cannot force another second of false happiness.

As soon as they clear the hedges, she drops her voice

to a whisper. "Of all the men in this world—" Melie stops herself, gritting her teeth. They continue deeper into the green maze, her rage finally getting the best of her. "I never imagined that Annalise would marry one like him."

Oliver's green eyes are wide with words he does not speak.

The princess knows she should stop there, but dealing with the insolence of the Eldric family for weeks now has consumed her supply of politeness, and for some reason, she doesn't think Oliver minds hearing her rant. She opens her mouth to continue spewing fanged words when a cold raindrop lands on her cheek, and Aimelie's anger softens into sadness. "I know my sister," she whispers. "I can't understand how Annalise could ever love Darren Eldric. She needs someone honorable, someone patient and intelligent and compassionate."

Aimelie's blue eyes meet Oliver's with something like sorrow. The princess doesn't know him very well, but just like she recognized goodness in Linden, she feels like she can sense enough of the same in Oliver to finish her thought:

"Someone like you."

ADRIANNA

"*I'm at the border.*" Adrianna recalls the only sentence she has had come through the bond in the past two days. "*I'm at the border,*" she repeats in her head. *But how am I supposed to know which side of Javir he is on?* Dria knows Desmond planned to meet with Edris Sharpkey in southern Javir, and she doesn't think her paramour would linger for longer than necessary in the territory. *But, on the off-chance he decided to keep moving toward Nesvla ...* Despite Desmond's ability to give Adrianna his vague location, his failure to follow up her subsequent questions has had the queen's heart racing for days. *And the idea that he somehow* can't *respond is even worse than those he doesn't share.*

A knock on her solar door has the Dark Goddess straightening her posture to prepare for company, as she wouldn't want anyone to see her like this. *The last thing I need is for gossip about a weak queen to spread through the kingdom.* She admits the guest with feigned confidence, but it is not who she expects.

"Your Majesty." The royal courier bows deeply, extending a hand cradling a finely stamped letter. *An orange seal* ... "A letter from the Nesvlan throne."

Adrianna tries to hide her shock. "Thank you. You are dismissed." With as much grace as a child, she rips the parchment open, sucking every bit of information off the page should it give some hint of Desmond's whereabouts.

Only, the contents inside reveal nothing of the sort.

The goddess lets her eyes rove over a gold-leafed announcement, one that brings a wicked smile to her crimson lips. *Annalise, you bloody fool!* Why her eldest sister would think it wise to advertise her upcoming nuptials to Prince Darren Eldric, Adrianna will never know. But the newly acquired knowledge has Dria beaming with something like excitement and self-satisfaction.

A second knock at Adrianna's mahogany door tears her gaze from the letter, which she folds and exchanges for the other one on her table. "You may enter," she affords.

When it opens, the man who walks through already knows he is doomed.

"Sit." The queen gestures to the red velvet chair opposite her own, to the one with a matching chalice of wine and a plate of fresh fruit. Adrianna watches Linden slowly seat himself on the cushion, as though the furniture itself would enact the justice he deserves. Tilting her golden curls, she lets him sit for just a moment longer before pushing the letter Renai gave her to the center of the table. "How long?"

Linden swallows. His caramel eyes read hers with a sort of brave anxiety, one that Adrianna knows won't budge unless she forces it to.

"I didn't bring you here for a full interrogation. If I wanted that, I would have handed you over to Calix. So." Jedda taps the letter with a manicured nail. "Perhaps you can work with me like I've decided to work with you. How long have you been spying on me for my sister?"

Her servant grinds his jaw closed.

The queen bites her lip. "Very well. Then I suppose I can continue talking." Dria opens the stolen letter, reading through Linden's words line by line, until she reaches the one that had her heart breaking in two the day she had received it:

"*My love for you continues to grow, even in your absence.*"

She pauses, fighting back tears. *Have I ever said anything like that to anyone before? Do I have to, or is it just assumed?* Adrianna faces Linden once more. "Do you really love her? Aimelie, I mean."

Tears fill Linden's steady gaze. "I do. I love her, and I would do anything for her."

A breathy laugh. "You don't say." Adrianna sighs, running a hand through the locks below the spot where her ruby-adorned crown rests. Normally, she would have stopped pressing here and sent Linden off to be executed. But this time … This time, things are different. This time, it has to do with Aimelie. "How long have you felt this way about her?"

His eyes peruse the painting on the wall in silent reflection. "The better half of a year."

The queen stares into the reflection of her wine. "And she feels the same way about you?"

It is not very often that Adrianna finds herself being examined by other people, but Linden gives her a look, nonetheless. "She does," he relents.

Something cracks inside the goddess upon hearing his validation, but Adrianna knows that where there is one exception, there will surely be more. *I cannot let him go,* she reminds herself. *No matter how much Aimelie loves him, I cannot let myself show mercy.* Such an act would open her up to being the sort of soft, spineless queen she so despises. Adrianna mirrors Linden's solemn expression. "As Aimelie's former mentor, I am certain you are aware of the consequences of treason."

A quiet nod, followed by an almost imperceivable laugh.

The queen stops. "I'm sorry, did you just *laugh?*"

Linden meets her gaze with eyes like fire. "Adrianna The Merciless, they call you. Adrianna The Butcher. Do you know why?" The queen's servant assesses her wide-eyed expression. "Because goddess or not, you don't care about consequences. You don't care about people. The only thing you care about is what they think of you—specifically, that they fear you." An audible swallow. "Well, I have news for you, Your Majesty. People who fear you will never admire you. People who fear have nothing to hope for. Take a page out of Aimelie's book. She should have been the one on the throne, if I had anything to do with it."

There is nothing for Jedda to say when he finishes, her confidence waving like a banner in the wind. Nothing for her to say at all, until the words come falling out of her mouth before she can stop them: "You're right."

Linden's face looks almost as awestruck as Adrianna's own, but the queen recovers almost instantly. She considers using her powers to finish his existence on this plane—*I could send a bolt of ice through his heart, or burn him to death*—but the idea of something that extreme doesn't sit well with Dria. *No, not for the love of Aimelie's life.* Taking a sip from her chalice, Adrianna settles on something less potent.

"You're very brave, I'll give you that," Dria points out.

"I can see why Aimelie was drawn to you." An honest frown. "It pains me that I have to kill you."

Linden has no retort, but his words continue to replay in the queen's ears: *Adrianna The Merciless, Adrianna The Butcher.*

The goddess's voice softens. "Is there anything you would like me to give to Aimelie in your absence?"

A huffed laugh, followed by what could be a small sob. Linden removes a golden ring from his finger, placing it gently in the center of the table between them. "It's the only thing I have to offer."

Dria nods, taking the metal band and setting it on his stolen letter. "I will also permit you to finish your wine before—" She recovers, remembering her position as queen and Dark Goddess. "Before I finish you."

The man stares at his chalice, then at Adrianna's own. Mournfully, he picks it up and drinks from it, frowning at the taste while his caramel eyes peer over the rim of the vessel. "I never thought I'd be having my last drink with the Crimson Queen," Linden japes darkly, taking another swig. "How will you end my life? Sword? Magic? Your blood-curdling smile?"

The queen chokes on a laugh while he finishes his wine. "Don't make me regret this." His confusion shines through while Dria fills her mouth with some of her own drink, drowning her minor humiliation. Running a finger around the rim of her chalice, she watches Linden's eyes begin to droop. "I wanted to do what Aimelie would have asked me to," Adrianna says quietly. "Something painless and peaceful."

Linden's brows push together while he opens his mouth, but no words come out. He closes it before the blinking of his tired eyes slows down, before his face begins to turn pale.

"Sleep well, dear Linden." Adrianna smiles kindly as he closes his caramel gaze for the last time. As soon as his body collapses onto the table, the queen stands, placing his golden ring in a silk bag and handing it to one of the guards she calls in. "I want this done neatly," Jedda orders him. "Place his head in a box and tie this bag on top of it with a pretty bow."

"Yes, Your Majesty." The guard moves Linden's corpse from her solar while Desmond's second-in-command enters.

"Sir Braydenton," the queen greets him with a letter burning in her palm. "Tell me, how much warmer is it in Nesvla this time of year?"

Sir Braydenton ponders for a moment. "I'm not sure, Your Majesty. I don't believe it is too much warmer."

"Good." Adrianna incinerates the announcement between her fingers, replaying Desmond's last words for the seventieth time: *"I'm at the border."* "Because effective immediately, that's where our men are headed—and I have a wedding to catch."

VEGA

"You're sure this is where she'll be?" Narelle pries from her and Eden's chestnut horse.

Elouthera sighs. "News spreads like wildfire in Nesvla, especially royal gossip. Besides," the goddess closes her lime-green eyes for one more second, "I can feel her." Some time has passed since her last attempt to find Dimity through the bond, but this morning, something felt ... different. The tether connecting Vega to her godly partner has grown stronger, like the hardening of a leather cord into steel.

"This is where Master Tasman and Captain Ivo wanted us all to meet, anyway," Modgen mentions in front of her. "Gods, I can't wait to see the look on Anna's face when she sees I brought back El—"

Vega punches him in the arm while a group of Nesvlan guards walks by.

"—my future wife!" Modgen exclaims through a wince, rubbing his arm.

Elouthera rolls her cat-like eyes until her gaze latches onto a series of smooth, golden domes, each one half-hidden by clusters of crimson and gold leaves. *Eldric Castle*, she notes. When she faces its direction, a string pulls taut through her heart, telling her one thing: *Dimity is in there.*

The clicking of their horses' hooves carries the weary travelers toward salvation, Vega's heart thumping in her chest with every stride toward the castle. Suddenly, self-consciousness gets the better of her, and for the first time on her journey of finding Dimity, she wonders what the goddess will think of *her*. She darts her up-tilted eyes between Modgen and Narelle. "Do you think we'll get along?" Vega poses her question quietly.

Modgen turns his head from the front of their horse. "Why wouldn't you? She's the Goddess of Wisdom and Justice. Unless you're into murdering people, I dare say you'll get along just fine."

Vega feels her stomach drop, her mind sailing back to when she trapped Anzac in an iron box a few days ago. She doesn't like to let herself think much on the subject— just like she tries not to remember the Nevs she hurt when her group was flanked in the forest—but at times like these, when she finds herself slumped in a pit of insecurity, she can't help a certain notion from crossing her thoughts: *What if I'm just as cruel as the deities I'm trying to save the world from? What if I am no better than Jedda and Anzac, myself?*

Elouthera knows that what she did to Anzac and the Nevs was justifiable, in that her opponents were out to cause serious harm to herself and her party. But the one action Vega didn't take is the one that weighs on her most heavily, the one that is bound to keep her awake at night for the indefinite future. *Why didn't I do anything? Why didn't I try to stop Anzac from suffocating my own mother?* Unbridled tears begin welling in her lime-green eyes, but Vega knows that nobody likes a weak leader. And right now, the goddess needs to lead.

"Have you met the Crown Prince of Nesvla?" Eden asks Modgen as they approach the foot of a large hill.

A shake of his reddish curls. "Nope. I didn't even know Annalise was supposed to marry him until today."

"I'm not sure she knew until recently, either," Narelle offers. "I don't think she would have been as insistent on building her empire from the ground up had she known there was an easier place to start."

Vega holds a breath when Eldric Castle comes into view above the hill, its mammoth domes like caps of sunlight gilding the white granite beneath it. *Dimity is in there?* The master manipulator had spent her childhood on her family's Nesvlan estate, but never had she the opportunity to visit the capital of the territory, nor bask in the presence of such magnificent architecture. "How does this compare to Larking Castle?" Vega wonders aloud.

"This one is a lot more lavish, if you ask me," Modgen Sprightly answers. "Larking Castle isn't as ornate, but it's taller and has more turrets."

Eden gazes in amazement as they approach the front gates. "I wonder what it looks like on the inside."

"Too bad you'll never get to find out." A husky guard moves forward from the entrance, his hand on the pommel of a sword.

"We haven't even stated our business." Modgen's fists curl around the reigns. "I'll have you know that our presence has been requested by Princess Annalise."

A slight lie, but that's all right.

The guard grumbles. "You think Her Highness would request the presence of the likes of you? Turn around and go home, before I give you a reason to."

Modgen whispers to Elouthera over his shoulder, "Can't you try using your magic on him or something?"

And risk exposing myself before I'm ready to? "What good would that do? I can take him down or bend his mind, but there will be plenty more if we make it inside the castle, and we don't even know where we're going."

A sigh of pure annoyance. Modgen pins his cobalt eyes

on the castle guard. "I demand to be let through these gates at once."

"Is that so?" The guard draws his sword, watching the horses jump backward with fearful whinnies. A few other guards move from their stations on each side of the irritated man, unsheathing their own weapons.

Vega holds on to Modgen to keep from being bucked off, their horses turning with little discretion before the group continues retreating back down the hill. With Narelle and Eden in tow, the goddess grits her jaw beneath the cloudy Nesvlan sky. "This is ridiculous," Vega says, stating the obvious. "How the hell am I supposed to get to her if she's a princess?" She swallows. "A *princess*, for the gods' sakes." She turns her small nose to the heavens. "What kind of sick joke is this, Lazarus? Anzac and Jedda get to spend most of their lives together, but I get to spend most of mine halfway across the world from Dimity, who just so happens to be in a social class unreachable from mine!"

The rest of the group is silent while Vega concludes her rant, her pale cheeks red from embarrassment or fury, she cannot tell. Eden toys with the glass vial around her neck. Narelle runs a hand through her horse's mane. Modgen keeps his mouth shut.

Until he doesn't.

"So, what's the plan? Sneak into the castle? Crash the wedding?"

"And ruin her wedding day?" Narelle shakes her chestnut locks. "There's no way we could make it in as uninvited guests. Everywhere around the castle will be under heightened security."

"Oh, I wasn't talking about using conventional methods." Modgen gives the tan woman a smirk.

Eden stirs. "Maybe it would be better to wait until after the wedding. It's only a week away."

Vega feels the horse lurch before she sees it, Modgen's shoulders broadening in sheer defiance while he whirls in Eden's direction. "I'll say this once. I've been busting my ass for Annalise this past month. I've brawled my way through Javirian fighting pits, broke into a gang-protected clocktower, and somehow evaded the God of Darkness and Decay for Lazarus knows how much longer." Modgen shoots Narelle a bitter smile. "Forgive me, Narelle, but I'm not particularly in the mood to care about spoiling Anna's wedding day. If anything, I'd hope my appearance would make her day that much more delightful."

For once, Vega agrees with her redheaded travel companion. *I've waited my entire mortal life to be reunited with Dimity. If crashing her wedding is what it will take, then I'd consider the scheme worth it.*

"You survived the Javirian fighting pits?" Eden questions in a shocked voice.

"Okay," Elouthera interrupts. "I have an idea." Pointing to an ornate building with vine-laced columns,

Vega faces her acquaintances. "Rumor has it that Princess Annalise and Prince Darren are to be married first at the Temple of Darrion before returning to the castle. If that's the case, we could be part of the onlookers, waiting for the right time to catch Dimity's attention on their way back."

"Perfect," declares Modgen. "What better way to start their celebration than with the return of some of her most valued people? And Eden, of course."

Vega gives him another punch in the arm, this time one that might leave a mark.

"And how will we ensure that guards won't get involved?" Narelle asks from her chestnut steed.

"That's where you and Eden would come in," Vega continues. "I'm still working on a plan to catch her attention, but in the meantime, I would suggest utilizing your connection with the Nevs by filling the surrounding crowds with as many allies as possible." The Goddess of Dreams and Mystery shrugs. "At the very least, they could help slow any guards who have detected us."

Narelle nods. "That should be our next stop. There is a Nevs' hall nearby that I remember seeing on Cyndeya's map." She gives an uncomfortable frown at Vega. "Your endorsement of Eden as High Priestess could prove very beneficial in getting more of the Nevs to stay—and to help your grand scheme."

Some dark part of Vega makes her want to say no, that

she will never help a Nev in the rest of her remaining mortality, or so help her Lazarus. But, given her party's current streak of bad luck—and being so close to Annalise—Elouthera decides it best to make an exception. *I will just have to set aside my petty feelings about the cult and do what I need to do to finally meet Dimity.* "If that's what it takes to get to Annalise, then I'll do it."

As the group makes it back to the main cobblestone road, the goddess turns her lime-green gaze toward the horizon with a sense of hope that she has seldom felt on her journey so far. *I'm coming for you, Dimity,* Elouthera tells her through the bond, casting away her doubts. *Somehow, someway, I'm going to meet you soon.*

ANNALISE

His chest presses against hers with an urgency Annalise has never felt the likes of before. Somewhere in the back of her racing mind, a small voice whispers that this might not be a good idea, but right now, Annalise is the last person to be convinced otherwise. Not when he kisses his way down the curve of her neck. Not when he brings his lips to hers and claims them with a force so powerful, it could shatter worlds.

It shatters her own world when he slips an arm around her waist, leaning her back in the chair while his other hand finds its way beneath her skirts. It shatters her sanity when his tongue glides over her own, until a certain movement has her spilling his name from her parted lips.

"Oliver," the goddess moans before she finds his mouth on hers again. "Oliver," she says between heavy breaths, rumpling the collar of his shirt. She lets her eyes roll in the back of her head while he kisses down the front of her throat, descending to her sternum. Her breath quickening, her heart ready to explode, she repeats his name once more, like a song, like a prayer. "Oli—"

Annalise wakes, clamping a hand over her lips after the last syllable of his name stumbles out. Warily, she darts her brown eyes around the room, hoping that for the love of Lazarus, nobody overheard her sultry moans. If the emptiness of her chambers is any indication, the princess would seem to be in luck. But if anyone *did* happen to hear her, Annalise knows exactly what they would say.

I'm damned, the goddess realizes, rubbing her eyes with her stomach fills with dread. The idea has her sprinting to a tub of cold water, splashing it against a crimson blush. Droplets drip from her cheeks like silent tears as she peers at herself in the mirror. *No,* Annalise corrects. She gives her reflection a wily chuckle. *It was just a dream! The gods know we all have uncomfortable dreams from time to time.* Although, the princess doesn't remember the last uncomfortable dream she didn't want to wake up from.

A feeling like shame has Annalise selecting her most modest gown for the day, calling on Sylvie to help her dress. *Maybe Tasman is right*, Anna thinks with embarrassment. *He seems to believe that I care for Oliver more deeply than I let on.* Her handmaid senses her dour energy, and upon securing a silver necklace, faces her in the floor mirror.

"An interesting choice of attire for your wedding rehearsal," Sylvie notes with curious eyes.

Oh, gods! I forgot that was today. A sudden urge to heave into a chamber pot has Annalise stepping off the raised dressing platform. "A little guessing helps keep people interested," she remarks, pausing for a moment at the implication of such a statement. *Gods, I need to get out of here.* Anna makes for the door, excusing herself from Sylvie's company before she paces down the stairs to the Great Hall, where the celebration of her wedding to Prince Darren will be held next week.

All around, the enormous room is being readied for the reception with swags of orange and gold satin, chocolate fountains, and cloth-of-gold tablecloths. Coupled with her gaudy, flower-ridden wedding gown, Annalise can't imagine how garish the whole scene will look. Guests clinking together their jewel-encrusted chalices, Nesvlan jesters dancing in clothes unaffordable by half the kingdom's population, a cake tall enough to dwarf the likes of Modgen Sprightly. If Anna could trade her entire wedding reception for donating the coin to the lower classes, she would. Only, it isn't exactly up to her to do such a thing.

"There's my future princess," Darren Eldric croons from halfway across the room. "You're a few minutes late," he reminds her quietly upon reaching her. "For a moment, I thought you'd jilted me a week before our wedding."

Annalise feigns a laugh. "I couldn't if I tried." *Because then I would be breaking the contract my parents thought it best to put in place, and apparently, I value their opinion above my own.* Wordlessly, she takes his arm, remembering his drunken advances from last week. Anna still hasn't raised the issue, but something tells her that bringing it up wouldn't do much good, anyway. She watches her betrothed run a hand through his night-black hair, shooting a bemused half-smile at a woman wearing burgundy. "Who is that?" Annalise asks from his side, trying to keep her lips from sneering.

Prince Darren pretends not to hear her, but the goddess has had enough. Not after his dishonorable act a few nights ago, not after Annalise has been playing the doting princess ever since she arrived here. *If he wants to play this game, I'm going to be the wildcard.*

"My *gods*, is that not just the most beautiful dress you've ever seen?" Annalise lies, enjoying the sight of Darren's face growing three shades paler. "My lord, you must introduce me to this fine lady. It's not every day that you find someone with such exquisite taste."

The prince's arm tenses under her own. "Of course, my lady." Darren straightens his spine, leading Annalise toward the burgundy-clad woman with leaden feet. His pale-blue gaze meets hers with noticeable discomfort. "Lady Catherine," he begins, "I'm afraid I haven't yet introduced you to my betrothed, Princess Annalise Larking."

Lady Catherine curtsies politely. She is beautiful, in a wicked sort of way; the kind of female who finds joy in spreading courtroom gossip and revels in the aftermath of her rumors. "Your Highness." She smiles widely.

"My lady." Annalise returns her grin. "I was just telling Prince Darren how beautiful your gown is. I must have my handmaid order me a similar color at once."

A forced laugh. "You have my thanks, Your Highness."

"Are you a part of the Nesvlan court?" Annalise pries, her dark eyes reading every unspoken word in her seductive eyes.

"I am, Your Highness. As I have been for the past seven years." Lady Catherine smirks at Anna's ignorance, giving Darren a subtle glance.

The goddess would blush, but she coerces a smile. "Wonderful." Annalise nods cheerfully. "It is always good to meet my future court members." She curtsies before excusing Prince Darren and herself, letting him lead their way to the Temple of Darrion in silence so they can rehearse their wedding in excruciating detail. *And rehearse, I shall, for I need to convince others, if I cannot be convinced myself.*

Annalise Larking drowns herself in lukewarm water, the suds of the bath muddling the surface into transparent clouds. *If only this is how clear court politics could be.* The princess scrubs at her hair, attempting to wash away the discomfort of her entire day, but for all her trying, she knows there is no reprieve from her thoughts on Prince Darren and Queen Minerva and Nesvla in general. What's more, is that this is just the beginning. This is to be her *life.* She sends her face underwater, the notion too powerful to think above the surface.

My parents could not have known how different Prince Darren and his reigning family would turn out to be, Anna reflects, stepping out of the bath to pull on an ivory shift. *Even Ivo and Tasman had high expectations when they rekindled my betrothal agreement with the Nesvlan throne, and that was only months ago.* The goddess stuffs her feet into a set of fluffy slippers, padding over to her feather bed while a single thought keeps her mind churning with ceaseless unease: *What would they think of him now?*

Instinct has Annalise brushing the scar on her left leg,

and she hikes up her dress to get a better look at it. Though the healing skin has begun turning white, it feels like only yesterday that she was breathing in the salty air of the Savek Coast, where her most pressing issue was strengthening her magic to stand a chance against Adrianna. *What will happen to my main objective once I marry Prince Darren? Will things remain the same as they are now, or will my control over the situation continue to drift from my grasp?*

Annalise knows that neither conjecturing nor reminiscing will do her any good, especially not with her wedding a week away. Instead, she climbs into bed, covering her face with the golden blankets, and pretending to fall asleep for the next hour. The plan fails more miserably than her plan to fall in love with Darren, then fails even more when there is a knock at her door. *A visitor, at this hour? Who the hell—* For a split second, Anna worries it might be the prince, but her decision to use magic should that situation arise again puts her anxiety to rest.

Another knock, this one more eager.

Groaning, Annalise crawls out of bed, wrapping a heavy cloak around herself before she opens the door to a frowning Captain Ivo.

"Your Highness." He bows, his grayish eyes less intense than usual. "I am terribly sorry for the late hour."

"Don't be." Anna waves her hand. "I couldn't sleep."

A brusque nod. "I ... I would have waited until tomorrow, but I thought you would want to be the first to know." Ivo's stare levels at her own with somber solidity. "Master Tasman has passed," he tells her quietly.

Annalise parts her lips, but no words come out. Within her chest, she can feel her heart tearing in two, a swell of tears ready to burst if she so much as breathes the wrong way. With an uneven sigh, she blinks back her sobs, nodding silently at Ivo. "Thank you for letting me know," Annalise manages.

Captain Ivo doesn't say anything, he simply reaches into his pocket to withdraw an emerald and onyx bracelet fit for a child. "He wanted me to give you this." Ivo drops the bracelet into Anna's extended hand, shaking from the intensity of the news. "It was yours, from when you were little. The one I used to narrow you down in the slums."

"I remember it." Annalise runs a thumb over the black beads.

Ivo continues. "You must have forgotten to pack it before you left for the Savek Coast, so Tasman had been ..." The man pauses to steady his breath. "He had been holding onto it for you until you returned."

Several tears escape her eyes while Annalise chokes back a larger sob, using the back of her wrist to dry her cheeks in vain. "Thank you, Captain."

But Ivo shakes his head. "If there is anything you

need, Your Highness," he gently places a muscled hand on her shoulder, "please don't hesitate to ask."

"Likewise," Annalise affirms, patting the top of his hand with as much ease as she can muster. The goddess watches him leave, closing the door behind him with careful softness before she releases a sob, letting her eyes overfill with the tears she had been trying so hard to hold back. When Anna finally catches her breath, she realizes that her chances of sleeping well tonight are all but none.

Placing her childhood bracelet beside her crown, Anna pulls her cloak tighter around her body, slipping out of her chambers. It would do her no good to sit alone with her thoughts, not when they were already dour even before hearing of Tasman's death. *Maybe a walk would help clear my head, or at least help me process what has happened.* Annalise rounds the bend quickly, shuffling down the dark corridor lest she be pressed against the wall again by Darren Eldric.

Only this time, it seems, the prince has found a different sort of companion. Slinking into the shadowed crook of a wall, Annalise holds a breath while Lady Catherine shares a passionate kiss with Prince Darren, her tan hands undoing the buttons on the top of his doublet. Shamelessly, Darren pulls her into his chambers, his partner all too eager to slam the door shut behind them.

A quiet pause. Then, a small laugh. Annalise finds herself smiling hilariously at the outside of Prince

Darren's door, laughing harder to herself while she passes it by. The servants must think her insane, but Annalise is well past the point of caring when she takes the castle steps in twos, pushing open the doors to the garden and forgetting to shut them on her way out. *I need to get out of here.* Trembling, she paces down the path to the beach with only the moon to light her way.

The closer she gets to the Falvedrie Sea, the more the temperature sinks, a brisk coldness seeping beneath Annalise's cloak and the silk of her chemise. But the goddess couldn't care less. As soon as she throws open the gate to the beach, Anna's feet take flight. She bolts toward the water, letting her cloak billow around her, willing every limb of her body to be constructed in a way so that like the birds, she could fly away from this nightmare of a place. *Couldn't I have been blessed with flight magic, or even shapeshifting so that I could leave this all behind me once and for all?*

Still, as appealing as the idea of running away sounds, Annalise knows she doesn't have the heart to do it. *I couldn't leave Aimelie. And what about when Modgen comes back?* If *he does. And what about—* Anna shoves the thought away, trying to avoid thinking about her Master of the High Council, until her hands begin to twitch and a cold fog escapes her mouth. She loses her train of thought as her heart begins to race, the breath in her throat growing shallower by the second.

Annalise brings a hand to her neck, witnessing the entire surface of the Falvedrie Sea begin to freeze over, her dark eyes nearly missing the black silhouette farther down the beach. The waves crack, ice splintering as her magic forces the water to lock its shape. For a moment, the world stands still and the sea is silent and even the stars seem to watch in awe, until the goddess's fingers tighten around her porcelain throat. *I ... can't ... breathe*, Annalise realizes with no small amount of fear. Clutching at her neck, the princess unclasps her cloak, shaking in her ivory chemise. She gasps, first from fear of not being able to breathe, then from a man approaching her with rapid steps.

"Annalise?" Oliver comes close enough for the princess to make out the perfect curve of his jawline. "Annalise, are you all right?"

If she could respond, she would, but first, she needs to conquer her rising panic. Annalise places a hand on her heart while pointing to her throat. "I ..." A gasp. "Can't ..." Another gasp. "Breathe," she finishes, even the damp sand beneath their feet crystallizing from her uncontrolled magic.

"It's okay." Oliver takes a cautious step across the frozen sand. "You can. If you couldn't, then you wouldn't be talking right now." A look of concern after seeing her cloak on the ground, then a glance at her nightdress. "Can you take a deep breath for me?"

Just try to calm down, Anna. You can do this. With a ragged inhale, the goddess draws a longer breath.

"How about one more?" Oliver encourages her, his green eyes continuing to assess her condition.

The princess hesitantly lowers her hand from her neck, managing to suck down more of the salty air than before.

Oliver watches the frozen water begin to melt, the waves lazily returning to their normal state while Annalise relaxes her muscles. He bends to retrieve her cloak, dusting off the sand before wrapping it around her shoulders and securing the clasp. "Might I ask why you're out at this late hour ... in your nightclothes?"

"I could ask the same of you," Anna rebukes. "Minus the nightclothes."

He gives her a look. "I take a walk on the beach if I know I won't be able to sleep. And you?" Oliver moves a half-step closer, peering into her brown gaze. "What's wrong, Annalise?"

Above them, only the half-moon bears witness to their interaction. She shakes her head while tears threaten her composure, though it's not like she had any to begin with. *I can't tell him,* Annalise reminds herself sorrowfully. *I can't.* The goddess pinches the bridge of her nose in a vain attempt to tether her mind to logic, but when Oliver adjusts her cloak to keep out more of the wind, her face cracks.

Without thinking, she throws her arms around him, releasing a sob into his shoulder. "Everything!" Annalise cries, breathing in his pine and cedar scent, shaking when his hands press against her back. "Everything," she repeats, while Oliver holds her tighter, his thumb brushing over the nape of her neck beneath tangled locks of hair.

VEGA

Modgen Sprightly chucks a pear at each of the females with a frown deeper than the Falvedrie Sea. "Well," he shakes his empty coin purse, "that was the last of it. We best pray that our plan will work."

Vega bites into her fruit, the sweet juice dripping down her petite chin. "It will. It has to." *If it doesn't, I don't know what we will do.* The master manipulator lets her eyes wander aimlessly around their rented room. The inn is much nicer than the one they stayed at in Javir, but there isn't much space to fit four people. *One more day,* Elouthera reminds herself. *One more day, and we will find out if the fates will allow me to finally be reunited with Dimity.*

"We should be heading out now to finalize plans with our girls," Narelle claims, standing from her seat. The tan woman turns to Eden. "Don't forget that necklace. I wouldn't dare want it falling into the wrong hands."

Vega watches with concerned eyes as Narelle and Eden ready for their departure to the Southern Hall of Nesvla. "Be careful," she needlessly reminds them as they slip through the door. Though, after the group's previous encounters with Anzac, it doesn't seem unnecessary.

Elouthera would go with them, but she has already paid her penance to the Nevs. *And, with any luck, that will be the last time I do.* It wasn't that the formerly employed fortune tellers gave her any reason to be unhappy with them, it is only that, against Vega's every intention, a wound still festers from the time when her mother chose them over her. *My mother*, Vega cringes inwardly at the thought of Cyndeya's death. She stuffs down the guilt before it rises to consume her.

If there is any good news, however, it is that the local guild of Nevs has decided to help Elouthera and her allies during the ceremony tomorrow, and potentially, when Dimity—*or Princess Annalise*—needs help collecting information about the kingdom. Vega convinced the oracles to concentrate their efforts on the areas surrounding Eldire, so with any luck, there will be an uptick in bawdy courtesans on every street corner around the Nesvlan capital. *It wasn't even that hard to sway them*, she recognizes. *I guess being the daughter of their original High Priestess had something to do with it.*

As though he could read Vega's thoughts, Modgen shifts against his post at the wall. "Do you think they will accept her? Eden, I mean."

The Goddess of Dreams and Mystery runs a hand through her shoulder-length black hair. "I hope so. From the way they reacted a few days ago, I assume they will." Vega can only pray that the Nevs' loyalty to Eden as their new High Priestess will remain untainted.

A pensive nod. "It helps that she has your endorsement."

Elouthera nods back. "She has the gift of sight; she just needs more practice. But I'm confident that one day, she will be as good a seer as Laraya Sharpkey was."

"She was able to channel Desmond."

Vega smiles softly. "And you, before you rescued us at the Oronian Clocktower. She said you came to her as a red knight."

Modgen betrays a wide grin, uncrossing his arms to shove his pale hands into his pockets. "A knight," the redhead reflects, mostly to himself. "That'd be the day. Women fawn over knights a lot more than they do a former royal treasurer."

A roll of Vega's lime-green eyes. "If you're that desperate, I'm sure they would accommodate you over at The Citrine."

"What kind of man do you take me for?" Modgen gives her a look of baffled reproach.

The goddess blushes. "I'm sorry." She tries hiding a smile. "It just sounded like you could use some help."

"Some help?" Modgen repeats with the faintest bit of amusement. "I can find myself a decent woman, thank you very much. It just takes a little more effort when I have to share a room with three females every night."

"A situation in which you can't even get one of *those* women to fall for you."

The redhead scoffs, failing to keep a grin from spreading across his otherwise shocked face. He stalks over to Vega, who sits perched on the side of the bed. "First, you call me insufferable; now you tell me I have no courting game." Modgen Sprightly leans forward to peer into Vega's cat-like eyes. "If I didn't know any better, I'd say *you're* the one with relationship problems."

Vega swallows, attempting to brush off the sting of his words. "Why? Because I'm good at pointing out the obvious?"

Modgen opens his mouth, then closes it. Slowly, he pulls away, sitting himself in a wooden chair to lean back and cross his boots. "You know, you really are nothing like Annalise."

Something in his tone makes Elouthera cringe, and the goddess folds her arms, if only to shield herself from more arrow-tipped words. *Gods, what am I doing? This is the exact opposite of why I came here, isn't it? I decided to help Dimity so that we could save these people, not become enemies with them.* Vega sighs deeply, turning her up-tilted eyes to face Modgen's blue ones. "I'm sorry for the way I've been acting recently." She shakes her head, locks of jet-black hair swishing with the movement. "I swear, this isn't how I really am." Vega leans forward, pressing her forearms onto her knees. "The truth is, I haven't exactly had an easy time making friends."

A sarcastic laugh. "You don't say."

She gives Modgen a look that has him shutting his lips for her to finish. "When my mother left me ..." A frown at the remembrance of Cyndeya's suffocation a few days ago. "I guess I began closing people off. And when I started going to school at the House of Perception, I finally made a close friend ... who turned out to be one of Anzac's shadow pawns."

"Good gods," Modgen curses from his seat. "I'm sorry."

Vega shrugs. "Don't be. It kind of worked out, I guess. Christa held me hostage on a ship headed for Empeirus, which just so happened to wreck near the Javirian coast. And once I ran into Eden there, and we were taken to the Oronian Clocktower, you eventually rescued us."

"Eventually," Modgen repeats with a smile.

The goddess returns it shyly. "And now, I'm the closest I've ever been to meeting Dimity, but I'm nowhere near the person I should be."

Modgen swats his hand. "It's never too late to start

over," he reminds her. "So, you haven't had the best luck with people so far. Well, I'm here to change that. And so are Eden, and Narelle, and Dimity."

Blinking her bright green eyes, Vega gives him a subtle nod.

"I can't promise that I won't hurt you," Modgen continues, "but I do promise that I won't do it intentionally."

She doesn't know why, but the sentence has Vega's lips blooming into a lovely smile, one that Modgen reflects with absolute enthusiasm.

His expression transforms into one of contemplation, a thumb and forefinger pressed around his chin. "I wanted to ask you about something."

A raise of Vega's black brows. *Oh, gods.* Her heart begins to beat ten times quicker.

"That thing that your mother said, right before Anzac intervened ..." Modgen shifts his cobalt gaze toward their room's small window. "Do you think it's true?"

Elouthera releases a breath. "About the demigod business?"

He nods his reddish curls.

A sigh. "I don't know," Vega admits. "She did also mention that your blood was valuable, just like Lillian did, back when we were ransacked in the forest."

For once, Modgen falls quiet, his thumb gently

tapping the arm of his chair. "You don't suppose she's right, do you? That I'm actually a demigod?"

The goddess shrugs. "There are legends throughout history that speak of them. Hell, before a few months ago, I wouldn't have believed in my own divinity." Elouthera offers him a thin smile. "I suppose anything is possible."

Modgen scoffs, palming his face.

"You said you never met your father, so that narrows it down to the male gods, at least. Now, we just have to figure out which one it could be." Vega bites a lip in thought. "Do you have any strange callings? An attraction to a certain element?" An ornery grin. "Magical abilities that you're keeping hidden?"

He gives her an unamused look. "Do demigods even have magical abilities?"

"No idea." Elouthera chuckles.

Modgen releases a long sigh, shaking his head. "Vega, I'm just a man who never met his father. It's as simple as that."

She would press further, but Vega is the last person who needs reminding that sometimes, it's easier to believe a harmless fib than the cold truth. "Okay," the goddess feigns agreement, letting their conversation drop into a comfortable silence.

It breaks when they hear a knock at the door.

Modgen reaches the handle first. Hesitantly, he twists it to reveal a stranger with a face as giddy as a child's.

"For after the ceremony, tomorrow!" the man exclaims, shoving two sets of orange and gold ribbon wands into Modgen's hands. "Wave them as Prince Darren and Princess Annalise journey back to the castle as husband and wife!"

No sooner do Vega and Modgen look up from the silk streamers than the delivery man disappears, leaving them to ruminate about tomorrow's plan.

Vega swallows. "Do you really think this will work?"

If Modgen's silence doesn't answer her question, his expression surely does. He tosses the ribbon wands onto the bed, bouncing his weight from heel to heel. Finally, he grabs Vega's hand. "Let's go."

"Where?" the goddess wonders aloud, following him out of their room.

"To the Nevs' hall, like Narelle and Eden have." Modgen kicks the door shut behind them. "The only thing that will help me sleep better tonight is if we go over our plan another twenty times."

Descending the stairs of the inn, Elouthera releases a sharp breath. "You're right," she admits. "Besides," her stomach tightens with unease, "I have a feeling we will need all the help we can get."

AIMELIE

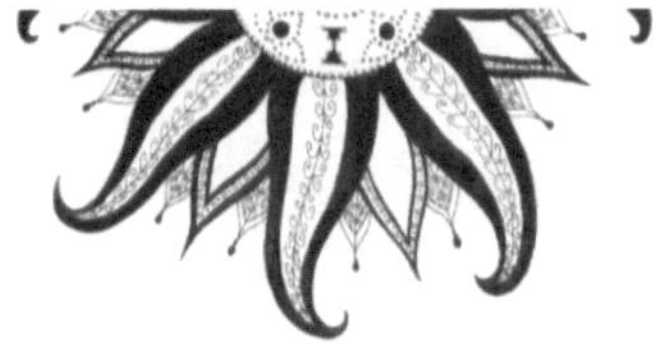

The mood is dreary for being the eve of the royal wedding, but if Aimelie had to guess, tomorrow will be even drearier. She peeks her head into the castle's temple, catching her sister's reflection in one of the golden mirrors while she prays for the fourth time today. Melie sighs, her heart aching at the loss of Master Tasman, but even more so for Annalise, whose grief has starved her of any socialization over the past few days. At any other time in life, Aimelie would have been content to let Annalise take as long as she needed to avoid dances and dinners, but … *Queen Minerva is starting to get antsy, I can tell.*

The clock chimes to announce the arrival of noon, and Melie opens her mouth before palming the side of her face. *No*, she decides, shaking her honey-blonde curls. *I'll give her until dinner before I bother her.* Leaving Annalise to her reverent thoughts, Aimelie makes the short trek back to the main part of Eldric Castle, just across a covered bridge. She meanders her way to the Great Hall with slow footfalls, letting the tension in her stomach loosen as much as she can allow. When the youngest princess of Empeirus arrives at the room, she finds it covered from floor to ceiling in lavish decorations and filled with about fifteen different people, almost none of whom she is familiar with.

"Your Highness." A kind voice from her left catches her by surprise.

Aimelie lets out a sigh of relief. "Master McHenry." She curtsies. "I'm glad to see you. I don't think I will know half the guests at the wedding tomorrow."

A light chuckle. "I don't think Annalise will, either." Oliver flushes. "*Princess* Annalise, please forgive my insolence." He shakes his head. "I don't know what's gotten into me, lately."

"I don't think Lady Catherine does, either." Aimelie exchanges an uncomfortable glance with Oliver while Prince Darren flirts with the scandalously dressed woman. "Do you think it's that he doesn't know we're here, or that he just doesn't care?"

Annalise's Master of the High Council opens his

mouth but thinks better of it. Melie wants to press him further, but Oliver's jaw seems to tighten even more when the Crown Prince of Nesvla sings across the Great Hall.

"Princess Aimelie, where is your sister? And don't tell me that she's still sulking in the temple." Prince Darren stalks toward them with perfectly combed hair and a dashing smile. "I hear it on good account that a wedding gift has been delivered for us today. Perhaps it would lift her spirits if we opened one a day early?"

Aimelie's frown is evident. "I'm sorry to disappoint you, my lord, but Annalise is indeed 'still sulking in the temple.'" *And to be honest, her energy might be better put to use there than it would be playing the witless fool when she's with you.* "She and Master Tasman were close. I dare say it will take some time for her to work through her devastation."

"There will be plenty of time for that after the wedding." Prince Darren begins heading toward the Great Hall entrance without so much as a goodbye, until his fleeting presence catches Queen Minerva's sea-blue gaze.

"Darren," she calls across the room from a table filled with corked champagne. "Wherever are you heading to?"

"To retrieve my future wife."

"Nonsense," Minerva tells him with a plastered smile. "We can send someone else to find her so you can continue to greet your out-of-town guests." The Queen of

Nesvla scans the room for her next victim. "Master McHenry, you don't seem too disposed at the moment. Would you care to scour Eldric Castle for its future princess?"

Prince Darren stops dead in his tracks.

Oliver points to his own chest with a stare so blank, it could make parchment look intricate. "Me?" A quick bow. "Of course, Your Grace." On a heel, he leaves, neglecting to catch the ire dripping from Darren's face.

Apparently, Queen Minerva doesn't catch it, either. She lets out a modest squeal when her royal courier places a painted white box onto a nearby table. "Darren, darling," she prefaces her command. "Come and open your first nuptial gift."

Aimelie squabbles. "Without consulting Annalise?" the princess asks shyly, but her attempt falls on deaf ears.

Rolling his eyes, Darren meets his mother at the table, pausing to bring a hand to his nose. Slowly, he untucks the fine white parchment from beneath a gold ribbon, reading aloud the writing on its front. "Happy wedding," the prince states, his gaze changing from annoyance to confusion.

"Who is it from?" Queen Minerva asks, peering more closely at the present, then taking a step back while she, too, seems to cover her nose.

Prince Darren shrugs. "There isn't any name." Carefully, he unties the silk bag on top of the box, withdrawing a piece of jewelry.

One of the guests leans forward beside the prince. "That's a nice ring," he comments, ignoring Darren's scoff.

"I'm a prince. I do not need more rings." Prince Darren hands it to the man for examination, unlacing the glittering gold ribbon.

Aimelie stares curiously as the nobleman holds the ring toward the ceiling, letting the skylight better illuminate it. "Huh," he sounds in the silence. "There's an engraving on the inside of it. Looks like it says … *Harwick?*"

Melie's face withers like a rose in winter. *Harwick.* For a split second, she is back at Larking Castle, standing in a warm embrace before a roaring fireplace. *Harwick.*

Prince Darren squints. A huff of laughter. "What an odd thing to give as a wedding present."

The youngest princess of Empeirus blinks, the words tumbling out of her mouth with a rattling breath. "Harwick?" she repeats, praying that she misheard every syllable of the name.

The nobleman nods.

Aimelie hikes up her pink skirts, crossing the room while every piece of the puzzle begins to fit together. The nondescript box, the ring, the lack of correspondence … She reaches the table, pressing her own hand to her nose at the hint of an ungodly smell. Prince Darren moves to open the lid, but Melie practically screams at his idiocy. *"Don't open that box!"* the princess orders, while the nobleman drops a golden band in the palm of her outstretched hand.

The metal lands with an imperceivable thud, but Aimelie knows exactly what it is before it even touches her skin, an exhale of dread escaping her lips. *Linden's family ring*, the princess thinks with horror. Closing her trembling hand, she ignores the prince's dark gaze, spinning in the opposite direction before she dares to see the contents of what is obviously Adrianna's gift.

Aimelie makes it halfway out of the Great Hall when she hears their gasps and curses, followed by an occasional gag. There is nothing for Melie to do besides will her slippered feet to move faster, panic clawing at the back of her throat when she catches the last of Darren Eldric's voice:

"What kind of person would *do* something like this?"

Something cracks inside of the youngest princess, tears flooding her big blue eyes. *A* monster *would do this.* Aimelie grits her teeth so hard, they could crush glass. *A heartless, merciless,* evil *monster. And by some cruel joke of the gods, that monster is my sister.* Thoughtlessly, Melie slips on Linden's golden ring before her groans of frustration turn into sobs, her cries muffled only by the hands over her ruddy face. Amidst her frantic mind, one thought rises above the rest: *I need to find Annalise.*

With desperate footsteps, Princess Aimelie Larking finds her way across the castle bridge, caring less about her appearance than Prince Darren's jokes. Her reddened eyes claw through the temple, but Annalise is nowhere to be found. On a whim, she decides to check her chambers, the Throne Room, and even the drawing room, to no avail. *Where is she?* Aimelie frets, waiting for a page to open the enormous mahogany doors before exposing her blotchy face to the outside world.

Aimelie whips her blonde curls to and fro, choking back tears during her trot past the gardens and toward the docks, even though it is likely the last place her sister would be. Rounding a tree, she searches the area surrounding a familiar vessel, locking eyes with Captain Ivo in front of their future ship. She hasn't mentioned her paramour to anyone other than Annalise, but the princess must tell someone about the news right now, lest it destroy her.

"She killed him!" Aimelie begins, her limbs quaking. "Adrianna killed Linden!"

Captain Ivo doesn't say anything before pulling her into his arms.

"I can't do it," Melie confesses into the sleeve of Ivo's shirt. "I can't live with what she's done."

"Yes, you can, Your Highness," Ivo tells her in the softest tones she has ever heard him use.

Aimelie lifts her gaze, releasing a loud sob.

Captain Ivo holds her forearms with reassuring stability. "You can, because you won't be going through this alone."

ANNALISE

Annalise Larking presses her forehead against folded hands, murmuring the same prayer that she has been praying for the last few hours. Having paused her reverence only to relieve herself, she continues nursing the hope that her words are reaching the ether. *Perhaps I should pray another to ensure that Lazarus hears me,* she deliberates. Though, for some reason, Dimity has a feeling that her godly father can hear her even when she isn't in the sanctity of a temple. In whispered tones, the Goddess of Wisdom and Justice sends up one last plea, asking the gods to guide her toward a destiny that will help her fulfill her mission of saving this world, however her own mortal story may play out.

The princess seals her lips, rising from the floor to

stretch her knees, which are sore from kneeling for so long. Padding over to an array of miscellaneously shaped candles, she lights one with a finger kissed by flame. *For Tasman*, Annalise offers silently. *May you find the peace this world seldom brought you.* She adjusts her crown before hearing footsteps click against the floor, tearing her brown eyes from the altar.

"How long have you been here?" Annalise asks her Master of the High Council, having seen him on the surface of the reflecting pool earlier.

"Only a few minutes. I didn't want to interrupt." Oliver paces a few steps forward from where he had been sitting at the far end of the temple. "Your betrothed has requested your presence in the Great Hall. Something about an early wedding present, I believe."

Annalise lowers her tired eyes to the floor, her lips set in an incessant frown. Smoothing out the wrinkles in her plain black gown, the princess starts walking, letting Oliver join her at her side. They walk in comfortable silence, their footsteps nearly in sync as the vaulted ceiling of the temple fades from view.

Oliver breaks the silence. "So," he begins softly. "Are you excited for tomorrow?"

Any other bride would grin with glee, but a sarcastic smirk rises to Anna's lips. "I'm excited for it to be over."

An awkward pause as Oliver rubs the back of his neck. "Would it be impolite to ask why?"

Annalise presses her mouth shut, shrugging her thin shoulders. "Wedding jitters," the princess suggests, her insides shriveling at the lie.

Oliver nods, eyeing the entrance to the Great Hall. "I, um ..." He stops his footsteps to reach into his breast pocket. "I got you something. A wedding present, that is."

The ivory silk bag is soft in Anna's palm, her fingers carefully untying its ribbon.

"I'm sure it's nowhere near as extravagant as the gifts you'll be receiving tomorrow, and it's certainly nowhere close to the Nesvlan throne," he flusters, "but I figured it would be a nice memento, of sorts."

With a fluid gentleness, Annalise withdraws a fine silver chain weighed down by a lavender pearl, its bail embellished with several sparkling diamonds. She releases a breath of awe, her dark eyes blinking at the sincerity of the gesture. "One of the rare lavender pearls of the Savek Coast."

A nod. "I wrote to the local jeweler in Cordel and had him design it." Oliver shrugs. "It had to be shipped here, but it's legitimate."

You're telling me that you put more thought into making this necklace for me than Darren Eldric has put into our entire relationship? Her brown eyes brim with tears. "It's beautiful." Annalise stares at it wordlessly for one moment, then two, pressing a hand to her stomach as a self-reminder to remain composed.

"It's also okay if you don't like it—"

"I love it!" Annalise bursts, a blush staining her porcelain cheeks. "In fact," she hands the necklace to Oliver while unhooking the gaudy one around her neck, "I'm going to wear it right now." The princess strips herself of a thick, citrine and gold collar, padding to the side of the corridor to drop it into a servant's trembling hand. "Go. Give your family the life they deserve." Annalise beholds the young Nesvlan glance between the jewels and herself until he disappears with hastened footfalls.

When Oliver meets her again, she retrieves his wedding gift, delicately clasping it around her neck and centering the pearl above her sternum. He is right. Compared to the Nesvlan jewelry Annalise has grown accustomed to wearing, it isn't anywhere near as lavish. The silver chain is fine and dainty, and the diamonds adorning the top of the pearl are petite like the rest of it. But for the first time in what feels like decades, Annalise almost feels like herself again. *It's ... me,* she reflects with no small amount of happiness. *Not the me that I am for Aimelie, not the me that Darren Eldric wants me to be. Just me.* Annalise meets Oliver's pine-green gaze. "Thank you."

"There's my blushing bride," Prince Darren calls to her from outside the Great Hall doors. "I'm afraid you've missed the festivities," he informs her, looking down his nose. "What took you so long?"

She ignores his pointed look at Oliver. "I've been at the temple all morning. What did I miss?"

A derisive snort. "Certainly not a warm gesture on behalf of your kindhearted sister."

Annalise presses her brows together. *Which one? Aimelie?*

Darren elaborates. "Queen Adrianna has sent us her well wishes by means of a rotting head. Some chap named Linden, if I remember correctly. Everything else after losing my breakfast is hazy. Anyway, I ..."

His voice trails off while Annalise processes the dreadful news, pressing a hand to her mouth. *Gods, no! Not Linden, not Melie's love.* She reopens her brown eyes to share a sidelong glance with Oliver, whose face reflects as much concern as her own.

"... the cake, and—*Look at me when I'm talking to you!*" Prince Darren spits at his future bride, jealousy staining every corner of his gaze. He moves a step closer. "The gods know I've dealt with enough in terms of this betrothal agreement. Your lack of an appropriate dowry, this godly madness between you and your deranged sister. I will not have you sharing your admiration with another man."

"You mean, the same way you share yours with Lady Catherine?" Annalise strides her own foot forward. "Believe me, we've both made sacrifices with this engagement."

Darren scoffs. "Please. One of these two parties could have had any princess in the kingdom, had your hundred-year-old master not been so desperate to rekindle our agreement."

"Desperate?" Annalise's brown eyes glint with the fire she tries so hard to keep inside. "You think I'd ever be *desperate* to marry you?" Her body shakes. "I'd rather *die* than spend the rest of my life chained to a whoring prick like you!" The last words echo against the castle walls, rattling the golden armor of eavesdropping guards.

Darren Eldric's black brows are raised so high above his eyes that they make the vaulted ceiling look low. "Well," the Crown Prince of Nesvla begins, his sea-blue eyes jumping between Annalise and Oliver. "Likewise." Prince Darren leaves their company without any formalities, being sure to shoulder Oliver on his way past him.

Something in the gesture makes Annalise snap. Without thinking, the goddess grabs Oliver's arm, guiding him toward a side door of the castle.

"What are you doing?" her Master of the High Council asks her cautiously. "Annalise," he murmurs, "you very nearly just ruined your chances of securing an unbreakable alliance—"

"To hell with the alliance!" Anna blurts, pulling him through the door and down the granite stairs. *Master Tasman was right. It's not like they would help me, anyway.* "Whether or not there will be a wedding tomorrow, I will leave that up to the fates to decide." She releases his arm, padding toward the dirt training ring in her black silk gown. "For now, I don't want to think about it."

Oliver examines her for a moment, letting his eyes read her own.

She knows what he will see: anger, resentment. *Disappointment*, Annalise realizes as the seconds pass. But she hopes he cannot read the one emotion she has tried so hard to snuff out, the one that had her freezing over the Falvedrie Sea, that had her in tears over a necklace on their jaunt back from the castle's temple.

Without a word, Oliver nods, walking over to retrieve a sword from the wall before tossing it to her. He withdraws his own, swinging the weapon in his hand casually while Annalise adjusts her own footing in the restriction of a corset. With serious green eyes, Oliver questions her from across the dirt: "Ready?"

But Annalise is already swinging, a grunt escaping her perfectly shaped lips.

ADRIANNA

Adrianna Larking cracks her knuckles from the top of her black horse, listening to the sound of five hundred Empeirian soldiers, their golden armor traded for the guise of dark, Javirian leather. She is sure that she has saddle sores from riding for six days straight, but the Queen of Empeirus could take no chances. *Not when Annalise has convinced the Eldrics to side with her. Not when Desmond, my* world, *is somewhere along the border, likely rotting in a prison cell.*

It has been one week since Dria's paramour has sent his message through their bond, and his cryptic words still plague her dreams at night: *"I'm at the border."* Adrianna spent hours focusing on their silent connection, grasping for any shred of additional information that might prove useful in determining which border

Desmond could mean, until at last, her lover divulged two words that changed the game: *"Near Nesvla."*

Hardly words, hardly a whisper.

The brief phrase was enough for Adrianna to temporarily transfer her queenly duties to Renai while she embarked on her mission to bring back the captain. Though Adrianna will not sleep soundly until Desmond is back in her arms, she passed the Nesvlan border days ago, forgoing a likely unsuccessful search in exchange for finding answers at their source. *For if I know one thing, it's that if anyone played a part in Desmond's condition, it would have to be Annalise or this so-called 'Vega.'* No human being could take down the God of Darkness and Decay like that.

Which is what brings Adrianna here, to the Nesvlan capital. That, and her mad idea of somehow managing to cease a royal wedding. The queen turns to her next-in-command after Desmond, her blonde braid swinging with every stomp of her horse's hooves. "Do you think they will suspect us?" she asks him flatly, her throat dry from days of hard travel.

Sir Braydenton shakes his brown ringlets, the scar on his lips shining in the cloud-covered sun. "Not if everything goes according to plan, Your Majesty."

Adrianna closes her icy-blue eyes. *Nothing ever does.* To maintain the element of surprise, the queen has merged her disguised Empeirian men with her Javirian recruits—courtesy of Edris Sharpkey—and exchanged her typical blood-red gown for a tunic and pants. The only difference between her outfit and that of a street pauper is that Adrianna's tunic is layered over golden armor, which the queen likes to remind herself of during the parts of this journey when she feels particularly unattractive.

In the distance, just over the horizon, she can make out the first sight of Eldric Castle's golden domes. The goddess hasn't set foot on Nesvlan soil before, but it would seem that the paintings do a decent job depicting the structure. She wonders what it must be like for her sister—or, *sisters*, since Aimelie has opted to side with Annalise—to live inside a castle other than their former home in Empeirus. *Is she happy?* Dria wonders, the tops of crimson-leafed trees bobbing in and out of her line of sight. *Does Aimelie enjoy spending time in this foreign territory more than she did at home?*

For some reason, her stomach clenches at the notion, but Jedda tucks the feeling away for the time being, trading it for the more comfortable and familiar emotion of anger. *If Annalise had any hand in hurting Anzac ...* Jedda inhales a breath of cold air while her army marches on. *I will make sure her death is long and slow; that she will miss the light of day so much, she will beg for the darkness.*

"Your Majesty," Sir Braydenton addresses her from her right. "It is time for your men to part ways. May I give them the order?"

Her cold blue eyes focus on the faint silhouettes of

archers along the walls of Eldric Castle. *How many men will be lost by the time this is through? Will it be worth it?* Adrianna swallows, pausing her horse at the peak of a hill. "You may."

Sir Braydenton blows a two-toned whistle through this horn, the dark army splitting into two groups. "With that Javirian leather, the Nesvlans should be none the wiser," he assures the queen. "They might conjecture that you gave the order for Javir to attack, but they shouldn't suspect *you* to be here, especially not without seeing any Empeirians on the field."

Queen Adrianna lowers her looking glass and nods her head. Just ahead, a rider retreats up the hill, his carthorse now void of a white box laced with gold ribbon. *Right on schedule.* Any other man delivering a nondescript box the day before the royal wedding would lose his head on the spot, but not one dressed as a royal courier.

"The gift has been delivered, Your Majesty," the messenger notifies his queen.

"Very good, Gareth." With a spine straight as steel, Dria presses her lips together as her army makes the trek toward Eldric Castle. Adrianna is ready to descend from her vantage point at any time, but the plan is to wait for the skirmish to begin. *Only then will I take the long way around the army to sneak into the capital as a civilian.* Logic dictates that Annalise won't be fighting alongside the Nesvlan men, not if the army isn't even hers yet. But if

Adrianna can find a way into the castle, or even a way to draw her out—

Jedda's thoughts freeze when she hears Anzac's voice echo faintly in her mind: *"She did this,"* he relays his message, his words labored but clear. The Dark Goddess panics, practically screaming in her head, *"Did what? What did she do?"* No response. *"Desmond,* please. *What did she do?"* The bond is quiet, its silence having returned to the same fruitless state it had been in for the past week.

Somewhere far ahead of her horse, the first arrow flings into the air, and a battle cry rouses the spirits of her hundreds of soldiers. Without a word to Sir Braydenton, Queen Adrianna Larking snaps the reigns with a vengeance the world has yet to see, sending herself barreling down the Nesvlan hills to plummet into the depths of war.

ADRIANNA

Adrianna slips three golden suns to the urchin under the secrecy of a dark cloak. "Whatever you do, don't stop running," she warns the girl. A drizzle of freezing rain lands on the top of her hood, the leaves of the crimson trees beginning to buckle under the constant pressure of precipitation. *Let us hope that Annalise will do the same.* With confident footfalls, the queen navigates her way through the swarms of Nesvlans plaguing the roads of Eldric, none of them the wiser that a vengeful goddess walks their very paths.

No doubt Annalise and Prince Darren have received their early wedding present by now, but Dria wonders if her army has caught the attention of the Nesvlan throne just yet. *My men were a good distance away from the castle when they split, but I still haven't heard any horn blares.* Her icy-blue eyes peer up at the golden domes of Eldric Castle for only a second, but it's long enough to trigger something like disgust. *How dare she and Aimelie run off to another territory, only to fall into the lap of luxury? How dare Queen Minerva and Prince Darren even accept them, after knowing how treasonous an act that would be against the Empeirian throne?* If Adrianna has anything to do with it, this mistake will be Nesvla's last. *Especially if I find out they had any hand in Desmond's detainment.*

At last, the queen reaches the castle walls, glimpsing the urchin out of the corner of her watchful eye as she stealthily takes position at a market stand near the entrance. With a clipped nod of her head, the girl runs between the first set of guards, then the next, leading them in a semicircle within the castle walls and back out the entrance.

"Get back here, girl!" the frontmost guard yells. "We brook no leniency for trespassers!"

What a pity, japes Dria, who waltzes into the unprotected tunnel.

"Hey, you can't—"

A close of her fist has the dirt beneath the cobblestones smashing its way to the top of the tunnel until the opening is sealed, snuffing out the cries of the townspeople like a candle in the wind. When Adrianna emerges on the other side, she lets the archers on the parapet share their sentiment before sending her own arrows of fire through each of their chests. Smoothing out the fabric of her cloak, Jedda cracks her neck. *Now, to find precious Annalise.*

Adrianna knows her troops will be flanking the front and back of Eldric Castle, so she points her feet in the direction of its lefthand side, hoping that one of the side doors will be unlocked. She pads through a garden in the icy rain, cautiously rounding the golden-domed castle until her gaze locks on a discreet door. *That should work.* She makes it all of two steps toward it before she hears the noise.

It sounds like the clanging of metal, but that isn't what catches her attention. No, that would have to be the female voice seeping through the cacophony, the same lady-like tone that keeps Dria up at night for hours on end. *No ... Could it be that easy?* The goddess swipes her feet over a patch of grass, stealing a glimpse of the scene while her blood begins to boil behind the cover of a tall shrub. Magic pulses through her arms when she finds Princess Annalise Larking swinging a sword beneath a glittering emerald crown.

It pulses even more when her blue eyes recognize her sister's opponent. *No bloody way.* Dria grits her teeth tighter than a vice as her feet carry her toward the training ring, launching her hands forward the moment her boots meet dirt.

Faster than a bolt of Lazarus's lighting, Jedda fires a

sheet of ice beneath Dimity's slippered feet, reveling in the scene of her sister stumbling across the ground. In a matter of seconds, Annalise recovers, dropping her sword to spin an arc of fire off her palm. Adrianna dodges it on quick toes, letting her black hood fall to her shoulders.

"Dria," Annalise whispers with wide eyes, eyes that the queen has never hated so much.

"Well, well," Queen Adrianna drawls. "Isn't this a happy reunion?" A pointed glance at her former Master of the High Council. "Master McHenry, it's nice to see you've chosen the losing side of the battle. Now, I don't have to make additional plans to take you out of this world, too."

Oliver steals a shield from a nearby wall of weaponry.

Jedda moves a step forward, letting a blood-curdling smile stain her face. "I don't know what you were thinking with this whole wedding business. I mean, *you* marrying a prince? And Linden?" A condescending laugh. "I mean, did you honestly think that you could get away with securing a spy in my castle?"

Annalise wrinkles a brow.

Does she not know that Aimelie's lover was collecting intelligence? Dria pushes the thought away to continue savoring the fearful look on her elder sister's face. "In any case, I have only one question which I require an answer to." The goddess lets her magic seep into her fingers. "Where is Desmond?" she asks Annalise, waiting eagerly for a reply to part her pressed lips.

The princess offers another look of confusion. "Dria …" Annalise shakes her head, "I don't know what you're talking about."

The Dark Goddess gives Dimity a somber nod, one that could be misconstrued as understanding by anyone else besides her sister. "If that's the way you want to play this …"

The ice sails past Annalise's head, missing by a margin narrow enough to skim her ear. Touching her fingers to the blood, Anna launches her own icy bolt, a frozen shield forming around her body. Adrianna fires rapid shots of flame to penetrate it, letting every ounce of her rage fuel her attacks.

"I'm in no mood for games, Annalise," the queen growls. "Tell me, *where is Desmond?*"

"I told you, *I don't know!*"

In the process of flinging more shards of ice, Jedda spots Oliver slowly backing himself toward a potential line of exit. She throws an additional bolt toward his head, Dimity tensing visibly when he blocks it just in time with his shield. *Oooh*, Jedda notes with a draconian smile. *You don't seem to like that much, do you?*

As if reading the queen's thoughts, Annalise sends a blast of flame Adrianna's way, the light almost bright enough to block her field of view. When Dria fizzles out the fire with icy palms, she finds her sister with arms tangled in vines, using them to tug on something behind

Adrianna. The queen has a fraction of a second to escape a falling statue, rolling out of the way for momentum to send it barreling toward Annalise.

What a grand idea! As the statue distracts Dimity, Jedda uses the same tactic to wrap her conjured vines around a different set of ankles—only this time, they are Oliver's. With adrenaline on her side, Jedda yanks Oliver off his feet, dragging him across the dirt of the training ring until he reaches her own. His punches are useless when she tangles her vines around each limb of his body. Gripping his brown hair between her fingers, The Dark Goddess presses the tip of an icy bolt into Oliver's neck, the blade sharp enough to draw a bead of blood. "Don't even think about it," she spits, before her sister tries to make a move she will quickly regret.

Annalise hesitantly drops her hands. "Adrianna, *please*." She swallows. "He has no part in this."

A condescending snort. "Oh, judging by the look on your face, I dare say he does." Dria's arms quake with the fury of ten thousand armies. "I'll give you one more chance," she permits Annalise, the last of her self-restraint evaporating with the statement. "*Where is he?*" Adrianna asks between clenched teeth, her unsteady breaths accelerating into panic. "WHERE IS DESMOND?"

"I already told you, *I don't*—"

Dria pulls the back of Oliver's hair, raising her dagger of ice to drive it toward his exposed neck.

"WAIT!" Annalise's scream echoes through the frigid air, the desperation in her eyes melting into a mask of calm when her sister halts her movement. "I'll tell you where he is," she breathes.

The queen's heart thunders in her ears as she waits for half a moment longer.

Annalise matches her fiery stare with unflinching poise. "Darren Eldric has him locked in the dungeon. He's torturing him as we speak."

In the two seconds it takes for Dria to process the statement, something breaks inside of her, the claws of fear gripping her tighter with every breath. Any other day, Adrianna would have second-guessed her sister's claim, but with her even tone and the severity of Desmond's situation ... Dria darts her blue eyes from Annalise to Oliver, then back to Annalise.

With the animosity of a goddess only heard of in legends, Adrianna thrusts Oliver toward Annalise, throwing a shield of ice around herself as she bolts toward the castle door. *A trade,* Dria thinks uselessly, without daring so much as a glance back at her sister and her former master. Using a fire-kissed hand, she burns a hole in the mahogany door large enough to walk through —the same idea she has in mind for Prince Darren's head.

DARREN

Darren Eldric casually re-laces the front of his trousers. He faces the bed, slipping on his undershirt and gold-spun doublet, letting his sea-blue eyes rove over every inch of Lady Catherine's tan body. She gives him a welcoming smile, one which he would gladly explore had he not just accepted her previous invitation.

"Do you think she suspects?" Catherine asks from the top of his blankets.

A huff of annoyance. Darren reflects on his lamentable conversation with Princess Annalise twenty minutes ago, to her last sentence in particular. He allows himself a meager smile. "I'm sure she has her suspicions. But," he rejoins her on the soft fabric, "you can rest assured that nothing will change when we marry." The prince kisses the top of her forehead. "You, first and foremost, are my top priority."

The soft hum of Catherine's voice has him reconsidering her recent proposition, but princes have some responsibilities that lie outside of their chambers, and Darren is no exception. Leaving his mistress to the alternative comforts of his bed, the Crown Prince of Nesvla sneaks out of the room, smoothing the locks of his black hair with deft fingers.

The castle halls are quiet today—especially after this morning's grotesque events and his debacle with his future bride—but Prince Darren still finds himself exchanging pleasantries with several nobles, including a fine-looking woman of about twenty years with eyes that could put the Falvedrie Sea to shame. *Since when have so many beautiful women graced these halls?* He is still caught up in this thought when he waltzes into the Throne Room, and any lascivious ideas shrivel upon the sight of a mass of courtiers.

They are scattered like fallen stars across the orange velvet aisleway, Queen Minerva listening attentively with a thumb and forefinger cradling her chin. *No doubt, this is all about the wedding tomorrow,* Darren believes with no small amount of displeasure. If it were up to him, he and Princess Annalise would have pushed their wedding until next year to avoid the immense stress of only a few weeks of planning. *Then again, if it were up to me, I wouldn't be marrying her in the first place.*

"Good afternoon, Mother," Prince Darren greets the queen from the side of the dais, but she can't seem to hear him over the ceaseless noise. Darren tries again. "How is your day going, Mother?"

Queen Minerva waffles her blue gaze between Darren and her courtiers, pressing her black brows together at her son. "Did you say something?"

The prince rolls his eyes, his perfect teeth gritting in frustration. "I asked how your day—"

The clang is loud enough to stall the words of thirty witless courtiers, every eye falling on a golden helmet rolling its way to the foot of the dais. *What in the name of the gods?* Darren moves a step closer to examine the guard's armor—

Until he chokes, something resembling the vines of a plant constricting around his neck, tight enough to turn his face purple. Somewhere in the background, the prince can see a crowd of people running for the door, the orange aisle runner erupting into flames on their way out, lighting up some of their garish dresses. And above Darren's fleeting breath, above the sound of his mother's frantic cries and the dissonance of their pompous nobles is a blonde woman, her body emerging from behind his shoulder to delight in his suffocation. The vines loosen their grip enough for Darren Eldric to suck down a gasp of air.

"What are you?" Darren chokes, the Throne Room burning before him. "Some kind of witch?" *A former lover?*

As if the state of the Throne Room isn't any indication of their misery, the frames of the stained-glass windows rattle at the sound of a deep horn blare, a noise Darren has never lived to hear until just now, but knows to mean one thing:

We are under siege.

The woman twitches her hand to guide the vines around his extremities, pinning his arms and legs to his body. "Now is not the time for questions, Prince Darren." She moves closer, Queen Minerva wailing behind her. Holding up an ivory hand, he watches claws of ice rise from her fingertips, each point sharp enough to draw blood with a single swipe. "Tell me where you are keeping Desmond, and maybe I will show you mercy."

Darren swallows. "I have no idea who Desmond is."

The pain is excruciating, every nail slicing through his cheek with ungodly force. Prince Darren bellows, his mother echoing the sentiment with her own mortified screams.

"*Please!*" Queen Minerva begs. "There must be some misunderstanding."

The woman whirls on a heel, her blonde braid swinging with the movement. "Misunderstanding?" she sneers with something like hatred. "My precious sister, Annalise, told me that your son has been holding Desmond prisoner in your dungeon. *Tell me if I'm misunderstanding.*"

"You are! I know all the names of our captives, and not one of them goes by Desmond!" Queen Minerva's eyes meet Darren's the moment she realizes just who this female is. She turns back to the woman. "Your Majesty," she adds haphazardly, stumbling into a curtsy.

Queen Adrianna snorts at her attempts at royal etiquette, pinning her icy-blue stare back on Darren. "You might be a pretty family to look at, but you have half the wit of a stone." Opening and closing her fist, a plethora of icy arrows hurdles toward the prince's head from all angles, his face contorting into the physical image of fear itself.

Queen Minerva's plea pierces the air of the Throne Room. "She lied to you! *Please,* I'll do anything to save my son!"

Darren Eldric releases a shriek at the last second, until the arrows suddenly stop, dropping to the floor to melt into shards. Heaving, the prince regards the Empeirian queen with a horrified gaze as she gives his mother a bone-chilling smile.

"I want that in writing."

ANNALISE

Annalise watches anxiously as Oliver catches his breath on the dirt floor of the training ring. The princess tries to pretend she isn't ashamed of what she's done, but she feels her stomach sinking into a pit of guilt the moment his green gaze meets hers.

Oliver rubs the back of his skull where Adrianna had held him by the hair moments earlier. "Prince Darren doesn't know what's coming for him," he says quietly with Annalise approaching on shaky feet.

"I know." A pained expression falls upon her elegant face. She turns her chin in the direction of the castle. "Maybe I should—"

"*Get down!*" Oliver tugs Annalise to the ground with a forceful hand, her crown tumbling across the dirt before an arrow plants itself into the nearest wall.

The princess drops her eyes to Oliver's, rolling off him with faint embarrassment. From her seat on the ground, she peers carefully over the hedges, until her dark gaze makes contact with something from her nightmares. On the far hillside, a Javirian army marches on Nesvlan soil, Annalise's heart pounding with every step it takes toward Eldric Castle. *Gods. It can't be.*

"We need to get out of here." Oliver gets to his knees.

Annalise follows suit, though her expression suggests otherwise. "But Aimelie; I need to find her!"

"You're no good to her dead, Annalise," he reminds her. "Right now, we need to get you somewhere safe."

Anna opens her mouth, but her voice is drowned out by the sound of a long horn blare. She meets his waning gaze. *Eldric Castle is under siege.*

As much as the goddess wants to argue, she can't deny the logic in Oliver's words. He helps Annalise rise from the ground, putting himself between her and the incoming army. Every footfall feels like a mile as she follows her Master of the High Council toward an opening in the garden, ducking behind each accommodating bush. Annalise keeps going until they reach the exit.

Her ears fill with a gruesome bellow.

The princess turns to behold a longsword slicing its way across Oliver's abdomen, the grin on the Javirian soldier's face all but the spitting depiction of victory. "*No!*" Dimity hears someone scream, realizing a moment later that the voice is hers. Without a second thought, the goddess summons a blade of ice and swipes it clean across the soldier's throat, his mouth filling with blood until his lips kiss the ground.

Oliver has met the earth, too, only his lips face the sky.

Annalise spills to the grass, crawling over to his body. "Oh, gods, *no!*" she cries, tears filling her eyes.

"*Go,*" Oliver tells her with pale lips, but the goddess shakes her head.

"I'm not leaving you." She clenches her jaw.

A wince through heavy breaths. "You said it yourself," Oliver reasons, "I have no part in this."

Annalise sobs. "I was wrong. You *do* have a part in this." She flusters, the tang of blood filling her nostrils. "I need you." She opens Oliver's doublet, peeling his undershirt halfway up his torso to expose the wound. It is deep, and bleeding heavily, as evidenced by his growing shades paler by the minute. *Gods.* Her dark eyes peruse every inch of his body as she looks for something that might help her keep him tethered to this world.

"Annalise," Oliver whispers to her, his unbloodied hand brushing her cheekbone. "I wish we could have had more time together."

But the goddess shakes her head. "No," she tells him under narrow eyes. "Don't you *dare* say that to me." With a slash of her hand, a wall of ice blazes around them in a circle, Annalise's hands deftly moving to unbuckle the belt around Oliver's waist. She pulls it free, opening his jaw to thread it between his teeth. "I already lost my parents; I'm not going to lose you, too." Huffing with fear and dread, Annalise hikes up her skirts, slipping a dagger from the garter around her leg. The light of blue fire dances against Oliver's tired face while she focuses on heating it.

When the silver metal is almost red, Annalise knows it is time. With a prayer to her father, she presses the molten blade to his open wound, watching it sear his skin. Oliver screams, his jaw deadlocked around the belt as his teeth sink deeply into the leather. Annalise withdraws the dagger, observing tendrils of smoke rising from his stomach while he catches his breath, the sound of his residual cries lessening by the second as she pulls his shirt back over the cauterized wound.

Oliver spits out his bit. "Some … warning … would have been … nice," he manages between breathes as the princess secures her dagger back under her skirts.

Wordlessly, she hauls Oliver to a seated position, his green eyes drooping with exhaustion. "Do you think you can walk?"

"Of course." Oliver sounds about as convincing as a blood-deprived man can be, but he manages to wrap his arms around Annalise enough for her to help him stand. He leans on Anna with heavy arms, his head tilting toward the earth.

"Stay with me, Oliver," she offers uselessly. He is practically a deadweight, but the princess shimmies him through a hole in her icy wall to spot the stables up to their left. *It isn't likely to be any safer than the gardens were, but if most of the fighting is taking place at the northern entrance of the castle, maybe we will stand a chance of securing a horse.* With the distant sound of war behind them, Anna carves another wall across their path, this one made of fire. *Perhaps that will help keep any more inquisitive soldiers from moseying their way toward us.*

Her feet peddling them to the now-unmanned stable, Annalise leans Oliver against the wall to untie a chestnut horse. She leads it out of its stall, hurriedly tacking it with a saddle and reigns before hoisting herself onto the animal. "I won't be of much help getting you up here, so—"

Oliver groans, hauling himself into the saddle behind her, nearly collapsing upon reaching a sitting position.

Okay. That will do. "Hold on!" Anna commands, giving the reigns a snap to send them trotting their way out of the stable. She leads them down to the beach, then through some untamed thicket, going out of her way to ensure she puts as much distance between them and the army as she can. Riding in silence, the princess ponders the bewildering nature of their situation, riffling through her memories for some obscure hint about a conflict between Javir and Nesvla, but finds none. The horse steps over a fallen log.

A horn sounds again, but this time, it is a single blare.

One horn blow, Annalise processes. *Two blows indicate conflict, but a single blow following the first pair means that the conflict has been resolved. What kind of castle can't defend itself for a whole ten minutes?* Anna closes her brown eyes, gritting her teeth as she puts together the pieces of the puzzle. "Didn't Adrianna have plans for acquiring Javir's iron ore production?" she asks Oliver over her shoulder.

A slight pause. "She did."

Annalise shakes her dark locks. "And she is here, now, at the same time a Javirian army is marching on Nesvlan soil." A bitter laugh, followed by a period of quiet. "My sister marched her army here after she learned I was to marry Prince Darren."

Oliver says nothing, the feeling of his arms around her waist the only assurance that he remains conscious.

"She has grown her army," she repeats, "and I threw away my shot at securing a Nesvlan alliance." *No doubt Adrianna will have done something to buy Queen Minerva's loyalty, especially after I sent her chasing down her son. Why else would the siege be declared null minutes after it began?*

They emerge out of the brush to meet a dirt road, not a single rider anywhere to be seen. Down the forested path they go, the sound of the horse's hooves lulling Annalise into a state of deep concentration. It breaks when Oliver leans his forehead against her shoulder. She tries not to think about it much, tries to tell herself that he does so out of blood loss, but it comforts her in a way she never imagined—a sentiment that scares her more than she wants to admit.

The trees open up at the bottom of a hill, the dirt path forking into two cobblestone paths, and Annalise does her best to remain calm and choose the one that feels more promising. *For now, we need to find somewhere to lay low until Oliver is well enough to travel a longer distance.* The town they reach is hardly bustling—a likely effect of the siege—but at the far end of the main road, smoke rises from what looks to be an inn. Annalise trots their horse to the livery stable next door, sliding off to help Oliver down. Digging into Oliver's coin purse, she tosses a few coins to the stable hand and places an arm under Oliver's shoulder to help him walk inside.

The inn brims with energy, its air smelling of sweet smoke so thick, one could cut it with a knife. The strumming of a lutist meshes with the gambling of men, and in every corner of the common room stands at least one courtesan—most of them taken, but some of them still searching for their next client with prying eyes. *I never thought it'd be this crowded,* Annalise thinks as they approach the front counter.

"How long?" the unenthused woman asks, one of her long fingers already looped through the hole of a key.

"Just one night." The princess exchanges a silver moon for the key, helping Oliver up the staircase with one eye watching their backs. A quarter of the way up the steps, Anna pilfers a pitcher of water from a half-empty table, tucking it as discreetly as she can into the folds of her black gown. When they reach the top, Annalise unlocks the door to their room, locking it as soon as they enter. She places the key and the water on a shoddy dresser before propping Oliver up into a seated position on the bed.

With his back against the wall, she opens his doublet to lift his shirt once again, monitoring the status of his wound. *It's not bleeding anymore, so that's a blessing.* Silently, she maneuvers Oliver's arms through blood-stained clothes, his green eyes still teetering on the edge of unconsciousness.

"Here." Annalise hands him the stolen pitcher of water. "Small sips. You need to recover your blood supply." She frowns, worry lacing her brown eyes.

As satisfied as she can be with his current condition, Anna pads to the other side of the room, retrieving her dagger from beneath her gown. Facing Oliver with her back toward the wall, she hikes up her dress to unlace the back of her underskirt, watching it fall to the floor like his jaw. Annalise drops the outer portion of her dress.

"Tell me." Oliver's green eyes are now fully awake. "How much blood have I lost?"

Annalise snorts. "A lot. I was just going to use some of the fabric to make bandages." The goddess retrieves her dagger, sinking to the floor to begin her best attempt at not cutting crooked strips off the bottom of the garment.

"Annalise?" Oliver asks quietly from the bed.

"Hmm?"

A moment of what feels like contemplation. "Why didn't you leave me behind?"

Annalise stops her cutting, glancing at him sidelong. "It's not in my nature to leave injured friends unattended," she repeats the words he once spoke to her what seems like decades ago.

Another second of pensiveness. "Is that what you would call me? Your friend?"

A blush makes its way to her ivory cheeks. "Of course. How couldn't you be, after all we've been through?" Annalise gathers her long strips of fabric and paces back to the bed. Her heart races more than it should when she sits on the edge beside Oliver, who is now shirtless. Carefully, she wraps the makeshift bandages around his waist, ensuring the damaged skin is completely covered. *He'll still need to see a medic, but this is the best I can do, for now.* When she is satisfied, the princess brings together the loose ends of the fabric.

"Annalise."

She looks up from her work to find Oliver studying her

face mere inches away, her brown eyes unintentionally dropping to his lips before meeting his gaze once again.

"You're a good liar," he grins, wincing the second Annalise ties the knot just a little too tight.

Immediately, she rises from the bed, doing her best to remain poised while she slips her tattered petticoat back underneath her dress. "I'm going out for a bit. To look for a medic. Or, to look for a new shirt for you." She scrambles. "One that doesn't smell like blood."

"When should I expect you back?"

"I don't know. Half an hour?" Annalise secures his own belt and coin purse around her small waist and presses the room key to her palm. "Keep drinking," she orders, slipping out the door.

A good liar? Annalise takes the steps in twos as she descends to the front door of the inn. *Does he suppose I'm lying about thinking of him as my friend?* But even Anna cannot pretend that she didn't catch his true meaning, and that specific implication is what makes her blood boil most. *He knows,* the goddess can feel her stomach tightening with embarrassment when she opens the door to fresh air. *He knows, and what's worse is that he's right.*

The runaway princess smoothes her fingers through her dark brown waves, traipsing toward the open-air market. *Why can't things ever be simple? Why couldn't I just love Darren, so that I could have a simple alliance with Nesvla and respect our parents' wishes? Why couldn't I have just left*

Oliver behind, so I could have continued traveling with a better chance of escaping? She tries to convince herself that she could have, but the idea that leaving Oliver could have led to his untimely death makes Annalise want to vomit.

Just ahead, an empty Nev's stand sits vacant from Adrianna's recent persecution of the oracles. Annalise wonders what the fortune tellers might have told her if she had chosen to live a life where her mind wasn't so overrun by her heart. Would a marriage to Darren have gathered her enough forces to stop Jedda and Anzac? Or wouldn't it have made a difference, at all?

Anna's gaze catches on a plain linen shirt in the shop next door, the merchant handing it over graciously for a small sum. "Thank you," she manages, emerging from her thoughts just in time to hear the whinnying of horses carrying three Nesvlan guards covered in golden armor. Discreetly, she turns her back toward them, pretending to be interested in some nearby fruit.

"We're looking for Princess Annalise Larking," one of them grumbles to one of the other merchants. "About twenty years, brown hair and eyes. Last seen wearing a black gown and keeping the company of a dark-haired man."

The princess rumbles the shirt in her hands. *I knew we should have gone farther.* Anna begins walking as casually as she can, slipping through a crack between vendor stands. Trying not to panic, she waits for the guards to exit the other side of the market, but presses her brows together when two emerge from the way they came. She grits her teeth when the guards dismount their horses to mosey through the front door of the inn, where she left Oliver, defenseless in their room. *Bloody hell. Now what?*

Just outside the building, a courtesan leans against the wall, her body draped in citrine-orange robes while she hums a sultry tune. Annalise scampers over to her, reaching once again into Oliver's coin purse. The princess hands her a golden sun. "This is for not asking any questions." She throws a silver moon on top. "And this is for giving me your clothes."

ANNALISE

The door slams shut with a thud, Annalise turning to lock it faster than what should be humanly possible.

"Everything all right?" Oliver questions, hardly catching his belt and the new shirt Annalise throws at his face.

"Put these on," is all she says, before setting down a bottle of wine and disappearing into the water closet.

Oliver slips the fresh linen over his shoulders, letting it hide his makeshift bandages. Waiting for Anna's return, the former master takes another sip of water from his pitcher. He still feels like hell, but at least he isn't as dizzy anymore. *I wonder if she happened to grab any food while she was out.* In less than a minute, the bathroom door opens again, and Oliver witnesses his most private of dreams come to life.

Princess Annalise Larking emerges with citrine-orange robes clinging to her body, the silk hugging every area Oliver has tried to keep himself from imagining. She frantically adjusts one of her sandals, hopping on one foot over to the bottle of wine she left on the dresser before gathering her hair into a top knot and pinning it with a golden hairpin.

On second thought, who needs food? Oliver clears his throat, pulling at his shirt collar. "Just so we're clear, this has absolutely nothing to do with our previous conversation, right?"

The princess smiles mischievously. "No, I just wanted to dress up like a courtesan for you while Nesvlan guards search the inn for our asses."

Oliver pinches the bridge of his nose. "They're searching for us?"

"Right here, right now."

He groans. *Why right here, right now?*

"But I have an idea." Annalise loosens a few strands of hair from her temples, covering the fresh cut on her ear. "If you want to get out of here, I need you to do two things: Follow my lead, and never speak of this to anyone. Understood?"

Oliver blinks his pine-green eyes. "Of course."

"Good. Now rub your eyes. I need you to look drunk." The goddess pinches her fingers around the wick of the bedside candle, using a pinky to smudge the inky soot along the rim of her dark eyes. She reaches over, mussing Oliver's brown hair before adjusting the ties holding the neckline of her silk robes together. The princess cracks her neck. "Well, how do I look?"

Oliver swallows. *Should I tell her the truth?* "You look … like a courtesan." The only discrepancy between Annalise's costume and an actual courtesan's outfit is her emerald and onyx bracelet and the lavender pearl necklace she left dangling around her neck.

The princess grins. "I never thought I'd say this, but … great! And you look like a passable drunk." She hands him the bottle of wine, which appears to be already opened. "Our goal will be to sneak out the front door, hopefully without drawing the attention of the Nesvlan guards. From there, we can grab our horse and head for the coastline." She glances at his abdomen, staring through the layers concealing his wound. "I know movement isn't easy for you, but you should be able to lean on me a little while I walk you down the stairs."

Oliver nods, doing his best not to grunt while the goddess helps him off the bed. She plants the wine bottle in his hand, linking her arm through his.

"Are you nervous?" Anna asks, the two of them pausing before the door.

Oliver sighs. "It's not my first time trying to pull off a

disguise." He remembers his adventures with Modgen Sprightly, back when he first met Annalise, wearing stolen servant's clothes. "First time with a courtesan, though." He tries to stifle a laugh.

Annalise blushes. "It's my first time being one." The door opens under her graceful palm, and the sounds of the bustling inn drench their ears. Sweet smoke rises from the opening of the staircase like a beacon to the common room, and Annalise guides them toward it. Suddenly, she stops, squeezing Oliver's arm. "They're searching," she whispers, cursing under her breath.

Through the thick haze, Oliver can make out two guards downstairs questioning guests, each of them holding parchment up to befuddled faces. *Damn it.* "We might be able to get by without them noticing. There are at least thirty people down there and only two guards."

The princess drums her fingers along Oliver's arm in thought. "Maybe, but—" She gasps, spinning him back around toward their door. "He's coming up the steps."

Oliver closes his green eyes in silent prayer. "Should I unlock the door?"

"He's halfway up already—just do as I say!" Annalise pins him against the wall, casually adjusting her posture to match her disguise. The pain in his side nearly disappears when she presses her body into his, her fingers toying with the collar of his new shirt. "What is he doing?" Annalise asks nervously.

Oliver glances to his left, but all he can think about is the warmth of her breath against his neck. "He's looking the other way," he manages, taking a long drink from his bottle of wine.

"I knew we should have kept traveling. *Gods!*" Anna vents quietly. Her dark eyes dare a peek in the guard's direction. "He'll be coming back after he questions that couple over there." She grabs Oliver's free hand, placing it on her lower back. "Make it look convincing," she flusters.

"Right." *Convincing. I could show you convincing, but it might cost me a sword to the throat.* Oliver watches the guard's interaction with the couple before he turns around to start in their direction. "He's headed this way, now."

"Good. Great." The princess forces a smile, running a porcelain finger along his collarbone.

Her voice sounds authoritative, but Oliver can feel Annalise's body tense against his. He sighs. *Gods, help me.* Oliver presses his cheek to her own, whispering into her ear: "Darren Eldric is going to kill me," he professes, pulling her hips flush against his own. He drops his mouth just below her jawline, pressing messy kisses down the length of her neck, feeling her hand crumple the fabric of his shirt collar. Oliver would stop if he could —if he didn't like the sound of Annalise's ragged breathing so much.

"I beg your pardon." The guard's voice makes them

both jump, and Oliver observes Annalise's entire disposition transform into the spitting image of a lower-tier courtesan.

"Oh!" A half-dazed smirk. "I'm flattered, really, but he found me first."

"What?" The guard clears his throat, shaking his head. "We're looking for Princess Annalise Larking." The Nesvlan man unrolls a worn sheet of parchment with a subpar sketch. "Early twenties, dark hair and eyes. Last seen with a ... man with brown hair ..." He eyes them both suspiciously.

Oliver takes a drunken swig from his bottle while Annalise swipes the drawing from the guard's grasp.

"Pretty," she claims with tired eyes. "But I haven't seen the likes of her around here."

Oliver tugs the parchment out of Anna's hand, squinting like his vision is fuzzy. "Can't say I've had the pleasure, but if I did, I'd trade you in for her," he japes at his courtesan.

The guard withdraws his sketch, analyzing the imposters with nerve-wracking intensity.

Annalise leans forward, her brown eyes trailing the length of the Nesvlan man's armor. "If you stick around long enough, maybe I can be the lost princess for you." She winks.

With an eye roll of annoyance, the guard rolls up his parchment, turning on a heel to retreat downstairs. Oliver releases a breath of air he didn't know he was holding, threading his arm through Annalise's as they hobble back to their room.

"I'm kind of offended," the goddess jests as Oliver opens the door. "Do I look that bad in this costume?"

The former master smiles, turning the key behind them. "I never said that."

Anna steals the bottle of wine out of Oliver's hand. "You said you'd trade me in for 'princess' me."

Oliver laughs, wincing in pain. "That's because 'princess' you is the *real* you. Well, if you don't count 'goddess' you."

Annalise palms her face, groaning quietly. Despite her divinity, she has never looked more human.

"For what it's worth," Oliver presses a hand to his wound, "Prince Darren doesn't deserve you. You're too good for him."

The princess is quiet while Oliver slowly seats himself at the foot of the bed. "Thank you," she states shyly, deciding to claim the spot beside him. "I wish my parents were here to know that."

Oliver nods solemnly, thinking about the absence of his own mother and father. "Your parents didn't know Darren, but they knew you. I'm sure they would trust your decision to void the arrangement, so long as you had the welfare of the kingdom—or, in this case, the *world*—in mind."

"You think my arrangement is now void?" Annalise follows the jest with a beautiful, radiant smile. "You know, you really are a diplomat at heart." Her grin fades. "Though, I'm not sure I had my fiancé's welfare in mind when I sent a pissed-off goddess after him."

"I'm not sure he ever had yours in mind." Oliver runs his fingers through his messy brown hair, desperate to change the subject. "So, now what?"

Annalise sighs. "Now, we wait. And hopefully, the guards will be on their merry way soon enough." She pushes a strand of dark hair behind her ear.

"Hopefully," Oliver repeats, distracted by the plunging neckline of her orange robes, his lips still warm from being pressed against her neck. *It's just a ruse*, he reminds himself, but his evergreen eyes can't help noticing the way Annalise's gaze seems to linger at his mouth, her chest rising and falling as fast as it had when the two of them were pressed against the wall moments ago. Slowly, she leans her body closer to his own, Oliver's heartbeat quickening as their breath mingles in silence. He waits, withholding his desires with every shred of self-control he has left while Annalise brings her lips an inch from his own.

A thunderous fist knocks at the door. "By order of the Nesvlan crown, you have ten seconds to open this room!"

Oliver meets Annalise's horrified stare. "Do you trust

me?" he asks, though, at this point, she doesn't have much of a choice.

"I do," the princess affirms.

In a matter of seconds, Oliver pulls the hairpin from her top knot and unlaces the top ties of her robes. "Do you still have that dagger?"

Annalise reaches beneath her robes to present him with the blade.

He slips it into his pocket, painfully rising from the bed. "Make it look like we just finished up," Oliver orders, taking his spot to the left of the door to unstrap his belt.

"Last chance!" the guard yells through the thin wood.

Annalise rumples the blankets on the bed, seating herself in the middle. "Just a minute!"

The door swings open under the guard's boot, his bloodshot eyes pausing on Annalise, whose fingers tremble as she re-ties the top of her bodice. "*Gods*," the princess swears, "I told you I'd make time for you next!"

But the jig is up when the Nesvlan guard unravels his parchment sketch once again, his sharp gaze shifting between the amateur drawing and the woman in real life.

Oliver makes his move. Kicking the door shut with a heel, he slips the leather belt around the guard's neck, tightening it as best as he can with a fresh wound. The guard reaches for his sword, but Oliver's foot finds the back of his knee, sending him to the ground gasping for air. No sooner does the Nesvlan man collapse than Oliver draws the dagger, angling it under his chin. The guard's eyes open wider, until—

By some curious grace of the gods, his expression goes blank, consciousness fading from his gaze like a sunset over the sea.

Oliver turns to Annalise, but she looks just as confused.

The door creaks open, only this time, soft footsteps emerge. Oliver moves beside the princess with the dagger still drawn, but the female in the doorway doesn't seem to pose a threat. With feline grace, she approaches them languidly, on near-silent feet.

"Please." The woman holds her small hands up in surrender. "I think we're all on the same side, here."

What in the name of Lazarus? "Do you know this woman?" Oliver asks Annalise over a shoulder, but the Goddess of Wisdom and Justice only presses her hand to his arm, urging him to lower his weapon.

Candlelight flickers against the female's dark hair, her lime-green eyes blinking with something like vacillating hope. "Princess Annalise?"

Annalise's swallow is audible. "Who's asking?"

A smile of relief. "Vega Kutchrik," she responds. "But you can call me Elouthera."

ANNALISE

Annalise hobbles across the road with Oliver's arm around her shoulders, her sandals almost too loose to keep up with Vega's scurrying. *Elouthera*, the goddess reflects with both astonishment and anxiety. *One minute, I was doing everything in my power to find her. Now that I'm with her, I don't have the slightest idea of what to say to her.* Regardless of Annalise's worries, however, one thing is for certain: the bond between herself and Elouthera has clicked fully into place, and Dimity has never felt as prepared to take on their enemies —immortal, or otherwise.

"It's right through here," Vega tells them, lifting a large pine branch to expose a door within the tree's trunk.

Anna shares a glance with Oliver.

"I know, I wasn't so sure of it at first either," Elouthera concedes. "But Narelle had been to a different Nevs' hall before."

The princess's eyes grow as wide as the moon. "Narelle?" *Could it really be her? But, how could she have broken free of my sister's dungeon?*

A kind nod. "I think you'll be pleasantly surprised by how much has fallen into place while we've been apart."

Annalise swallows, pressing her feet into the forest floor until they reach the solidity of wood. Within the hollow tree descends a spiraling set of stairs, which she opts to climb down first, keeping Oliver behind her. If the journey down the tree is arduous for her, Annalise can't imagine how troublesome it must be for her wounded friend.

"*Gods,*" she can hear Oliver grunt, leaning one of his palms on Anna's shoulder.

The goddess slows her pace, letting her brown eyes fall on an open doorway carved into the dirt. *What the hell?* A few more footsteps reveal an underground cave, its ceiling held up by the root system of the tree. Upon flat ground, Annalise laces her arm back underneath Oliver's, shuffling them into the earthen room.

About thirty-or-so eyes pause their conversations to meet her with stares more uncomfortable than the ones she endured in Adrianna's Throne Room. It takes Anna half a moment to decipher why. Almost every one of the women in the Nevs' hall is dressed in the same citrine robes that she currently wears—almost every one, except for a tall, redheaded man with a grin bright enough to fuel the sun.

"By the gods!" Modgen Sprightly beams. "If it isn't my beloved Annalise ..." He blinks. "... wearing courtesans' robes, with her arm around Master McHenry ..."

Annalise laughs, releasing Oliver to embrace Modgen in a hug. "It's not what it looks like."

Her childhood friend squeezes her tightly, pulling away to assess her with shrewd eyes. "So, what did you in? Peer pressure? Bad round of *halsen?*"

"Nesvlan guards, actually."

Vega gives a blink of her lime-green eyes. "This is an odd group."

Annalise would reassure her otherwise, if she didn't believe the same thing, herself. The goddess opens her mouth when a blur of chestnut hair and tan skin bursts from the former Nevs, the woman's face on the verge of tears. Anna lets her own flood down her cheeks.

Narelle wraps the princess in greedy arms, choking on her sobs while the rest of the onlookers whisper.

"I am so sorry," Dimity cries into the courtesan's cloaked shoulder, breathing in her scent of lilacs and lilies. "I should have done more, I should have—"

"With what? Your vast supply of resources?" Narelle looks the goddess in the eyes. "It was my choice to do what I did for you. I knew the risks involved. And believe it or not, I'd do it again."

A larger sob slips from Anna's throat, her eyes closing from both gratitude and guilt. *How can she forgive me after I failed to rescue her from the dungeon?* Before she can ponder too much on the question, another female surfaces from the Nevs, her mismatched eyes filled with shy curiosity.

Narelle pulls away from Annalise to place a hand on the woman's shoulder. "Annalise, this is Eden Sharpkey, High Priestess of the Nevs. Eden, meet Princess Annalise Larking."

"Your Highness." Eden curtsies politely, her Javirian accent strong and rolling.

Eden Sharpkey ... Laraya's daughter? "It's a pleasure to meet you, Eden." Annalise bows her head. "I can assure you this isn't my typical attire," she quips.

A reserved smile. "It's a good thing you chose it, today," Eden proclaims. "Otherwise, we may not have found you."

The princess wrinkles her forehead.

"When the Nevs were banned," Narelle explains, "I agreed to teach them how to blend into society as courtesans, collecting information across the kingdom. They could gain employment, and you could benefit from their intel."

Vega chimes in, "The courtesan you bought your outfit off of—that was one of our girls." She smiles. "So, when she reported the incident to us, I headed to the inn right away."

Annalise balks. "Narelle, I don't need to remind you of what happened the first time—"

"I am well aware, Annalise." Narelle cups the side of her face, a fragment of motherly nature from their past. "You don't have to worry about me, Piper," the former courtesan tells her with a caring smile.

The goddess nods, despite her hesitancy to believe it. She turns to Vega. "That guard back at the inn," Annalise begins. "Did you …?"

"No," Vega clarifies. "It was just mind control. One of my abilities." She blushes faintly.

Oh, that's not horrifying at all. Then again, people could say the same of me, throwing flames from my hands. "I see." Anna smiles. "It sounds like we have a lot to catch up on."

"Uh, I hate to interrupt," Modgen interjects, "but Oliver doesn't look as well as usual."

Anna turns her head to assess her Master of the High Council, who looks like he is in far more pain than he was in an hour ago. "Gods," she curses, moving to his side. "There wouldn't happen to be a medic down here, would there?"

"Ooh, I'm a medic!" one of the Nevs coos from the wall.

"Don't pay any attention to her," another croons with a serpentine smile. "I'm told *I* can cure anything."

Something shamefully close to envy has Annalise tightening her grip around Oliver's waist. "Sounds like their training is paying off," she tells Narelle.

"That's quite enough," a woman from the back spits, elbowing her way to the front of the group. She looks to be about fifty years old, and, to the appreciation of most, does not wear the robes of a courtesan. The woman gives a swift curtsy. "Elda, at your service, Your Highness. I've been the medic for these girls for the past twenty years."

Dimity helps Elda lay Oliver on a bed of low cushions, rolling her eyes at the fawning women behind her when the medic removes his shirt to unwrap his bandages. "I cauterized it," the goddess declares louder than she intends to, but at least the voices of the crowd drop to whispers.

"I see that," Elda notes. "You did a good job, too." She winks a wrinkled eye at Oliver. "You're a lucky man." A snap of her fingers. "Bridget. Brew him a cup of *veltrad* tea, will you?"

"Speaking of lucky men," Modgen intervenes, "what the hell happened with Prince Darren? I can't imagine you're getting married tomorrow after being chased by Nesvlan guards."

Annalise groans, her fingers meeting the crooks between her eyes and nose. "It's a long story." She does her best to fill the gang in on the overarching details of her time spent at Eldric Castle—from the very beginning, when she was reunited with Aimelie, to the grim ending, when Annalise sent a wrathful Adrianna after her betrothed. "Needless to say, I don't think Prince Darren is expecting me to meet him at the altar tomorrow. And, as if Adrianna's bounty wasn't enough, I have an entire slew of Nesvlan guards after me."

Modgen snorts. "What's new?"

Elda leaves Oliver's side to let him continue sipping his tea, setting to work in the corner of the cave.

"So." Vega crosses her arms. "The Crown Prince of Nesvla isn't all he's cracked up to be?"

"He's a prick," Oliver laughs over his half-empty teacup. "Isn't that right, Annalise?"

Anna raises her brows.

"A *whoring* prick, that she'd rather die than marry." He covers his green eyes while descending into absolute hysteria.

Eden echoes his humor with resounding giggles.

"I think that's enough tea for you." Annalise swipes the cup beneath burning cheeks.

"He was that bad?" asks Narelle. "I'm sorry, love. But I'm glad you were able to meet your youngest sister, again."

Annalise relents a faint smile at the thought of Aimelie. It disappears when she realizes that she has lost her, again. "Oliver and I ran as soon as Adrianna departed for the castle." A somber gaze. "Melie could be anywhere, by now."

Modgen shrugs. "I wouldn't get yourself too worked up about it. Didn't you say she and Ivo were leaving on a trip to Calleeit the day after tomorrow?"

The princess blinks, considering the likelihood of them setting sail two days early. "If their ship was already stocked with food and supplies, that would be a reasonable means of escape." Annalise rubs the back of her neck. "I just wish we could have said goodbye."

Elda returns with a poultice, which she carefully wraps around Oliver's abdomen with Anna's help. She hands her a cloth bag when she finishes. "Change the poultice daily for the next three days, then switch over to the salve for a week. I gave you a stash of more *veltrad* leaves if he needs them, but make sure he's drinking plenty of water." The medic regards Oliver with concerned eyes. "He'll be quite sore for the next week."

Annalise nods, taking the bag without a thought.

"And, this goes without saying, but intimacy is off the table."

If Annalise's eyes could be any further out of her skull, they would be on the floor. "It is *always* off the table." She recovers herself quickly.

Until Oliver bursts into another spell of laughter, this one inducing tears.

"How much of that did you give him?" Vega asks the medic.

"Bridget does tend to make it a bit strong," Elda answers. "The strength should diminish within the next half-hour, or so."

"Half an hour, huh?" Modgen rubs his palms together. "I suppose that's enough time to come up with our next steps."

"Next steps?" Vega repeats with surprise. "What kind of next steps can we take with a kingdom-wide bounty out for Princess Annalise?"

The Goddess of Wisdom and Justice tucks a lock of loose hair behind her ear. She sighs. "Maybe we don't have to take them in the kingdom, at all."

The rest of the group falls silent, every gaze resting on hers.

"If the correspondence Aimelie had received holds true," Dimity elaborates, "then there is a chance they might accept us in Calleeit."

"And if they don't?" Modgen crosses his lean-muscled arms. "It's not that I don't trust Aimelie, but there's a reason why Calleeit broke away from the kingdom."

Annalise nods. "Yes, and it was Adrianna." She crosses her own arms, tapping a finger in thought against her elbow. If Melie was right about the possibility of an alliance with the island territory, it could present numerous opportunities for Anna's cause. *But if she was wrong, it could spell doom for us all.* The princess shrugs her shoulders. "What other choice do we have?"

Modgen and Vega share a glance, as do Narelle and Eden. Oliver gives Annalise a drunken smile.

"As much as I would love to go with you," Narelle starts, "I think it's best if I remain here, with Eden. Our work with the Nevs has just begun, and someone needs to oversee the operations of your network."

Annalise would counter her decision, but despite her broken heart, it makes too much sense. *Even if she stayed with me, there is no guarantee I would be able to protect her. Hell, I couldn't even save Narelle when I lived a few miles from her.* With as much grace as she can offer, Annalise nods her head. "I understand," she relents.

Somewhere beneath her citrine robes, Anna's stomach begins to churn. *So many things could go wrong with this plan,* the princess broods with compounding fear. Weather, supplies—*pirates,* Annalise reflects on her previous encounter with Captain Garin on her way to the Savek Coast. But if there is one thing the goddess has learned, it is that time is sacred, and idle minds make for idle change. *If we do nothing at all and spend the rest of our days hiding under Adrianna's nose, my chances of taking back the Empeirian throne are as good as gone. It is this, or nothing.*

"Well, at least we have Elouthera, now," Modgen

points out, "so we'll be traveling under the protection of *two* goddesses."

"*We?*" Annalise squints. "You've done more than I could ever ask for, Modge. I'm not asking you to take a trip across the Falvedrie Sea to *Calleeit*." *Javir was bad enough.*

"I wasn't expecting you to ask." He gives her a light-hearted grin. "Consider it a bonus for having such an amazing friend. Besides, I don't care if you and Vega are deities. You'll need all the help you can get. Which is why Oliver and I are happy to join you." Modgen gives Oliver's shoulder a playful punch, the latter's green eyes fluttering open to consciousness.

"Oh, good," Vega jokes. "I can feel your helpfulness, already."

Modgen chortles. "Hey, I already saved your ass once."

"All right." Annalise sighs, bringing her hands together. "I'm sure we can gather enough supplies and perseverance to make it through a few weeks at sea." *Even if I will loathe every second of it.*

"We just need to book passage for a vessel without drawing attention at the harbor." Vega twirls a lock of short black hair. "How will we be able to get away with that, considering the Nesvlan throne probably has more guards looking for you than the few that were back at the inn?"

Every mouth falls quiet at the question, every mouth except the one that Annalise likes hearing most.

"Easy." Oliver shoots her a winsome grin. "We can take my ship."

ADRIANNA

Dria withdraws the emerald and jet crown from her satchel, running her fingers over the jewels from the saddle of her swaying horse. It doesn't take a genius to recognize Annalise's royal colors, so Adrianna wonders what fool committed high treason to forge her this crown. *Was it the Nesvlans? Queen Minerva was already willing to marry her son to Annalise.* Her mind begs to explore every possibility, to figure out which person she needs to weed out of her kingdom next, but nothing concerns her so much as the current task at hand.

She left Eldric Castle as soon as she heard his voice through the bond, the god's words stronger and clearer than they have been in weeks. Whether Nesvla will continue to come to her aid, Adrianna can't say with certainty, but the three hundred-some men trailing her remaining army give the queen hope. *And even if Queen Minerva wants to break our treaty, she won't. Not with the reminder of Prince Darren's fragility staring her back in the face.* Jedda concedes a dark smile at the remembrance of his marred cheek, the way the blood pooled on the Throne Room floor beneath his petrified eyes.

Adrianna pats the sealed agreement through her cloak. "How much longer to the border?" she asks Sir Braydenton, her body yearning to quicken the pace as they approach the town that Desmond disclosed to her through the bond.

"Only a few more minutes, Your Majesty." Her second-in-command's hair billows in the brisk wind, the weather getting colder by the day. "You're sure this is the town?"

The Crimson Queen gives him a look. "I *know* this is the town," she corrects him, rolling her blue eyes. She entertains the idea of refilling his position the moment Desmond has returned. *"I'm almost there, my love,"* she whispers to him silently.

"I'll be waiting," Anzac responds, Jedda's heart firing rapidly at the fact that he is conscious, that he is *alive.*

Cresting above the dirt path is a tall, worn sign, its letters smudged with dirt and grime. *Iltag, Javir,* the goddess reads, pivoting her horse. "You three." Adrianna points to her closest soldiers. "Come with me. The rest of you will wait here until we return," she mostly tells Sir

Braydenton. With a snap of her reigns, the queen leads them down the hill and into the small town, the hooves of their horses clacking against every uneven cobblestone.

His voice permeates her mind. *"The old woman will let you in."*

"Okay," Dria confirms. On the main road, a cemetery on their right grabs her attention, particularly the missing gate along its entrance. *How odd. They should consider replacing that, at the very least to make it look nicer.* But Adrianna's eyes land on a large, rectangular box lying on its side between the headstones. The metal is dark enough to drown out the sun, but that is not what catches her eye—that would have to be the small holes in the visible end. Dria's stomach anxiously fills with disturbing ideas.

"Your Majesty?" an old crone questions from the rickety porch of a townhouse.

Adrianna dismounts at once, her feet striking the ground before hastening into a trot. "Where is he?" she asks the woman when she reaches the steps.

"Inside, to the left."

The goddess throws open the door to the house, nearly tripping over the rug as her eyes frantically search the interior. "Desmond?" Adrianna calls, making a left down the hallway. She spurs her feet across the rickety floorboards, until her blue gaze floods with tears when at last, she spots him sitting upright on a cot, sliding his foot into a boot.

"*Dria,*" her Captain of the Guard reveres, catching her when she collapses into his arms. Every muscle in Desmond's hands grip her with unmatched intensity while she stains his sleeve with loud sobs.

Adrianna doesn't even care if people can hear her; she only needs to be nearer to him, closer to him to forget about the dreadful time they have spent apart. Pulling back only to examine his tan face, she runs a hand through his charcoal waves. "What happened to you?" she sobs.

A matching set of tears slips down Desmond's own cheeks, his handsome lips pressing together in something like disdain. "Elouthera," the captain whispers. "If she and her ilk hadn't trapped me in that damn cage, I would have been able to visit a medic for my leg." He runs a hand over the fabric covering his left thigh.

Jedda's tears turn to ice, freezing to her skin. She melts them away with magic-ridden fingers. "We'll find her," she swears to him in a tone potent enough to raise the dead. "I promise."

"And Dimity?" Anzac gazes at her with his quicksilver eyes.

Adrianna tries not to think about the mercy she showed her sister two days ago, before she stormed Eldric Castle in hopes of rescuing Desmond from its dungeon.

She lied to me, Dria recalls with no small amount of astonishment. *Annalise lied.* "We'll find her, too." The queen's icy gaze melts the longer she lets it wander over her lover's face. "Who saved you?" she asks, running her thumb over the familiar shape of his cheek.

Desmond shrugs. "My shadow pawn brought a group of men to me, but the old woman healed me. She must have worked some kind of miracle." He presses his black brows together. "I could have sworn I was going to die."

"Not if I had anything to do with it," the elderly woman says from the doorway, a soft smile painting her lips.

The goddess stands from Desmond's lap. "My lady, I owe you—"

"Yes, you do."

Adrianna's confusion must be evident, but it dissipates the moment the woman hovers a wrinkled hand over her leathery face, revealing pale skin, caliginous lips, and citrine eyes. The transformation is almost enough for Dria to gloss over the amethyst-encrusted crescent hanging around her neck.

Adrianna swallows. "Cyndeya," she names her at last. *Where is the vial of my hair?*

"How?" Desmond begins. "I thought I killed you."

"By suffocation?" A nod of her black ringlets. "I thought so, too, until I woke up in the dirt."

The High Priestess takes all of one step before Jedda

throws out a hand in warning. "Don't you dare," the goddess spits.

"Oh," Cyndeya starts, "I wouldn't do that, if I were you." A pointed glance at Desmond. "After Vega proved herself unsympathetic to my cause, and your captain left me for dead in the street, I did a lot of thinking. Existential pondering, if you will. I thought, there must be some greater use for me if I was able to live through the wrath of a god, but nobody has ever seemed to take me seriously. So, when I saw your shadow pawn waltzing around town, I saw it as the perfect opportunity."

"Opportunity?" Desmond repeats from the cot.

"Exactly," Cyndeya confirms, her orange eyes glittering. "The opportunity to make myself respectable in other people's eyes. The opportunity to make myself as vital as a *deity*." She smoothes out the pleats of her dress. "You see, Captain, there was no way you were going to run off with an infected wound and live to tell the tale, so ..." A swoop of her hands. "I had the men who rescued you bring you here, to this deserted house, and then I took the time to heal you."

Adrianna squints, holding Desmond's hand. *She is far too smug about saving someone's life.* "What aren't you telling us?"

The High Priestess grins. "I thought you'd never ask. Like I mentioned previously, Desmond would have died if I hadn't intervened, so—"

"*What did you do?*" Queen Adrianna cuts through her words.

"I used a spell, one that would bind his life to another living thing, and then I had a local medic treat his condition as they normally would."

Desmond scrunches his forehead in thought. "The woman with the blonde hair," he recollects.

But Adrianna isn't as satisfied with Cyndeya's response. *She saved him with some sort of black magic.* "You freed Narelle Lambric and Robbin Flangham from the dungeon and helped them escape, two prized sources of information on Annalise. Give me one good reason why I shouldn't end you right now."

She chortles. "Well, that's just it. You can't. I bound Desmond's life to my own, which means that if you kill *me*, you kill Desmond."

Panic seizes Adrianna's throat, her breathing heightening every second she holds Cyndeya's prideful stare. "You did *what?*" The queen's shoulders quake as she realizes the consequences of the oracle's actions. *I couldn't even keep Desmond safe; how am I supposed to protect two beings at the same time?* The goddess seethes. "I don't believe you."

The oracle nudges her chin at Desmond. "Look under your left shirt sleeve."

Exchanging a glance with her captain, Adrianna watches Desmond roll up his sleeve to expose a line of rune-like symbols carved into his flesh, the marks beginning to scar over. *Gods, no! No, no, no, no, no!* She lifts her gaze to the witch, her eyes roaring with fire, dropping her voice to a tone that is sure to make her skin crawl. "I may not be able to take you out of this world, Cyndeya, but I *can* make you wish you were never born into it."

"My darling," she gives Dria a sparkling smile, "I already do."

The queen's breathing is audible. "You're insane."

"No one ever said I was sound of mind, only that I had one I wasn't afraid to use."

On the cot, Desmond holds his face, bringing his silver gaze to the High Priestess. "I suppose you'll be coming back to Empeirus with us, now that we can't let you out of our sight."

Cyndeya's victorious grin makes Dria's fists curl. "That would probably be for the best. Oh, there is one part of this scenario that should please you, Your Majesty." Shadows creep their way into her expression. "This time, I won't just help you *find* Elouthera. I'll help you *end* her."

EPILOGUE

The southern wind whips Aimelie's blonde hair with a ferocity outmatched only by her heart. Just ahead, in the raging afternoon sun, the desert island of Calleeit stares back at their Nesvlan ship in the same defiant manner it has had throughout history. The deckhands are quick to exchange hearty cheers, but the youngest princess observes her protector in somber silence, the brutal rays of the sky already burning her freckled, ivory cheeks.

"Put these on," Captain Ivo encourages her.

Aimelie eyes the leather boots with little interest.

He drops them on the ship deck before her. "You'll need them to walk across the sand."

Only after he stalks away to prepare for landfall does Melie bow to remove her silk slippers, replacing them with the high boots. She drops her dress over her new garments, meeting Ivo at the front of the ship. "Tell me this was a good idea," Aimelie whispers to him.

Ivo straightens his spine, crossing his hands behind his back. "It is a crime to lie to a princess."

They left as soon as they heard the horns blare outside of Eldric Castle, uprooting without so much as a goodbye. With the ship already stocked for their departure, it made more sense to leave unexpectedly rather than risk being delayed by an army of unknown proportion. *Or risk being killed by them.* Even if Aimelie secretly welcomes the distraction from Linden's death, her heart aches at the misfortune of parting ways with Annalise for the second time in her life. But, at least now, she should know where to find her.

The deckhands signal that their ship has successfully docked, and a wooden plank is provided by one of the Calleetian locals to begin letting off passengers. The crew files off one by one, singing with glee at the feeling of solid ground beneath their toes. With Ivo close behind, the princess crosses the docks to take her first step on Calleetian soil. *Or sand, rather.*

Her boots sail across the shimmering abyss of gold and white, marred only by the occasional tent or swaying palm tree. The heat is scorching, even in light colors, and the princess puts a hand to her brow only to realize that the sweat has evaporated. A mirage sparkles in the distance on the outskirts of town, and upon entering, Aimelie quickly realizes how welcome she really is.

The first thing she notices is their attire. Nowhere to be seen are the heavy, multilayered silk dresses of the mainland. No corsets or heels or emblazoned doublets. All the courtroom finery has been replaced by loose, flowing fabrics of cream and gray and blue, their ebony feet adorned with golden sandals or the same leather boots that Aimelie, herself, has taken to.

She turns to Ivo. "Perhaps you should have given me a change of clothes, as well," Melie snaps quietly.

The second, and more concerning, thing the princess notices are the locals' expressions. The Calleetians peer at Aimelie and her posse waltzing into their town with a gaze as unsettling as one of Adrianna's childhood melt-downs. *I shouldn't be here*, is all Melie can think while she tries to ignore their beady stares, but the throbbing pain in her heart is enough to justify her insolence. No sooner does the princess spot the beginning of a path leading to a domed fortress than a pair of armed guards blocks the way.

"No farther than here," the guard on the left orders, the scales on his armor unsettlingly sharp.

Aimelie clears her throat. "Please, sir. You mistake our motive. We come here by the authority of Queen Haraja. I am Princess Aimelie Larking, of Empeirus."

The guards exchange glances. "Only you two," the second man commands.

Melie would try to bargain, but for some reason, she doesn't think these guards are in the mood to negotiate. *That, and I probably wouldn't be successful.* "Very well," she deigns. She can only pray that the queen will be more forthcoming to her company. Their footsteps in a soft harmony, Aimelie and Ivo make it to the entrance of the wide fortress, its turquoise domes a stark contrast to the golden ones of Eldric Castle. The two exchange glances before the open, oversized doorway.

Ivo observes her carefully with his grayish-blue eyes. "There isn't much I am going to be able to do for your safety, Your Highness. I am only one man, and the throne is bound to be surrounded by countless guards."

Aimelie swallows, her hands finding the golden pendant around her neck that had been given to her what feels like a lifetime ago. "I must do this. If even for the sake of trying. And if I don't come back out, at least I will have done everything I could for Annalise, and for this world." Taking Ivo's hand in hers, she shares a smile, even if it doesn't reach her eyes. "Thank you for all that you have done for my family, Captain Ivo."

He regards her with wide eyes as she takes the lead, stepping foot into yet another royal home. Her boots slip over one hundred cobalt tiles, each one decorated with a white star. With ragged breaths, her blue eyes follow the cosmic path until it ends at the foot of a dais, Aimelie's heart rattling with unmatched anxiety.

Twenty or so guards in the same scale-adorned uniforms she had seen earlier stand in perfect lines before the throne, its occupant lifting her head in what Melie hopes is great interest. The Calleetian guards stiffen almost imperceptibly, their hands tightening around each of their spears. And between these walls of protection, Queen Haraja of Calleeit pins her lined brown eyes on the princess and Captain Ivo.

"Your Grace," Aimelie begins, but the queen pays her no heed. She can only guess what Queen Haraja is yelling at her guards. *Probably something along the lines of "Who let this lot of Empeirian scum into my Throne Room?"*

The guards' eyes dart back and forth.

"Your Grace, my name is Princess Aimelie Larking, of Empeirus," she tries again. "We agreed to negotiate an alliance during our correspondence over the past few months ..."

Not so much as a glance in her direction. *Does she not speak the common tongue? I don't think Captain Ivo knows Calleetian, either.* The princess begins to panic, her doe eyes searching for any sort of response to keep her from feeling insane. She feels Ivo place a hand on her shoulder, his expression doubtful of the situation.

"Is this the way we treat guests in Calleeit?" a strong male voice bellows from Aimelie's left. His navy tunic and proud stance lead her to believe he is of royalty, especially if he is speaking to the queen in such a tone. The young man covers the distance between Melie and Queen Haraja in quick strides, rattling off a few additional sentences in the southern tongue before turning to face Aimelie.

He doesn't look much older than me, Melie notes, and despite her aching heart, she must admit that he is handsome, too. His dark brown eyes and tawny skin mirror the queen's, but his demeanor has a sort of kindness to it, something that Aimelie finds refreshing after her experience in this territory so far. She straightens her posture as he approaches.

"Forgive me, Your Highness. My mother was not aware of your arrival," he begins in a Calleetian accent.

Aimelie presses her blonde brows together.

"Allow me to introduce myself." The gentleman extends a hand. "My name is Zenebe Bahiti, Crown Prince of Calleeit."

Aimelie shakes his hand in shock. First, at the oddity of shaking hands, then, at the notion that Queen Haraja didn't know she was coming. "I ..." She clears her throat. "Aimelie Larking, Princess of Empeirus."

"You need to tell me what is going on right now," the queen commands her son in the common tongue, the sapphires in her golden crown gleaming with impatience. "Why is she here?"

The princess startles. "Your Grace, we've been corresponding for months—"

"You weren't corresponding with her," Prince Zenebe interrupts. His dark eyes glance at his mother's. "You were writing to me."

Melie gawks. The tension in the Throne Room is thick enough to be sliced by one of the guards' spears.

Queen Haraja shifts her cutting stare directly to her son. "We will discuss this matter in private," is all she tells him. "And as for you," the queen addresses Aimelie, "I want nothing to do with whatever Empeirian troubles you bring with you."

"Which is exactly why I took up the quill myself," the prince spits. "Because I knew you would think that way."

"And I will continue to think that way for as long as I shall live." The queen stands from her throne. "I fought alongside our people to break free of their tyranny. What makes you think that we should concern ourselves with anything that has to do with the Kingdom of Empeirus?"

Prince Zenebe palms his forehead. "The war has been over for *years*, Mother—"

"And yet, the scars we bear are eternal," Queen Haraja replies, gesturing to a long white line running the length of her upper arm. Her dark gaze finds Aimelie again. "Get out! You are not welcome here, and you never will be."

The princess blinks. Her chest begins to rise and fall like the sea she just sailed for weeks over to reach this gods-forsaken island. Ivo places his hand back on her shoulder, turning her around successfully this time. *But the letters ... The prince wanted to negotiate ...* Step-by-step, Aimelie's leather boots pad their way down the same cobalt tiles she had traversed on her way into the Throne Room. *It was Adrianna who started the War on the Horns; Annalise and I had nothing to do with it. I understand being hesitant to support an Empeirian, but Annalise would be fighting against the very monarch who caused them so much strife in the first place.*

Melie prepares herself for another ceaseless boat ride, for an even more hopeless war. Such ideas make her want to weep with defeat, but her stomach roils at the thought that bothers her most: *What will Annalise think of me? Fleeing on a whim and then failing in my attempt to gain her the only ally who could help her, who could help the world.* Her heart has been broken for weeks now, but somehow, it manages to fracture even more.

Aimelie's fingers find the golden ring on her opposite hand, burning at the idea of her failures, none more so than Linden. Her doe eyes begin to well with tears, but she has shed too many. Now is not the time to be sorry for herself, not when there is a world that needs saving. The princess slows her pace. *Now is not the time to leave, when there is a world that needs saving.*

"Princess?" Ivo questions quietly, his hand gently urging her to keep moving forward, but Aimelie stops.

Her heart rattles in her chest, but Aimelie Larking forces her body to face the dais one more time. "No."

Queen Haraja opens her lined eyes wider than ever. "*What* did you just say to me?"

The youngest princess swallows. "I said, *no*."

The guards shift in their positions, but Aimelie swears that Prince Zenebe betrays just a hint of a smile.

The queen raises a black brow.

"Your Grace, you must forgive me. I did not fight in the War on the Horns; didn't so much as have a say in the matter, because I was a child. I am sorry for the pain and suffering it caused to both sides. But right now, a war is being waged with an outcome far greater than the simple gain or loss of territories." Aimelie moves forward a step.

"The rumors are true," she continues. "Gods and goddesses walk this Earth, and they have agendas that each will stop at nothing to fulfill." Melie closes her blue eyes for a moment, stealing a breath. "I am not asking for you to get involved in a trivial matter of the Empeirian kingdom, Your Grace. I am asking for you to help us save the *world*."

Queen Haraja slowly leans back on her throne, her dark eyes assessing the princess and Captain Ivo. She looks to her son, who stands strong as ever. "Zenebe, retrieve your father from his study and bring him here." She lifts her chin at Aimelie.

"Go on, Princess. I'm listening."

ACKNOWLEDGMENTS

"When do you sleep?" my aunt asked me during the midst of wedding planning, working a full-time job, and writing this book. In truth, I probably don't sleep enough, but at least I daydream while I'm awake! Although I wrote *Daughter of Daybreak* during the busiest time of my life, somehow, I enjoyed writing this novel even more than my first. That said, its successful completion would not have been possible without the help of so many remarkable human beings.

To my killer beta reading team: I can't thank you enough for your valuable honesty, your exceptional feedback, and for showing as much interest in making this book a success as I have. Your excitement and support mean the world to me!

To my amazing editor, Lucia Ferrara: I'm so grateful that the stars aligned in such a way that you were able to continue working on this series! Thank you for helping me make this story as polished as it can be.

Thank you to my ever-talented cover artist and designer, Agata Broncel. It's always a pleasure working with you and getting to dress my book in such gorgeous artwork! I can't wait to put this one on the shelf next to *Daughter of Lazarus*.

To my cherished family: Your endless love and support is the reason why I am here today. Thank you for raising me to believe in myself enough to bring my dreams to life—and then, to do it all over again. Mom, your boundless devotion to helping others inspires me every day, and Dad, anyone who has ever asked where I get my work ethic knows it was passed on by you.

To Eric, my beloved husband: Living with you is more of an adventure than the one Annalise had in this book. Thank you for your awful guy jokes, for cooking dinner for me every night, and for the silly dances you won't share with anyone else. I can't begin to describe how thankful I am that Courtney wanted me to work with her. I love you more than the world.

Finally, I wanted to give a special thanks to all my fabulous readers. I consider myself the luckiest woman alive to be doing what I love, and it is only through you that this is possible. Thank you for believing in my stories as much as I do.

DON'T MISS THE LATEST NEWS ON **ARDEN'S EPIC SERIES** ...

BOOK
THREE
COMING SOON!

Sign up for her newsletter at

WWW.JUNIPERARDEN.COM/CONTACT

Follow Juniper on social media!

@JUNIPERARDEN

ABOUT THE AUTHOR

Seasoned traveler, dog-lover, and drinker of fine teas, Juniper Arden spends each day dreaming up her next ambitious idea like she has since she was a child. When she isn't putting pen to paper, you can find her braving mountains and meadows, cuddling with her fur babies, or whipping up a batch of her famous chocolate cupcakes. *Daughter of Daybreak* is her second novel and the second installment in the *Daughter of Lazarus* series.

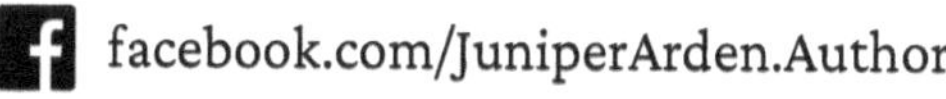

facebook.com/JuniperArden.Author

instagram.com/juniperarden